Also by Carolyn Brown

What Happens in Texas
A Heap of Texas Trouble
A Slow Dance Holiday (novella)
Christmas at Home
Summertime on the Ranch (novella)
Secrets in the Sand
Holidays on the Ranch
Red River Deep
The Honeymoon Inn
Love Struck Café (novella)
Bride for a Day
Just in Time for Christmas
A Chance Inheritance
The Third Wish (novella)

LUCKY COWBOYS
Lucky in Love
One Lucky Cowboy
Getting Lucky
Talk Cowboy to Me

HONKY TONK
I Love This Bar
Hell, Yeah
My Give a Damn's Busted
Honky Tonk Christmas

Spikes & Spurs

Love Drunk Cowboy
Red's Hot Cowboy
Darn Good Cowboy Christmas
One Hot Cowboy Wedding
Mistletoe Cowboy
Just a Cowboy and His Baby
Cowboy Seeks Bride

Cowboys & Brides

Billion Dollar Cowboy
The Cowboy's Christmas Baby
The Cowboy's Mail Order Bride
How to Marry a Cowboy

Burnt Boot, Texas

Cowboy Boots for Christmas
The Trouble with Texas Cowboys
One Texas Cowboy Too Many
A Cowboy Christmas Miracle

One Hot Cowboy Wedding

CAROLYN BROWN

Cover design by Eileen Carey/No Fuss Design
Cover images © Rob Lang and by Barvista/
Shutterstock, jaclyn young/Shutterstock

Published by Sourcebooks Casablanca, an imprint of Sourcebooks
P.O. Box 4410, Naperville, Illinois 60567-4410
(630) 961-3900
sourcebooks.com

Originally published in 2012 in the United States of America by Sourcebooks Casablanca, an imprint of Sourcebooks.

Printed and bound in Canada.
MBP 10 9 8 7 6 5 4 3 2 1

To Charles Brown
With love and thanks for all you do to make my world run smooth!

Chapter 1

SHHHH! IT'S A SECRET!

That line had run around in Jasmine's mind all day on a continuous loop. She imagined two little girls playing out on the grassy lawn with their Barbie dolls, and it was a secret where Barbie and Ken were going for supper. Then two middle school girls in her bedroom gossiping about boys, and it was a secret.

Oh, the secrets she and Pearl had shared through the years, and now she had one that she couldn't share with anyone, not even Pearl.

"No one in Texas is ever going to know. Not even Pearl. I'll go home and everything will be the same. I'll wake up Monday morning, open the Chicken Fried Café, and business will go on as usual and by then I'll forget all about this wedding. It'll be a secret, all right, but between me and Ace, and no one else will ever know." She talked to herself as she flopped her suitcase on the hotel bed and unzipped it. Her hands were shaking. A fine bead of moisture covered her upper lip, and second thoughts were about to smother her plumb to death.

She and Ace had taken different flights. He'd

flown out of Dallas on Friday and gotten their rooms. She'd arrived late Saturday afternoon and caught a taxi to the hotel. It was down to the wire, swim or drown time, red light or green light. Her hands were clammy and sweat was pooling up around the band of her bra. Nervously, she looked at the clock. The hands whipped around so fast that it made her dizzy. Where had the time gone?

She took a quick shower, washed and dried her long, dark hair, and applied makeup. Then it was time to dress. Thank God the plane had been on time or she would have been rushed. She couldn't have stood a dose of nervous and one of hurry-up at the same time.

The white satin dress fit tightly to the waist with a hem that stopped right above her knee. Filmy illusion was attached to a white Stetson hat in a big bow with the streamers hanging to her waist. The dress was sprinkled with pearls and edged with lace. The shoes were white satin with beadwork on the high heels. But Jasmine didn't feel like a bride. She felt like an imposter.

A rapid *rat-a-tat-tat* on the door said time was up. She opened the door to find Ace smiling from ear to ear and holding a black Stetson. He was sexy in his black western-cut jacket, creased black Wranglers, and white shirt unbuttoned at the collar. His blond curls were almost tamed with a healthy dose of gel, but a few still escaped to float playfully on his forehead. But then it was common knowledge that Ace Riley was a player, so he would know exactly how to dress, how to swagger, how to use that Texas drawl, and how to smile to attract the women.

He braced an arm against the doorjamb and let his gray-blue eyes slowly scan her from high heels to Stetson. That didn't surprise Jasmine either. Flirting came as natural to Ace as breathing. The first thing he did when he walked into the café was scope it out for new skirt tails; the second was turn on the charm.

"Whew! You clean up pretty damn good, Jazzy." His sexy Texas drawl was deep, and his words came out slow. Most women melted when he walked through the door and swooned when he opened his mouth. He'd never affected Jasmine that way, not until that moment.

She'd seen him before in dress jeans and crisply ironed shirts but never as fancy as he was that day. Most of the time he came into the café in his scuffed work boots, faded jeans, and shirts with the sleeves cut out; the barbed-wire tat around his arm was a constant reminder that he never intended to let a woman anywhere near his heart. A motel bed or her bed, yes, but never his heart or his bedroom.

"Those are two places I'm saving for the love of my life if I ever meet her," he'd told Jasmine once while he was eating hamburgers in her kitchen.

Jasmine struck a pose for him. "Do I look like a

blushing bride? You know you shouldn't be seeing me before the wedding. It's bad luck."

He fanned his face with his black Stetson and whistled through his teeth. "Oh, darlin', you look every bit the part, and don't worry about bad luck. We're in Vegas and no one knows what we're up to. You know what they say: *What happens in Vegas stays in Vegas!* We ain't got a thing to worry about. Let's go get married?"

She looped her arm into his and pulled the door shut.

The elevator was right across from her room and opened immediately when he pushed the down button. "See, it's an omen. Nothing bad is going to happen because I saw you in that cute little dress. Besides, the rules are different in Vegas."

She looked up at him. "Oh yeah?"

"Sure they are. Didn't you read the rule book in the drawer right beside the Gideon Bible? God, Jazzy, this ain't your first time in Vegas, is it?"

"Hell, no! I've been here before and you are full of crap! There is no rule book in the drawer." She giggled.

"Did you even open the drawer and look?" Ace demanded.

"Yes, I did," she lied.

"Well, crap!" Ace teased, "If it had been there, you would have seen that on page five, paragraph six, it says that the groom can see the bride on the wedding day and that it will bring them good luck. Paragraph seven says that the only thing they have to be careful with is the blackjack tables. If the bride is wearing her wedding dress, they will lose their money there. So, all we have to do is stay away from the blackjack tables. Besides, what bride and groom would spend their time gambling anyway? They'd be rufflin' up the sheets with some hot-as-hell sex," Ace said.

"Nothing, not even a fake marriage, will ever change you, Ace," she said, laughing.

The elevator doors slid open, and he strutted out with her on his arm. Heads turned as they walked past the blackjack tables, the roulette wheels, and the slot machines. One woman fanned herself with the back of her hand; another licked her lips as if she could taste his kisses; and at least two wiggled as if they needed to make a dash to the bathroom and change their underpants.

Men seemed to be ogling Jazzy as if they'd like to lay her down on satin sheets and peel that tight-fittin' dress off her slow and easy. Truth was that Ace was thinking about how those full lips would taste; if that long hair would feel like silk as he tangled it up in his fingers; or how slick those legs would be wrapped around him in a Jacuzzi. He shook his head to knock out the vision, and another kinky blond curl fell down on his forehead. He didn't bother pushing it back. After the wedding he would settle his black Stetson on his head, and that would keep the pesky curls away from his eyes.

At the curb, he raised his hand and a taxi pulled right up. “See, more good luck. Elevator right there waiting for us and now a taxi is Johnny-on-the-spot. I tell you, this is our night, Miz Jazzy.”

“Okay, I believe you, Ace. Nothing can go wrong, and what happens in Vegas stays in Vegas. Shhh, it’s a secret.” She held one finger to her lips.

He opened the door and held the streamers from her hat while Jasmine crawled into the back seat and then he followed her.

“Yes, it is a secret. Our secret and we’ll leave it right here, so don’t worry, darlin’,” he whispered.

His warm breath started something boiling down deep in her stomach. But that shouldn’t come as a surprise. She had dated four men in the past year and a half. One of them got past the second date. None of them got further than a good-night kiss.

“Cupid’s Wedding Chapel,” he told the driver.

“I’ll have you there in twenty minutes. Traffic is pretty bad this time of night,” he said.

“We need to be there at seven.” Ace checked his watch. They had fifteen minutes. *Dammit!* He’d forgotten to figure in traffic. He’d just figured on getting there right at the time, doing the deed, and getting back to the hotel where he would play the slots for a couple of hours and go to bed.

“Then we’ll take a shortcut. Hang on to your hats.”

"What happens at the chapel?" Jazzy asked.

"I bought a package deal. Pictures. Bouquet for you. License in a cute little folder with a seal on the front. And the ceremony. The lawyer said to bring him a valid marriage license, but I'm taking pictures so Cole can see it was a real wedding. I appreciate you getting all dressed up, Jazzy," he said softly.

She punched his arm playfully. "What are friends for?"

He grinned. "God knows I don't want you to back out, but I wouldn't blame you, and we'd still be friends if you are about to change your mind."

She shook her head emphatically. "Hell, no! That sumbitch Cole isn't getting the farm. But I do have one question, Ace. How is it that he won't be tellin' the whole family anyway?"

Ace graced her with his brightest smile. "Ranch, darlin'. Not farm."

"Okay, let's put it this way: That sumbitch Cole ain't gettin' your Texas dirt whether you grow potatoes or Angus calves," she said.

He chuckled. "I like the part about sumbitch Cole, and I'll stick to Angus. And I'll explain the Cole situation to you after the wedding. Don't worry. He won't tell a soul about the ranch if he doesn't get it."

The taxi pulled up in front of a sweet little white chapel and parked behind a long, white limo with a driver standing at attention beside it. Ace gave the driver a bill. Jasmine scooted out of the taxi. She hadn't planned on moving so much in the tight-fitting dress when she bought it the previous spring. It was supposed to be worn to a personal shower for a friend, but they'd changed their minds, decided to have the shower at a honky-tonk, and everyone wore jeans. It had hung in her closet until that morning when she went looking for something to wear to her wedding.

Ace tucked her arm into his again. "Love the hat thing," he said.

"Spur of the moment. Pearl was going to use it for her wedding and Tess pitched a fit, so she told me to do something with it. It's my something borrowed," she said.

"What's blue?"

She hooked a finger under her skirt tail, raised it a notch, and showed him a blue garter.

"Old?"

"Bra and underpants." She giggled.

"New? The dress?" Ace asked.

"Yes, it is. Never worn, so it's still new," she said.

"Then we've got it covered." He slung an arm around her shoulder. It wasn't the first time Ace had hugged her or even walked across the café floor with his arm around her, so why did steamy little hot tingles dance up and down her spine?

The door opened at the exact time they stepped through the archway onto the porch, and a smiling woman motioned them inside. "You'd be Ace and Jasmine. You are right on time. I'm Harriett and I'll be acting as your wedding planner tonight. My, don't you both look beautiful."

Ace cleared his throat.

Harriett laughed. "Handsome, then. Does that work better for you, cowboy?"

"Yes, ma'am, it surely does."

She picked up a nosegay of red roses with streaming satin ribbons that matched the roses perfectly. "Hold them at waist level and loop your arm though his. It makes for prettier pictures and gives me time to get to the front of the chapel before you start down the aisle so I can get good pictures of you."

Jasmine nodded. Harriett didn't look a thing like Marcella, her mother's cousin and the most sought-after wedding planner in Sherman, Texas, but the authority in her voice sure reminded Jasmine of Marcella.

The lady hurried across the small foyer to swing open double doors into a tiny chapel with twenty white folding chairs on each side of the short center aisle. The traditional wedding march started playing softly from speakers attached to the pulpit at the front the moment the doors opened.

Jasmine wondered if they were on a timer—kind of like a clock wired to a bomb. If so, what detonated the bomb? The words *I do*?

The preacher motioned them forward. Harriet rushed down the aisle in front of them, turned around, and started snapping pictures. Cole wouldn't have a leg to stand on if he contested the marriage with all the pictures the woman took between the back of the chapel and the pulpit.

Jasmine was amazed to see that the chapel was completely full of people but figured they must be waiting for the next wedding, the one with the bride and groom waiting in the white limo out front. She wondered if they were movie stars or celebrities who had snuck off from Hollywood for a quickie marriage, and if the people in the audience were paparazzi from every ragtag gossip paper in the whole country.

They barely made it to the front when the preacher intoned in a loud voice, "We are gathered here this day to unite"—he looked down at the marriage license on the pulpit—"Jasmine King and Ace Riley in holy matrimony… Hand your flowers to Harriett," he whispered.

Jasmine looked around to find Harriett reaching for the flowers. She laid the bouquet on an empty chair and went back to taking pictures.

"They'll send them to my computer via email. Be there when we get home. I wasn't expecting so many, though," Ace whispered.

The preacher went on. "Now, Ace, take her hands in yours and face each other."

When they were facing each other, the preacher smiled and a flash went off behind Jasmine. These people really took the business of quickie marriages seriously.

"In this time-honored tradition of a wedding ceremony, Jasmine and Ace have come before me to recite their vows to each other and to exchange rings. If there is anyone who has a reason they shouldn't be married, please step forward now and state your cause or forever hold your peace."

He paused for a minute, wiped his sweaty face with a white handkerchief pulled from behind the oak pulpit, and used both hands to slick back his thick black hair. The smile never left his face, and Jasmine heard several clicks behind her. Surely, those crazy people didn't think she and Ace were the celebrities. Granted, she'd been asked before if she was kin to Dr. Cuddy on *House*. Maybe she should stop the wedding and tell them that the real celebrities were hiding in the limo outside, and they were wasting their batteries on a cowboy and a café owner from Ringgold, Texas, population less than a hundred.

"No one to protest?" the preacher asked again.

Jasmine bit back a giggle. Her four best friends, Liz, Pearl, Austin, and Gemma, would be stampeding through the chapel like a herd of longhorn heifers if they had any inkling what was going on that minute. But they didn't and wouldn't ever. Maybe someday when they were all sharing a room in a nursing home she'd tell them about the year she was married to Ace Riley. The vision that popped into her head was of five old ladies sitting around a domino table. Pearl was the one with lightly frosted, red kinky hair, shooting daggers at the old man winking at them; Austin and Gemma would have gray streaks in their dark hair, but Liz, gypsy that she was, wouldn't have changed all that much.

"Yes, well, apparently no one wants to object, so we will continue," the preacher said. His smile was plastered on as if he expected it to get him through the pearly gates of heaven that very night, and the cameras all over the chapel kept up a steady clicking noise.

Jasmine was giddy with nerves over repeating vows right there before a certified preacher—and even God—that she had absolutely no intentions of keeping. Why didn't the preacher tell those people behind her that they were photographing the wrong wedding, and why was he smiling like he'd just won the lottery?

She wasn't the only one with a case of jitters. Ace was rubbing her palm with his thumb because he couldn't be still. She wished he'd stop because it was shooting so much sexual energy through her body that she could have jumped him right there in front of the pulpit before the vows were said. The white dress and veil didn't make her a real bride, but evidently her hormones thought so. Maybe all brides felt like that when they were about to say vows before a grinning preacher and in front of a bunch of crazy people with cameras.

"Okay, Jasmine, repeat after me," the preacher intoned.

Jasmine repeated with a heavy dose of guilt.

The preacher turned to Ace. "Repeat after me."

Ace repeated without a single bit of guilt.

"Rings?"

Ace dug in his pocket and brought out a set of matching plain gold bands he'd picked up at the Walmart jewelry counter on his way to the airport. He handed them to the preacher who blessed them and told everyone in the chapel their meaning before he handed the smaller one to Ace.

"Repeat after me as you put this on her finger. With this ring..."

"With this ring..." Ace said.

Jasmine kept expecting lightning to zip down through the cathedral ceiling, shatter the crystal chandelier, and fry poor old Ace deader'n a roadkill skunk for vowing things he had no intention of doing.

The preacher handed her the larger gold band. "Jasmine, you repeat after me as you put this ring on Ace's third finger."

"With this ring..." She slipped the ring on his finger.

Her chest constricted like a two-hundred-pound sack of potatoes had been slammed against it. Maybe God and all the angels had long since given up on Las Vegas and let Lucifer have it.

"And now I pronounce you husband and wife. Mr. and Mrs. Ace Riley. Go forth and be happy! But first, Ace, you may kiss your bride."

Jasmine looked up and he looked down into her green eyes. She hadn't planned on this part. The preacher would say they were husband and wife, and that would be that. But from the look in Ace's sexy eyes, he was going to seal the deal with a real kiss.

She shut her eyes and moistened her lips. Lights started flashing and wedding music began playing, this time louder than before and with lots more jazz. Lord, a kiss had never affected her like that before.

Holy crap! That wasn't supposed to happen! Jasmine thought.

But when she opened her eyes, it wasn't just the sparks of a kiss setting off music and stars. All the people in the church were holding cameras and talking all at once. Someone with a video camera and a microphone on a long stick shoved chairs to one side so they could get closer. Red dots danced in front of Jasmine's eyes, and she wondered if it was the result of flashes and bright lights or if Ace was really that good at kissing.

"Hell's bells, Ace, does this come with the package too?" she asked.

"I have no idea what this is all about," he said.

"Mr. and Mrs. Ace Riley from Ringgold, Texas, you are the winners! You are the five thousandth couple to get married in my chapel," the preacher announced in a booming voice full of excitement. "We've been advertising for weeks and you've won the prize! Today is mine and Harriett's twenty-fifth wedding anniversary, so it's perfect."

Cameras seemed to light up the whole state of Nevada, and suddenly the preacher's perpetual smile made sense. He wanted to look good for the cameras. He had his arm thrown around Harriett and they were posing for pictures.

He talked out the side of his mouth as the flashes kept going off from different directions. "This service will be credited back to your charge card. The prize includes a limo for the rest of the evening, complete with champagne and the honeymoon suite at the Bellagio where dinner will be served in your room. Keep smiling. I'm a lucky man that you are both so photogenic. Your picture will look beautiful in my foyer and in the morning papers."

A reporter shoved a microphone near Jasmine's face. "Why did you come to Vegas to get married?"

She swallowed hard but nothing came to mind other than *Shhh, it's a secret.*

"It's so romantic," she said.

"And we only had the weekend so we wanted to plan a short honeymoon as well as a wedding," Ace said.

"I hope to hell this never goes any further than a picture in the foyer," she whispered to Ace.

Someone yelled from the back of the chapel, "How long have you known each other?"

Ace hugged Jasmine up to his side. "A long time. We were friends first, and we fell in love."

He tipped her hat back, kissed her again for the cameras, and whispered, "Play along. We get the honeymoon suite and a limo. And it's just a local contest thing."

A petite lady in a cute blue suit with a multitude of support cameras asked, "When are you going back to Texas?"

Ace ran a hand through his blond curly hair, then settled his Stetson on his head. "We have to fly home tomorrow. So if y'all will let us get on with our honeymoon, we'd be much obliged."

Jasmine turned around when one of the reporters asked, "Isn't she the doctor that plays on that old television show *House*?"

Another one answered before she could assure them that she was not a movie star, "No, but she does look like that doctor. I can't remember her name, though. Hey, Mrs. Riley, are you any kin to an actor on *House*?"

Jasmine shook her head.

"Okay, guys, make an aisle for the bride and groom so they can get on with their honeymoon. Thank you for accepting my invitation to be here for this momentous occasion tonight," the preacher said.

The photographers separated for the newlyweds but kept shooting picture after picture. So many lights went off when Ace scooped Jasmine up in his arms that she saw big red streaks behind her eyelids. The limo was waiting and the driver opened the door when he saw them coming.

"Who is that?" a lady in a long, white dress asked the man in a tuxedo beside her as they were going into the chapel.

The groom answered, "Must be movie stars or something for that much publicity. I told you we were getting married at the right chapel."

Ace put Jasmine inside the limo and then crawled in beside her. One reporter stuck his head in the door and held up a small recorder. "Have you ever been in a limo before?"

"Limo? Honey, this is a limo! I thought it was that Pallatio suite that preacher man was talkin' about," Jasmine said in her best Texas redneck drawl. "Ace. This is just the car. Wonder what that other place is?"

Ace guffawed. "I think it's Bell-a-gio, darlin', not Pal-la-tio. It's a fancy hotel."

"Well, how about that? Are you going with us?" she asked the reporter.

When he started to get inside the limo, the driver quickly shut the door.

"Jazzy, you are a hoot!"

"Hoot nothing. This is a holy mess we've gotten ourselves into, Ace! Now what? Does the paparazzi follow us all the way to the hotel? Or do they come right into the honeymoon suite and take pictures of us in our jammies? All I brought was boxer shorts and a tank top. If I'd known I got to be a star, I'd have bought a black lacy teddy," Jasmine said.

"Now you know how the real Cuddy on that television show feels." Ace laughed. But an instant picture of her in a black lace teddy on a big bed with gold satin sheets started an arousal, and he had to think about something else in a hurry or be in misery all the way to the hotel.

Jasmine shot him a look that said funny was over.

"Don't look at me like that. I didn't do it. And I'll protect the door of our honeymoon suite like a dragon protectin' a princess. One thing for sure, darlin'—there ain't no way that smartass lawyer can take my ranch away from me now. We've got pictures, and I'll buy whatever newspaper the article is in tomorrow morning about us winning the prize. Who would've thought we'd fall into a deal like this? Right now I'm telling the limo driver our first stop is our hotel to get all our things. We've got luxury waiting at the Bellagio. Champagne first?"

He removed a bottle from the ice and held it up.

She nodded. She sure needed something to calm her nerves.

He poured two flutes and handed her one. "To a happy marriage, Jazzy."

She touched her glass to his. "And to a happier divorce."

Chapter 2

The suite was stunning. The king-sized bed faced a wall of glass windows with a view of the Las Vegas night lights. The seating area included a big-screen plasma television, a fully stocked minibar, comfortable furniture, and a thick, plush carpet.

Jasmine tossed her hat on the bed, kicked off her shoes, and sank her feet into the carpet. "Thank God that's over."

"You didn't even look at the fancy digs. You've been here before." Ace removed his jacket and hung it in the mirror-fronted closet.

"Your jaw didn't drop either, so you've been here too. Right?" she asked.

"I've been in Vegas for the Professional Rodeo several times, and yes, I've been here," he said.

"But you didn't book a room here for your wedding, which tells me that you didn't book the room the time you were here," she said.

"I'm not talking about past women on my wedding night, if that's what you are angling for." He sat down on the sofa and picked up a menu from the glass-topped coffee table. "What would my new bride and best friend like for supper, or is it dinner in a place like this?"

She sat down beside him. "I'm not a bride in real life. I am your best friend—at least as long as you are a dragon and I'm the princess the rest of the night—and it is supper. You let all those cameras come through the door, and I'll turn into a dragon and you can be the princess."

"Never been a drag queen. What color dress do I get to wear if I'm a princess?" he teased.

"I think apricot taffeta and a corset, or at least a good tight-fittin' bra." She giggled. She'd only had two glasses of champagne, but they'd been on an empty stomach.

Ace kicked off his boots and leaned his head back on the sofa. "I was thinkin' maybe I'd be a sexy princess and dress in black lace with one of those big floppy hats."

His eyelashes fanned out on his cheekbones. Strange, she'd never noticed before how thick they were. His thigh pressed against hers and created another spasm of desire. It was a helluva time to decide that she was attracted to Ace Riley. All those months he'd teased her about a date and she'd held him off. Put him in a fancy hotel and her in a wedding dress, and suddenly she would like to have wild, passionate sex with him? God, what was wrong with her? Hopefully, it was a combination of nerves and hunger. Now that the whole thing was over and food would be coming soon, she would get over the craziness.

He opened his eyes, sat up, and looked at the menu. "So we've moved past the drag-queen conversation and on to the dinner?"

"Looks that way." She moved even closer to study the menu with him.

There were dozens of women in north central Texas that Ace could order for. Gracie liked chicken fettuccine; Karly, seafood, preferably lobster; Macie, burgers and fries and banana splits afterward. But he had no idea what Jasmine liked or hated.

"Steaks. Seafood. Wine list. Beer, imported and local. Appetizers. Sushi," he rattled off to cover the guilt trip.

"I don't want sushi," Jasmine said.

"Steaks?"

"Sounds good. Appetizer of those little pepper poppers," she said.

Something hot in her mouth might take her mind off the hot cowboy beside her.

She hiked up her dress, removed the garter, and slipped it over his hand and up his arm to his bicep. "I won't go past the barbed wire."

"Good, because ain't no woman going to get under the barbed wire and capture my heart." He popped the garter and made the mistake of looking at her long legs, stretched from sofa to coffee table.

Would those red toenails taste like strawberries? What would they taste like if he dipped them in warm chocolate syrup?

Stop it, right now! Think about steak. Think about fifty-yard passes. But not Jazzy. She's only a bride to save the ranch, not because she's attracted to you, cowboy. If she was, she would have let it be known months ago. This is like the old western movies when the villain tries to take the farm and the cowboy rides in with his white hat and saves it for the damsel in distress. Only with a twist. I was the cowboy in distress and Jazzy is the cowgirl in the white hat who's ridden in to save the poor old cowboy. But rest assured, there sure won't be any ridin' off into the sunset.

"Medium rare. Baked potato. Salad with ranch dressing and whatever dessert is chocolate and sinful. And don't forget the pepper poppers," she said.

He picked up the phone, ordered, and turned back to find her green eyes locked with his. Something flashed between them like a forked bolt of lightning. She wet her lips like she had at the wedding chapel, and her eyes went soft and unfocused. He was leaning in for the kiss. Hell, he could taste the kiss, and the arousal beginning to put pressure on his zipper was proof that he wanted even more than one kiss, but he drew back at the last minute.

Jasmine felt cheated and relieved at the same time. Cheated because she really wanted his lips on hers; relieved because he blinked and quickly made an excuse to go to the bathroom. She went to the bedroom side of the wall splitting the room, opened her suitcase, and hurriedly changed from the white dress into boxer shorts and a gray tank top.

Get the thing off and the vibes will go away, she thought.

She heard the shower running and thought back to the first time she met Ace Riley. He had been one of the first people she'd met at the Chicken Fried when she bought the place and found out that the café was his second home. He often stopped in right about closing time for a hamburger and ate it in the kitchen while he talked about his women problems, his ranch, or his family. When he came in just before closing last Thursday looking like he'd lost his last friend, she'd asked him what was wrong.

He'd sat down at the prep table and put his head in his hands.

"Okay, spit it out. Did your best friend die? Oh my God, he did, didn't he? Please don't tell me it's Wil. I've got to call Pearl right now."

He put out a hand and touched her arm to stop her. "It's not Wil or any of the O'Donnell brothers. It's no one. I'm goin' to lose my ranch, Jazzy."

"Foreclosure?" she whispered.

"Oh, no, I'm not rich but I've got money, and the ranch is paid for. My gramps left me everything he had. Cows, bulls, land, house, barns. All of it. I moved my stock and equipment in, kept the best, and sold the rest. He used an old lawyer that was half-senile and half-alcoholic, and I signed all the papers the week after Gramps died. Without reading any of it," he'd groaned.

She'd finished grilling a thick hamburger patty, toasted a bun, and put the burger together: mustard, meat patty, tomato, lettuce, pickle slices, and the top bun, added a double handful of chips on the side of the plate, and set it before him without even asking. She knew him so well that she even knew how many pickle slices he wanted on his burger.

"That wasn't very smart, I take it?" she asked.

"No, the lawyer asked me if I understood all of it and I said I did. I'd worked for Gramps for years and knew it was mine when he passed on. We'd talked about it lots of times. I didn't need to read all that legal jargon."

"And what came back to bite you on the butt?"

He'd bitten into the burger without his usual happy *mmmm* noises. "Old lawyer died. His nephew takes over and is closing his files. He reads the will and then calls me to make sure I'm married. When I told him 'hell no,' he said I was in big trouble. I have this cousin, not first cousin but second or third. His name is Cole, and the small print in the will says that if I'm not married within two years of Gramps's death, then Cole gets it all, lock, stock, and barrel. That means he gets what I've worked for because I sold off a lot of Gramps's old equipment and the cattle culls, and in the past two years I've built the place up."

Jasmine replayed the events in her mind while an old rerun of *Bones* played on television. How had she missed noticing how sexy Ace's eyes were or how cute his butt was in those old faded Wranglers that day?

"How long you got?" she'd asked.

"A week and I don't even have a girlfriend. And you can bet that Cole is gloating. That bastard hates ranchin' but he hates me even worse because I was Gramps's favorite. He's not even a Riley. He's kin on Granny's side so he's a Nelson, and Gramps knew exactly what he was doing. I'd fight a forest fire with nothing but the spit in my mouth to keep Cole from having my ranch."

"So a week from today?" she'd asked.

"That's it. I might as well start packing."

"Where's Cole from? I haven't ever met him, have I?"

"Oh, no! That slimy bastard lives in Dallas, and according to what he told the lawyer, the place and everything on it will be sold at auction before the end of summer. I can buy it or get out."

"I'll marry you," Jasmine had said without a second's hesitation.

He'd almost choked. "What did you say?"

"I said that I'd marry you. You know the story

of me and Eddie Jay. I don't have any intentions of getting married or even involved with anyone for at least a year. I'm on the wagon. How long do you have to stay married before you can get a divorce?"

"At least a year. Jazzy, a year is a long time," he said.

"Depends on what you are doing. We won't be doing anything different than we are right now. So it'll go by just as fast if we're married or if we aren't. It's a secret that only you and I will know about. Let's go to Las Vegas and get married. We'll bring home a marriage license and give it to the lawyer. Cole can crawl back under his rock and forget about taking your ranch, and in a year we'll get a very quiet divorce," she'd said.

It had sounded like a beautiful, golden plan at the time. No one other than the lawyer and greedy Cole would even know about the marriage. The lawyer would file the papers and forget about them. Cole could lick his wounds and forget about padding his bank account with the proceeds of the Double Deuce.

"Are you sure, Jazzy?" Ace had whispered.

"Hey, what are friends for?" she'd said with a big grin.

Now she wasn't so sure that it had been a golden moment. More like a fool's-gold moment!

Ace took a long, cool shower and had things under control when he wrapped a towel around his waist. He poked his head out of the bathroom and yelled, “Hey, Jazzy, would you pitch my duffel bag in here?”

In a minute she stuffed it through the small slit and he shut the door. He dug around in the bag until he found his cotton pajama bottoms and a white tank top. He combed his curls back with his fingertips and brushed his teeth.

He’d never had a friend like Jazzy before. They’d hit it off from the day they met when he came into the Chicken Fried Café and ordered a burger. She was cute as a new baby kitten, tough as nails, and sweet as ice cream, and he’d flirted some those first few days. But they’d become friends and he didn’t want to ruin that. He could take any problem to Jazzy and she’d help him work through it. He’d eaten lots and lots of burgers in the middle of the afternoon in her kitchen while he talked about cows, bulls, hired help, and even women.

He’d never thought for a minute about him and Jazzy getting hitched. He wouldn’t have asked her, not in a million years. But now they were and there had been that crazy, topsy-turvy moment when he kissed her at the chapel and another one when she sat down so close that their legs touched. Fire and ice shot through his body, and there wasn’t a thing he could do about it. Jazzy was his friend, the only woman he’d ever trusted. And she’d only married him because of that friendship. So he'd had to shake that crap out of his mind about kissing her again to see if it felt as good the second time around.

He was just coming out of the bathroom when someone knocked on the door and yelled, "Room service!"

Jasmine started to stand up but noticed that he was closer to the door. He was one hot cowboy with water droplets still clinging to his hair and that thin tank top stretched across an acre of chest. She wondered if that soft blond hair peeking out the top would feel like velvet on her fingertips.

Common sense told her to kick Ace right out in the hallway, lock the door, and tell him by cell phone to sleep in the hall or go book another room. It yelled loudly that she was playing with fire and she would get burned. Ace Riley was a player. Ace Riley had a barbed-wire tattoo on his arm, testimony that no woman would ever get near his heart.

Desire sending out delicious little liquid spasms down low in her belly told her to hang a "Do Not Disturb" sign on the door and consummate the marriage in at least three different positions. It whispered softly that what she and Ace could do in that big bed would make red-hot flames.

It wasn't easy but she ignored both of them and concentrated on her hungry stomach. Dinner smelled heavenly when the waiter pushed it inside. The table was lined in virginal white, and silver domes covered their plates, with napkins, crystal, and silverware all at the ready. A basket of bread sat in the middle. An ice bucket with crushed ice and six Coors longnecks was beside it. And a three-tiered silver server held a whole array of miniature chocolate delights—from bite-sized cheesecakes to chocolate-covered strawberries.

Ace pulled a straight-backed chair up to the table and motioned for her to sit. "I'm glad you're willin' to give up the good life and drink beer with me."

"The champagne we had in the limo was very good, but I really do like beer with steak. It's the redneck in me," Jasmine said.

Besides that, two glasses of champagne had put wicked desires in her heart and body. Beer, steak, and at least half of those rich, sinful delights afterward should take her mind plumb off sex for at least a week. By then she'd be back in her routine and Ace would be the fellow who came in for burgers and bantering.

He brought another chair from the other side of the room and sat down across the table from her. "Ah, come on, you ain't got a drop of redneck. You come from the high-dollar side of life. I knew that the first time I met you. You never do talk about your upbringin'. Maybe I ought to get to know you better now that we're married."

She cut a piece of rib-eye steak and chewed it slowly. "God, this is good. I'd marry you all over again just for the steak."

He laughed out loud. "And I thought I was a ladies' man."

"Sorry to bust your bubble, but the steak is better than any man I've ever met, including you, my friend." She checked the windows to make sure the stars were shining in the sky. In that flat desert, a storm could travel really fast, and she'd already tempted the Almighty God once that night when she vowed to love Ace and respect him through all eternity.

But I do love him as a friend, and I do respect him as a rancher and a cowboy, she argued.

Stop justifying. You also promised that 'til-death-do-us-part crap, her inner voice whispered.

I will respect him until the death of the marriage parts us. That's called a divorce.

"Now that my ego is in shambles, tell me about you in case Cole says this is just a marriage on paper and contests it," Ace said.

"Poor baby! His ego has been shattered," Jasmine teased as if they were in the café kitchen instead of the honeymoon suite at the Bellagio.

"Come on, Jazzy. I don't know jack crap about you. A man should know the woman he's married," Ace said.

"Okay, but only because you are pouting. I was born and raised in Sherman, Texas. My mother and Pearl's momma were best friends so it just fell into place that we spent a lot of time together. I have a graduate degree in business management and accounting. Came right out of college and went to work for Texas Instruments and gradually worked on my master's degree. I like what I do now much better than what I did. Cooking has always been my passion."

"Men?" Ace asked.

"Five years with Eddie Jay. I've mentioned him before, remember? Three dating him and two living with him. That broke me from sucking eggs, I'm here to tell you. Evidently he's been in love with Jadeen Jones since high school but wouldn't buck up against his folks to have her because she came from the wrong side of the tracks. She had his baby last year. Cute little boy that looks exactly like him. We broke up and he married her. End of story."

Ace frowned. "He had a baby with another woman while he was with you?"

"Seems that way."

"Crap, Jazzy! You let him live?"

She buttered a yeasty-smelling roll with a crusty top. "He wasn't worth the bullet to put him down. We had this big fight but not like the one between Pearl and Marlin Johnson. I just pitched a bitch fit, which is about ten times bigger than a hissy. Pearl had to pay a fine for domestic abuse, and he got a restraining order against her. I told everyone that our relationship died in its sleep and neither of us really knew it was dead and didn't care enough to mourn. But my heart was cut up in little pieces, and I'm never trusting another man. You are all—"

Ace threw up a palm. "Whoa, there! I'm sitting right here."

"Darlin', I'd trust you least of all. You are the biggest player and flirt in the whole big state of Texas, even if you are my best friend."

Ace slapped a hand over his heart. "I'm hurt."

"But you won't be in pain a minute longer than it takes to pick up the next woman. Betcha dollars to buckets of cow crap that you are flirting with one by the time we get off the plane tomorrow afternoon."

Ace chuckled. "You know me too well, darlin'."

She nodded. "Yes, I do. Now tell me about you in case the lawyer grills us...kind of like in that old movie *Green Card*."

"I saw that. Felt sorry for them in the end," Ace said. "So you are from Ringgold?"

"Born right on the ranch. When my folks got married, Gramps gave them a start with a section of land, a trailer house, and forty head of Angus. By the time they had three boys, they'd built a house and the herd was growing. Momma was still trying for a girl and got pregnant a fourth time. She went into labor but thought she had plenty of time to get to the hospital, so she didn't get in a hurry to call Daddy out of the field. She got my three older brothers ready to take over to Gramps's place, and by the time they got there, it was too late to go on to the hospital. Granny delivered me in her bedroom, and the ambulance came and took me and Momma to the hospital. Doctor said Granny did a fine job, and Gramps said he got to name me since I was born on the Double Deuce.

"That's why I'm named Ace and why I was his favorite. That and the fact I'm the odd child in the family. Three older brothers who stuck together, then three younger ones that came along after I was a big kid, and they hung together. I was truly the middle child in my family but the only child when I was over at Gramps's place. Momma let me stay over there a lot after Granny died when I was twelve because Gramps was lonely. I have a tat on my arm, which you've seen, and a birthmark behind my left knee that looks like a lopsided set of bull horns. Other than that, I am what you see. I like steak and beer and hamburgers. I ride bulls in the rodeo, and you know who my friends are."

She reached for another bottle of beer at the same time he did. Their hands brushed and the air crackled. She jerked her hand back. It might be a long night, but she wasn't giving in to the desire. He'd married her to keep his ranch, not because he was attracted to her. If he had been, he would've seriously asked her out months ago. He was constantly teasing her about going out with him but she knew it, he knew it, and so did everyone else.

Everything was surreal to Ace. He'd been a

player since he was old enough to chase women, and he loved them. He loved the way they smelled. He loved the way they felt. He loved the chase and the score. All of it, but that night something was happening that ran deeper. Ace Riley, experiencing something new at the age of thirty-two with a woman, and having that woman be Jazzy, put him in brand-new, unmarked territory.

He tried analyzing the situation while he ate. He'd hugged Jazzy lots of times, thanking her for making him a burger after the Chicken Fried was officially closed or comforting her when she looked worn down to a frazzlin'. How could a white dress, those white satin high-heeled shoes, and a Stetson hat have made such a difference in the way he felt?

"Okay, I think we've got that all cleared up. We're good enough friends that if the lawyer asks us those green-card questions we can pass the test without studying. Nothing can go wrong." He grinned.

"I think I heard those four words earlier today," she said.

"What four words?" he asked.

"Nothing can go wrong. I don't believe in the magic of Vegas anymore," she groaned.

"Come on, Jazzy. We'll go home and the only one who will know is Cole. He'll keep his mouth shut, believe me, because he won't want his dignity hanging out on the line like dirty underwear, and he's already made his claims about what he's going to do. He'll slink off like a wounded coyote and lick his wounds. And the lawyer don't care who gets the ranch. He just wants to close the paperwork and go on."

"And why won't Cole broadcast it to the world just to make you look bad?" Jasmine asked.

"Because there's a history with him and the ranch. He never wanted it, still doesn't. I'm not sure what happened, but there was a big problem with Megan after she married Garrett. It wasn't her fault, and it had something to do with Cole being drunk and insulting her. Garrett wanted to kill him. Daddy told Cole to get the hell out of Montague County. Cole would love to get his hands on the ranch, but he would never tell anything. For one thing, no one would believe him; for another, if Garrett ever finds him, he'll still beat the crap out of him."

"Sounds complicated," Jasmine said.

"It is."

"Oh my God!" she said around the tasty little petit-four cake she'd popped into her mouth. "Ace, taste one of these. They're wonderful."

She picked up the tiered tray and carried it to the coffee table. "Push the cart out in the hallway, but we're keeping these in here. If we don't eat them all, I'm taking them home with me tomorrow."

He wheeled the cart out and came back inside but was careful to sit on the other end of the sofa away from her and not right in the middle. He turned up the volume on the television when the ten o'clock news came on. The weather was going to be hot and sunny, but that was to be expected in Nevada as well as Texas the first week of June. Someone had won a half-million-dollar jackpot at the slots at one of the casinos. Jasmine listened with half an ear but didn't pay much attention when the anchorperson didn't mention the Bellagio.

And then that cute little lady who'd been at the wedding chapel came on the television with her big smile said, "And for our human-interest story today. A couple from a tiny little town in Texas called Ringgold that has only about a hundred people in it..."

Ace and Jasmine both sat straight up and held their breath.

"Got the ultimate honeymoon in Las Vegas tonight. We have live footage of the whole wedding ceremony and their surprise when they found out that they'd just won a honeymoon package, compliments of Cupid's Wedding Chapel, for being the five thousandth couple to get married at the Cupid's. The owner presented them with a surprise package including the honeymoon suite at the Bellagio, dinner, a limo, and champagne. Congratulations, Mr. and Mrs. Ace Riley from Ringgold, Texas. May you have a long and happy life and come back to Las Vegas on your fiftieth anniversary."

The whole time she was talking, live footage of the wedding flashed across the screen. Jasmine's first thought was that the camera didn't add ten pounds but twenty. Her second was something that had to do with hell being holy! She pushed her chair back, stood up on weak knees, and paced the floor. Ace followed Jasmine's example and kept in step with her back and forth across the floor.

"Please tell me that is not national coverage, that it's a local, preferably a Bellagio-only station," she moaned.

Both of their cell phones rang at the same time. His ringtone was "Mammas, Don't Let Your Babies Grow Up to Be Cowboys." Hers was "Baby Girl," which meant her mother had her father's cell phone in her hand and not her own.

"Don't guess it is," Ace drawled.

"You goin' to answer yours?" she asked.

"Not right now. We got to get our stories straight before we answer anything. That was Momma. Who was yours?"

"Momma on Daddy's phone. Hers is always in her purse, and his is on the end table between the sofa and his recliner," she said.

Jasmine threw herself back on the sofa. "We are up crap creek without a paddle and I see the rapids ahead. Dammit to hell, Ace. I can't do this! I can't be married to you in real life. This was supposed to be a secret! I've got a café to run."

Ace followed her lead again, landing beside her so close that their entire sides were plastered against each other. "Guess we're goin' to have to pretend to be married for a year. I'm sorry I got you into this mess, Jazzy."

"I'm the one who proposed to you, if I remember right, so you don't get to be sorry about that." She jumped up like a windup toy and paced back and forth across the floor again, mumbling and cussing alternately.

His phone played the first bars of Blake Shelton's "Hillbilly Bone," and he picked it up.

"Hello."

She stared right at him and he grinned.

"Yep, that was me, all right. I guess she did get past the barbed-wire tat. Nope, honey, I guess I won't be seeing you again. I'm sorry that you are disappointed. Got a call coming, 'bye now." His voice was low and sexy.

She glared.

He poked a button and said, "Yes, ma'am. That was me and yes, ma'am, I'm married. No, it's not a joke. Yes, I guess we are canceling our date for the rodeo. Sorry that you think I'm a sorry bastard. Got another call."

Jasmine glared harder.

"Hello. Don't think so, darlin'. I hear that rotting in hell involves sitting in flames, and I really don't like that."

He laid the phone down after that one and said, "She hung up on me after she told me to rot in hell."

"Crapstorm, Ace. We've stirred up a big, old crap tornado! What in the hell are we goin' to do? I don't have an extra bedroom."

When Ace shrugged, she went on, "Dammit! We might as well have gotten married at the Montague County Courthouse and put it on the front page of the Bowie newspaper. Momma is going to be furious."

Ace chuckled.

She pointed her finger at him and narrowed her eyes. "It's not funny. It's *not* a secret after all, and what happens in this town isn't supposed to be broadcast on national television. We are married and you, darlin', are going to have to be celibate for a whole year!"

Ace groaned. "Oh my God! Jazzy, what are we going to do?"

"I don't know. But I do know if you cheat on me, Pearl and Gemma will kill you." She threw herself back on the sofa for the second time, keeping a foot of space between them. "Why in the hell did you pick that chapel?"

Ace threw up his palms defensively. "Hey, it looked like the least known one in the whole town. How was I supposed to know it was having a contest? You can live at the ranch. I've got four bedrooms. Three are empty right now. You can take your choice."

"I don't want to live at the ranch! I like my

apartment and it's convenient above the café. And you said nothing else could go wrong. Guess what, cowboy?"

His phone rang again. "I will never utter those words again, Jazzy. I promise. That's my mother."

She pinched the top of her nose. The headache was coming on strong. "There's no getting around it now that it's been on television. You're going to sleep on my sofa for a year, boy!"

Ace sat up straight and shot her a dirty look. "I'm not sleeping on a sofa when I've got a king-sized bed. And don't call me 'boy'! I'm a full-grown man, and if you doubt that, I can prove it right now."

"No thank you," she said.

"*You* can live at the ranch. You don't have to do jack crap in the way of cooking or cleaning. You can go to your café every morning and come back at night when you get finished. Sleep in one of my guest bedrooms and pretend to be my wife. It's no big deal!"

"No big deal!" she squealed. "That's what you think, buster!"

He shook a finger at her. "Stop being dramatic, Jazzy."

She dropped her hand and glared at him. "Me, dramatic? I'm barely scratching the surface of drama."

"Oh, really?" he said coldly.

"You don't have any idea what you are about to

walk into. My mother will plan a big party and may even make us repeat our vows in front of a Texas preacher so it will be legal in her eyes. And dear Lord, what about Gemma and Austin and Pearl! God Almighty, crap tornado doesn't begin to cover what's going to hit you!"

He ran a hand down his face, but it didn't erase the worry. "If we tell them it's a farce, then Cole will figure out some loophole way to take the ranch and all this will be for nothing."

Both phones continued to try to outdo each other. The room sounded like two country-western concerts in one bar at the exact same time.

Jasmine took a deep breath. "Okay." She sighed.

"Okay what?" Ace asked.

"That sumbitch ain't takin' the ranch. We'll just have to suck it up and endure each other. I'll stay at the ranch but only from bedtime to dawn. Story is that we've been seeing each other for a couple of months on the sly and decided on Thursday that we'd fought our love long enough and would get married. Simple but almost true," she said.

"A whole year!" he groaned.

"Ace Riley, you will be celibate for a year. And before you roll your pretty blue eyes, yes, I have mommy issues and no, they are not resolved, and you will understand when you meet Kelly King that she gets her way, so you might as well let her have it to begin with."

He moaned loudly and rolled his pretty blue eyes anyway.

Blessed silence filled the room for all of five seconds, then her ringtone told her that her mother had fished her phone from her purse. If a ringtone could sound angry, it did.

She answered cautiously. "Hello, Momma. It's awful late for you to be callin'. Everything all right?"

"Jasmine Marie King, don't you play dumb with me. I've been callin' you every two minutes for half an hour. Have you seen the news? That is you, isn't it? Marryin' that blond-haired cowboy?"

"Yes, ma'am, it is. I married Ace Riley at Cupid's Chapel tonight. You want to meet him?"

"I'm cussin' mad right now, girl. Are you pregnant?"

"I am not!" Jasmine choked out the words.

"Well, why'd you go off and do a dumb stunt like that? We've been saving for thirty years for your wedding."

"Take the money and go on a cruise."

"I hate boats and your dad refuses to sleep anywhere but in his own bed. I knew when you went off on that fool notion to buy a café that nothing good would come of it. We *will* have a wedding and a reception in Sherman. One of those fly-by-night things in Las Vegas can't be legal and binding. Besides, I don't care if it is. It's not legal and binding in my eyes until the marriage license says 'Texas' across the top, so you will redo it, Jasmine.

"There's no room for argument, so either you pick out a dress or I will. That's all you get to choose since you and your groom decided to elope off to Las Vegas. What in the hell were you thinking? I'm planning it for one month from today. We'd do it sooner, but it'll take at least that long to line up a caterer and get things arranged. It'll be a true Texas wedding with all the trimmings, and I'm spending every dime we've saved for it. The guest list is going to be huge and I've already called Marcella."

"Four weeks from today is Saturday, and I'm not closing the Chicken Fried." Jasmine's headache approached a full-blown migraine.

"You know that I've been planning your wedding since you were born, and if I decide to have my reception on Tuesday morning at ten o'clock, you'll close that restaurant and come to it, young lady. And you'd better have a decent dress for the wedding. Not some hooker dress like you had on in that wedding tonight."

Jasmine shut her eyes. She had a month to come up with a decent dress to wear to another farce, or her mother would pick out a ridiculously fancy dress with a train that stretched from Amarillo to Beaumont.

Ace chuckled and she snapped her eyes open long enough to give him a go-to-hell look that was meant to leave nothing but a silver belt buckle and pearl snaps on the fancy velvet sofa.

"Did you hear me?" Kelly King said.

"Yes, ma'am," Jasmine barked, then softened her voice and said with sugary-sweet sarcasm, "Momma, could we have the wedding on the first Sunday afternoon in July? You choose the place and the hours. We'll come home to Sherman Saturday as soon as I close the Chicken Fried and stay 'til the last dog's dead at the reception. I'll bring the dress."

"I'm looking at a calendar and Sunday, July 1, is out of the question. Your father is scheduled for a conference in Boston. We'll have it on July 8." Kelly huffed. "What's done can't be undone. Tell my new son that I'm lookin' forward to meeting him. And I will have a backup dress on hand in case you show up with something too plain."

Jasmine rolled her eyes and said very slowly with gritted teeth, "I will tell Ace, Momma," and then hung up.

Ace threw an arm around her shoulder. "That sounded horrible."

"It was. In one month we are having a wedding reception that will straighten every blond curl on your head, and we will be getting married again in the great state of Texas because if the marriage license doesn't have 'Texas' across the top, then it's not good for anything but to put in the outhouse to use when you run out of toilet paper."

He groaned. "Dammit! Jazzy, I'm sorry. Just tell her no, that we're already married and it is legal."

"It's complicated and she is right. I do know how long she's waited for this and how important this wedding is to her. I'm her only child and she didn't have a big wedding, so she's always said mine would make up for hers. I told you, it would be hell to pay! Momma will invite everyone in the state of Texas including the governor, if she can get Daddy to make the call. And if you think this is a mess, wait until we file for divorce."

"Your momma goin' to put out a hit on me?" Ace groaned.

She pointed. "Probably. She might even hire Cole to do the killin'. And you can bet that she will start in on me the week after the Texas wedding about my biological clock ticking and wanting a grandchild. She'll say I owe her one because Pearl got married the right way in Texas and she's already giving Tess twin boys so we'll have to deal with that too."

Ace wiggled an eyebrow and glanced at the king-sized bed. "Does that mean...?"

"It means you can sleep on your side and I'll stay on mine. It means nothing has changed," Jasmine said. "I don't do booty calls for friends."

He laughed. "Well, at least you are still calling me a friend." His phone rang and he rolled his eyes.

"Your turn," Jasmine said.

"Hello, Momma," he said.

"Ace Thomas Riley!" She yelled so loud that her words bounced off the walls.

"That's me, Momma," he said, "all three names and in the flesh. Right here in the fanciest hotel in Vegas in the honeymoon suite with Jasmine King Riley, my new bride. I'll bring her by tomorrow evening when we get back to Ringgold so you can meet her as my bride. I'm sure you've run into her at the café, but I'd like to introduce you formally."

"I would have liked to have talked to her and met her formally before you married her. I didn't recognize that name. You say she works in a café?" Dolly Riley's voice was two octaves higher than normal.

"She owns the Chicken Fried and she's the cook."

"Dear God, Ace! Did you draw up a prenup?"

"Never crossed my mind."

"I'll talk to you when you get home. Any other surprises in store?"

He chuckled. "Momma, are you askin' me if we're going to make you a grandmother real soon?" Ace went on. "The answer is no. We did not get married because Jazzy is pregnant. Sorry to disappoint you."

"Disappoint! Praise the Lord for that small favor!" Dolly snapped her phone shut.

Jasmine laid her head on Ace's shoulder and it felt right, proving that friends were a helluva lot better than lovers. "We've eaten our horny toads. The rest of the calls can't be that bad."

"Horny toads?" he asked.

"Granny Dale, that would be Momma's mother who lives in west Texas, says that if you get up every morning and eat a live horny toad, nothing the world can throw at you the rest of the day is so bad."

Ace laughed, letting out the pent-up tension. "I am imaginin' both our mothers with horns on their heads."

"Well, the cat's definitely out of the bag and we can't put it back inside," Jasmine said.

"Not without getting clawed all to hell," he answered. "Let's turn our phones off, unplug the room phone, and let them all think we're usin' that bed for something other than sleepin'." He patted her arm.

She promptly pushed the button on her cell phone. "I wish I'd have thought of that before the news."

Chapter 3

THE BED WAS SO SOFT AND JASMINE WAS SO worn out physically and mentally that she wished she could slip beneath the duvet and sheets bare-butt naked instead of wearing plaid boxer shorts and a gray tank top. She'd worked until two that day, flown from Dallas to Vegas on a nonstop flight, and gotten married, and then dealt with the fallout all evening. She picked up the tiered server and carried it to the bed. Ace was already on his side of the acre-sized bed, his hands laced behind his head and his eyes on her.

She set the goodie tray in the middle of the bed and settled down, cross-legged, beside it. "You guys cheat. It's all right for you to go to bed naked from the waist up. Girls don't get to do that."

"Hey, I got no problem with you coming to bed naked all over." He grinned and chose a bite-sized turtle cheesecake from the server.

She bit into an enormous chocolate-covered strawberry. "I deserve every bit of this. Stress destroys fat grams and calories."

"And there's a book in the bedside table..."

She air slapped him on the tattoo. "Tell me

about that thing. Austin says that Rye's got one too. I know they protect you from women but that Rye's didn't work with Austin. When did you get them, and are you BFFs or something?"

Even that close, her almost-touch heated the barbed wire up to the burning point.

"In guy language, that BFF crap means something different than you girls' stuff about best friends forever," he said.

"What does it mean?"

He ate another cheesecake bite. "Can't tell you. It's a big secret and we have to sign our names in blood before we can be a member. Part of the code is that girls don't get to know what it means."

"Oh?" She tucked her chin in and looked up at him through heavy lashes.

"Have to prick our finger with our own spur. No sissies or preppies can be in our BFF club," he said seriously.

"Ace Riley, you are full of pure old stinky bullcrap."

"That's what the first letter stands for. Want to keep guessing on the two *F's*?" When he grinned his blue eyes sparkled.

"No, I do not. Any members of your club women?" she asked. "I figured a flirty player like you would let women in just to seduce them."

"Hell, no! This is a guy's club," Ace said.

"You wear cute little necklaces to prove it, or do

you all have barbed-wire tats?" She tried to decide between a tiny cheesecake or a bite-sized tiramisu.

"Hell no again! And my tat don't have a thing to do with our BFF club," he declared.

"Okay, tell me why you and Rye have one, and Wil doesn't have one. I've never seen one on Raylen or on Dewar either. Are they members of your club?"

"We're all members of it. We meet at least once a month, and everyone tells their wives or girlfriends that they're goin' coon huntin'. The tat is something different than the club. Just me and Rye got them."

She propped up on one elbow. "You better tell me because if Cole or his lawyer ask about it, I need to know."

"It's a crazy kid thing."

She cocked her head to one side, her dark-brown hair curling up on the pillowcase. "I'm listenin'."

Ace sat up and faced her. His arms were muscled from hard work, his abs ripped, and a fine line of soft brown hair trailed from his chest down beneath red-plaid pajama bottoms with a drawstring. Jasmine's fingers itched to go exploring where that hairline ended. She sat up and laced them together to keep them out of mischief.

He sighed. "It was eleven years ago. Rye is actually the youngest among me and him and Wil. Dewar is just younger than him, and Raylen comes in after that. We all ran around together, but it was me and Wil and Rye who were the same age. Rye'd just turned twenty-one and we'd been down to Mesquite to the Resistol Rodeo. Not a one of us did a bit of good that night. None of us had enough points to even go on to the next round of bull riding. Raylen and Dewar are both younger than us, and they ride broncs and would put us plumb to shame. So we were whinin' around like three little girls. We were big boys so we could go to the bars and Raylen and Dewar couldn't, so we left them behind and started home."

Jasmine was reminded of what her mother said about Granny Dale. "Don't ask her a question because she begins everything with, 'In the beginning God made dirt,' and it'll take her five years to get the answer out."

"Anyway," Ace went on. "We were hitting every bar from Mesquite to Dallas. It was very late or very early, depending on how you look at it. But it was way past two because all the bars were shut down. None of us were sober enough to drive, but it was my truck so neither of them was going to get behind the wheel. Rye was carryin' on about this girlfriend he had. Sabrina? No, her name was Serena. They'd been in love since grade school and she'd up and married another man. Wil had passed out in the back seat, and I looked up to see a twenty-four-hour tattoo parlor right there on our side of the road. I pulled the truck into the parking lot and told Rye all three of us were getting barbed-wire tats around our left arm so no woman could ever hurt him again."

"But why would you and Wil get a tat? Serena didn't break your hearts," Jasmine asked.

"Did I say we were very, very drunk? And remember, we'd stabbed our fingers with our spurs and written our names on the BFF roster sheet, which is in a bank vault under lock and key and protected by armed guards, so in my drunken state I thought I had to take care of Rye."

Jasmine giggled. "How on earth did you get home without wrecking your truck?"

"It was a real job, I'm tellin' you, darlin'. A real trick that took an excellent driver to pull it off, but I can drive anything with four wheels or ride anything with four legs."

"And two legs?" She raised a dark eyebrow.

"I'm a sweet-talkin' son of a gun with anything that has two legs." He grinned.

"Go on," she said.

"Well, Wil woke up enough to tell us he wasn't getting no tat and went back to sleep. Me and Rye staggered into the place. Hell, we didn't even look around to see if it was decent. It's a wonder we both didn't catch something horrible, but anyway, we told the lady what we wanted. You should've seen her, Jazzy. She had tats all over her body, at least the parts we could see, and that was a helluva lot of skin. She took Rye to the back room and I followed. She put a barbed wire around his left arm and I bared mine to get the same thing. Wil didn't even feel sorry for us when we carried on the next day about them hurting."

"That was pretty stupid, and I wouldn't have felt sorry for you either," she said.

Ace propped the pillows against the headboard and leaned back. "Okay, now you have to share. You got any tats?"

"One," Jasmine said.

His eyes scanned what he could see. "You're lyin' to me—and on our wedding day. I might divorce you in a year rather than you divorcing me."

"I've got a tat. I'm not lyin' to you."

"Where?"

To Jasmine, his gaze felt like a blowtorch. It had to be that dress and veil. She'd been a fool to wear the thing and it was supposed to stop making her hot when she took it off. She should've worn her jeans and a tie-dyed knit shirt and sneakers. But there it was hanging in the closet when she'd started packing for the overnight trip and she'd decided to play dress-up.

"Where?" he asked again.

"On my butt, and nobody, not even Pearl or Momma, knows it's there. I got it when I bought the café."

He grinned. "I didn't know they made a tat of a chicken fried steak. Show it to me."

She shook her head. "It's not a chicken-fried steak."

"Then what is it? Show me. You promised to love, honor, and *obey* me. I'm orderin' you to show me that tat. I still don't believe you've got one!"

Her eyes widened. "You vowed to love, honor, and *respect* me. I'm callin' in that last vow about respectin' me and my tat."

He inched over toward her with a wicked gleam in his eyes.

"Oh, okay. It's not that big a deal," she said.

"I'm the very first one to ever see it, so it's a big deal to me," he said.

She flipped around and jerked down the back of her boxer shorts.

At first Ace couldn't believe his eyes. He'd expected a butterfly or a heart, or perhaps the Chinese symbol for love, but not what was right there in bright green and yellow high up on her hip. He moved closer and blinked several times, but it was still there. Why in the world would she get a tat of the John Deere tractor logo: a bulging green square with a yellow deer silhouette in the center?

She flipped her shorts back up and turned to face him.

"Why?" he asked.

"Why did I get a tat? Why is it a tractor logo? Which one?"

He wasn't grinning anymore when she looked up. "All of the above."

"I got it because I quit a six-figure job to buy a café that won't make half that in a year. And I'll work twice as hard and twice as many hours to make half that much. A tractor logo because one time back when Pearl and I were teenagers we got into trouble and her dad decided our punishment was plowing a field in a John Deere tractor with an open cab. No air-conditioning and no CD player, not even a radio. And it taught me a lesson I'll never forget. Either be smart enough not to get caught, or suffer the punishment without bitchin'. But mostly it was to remind me that I'm in control of where this tractor called life is taking me. And if I've ever got a doubt, all I need to do is look in the mirror at my butt."

"Fine-lookin' butt and fine-lookin' tat," Ace said.

"You are a good friend," Jasmine said.

"Not as good as you, darlin'. You saved the ranch, remember?"

She laughed. "Guess neither of us are as smart as we thought we were, though, are we?"

Ace snuggled back down in the bed and laced his hands together behind his head again. "Guess not. What was it that got you and Pearl in so much trouble that you had to plow all day?"

"All day? It was all week." Her voice raised at least three octaves.

Ace rolled over to face her. "What in the hell did you two do? Wreck his brand-new pickup?"

"No, we got into his very expensive bourbon and got pretty well wasted, then we filled the bottle up with water," she said.

It started as a chuckle down deep in his chest, but when it erupted, it was a full-fledged guffaw that he couldn't control. "I didn't know I'd married a whiskey girl," he finally got out.

"That's what you get for sayin' yes when I proposed." She yawned. "Confession must be good for the soul because I'm sleepy now, but if you tell anyone about my tat I'm going to divorce you before the year is out."

Ace rolled his eyes in mock horror. "She has ice water in her veins. She's threatening me before the marriage is even consummated."

Jasmine shot a look his way and turned over with her back toward him, curled up in a ball, and shut her eyes. Knowing that Ace was only a couple of feet from her, visualizing that broad chest, a big bicep with the tat wrapped around it, and catching a whiff of his shaving lotion every time she inhaled did not bring on instant sleep.

Ace looked his fill of Jasmine. She did look like she could be that actress's sister with her small waist, well-rounded cute little butt, shoulder-length brown hair, and those eyes. But he bet dollars to cow patties that Greg House never found a John Deere logo on Cuddy's butt. He had to force himself to stop thinking about Jasmine, but it sure wasn't easy. Not when he was semi-aroused and wanting to do much more than sleep with Jasmine—as in shut his eyes and really, really just sleep.

When she awoke the next morning, sunlight was streaming in the window. Ace was spooned up next to her back with an arm thrown around her midriff and his face buried in her hair. She was afraid to breathe after the dreams she'd had all night. All she had to do was pretend she was still dreaming, roll over into his arms, and whisper his name and the hardness pressing into her back would take care of the rest.

Every hormone in her body had set up a chant: *It's okay. You are married. It's okay. You are married.*

She tried to wiggle out of his embrace, but he mumbled something and wrapped her up even tighter and mumbled something about her being beautiful. Jasmine had no doubt that he was having a very good dream. Was she anything other than a cook slash waitress in the dream, or was she even a character in it? Most likely he was talking to Gracie or one of those other women who'd called him the night before.

She pushed backwards, which was a horrible

idea. Heat practically set the fancy duvet into blazes. "Ace, wake up!"

"Do I have to?" he whispered.

His warm breath heated up the sensitive skin under her ear.

She pushed backwards again. "Yes, you have to wake up. We've got to be at the airport in two hours and I'm hungry, so we need to pack things up, check out, and get some breakfast."

He still didn't open his eyes. "Let's stay here all day and have breakfast brought in and catch a redeye home."

She relaxed and stopped fighting against the strong arm that held her. "We've got to go home and face the music sometime. Might as well get it over with. We got caught."

"I know, but we could put it off one more day. You think they're goin' to make us plow the fields?" He nuzzled against her neck, liking the way his face fit as if they'd been made for each other.

"Hell, I hope not. I need to make desserts for tomorrow's lunch run when we get home. I sure don't have time to plow fields," she said.

"And when you get finished at the café you're coming to the ranch, right? You can have a guest room or sleep with me. Your choice," he teased but held his breath until she answered.

Jasmine was barely surviving sleeping with Ace one night. Two nights would be stretching it. Three and the marriage would be consummated multiple times. "I expect we'd best plan on me sleeping in the guest room. I'd never get up and get to work at five in the morning if I was sleeping with you. Besides, you've got barbed wire protecting your heart."

"And you've got a tractor symbol on your butt to prove that you can control your own destiny," he said.

"We're quite the blissful newlyweds, aren't we?"

He kissed her on the neck, his lips lingering awhile as he tasted the softness of his pseudo-bride. "What would you like for breakfast? Your wish is my command."

She laughed and rolled away from him, standing beside the bed and stretching like a cat. "Bacon, eggs, potatoes, biscuits, gravy, and the works."

"I was hoping you'd want something a little closer to this bed," he whispered seductively.

She pointed at him. "Don't tease me, Ace. You want first shower?"

"How about a together shower? See if your tractor can run over my barbed wire," he said.

Who said he was teasing? Jazzy was a fine-looking woman even in a gray tank top and plaid shorts. He could have both off and thrown in the corner in five minutes if she'd just cooperate a little bit.

She picked up her cell phone from the nightstand. "You really are a good friend. You're trying to take my mind off what we're walkin' into and I appreciate it. Just remember, as long as we stick to our story and stand by each other, you won't lose the ranch. Good grief! I've got fifteen missed calls and ten voice messages."

He rolled over and grabbed his phone from the other side. "I beat you. I've got sixteen of each. Looks like ten of the missed calls are from my mother, and oh, now isn't that a sweet surprise. Four from Cole." He flipped the phone open and hit the recall button on Cole's number.

"This is Cole Nelson," the voice on the other end said.

"This is Ace Riley. I missed your call last night, but a groom doesn't answer the phone on his honeymoon."

"I saw it on television," Cole said icily. "What'd you do, marry a cocktail waitress just to keep the farm?"

Ace handed the phone to Jasmine. "It's Cole. You talk to him."

"Hello, I'm Jasmine. I haven't met you but my mother has insisted we have a real wedding in Sherman, Texas, next month where we will be saying our vows again before family and friends, and we'd be so glad for you to attend," she said sweetly.

"You made a big mistake, lady. What'd he promise you?"

Ace jumped out of bed and bowed from the waist down.

Jasmine stuck her tongue out at him.

"To love, honor, and respect me."

"Did he make you sign a prenup?"

"Of course not! We trust each other implicitly," she gasped.

"My lawyer will require proof," Cole said.

"Will the marriage license and pictures do, or should I bring the bedsheets?"

He hung up without another word.

Ace laughed until his side ached. His cousin had met his match when he meddled with Jazzy.

Jasmine fussed and fumed as she paced beside the bed. "Rotten idiot anyway askin' me if we signed a prenup. As if I'd take a dime of your money or land. Hell, I'm protecting it from him. He's stupid. He doesn't know what good friends we are or that this was all my idea."

She mumbled all the way to the bathroom. She was still talking to herself when she came back out with a towel around her head and one tucked around her body. "Your turn."

Ace picked up his shaving kit from his suitcase and started that way. "Your phone rang twice while you were in there. One was Gemma and the other was your mother. I didn't answer either one."

She made sure the bottom towel was secure, then dried her hair vigorously. "Well, I'm sure not ready to talk to Momma yet, and Gemma can wait until I get home. Which reminds me of something I've been wondering about for months. You and Wil were in and out of the O'Donnell's place for years. Why didn't either one of you hook up with Gemma or Colleen?"

Ace stopped at the bathroom door and watched her, his mouth going dry at the sliver of thigh that peeked through a slit in the towel. "It would be like dating my sister."

"You got a sister? You said six brothers, but you didn't mention a sister," Jasmine asked.

"Hell, no! Thank God for small favors. Putting up with Rye's sisters was a cross to bear." Ace whistled into the bathroom. "Hey, Jazzy," he yelled above the sound of his electric razor. "When do you want that shindig thrown with my side of the family? I'll try to talk Momma out of another wedding, but I ain't makin' no promises. She probably thinks we have to do it all over again to make it legal in Montague County, not just the state of Texas."

"Oh, sweet Jesus," she moaned.

"I'm waiting," he yelled again.

"Momma is having one July 10. Just make it on a Sunday afternoon."

The hum of the razor stopped and the whistling started again as he turned on the shower. It was replaced with a deep voice singing, "Hello, Darlin'," a song Conway Twitty made popular years and years before.

Jasmine hurriedly slipped into bikini underpants, a bra, jeans, and a knit shirt while he finished the song and his shower. She was drying her hair when he came out of the bathroom smelling like a mixture of soap and sexy shaving lotion. He was dressed in jeans, shirt, belt, and boots. His hair still had water clinging to a few curls.

She reached up and brushed them away, then quickly drew her hand back. How in the devil could plain old water, no more than dewdrop in size, send shivers down her spine? And how in the hell was she supposed to live with him in the same house for a whole year with these newfound feelings?

Chapter 4

Ace worked on a platter of food that would choke a good-sized horse while Jasmine nibbled at some fruit and a crepe from the breakfast bar. That she was nervous angered her as much as anything else. She was thirty years old, for heaven's sake. She'd been running her own business for a year and a half and she hadn't asked anyone for anything. So if she wanted to pick up a hitchhiker in Nocona and take him down to the Montague County Courthouse and marry him that afternoon, it was her business. At least she knew Ace and he was a decent guy, a fine friend, and a gentleman even if he did have a sexy sense of humor.

The internal pep talk didn't do a bit of good. She was chewing at her thumbnail when Ace hailed a taxi, and by the time they reached McCarran International Airport she felt like she was walking on the edge of a barn roof in three-inch spike heels during a class five tornado.

They checked their bags, hurried through security without a hitch, and got to the waiting area just as a young man announced that the flight to Dallas was boarding. Ace followed Jasmine down the corridor and into the plane and found their seats.

"I've got the window seat but I usually sleep on airplanes. You want to sit there?" he asked.

"Thank you," she said, not eager to sit in the middle seat with Ace on one side and someone else on the other.

She was glad she didn't have extremely long legs like her friend Austin, who was almost six feet tall. At five feet two inches, her knees came within three inches of pressing against the seat in front of her. Austin would be biting her knees unless she flew first class. She snapped her seat belt shut and looked out the window instead of listening to the blah-blah-blah customary cautions.

Ace settled into the seat next to her and got comfortable. He buckled his seat belt, leaned his head back, and shut his eyes.

Jasmine envied his ability to doze while the flight attendant gave the "hang onto the seat cushion and use it for a flotation device" speech. He didn't even open his eyes when the captain's deep voice came over the intercom and said that they would arrive in Houston, Texas, in two hours and forty-three minutes.

When they were in the air, Ace roused up enough to unfasten his seat belt, order a pillow, and in less than two minutes had slung his legs over into the empty space beside him and slept soundly. How he could sleep with those three teenage girls behind him was a mystery to Jasmine. She tried to tune out the giggles and the "OMG, she's not even hot. How could he like her?" and "FYI, she's sleeping with Freddy," but she couldn't sleep.

Suddenly she was pissed at everything and everyone... starting with herself for volunteering for this fiasco and ending with that television station that told the whole world.

She could not let Ace lose everything he'd worked for his whole life over a piece of paper and a few promises. Who was it that said, "Promises are like pie crusts—made to be broken?" Well, he was a genius today. Tomorrow he might be the biggest idiot in the state of Texas, but right then he deserved that big Nobel award for the most profound statement ever uttered.

Ace flipped the pillow on her shoulder and snuggled down into it with a sigh.

"OMG, he's like so sexy. I wonder if he like really rides horses. I bet he's a country music star. OMG, he is, isn't he? Is he Keith Urban?" one of the teenagers whispered.

Jasmine frowned. Ace was a helluva lot sexier than Keith Urban.

"Shhh, she'll, like, hear you," another one said.

"FYI, I don't care. She's like an old woman and he's, like, too sexy to be with her."

Jasmine held up her left hand and wiggled her fingers until she heard gasps behind her.

"OMG, she, like, heard you. And that's, like, a wedding ring."

"BTW, like, I don't care about that, like, either. He just married her for her money, I bet. OMG, I bet she's his manager and she made him, like, marry her."

Jasmine was glad that Ace was sleeping. If he'd been awake, he would have teased her for weeks about the teenyboppers. (Did they like call them that, like, still or was that, like, OMG too ancient of a term for, like, pubescent girls?)

Evidently they all had ADD because Ace's sexiness only lasted a few more minutes and they were off on another tangent. Jasmine wondered briefly if symptoms of attention deficit disorder included abbreviated conversations and overuse of the word *like*. Then everything got quiet behind her and she heard faint noises that meant they were texting.

Probably to each other, Jasmine thought.

She lost interest in the BFFs behind her when she turned toward Ace and got a whiff of his shaving lotion. Ace had never affected her before she put on that wedding dress, so there must have been some kind of biological sex dust crap sprinkled in it that heightened her senses.

Did they spray down all white dresses that had the remote potential of becoming a wedding dress with some sexuality-enhancing pixie powder? She'd like to have the mad scientist who invented this crap by the balls. Oh, yes, it was most definitely a male scientist, one who couldn't attract a woman if he was the only guy on an island with a million women on it. So, he'd invented a little dust to sprinkle in the seams of white dresses that had some kind of weird timing device that set it off on the actual wedding day.

She hoped his invention came around and bit him squarely on the butt.

She turned her head slightly and looked at Ace. His eyes were shut so she could stare as long as she wanted. She held her hands tightly in her lap to keep from running her fingers through his hair. He needed a haircut but she liked his blond curls just the way they were.

She blinked and looked down at the new wedding band sparkling in the sunlight flowing through the small window. Married! She was married. The *m*-word was now a real word. Married to the biggest player she'd ever known. She wouldn't even date him because he chased every skirt that walked past him and flirted with anything that had boobs. No way would she get into a committed relationship with Ace Riley, but she was sure married to him.

She looked back at his lips and wondered if another kiss like they shared when the preacher told him to kiss the bride would make her as feverishly hot as that first one had. The way that man could kiss, it was no wonder the women took numbers and waited by his bedroom door.

If thinking about another kiss could cause her to pant, then a romp in the bed with Ace would set the sheets to flaming. He wiggled and his thigh plastered against hers and that heightened-sense syndrome kicked right into action.

Thigh against thigh.

Bursts of white-hot heat that took her breath.

"Well, crap," she mumbled as she scooted her leg away from his.

The girls behind her were now sighing and talking about how boring flights were and how they wished they were home so they could see their boyfriends. They would say that Jasmine had an acute case of SMI (severe mommy issues) and she was really too old for such things.

"And I am," Jasmine whispered.

She'd been fighting SMI issues her whole life. As an only child to a mother who was used to getting her way, she'd learned a few tricks. And more than once she'd stood up to Kelly King. When Kelly had pitched a Texas-sized hissy about her quitting a fine job to buy a café in a town that boasted a population of one hundred people, Jasmine had pointed out that Thurber, Texas, had a population of five and the Smokestack restaurant in that town was a booming business.

Kelly had thrown out the guilt trip of "I sacrificed

so you could have an education and make something out of yourself," but Jasmine's mind was made up. She'd bought the café and never looked back at what she'd left behind.

But this wedding business was the SMI that had Jasmine pissed off. She never did want a big wedding. When other little girls were putting pillow cases on their heads for veils and picking dandelions for bouquets, she'd been more than happy to cater their make-believe weddings with her Easy Bake Oven.

That's how long Kelly King had been talking about her daughter's wedding. She had been planning it as the event of the century in north central Texas for as long as Jasmine could remember. Maybe it had to do with the fact that Kelly's wedding hadn't been such a big deal and she regretted it, but whatever created it, the end result was one of those SMIs and Jasmine hated being out of control.

"Which brings me back to these crazy feelings," she mumbled.

"What'd you say, darlin'?" Ace asked without opening his eyes.

"Nothing, I was just talkin' to myself," she said.

He made a noise like *uh-huh* and shifted into a more comfortable position without moving the small pillow from her shoulder.

Warm breath on her neck.

All they were going to find was a pile of ashes in the seat when the plane landed.

Ace roused when the plane landed. He stretched as much as possible in the tight space, tossed the pillow over on an empty seat, and looked at Jasmine.

"Guess it wasn't a dream, was it?" he said.

Her hands were clenched together so tightly that her knuckles were white. "It wasn't a dream. We are married."

He covered her hands with one of his big rough paws. "We'll get through this, Jazzy. You are the strongest woman I know."

"Well, thank you for that vote of confidence." She managed a weak smile.

Her hands relaxed and he moved his away. "Hey, lady, any woman who could resist my charms for more than a year has to be strong."

"Have I told you today that you are the most egotistical cowboy I've ever met?"

He grinned.

Why in the hell was a simple smile so different that day than it had been on Thursday last week, or even the first time they met?

"We've got an hour and fifty minutes here in Houston. What do you want to do?"

"Eat!"

The girls who had sat behind them giggled and threw flirty looks toward Ace as they left the plane in a pack. Ace waited until everyone behind them had already gotten off before he stepped out into the aisle and offered Jasmine his hand.

"Thank you," she muttered.

"Us sexy cowboys who marry old women try to be obligin'." He grinned.

"You demon! You weren't asleep."

His eyes sparkled. "I was some of the time, but a sexy cowboy likes to listen to his little groupies. I know I slept some of the time because I'm hungry. I always wake up starving from a nap."

She put her hand in his. "It's not funny, and I'm not old. And you are two years older than me, so there."

"But my groupies think I'm sexy. Did I hear your bones creaking when you stood up? I told you we should have brought your cane."

"It's not going to work, Ace," she said softly.

"What? Walking?"

"You know what I mean. You've always teased me out of bad moods. This one is too big and too black," she told him.

"Food! That will help. When there's a big old scary monster in my path, I go to your café and you kill it for me by making me a double cheeseburger and fries. You didn't eat three bites of breakfast. Let's go get something fast and hot."

Fast and hot! Hmmm, I could go for that. She quickly lassoed the thoughts before they could materialize into Technicolor.

"Well, halle-damn-lujah!" Ace pointed toward the board in front of them as they stepped out into the terminal. "Our next flight is on time and leaves from next door. And there is a McDonald's. We are two lucky people today, Jazzy."

She didn't feel so lucky. She felt like she was sitting on top of a keg of dynamite and the fuse had already been lit.

He led the way to the counter and turned to Jasmine. "What'll it be?"

"An order of fries and a chocolate shake."

"Give her a number one, supersize it, and two of those apple pies," he said.

"Ace!"

"You've got to eat or you won't have the energy to help me take care of the crap storm waiting on us," he said.

"It'll take more than food to build up that much energy. Honey, it's bigger than Katrina and dumping something far worse-smelling than a hurricane." She managed a weak smile.

He pointed toward an empty table and let her lead the way. He pulled out a chair for her and then sat down across from her while they waited for their number to be called. "Come on, Jazzy. You can give me a bigger smile than that. You are the strongest woman I know. Laugh at the situation. Get mad. Do something other than pout."

She exploded right there in the airport. "Pout! I'm not pouting! Have you ever seen me pout? I'm not a whimpering woman."

"That's better," he said.

One cowgirl in tight-fitting jeans and bright red boots winked at her and gave her a thumbs-up sign.

That put more courage in Jasmine's backbone than all the inner arguments had done since the television broadcast the night before. She threw back her head and laughed. "I. Am. Not. Pouting," she said again between giggles.

"And that is funny? Why?" Ace asked.

"You wouldn't understand. It's a woman thing," she said. "But now I'm hungry and they are calling our number. I hope you didn't order all that food for me in hopes you'd get to eat half of it."

"That's my Jazzy," he said.

When they were back on the plane, in the air, and on the leg of the journey from Houston to Dallas, Jasmine motioned to the flight attendant with a stack of pillows in her hand.

"My turn," she said.

"What?" Ace asked.

"I'm taking a nap. No groupies behind us for me

to have to protect you from so, darlin', be a good husband and don't wake me until it's time to buckle up for the landing," she said.

Ace took the pillow from the attendant, fluffed it up, and put it on his shoulder. "Put 'er here, pard'ner."

She rolled the kinks from her neck and rested on his shoulder, shut her eyes and went right to sleep, only to dream of a tornado hitting the café and Ace carrying her out the back door to safety.

Ace could tell by the way she was breathing and her eyes were dancing behind her eyelids that she was dreaming. Long, thick eyelashes rested on her high cheekbones framed by dark hair. Her lips were full and oh so kissable, and her body was made for a man's hands to explore.

Got to stop it or I'll be in misery, he thought. He looked out the window at the ground below and imagined getting stuck out in one of those lonesome places with Jasmine—a willing Jazzy who'd want him as much as he'd wanted her since that wedding kiss.

The landing wasn't smooth, and Jasmine awoke with a start. "Did we make it?"

"I believe we did," Ace said.

"I was afraid that it was going to blow us away." Her eyelids fluttered and then snapped open. "I was dreaming."

"About what?" he asked.

"A big storm. We were the only ones in the café and it was coming on fast. The wind was howling and everything was this strange, eerie shade of green. The funnel was touching down and then going back up, and I couldn't move. You grabbed me and carried me out the back door. We were going for your truck to outrun it when I woke up," she said.

"See, I told you I'd protect you," he said. "Ready to go home?"

"Yes, I am," she said stoically.

Chapter 5

THE PARKING LOT AT THE CHICKEN FRIED WAS not empty. Jasmine nosed her truck in beside a whole line of other vehicles. There was Gemma's little red truck, Rye's black truck, and Pearl's vintage Caddy. She loved her friends, every one of them, but after the past twenty-four hours and fighting Dallas traffic, she would have gladly driven into a parking lot that was completely empty.

She'd followed Ace all the way from the airport, up I-35 to Gainesville, and across on Highway 82 to Ringgold without stopping, keeping her eyes on the tail end of his truck and wishing the trip would last five hours instead of one. Normally, she hated Dallas traffic and would rather fight a hungry coyote than drive to the Dallas Fort Worth airport, but right then she'd gladly drive right back down there and get lost on every one of the loops around the city.

At least her mother's car wasn't among them, and she'd been spared that for a few days. Ace opened her truck door and stood to one side. The sun was bright and the day hot. The wind that rushed into the truck was hotter than Ace, and that was scorching hot.

She could've slapped that grin right off his face, but it wasn't his fault that she was in this mess. She'd volunteered for the job. But in her own defense, she hadn't expected it to be anything more than a twenty-four-hour lark and a big yearlong secret.

"You ready for this?" he asked.

"Hell, no!"

"You want to get in my truck and we'll run away and hide out until they go home?" he asked.

She rolled her green eyes. "They won't go home. They'll chase us down and make us be happy ever after. Ace, they think we are really, truly married. The real kind where everything is kissy-kissy happy."

Ace snapped his fingers. "Okay, Jazzy, get into character. You are a new bride who just had an amazing night of sex in a big, fancy hotel. You can play the wife role for a year. I know you can! Remember, those people in Vegas thought you were an actress. You can do this."

"I'm feelin' pretty bitchy for a wife who just had sex. Strange, I don't remember it and I've always had the impression you were pretty good in that area," she said.

Ace slung an arm around her shoulder. She was exactly the right height for a comfortable hug. "Just pretty good? I thought I was dazzlin' good."

"I guess I can pretend." She sighed.

"That can be remedied anytime you want a taste

of the real thing, so you don't have to pretend. That sounds like the beginnings of a good country song. Think I should call Josh Turner and see if he wants to write the rest of it?"

"Don't tease me!"

The front door of the café swung open, and Gemma raced out on the porch to wrap them both in a hug. "Y'all pulled a sneaky on us. We would have all flown out to Vegas with you if y'all had let us know. Come on in. We've got wedding cake and cold beer."

"How long have you been here?" Ace asked.

"Thirty minutes. I figured if you had to check out of the hotel at eleven and your flight was about noontime, with the layovers and all that you'd be home about now," Gemma said. "Remember, I've flown in and out of Vegas for the Pro Rodeo twice now."

Pearl was first in line to hug Jasmine when she was inside the dining room of the café. "I bet your momma is livid."

"Worse. We have to get married in Texas and she gets to pick out the dress." Jasmine giggled nervously.

"Dear God!" Pearl gasped.

"Eloping was not her idea of an only daughter's wedding," Jasmine said.

"It'll be horrid," Pearl said.

"Yep, with a train from Amarillo to Beaumont.

And you are going to be the matron of honor and she's picking out your dress too."

"Crap!" Pearl gasped.

"Now you are beginning to get the picture. One month from today on the second Sunday in July. Marcella is helping."

"Holy crap!" Pearl whispered.

"Yes, ma'am," Jasmine said.

"I love a party. Do I get to come?" Gemma asked.

"Me too. Who is Marcella?" Liz asked.

"Momma's cousin who fancies herself a wedding planner. I swear she has every wedding magazine subscription for the past five decades, and if there is anything newfangled, she will fit it into the wedding. You can bet we'll have a unity candle; we'll scatter sand with our parents to blend two families together; we will have a fancy prayer bench to kneel on while the preacher blesses the rings... You name it and we will have it. It will take two hours to marry us and five hours' worth of reception if Marcella has her way. She says anything as expensive as a wedding should be memorable."

"Jesus!" Ace said.

"He can't help you, honey. But if you want Marcella to invite Him, she will and Momma will demand that God let Him attend," Jasmine said.

Gemma threw her hand over her head. "Girl, I'm pretty good at stayin' on a bronc's back long enough to win, but I'm not so sure about dodgin' lightnin' bolts."

Jasmine could vouch for the fact that God was takin' care of heavier matters than weddings and blasphemy that day. "You and Austin are bridesmaids, and I may need to get out the phone book to have enough women beside me to make Momma happy. She will insist that all of Ace's brothers serve as groomsmen, and then there is Rye and Wil, so I'll need lots of bridesmaids. And Momma loves taffeta!"

Pearl shuddered. "Please not apricot-colored."

"That's Momma's favorite." Jasmine shouldn't have taken pleasure in tormenting Pearl when she was nine months pregnant, but she sure couldn't share the real story with her. And it was the first time anything happened in Jasmine's entire life that she couldn't share, so Pearl could just be miserable with her over the color of the dresses. It was a small price for a friend to pay.

Ace squeezed her waist. "How many? Did you say all my brothers? I was thinking maybe just Wil and Rye."

"Momma may decide we need a dozen of each. It ain't legal unless it's registered in the great state of Texas and has enough bridesmaids and groomsmen to fill up the whole front of the church. And it's a big wide church, let me tell you. Momma ain't havin' grandkids that are the result of a questionable marriage. It could be they might want to run for president, and a Las Vegas marriage license wouldn't be worth the paper it's written on."

"For real? Are you kiddin'?" Gemma asked.

Jasmine pointed at Pearl. "It's the pure, unadulterated God's honest truth. You better have those twins next week."

Rye clapped a hand on Ace's shoulder. "We had no idea you two were even seeing each other."

"Or that you were thinkin' about getting married. Was it a big surprise, really a surprise, when you won that package deal at the chapel?" Austin asked.

Rye and Austin had only been married a couple of years. She'd inherited a watermelon farm over in Terral, just five miles from Ringgold, across the Red River into Oklahoma. She'd intended to come to southern Oklahoma and sell the place, but Rye lived across the road and she fell in love with him and the watermelon farm.

All of the O'Donnell men—Rye, Dewar, and Raylen—were tall, dark-haired cowboys that had a swagger in their walk and a drawl in their talk. Handsome beyond description they were. But not one of them made Jasmine's pulse race like Ace did when he took her hand in his.

Raylen patted Ace on the back. "Ace has always been the sneaky one of the bunch."

"You got a lot of room saying that," Dewar said.

Raylen grinned. "Guess I do. Me and Liz pulled off a sneaky wedding too, didn't we?"

The Christmas before, Raylen had married Liz

with no family or friends at the wedding. Liz's uncle left her twenty acres adjoining the O'Donnell horse ranch. She had been born and raised in a traveling carnival, but she'd always dreamed of putting down roots. When her mother asked her what she wanted for Christmas every year, she'd told her that she wanted a house with no wheels and a sexy cowboy. Her Uncle Haskell gave her the house; Raylen O'Donnell supplied the rest.

Dewar handed Ace a beer. "Here, man. You probably need something cold after that stunt. And I believe the last number we talked about was a hundred dollars?"

Dewar was the last of the O'Donnell male offspring not married. He had jet-black hair, green eyes, deep dimples in a square face, and a scar on his cheek. He and Ace had a running bet as to which one would outrun the women the longest.

Ace let go of Jasmine's hand long enough to draw his wallet from his hip pocket and put a bill in Dewar's hand. "You'd better go home and take off them boots and get on some runnin' shoes because you are the last eligible bachelor in Ringgold."

"Hell if I am. You still got three younger brothers," Dewar said.

"Okay, then among the five of us." Ace recounted and slipped Jasmine's hand back into his.

Wil grinned. "That is four down and one to go.

Dewar, you got something you want to tell us so we aren't shocked all to hell again in a few weeks?"

Austin grabbed Jasmine's arm and pulled at her. "Come on. You can leave your new husband for a few minutes and tell us how this all came about."

Ace held on tightly. Together they'd work their way through the next year. He wouldn't forsake her.

"Ace, darlin', look at that cake. How did y'all get something on such short notice?" Jasmine changed the subject.

Pearl beamed. "There's a bakery in the grocery store in Nocona. The minute Gemma saw the news she called, and she and Liz made a trip over there this morning."

Gemma O'Donnell was the same height as Jasmine. She had dark hair, green eyes, and a wide smile that lit up the whole café. She owned the beauty shop next door, and she and Jasmine were good friends—both full of spit and vinegar, and together they plowed right through every obstacle that got in their way.

Jasmine kept the whine inside, but she really wanted to let it out. She couldn't even tell Gemma, and when the year was up, Gemma was going to be livid.

"Bet that fancy hotel didn't have a wedding cake, did it?" Liz asked.

"No, ma'am, it did not. Who's goin' to cut that thing? I love cake," Ace said.

He wasn't sure he could actually swallow a bite, not after what Jazzy had said about the next wedding. Lord, he'd pictured it as something small with one person to stand up with him and one with Jazzy and a cake and some punch. Not a full-fledged shindig that would last two hours in the church and another five at a reception.

Gemma picked up the knife. "I'm going to cut it, and you are going to feed each other so you'll have lots of good luck and this marriage will last forever. Pearl, you pour some beer in these two glasses and they can toast too. I thought about champagne, but you've already had that with the fancy limo and room. Besides, you are back in Texas so it's beer! But the cake feeding is going by the books because I intend for you to stay married because you couldn't have picked better soul mates."

She set the top layer of the small three-tiered cake to one side before she cut the next layer. "You have to freeze the top layer and eat it on your first anniversary for good luck."

"Did you do that?" Jasmine asked Pearl.

"It hasn't been a year yet, but it's in the freezer. How about you?" Pearl asked Liz.

"We only been married five months, but I didn't freeze any cakes. Remember, we got married on Christmas by the judge and we didn't have all the hoopla. We don't have a wedding cake topper, but if it's important I'll freeze a Ding Dong and we'll share it on our first anniversary."

Wil twisted the top off three bottles of Coors. He filled nine glasses with beer and one with ginger ale for Pearl. Wil's tall, dark good looks complimented Pearl's flaming red hair and green eyes. Jasmine had decided months before that she wasn't having a husband until she could get a cowboy that looked at her like Wil looked at Pearl. Now she had a husband who didn't want to be married and who sure wasn't happy about a big foo-rah over in Sherman in a month. Yep, it was fool's gold day for sure!

That which does not kill us makes us stronger, her grandmother's voice whispered in her ear.

Well, Granny Dale, I will be the strongest woman or else the deadest one in Montague County in a year's time.

She could've sworn she heard her grandmother giggle.

Gemma cut one small piece of cake and handed the plate to Jasmine.

"Is this all I get?" Jasmine asked.

She'd married Ace and now had to live with him for a year, in the house with him, and see him wandering around without a shirt, showing off his muscular chest, and she couldn't even touch it. And all she got was a piece of cake the size of a silver dollar?

"No, that's what you and Ace are going to feed each other. You go first," Liz said.

Jasmine used her fingers, broke off a piece of cake, and hurriedly shoved it toward his mouth. The sun was shining but lightning could still come through the window and strike her dead as a doornail for pretending to be happily married.

"You get a drop of that icing on my face and you have to lick it off," Ace said with an evil grin and a wiggle of the eyebrows. If awards were given out for acting out the role of a love-drunk husband, Ace Riley would have it nailed.

Jasmine slowed down and carefully laid the bite on his tongue. He grabbed her wrist to hold her fingers in his mouth, wrapped his tongue around the finger and thumb, and sucked off all the cake icing.

Liz's dark eyes widened as she looked at Raylen. "Now I wish we would've had a cake."

"Bring out the Ding Dongs when we get home, darlin'." He kissed Liz right on the lips.

"Now be nice. All that lovey-dovey stuff might slow Dewar down and the wrong woman will catch him," Rye teased.

Ace picked up the rest of the cake, deliberately missed Jasmine's open mouth, and smeared icing on her upper lip. He tipped her chin up and slowly licked every drop of it off, ending with a hard, passionate kiss.

Lights didn't flash and wedding bells didn't ring like they did in Vegas when he kissed her, but they didn't miss it by far. When he broke the kiss and looked into her eyes, her knees went weak. So it wasn't the white dress and the moment after all. Ace Riley, her new husband, had just knocked her socks off.

"Now can we have a real piece of cake?" Ace asked hoarsely.

Jazzy was doing a fine job of acting like a new wife. Too fine! That kiss caused a stirring that was uncomfortable. Thank goodness his shirttail was hanging out over his belt and covered the evidence.

"Not until you drink out of each other's cups," Pearl said. "The trick is to lock arms and drink out of your own glass."

Rye refilled fluted glasses that Austin had brought over for the occasion, making sure Pearl got the ginger ale and waiting until the bride and groom had done the traditional thing, then he held up his glass. "To Ace, a branded cowboy!"

Everyone tossed the beer back like shots of whiskey.

Liz refilled everyone's glasses with beer and Pearl's with ginger ale. "Here's to a lifetime of happiness with your branded cowboy, Jasmine."

Jasmine looked at Ace. Surprising enough, no hot anger was shooting out of his eyes. Most men would be madder than a wet rooster in a thunderstorm at being called branded. But his eyes were still soft and dreamy from the kiss.

Gemma cut big chunks of the wedding cake and

handed the first two pieces to Ace and Jasmine. Liz popped the tops off several more bottles of beer.

Jasmine loved every one of the O'Donnells: Raylen, Dewar, Rye; Colleen, who was missing from the party because the previous February she'd married Blaze McIntire and joined the very carnival that Liz had left behind; Gemma; and of course Austin. She really loved Pearl because she'd been her best friend forever, and Wil, because he made Pearl happy. And Liz because she had worked for several weeks for Jasmine when she first moved to Ringgold and they'd become such close friends.

But she wished the whole lot of them would go home. Her world was upside down and inside out. She needed some time to process it all before she opened the café the next morning.

Crap! Tomorrow morning bright and early I have to face Bridget, plus all the Monday morning regular coffee drinkers. And Ace won't be anywhere around, not until midafternoon.

Ace set his empty plate on the table, put his arm around Jasmine's waist, and drew her close to his side. "Good cake and good friends. Thank you all for this."

"You are very welcome," Gemma said. "And now it's time to turn out the lights, like that old song says. I'll see you," she pointed at Jasmine, "on Tuesday unless Momma throws a fit to come for lunch tomorrow."

Jasmine nodded. Ace's hand was hot against her back, sending rippling tingles from his fingertips to her neck and down to her toes, and reminding her that his kiss had been every bit as hot as his hand.

Pearl looped her arm through her husband's. "Okay, Wil, it's time to take your fat wife home."

"My wife is not fat," he protested.

"You blind or something?" Austin asked.

"I'm with Rye. I think Pearl is beautiful pregnant," Raylen said.

Liz and Gemma were busy carrying the dirty plates to the kitchen and loading the dishwasher. Gemma wrapped the small top layer of the cake in plastic wrap and then slipped it into a gallon storage bag before she stored it in the freezer. Liz wiped down the table, threw away the beer bottles, and swept up the crumbs. When everything was put to rights, Liz wrapped her arms around Jasmine and Ace in a three-way hug.

"I really hope you are happy," she said.

"Why wouldn't we be?" Ace asked.

"It's so sudden," she said.

"After what you and Raylen pulled off, don't talk to me about sudden," he teased.

"Guess you are right." She giggled.

Ace kept his arm around Jasmine until the last truck had pulled out of the drive. He was reluctant to remove it even then. It felt as if he was really the branded cowboy and she was his bride, as if they were soul mates who'd finally found each other.

"Was that our horny toad?" he asked.

"That wasn't even a cricket. The real horny toad is our parents," Jasmine said.

Ace rolled his pretty blue eyes up toward the ceiling.

"Won't do a bit of good. Prayin' or cussin', either one. We got to get it done so we might as well get on with it," she said.

He grinned. "I told you that you were strong as steel! Throw some things into a bag and we'll go by the folks on the way to the ranch. If we make a stop there we can always plead that we're tired and have to get things ready for tomorrow. If we don't, they'll come to the ranch and stay until midnight."

Jasmine stepped away from his arm, amazed that the heat from his hand was still there even when she was two feet away. "I've got most of what I need out in my truck and I'll go get the rest. Want to come up or wait here?"

He shot her a wicked grin. "Need me to undo your bra?"

"In your dreams, cowboy!"

Methinks thou didst protest too quickly, her conscience giggled. Until that moment, Jasmine didn't even know that her conscience had a sense of humor.

Yes, I did, she agreed as she raced up the stairs

and into her apartment. *If Ace undid my bra, I'd have his belt buckle undone and him lying on his back so quick he wouldn't know what hit him. This craziness will pass. It's the dress and the cake.*

"Hell, he might end up with Gemma yet," she whispered as she packed several pairs of underpants, an extra bra, and a few more clothes in a small suitcase. A jolt of pure unadulterated jealousy tightened around her heart like a hangman's noose.

Whoa! You have no right to be jealous of either Ace or Gemma. They are both your friends, so stop this crap right now.

Ace sat down at the table nearest to the door and put his head in his hands. If things had gone right he would have been on the Double Deuce shooting the breeze or playing a Sunday afternoon game of poker with his foreman and hired hands out in the bunkhouse.

He lifted his head when he heard her coming down the stairs. Not another woman in the world would be giving up her life for a whole year for him. But celibacy for a whole year? No flirting, which was as natural to Ace as breathing. No kissing or chasing a woman. He probably shouldn't even be opening his little red leather book with all the names and addresses in it. God Almighty! It was going to be a long, long year.

"Do I need to put on body armor?" she asked.

He chuckled. "Naw, just stand behind me. They won't shoot me. I'm the fair-haired child."

"That's real comforting," she told him.

"I really am the spoiled middle child, and if you don't believe me, ask my older brothers who did not get a ranch handed to them free and clear of debt. They'll crawl up on their soapboxes and bitch like little girls if you lend them an ear." He picked up her suitcase and carried it for her. "Guess we'll have to take both trucks since you'll be coming in to work early."

"Guess so," she said.

"Then let's go by the Double Deuce first. When we drive up in my folks' yard we should be together," he said.

She followed him to her little truck. He slung her suitcase into the back and then opened the truck door for her. When she was settled in with her seat belt fastened, he leaned inside and planted a hard, wet kiss on her lips.

"Don't slap me. Gemma just pulled up in front of her beauty shop. Can't have her suspicious," he whispered.

Jasmine whipped her head around to see Gemma waving from the Petticoats & Pistols beauty shop next door to the Chicken Fried Café. Both places had started out as a car dealership many years before. The beauty shop had been the office for the dealership, and the café had been the home of the people who owned the business. The parking lot served both places back then and now as well.

Jasmine waved as she backed out of the lot and turned south on Highway 81 toward Bowie. Granny Dale told her once that no one could eat an elephant all at once but they might eat the whole thing a bite at a time. Going to his ranch was the first bite in the elephant that she'd have to eat in the next year, and she wasn't even sure she liked elephant. Was it served grilled, fried, or ground up into hamburger? Did she put barbecue sauce on it or cook it in soup?

She passed the O'Donnell horse ranch on her right. The countryside wasn't so different from where she had grown up in Sherman, except that she was a town girl. She'd always loved to visit Pearl on her family ranch, loved horses and the smell of a barn. She'd liked Tess, Pearl's southern momma, who was always giving them advice on how to be a real lady. But she'd loved John, Pearl's dad, who talked with a slow drawl and taught the girls how to ride, both horses and tractors.

When Ace made a left turn off the highway onto a section line road, she followed. The road turned to dirt half a mile later. Another quarter of a mile and Ace turned right into a gravel lane with barbed-wire fence on either side. She could see the house, and it wasn't anything like the big brick two-story Pearl had lived in out on the ranch. It was long, low-slung, and painted white. It looked more like a bunkhouse with a wide front porch open on the north and south ends to catch whatever summer breeze could be cussed up.

"Welcome home," Ace said when he opened the truck door for her. "Those are my hired hands on the porch so I reckon I'd best carry you over the threshold once you meet them."

"Ace?" Sam pushed his tall lanky frame out of the rocking chair. His bright blue eyes sparkled in a face full of wrinkles and wisdom. His thick gray hair was parted on the side and combed back; his jeans and chambray shirt were both clean and pressed. Cowboy boots were scuffed and spurs jingled when he crossed the porch.

"Sam?" Ace laced his fingers in Jasmine's and led her up on the porch. "Dexter, Buddy, Tyson?"

"We s-s-saw the n-n-news last n-n-night." Buddy grinned and pushed a strand of brown hair back out of his eyes. Like Sam, he wore jeans and a chambray shirt, both clean but not ironed. His eyes were the same shade as his hair. Even with his cowboy boots he wasn't more than three inches taller than Jasmine but his arms bulged the fabric of his shirt, and there wasn't a bit of spare fat on him.

"You goin' to introduce us or what?" Dexter asked. He was only slighter smaller than King Kong, had arms the size of hams, and a big, round bald head. He looked like a bouncer or maybe a wrestler.

"This is my new wife, as you all know, since it was on last night's news. Jasmine owns the Chicken

Fried Café south of Ringgold, so you might have seen her there," he said.

"I'm Tyson. I been in there a few times, but I ain't never seen you." The youngest of the four stepped forward. His red hair was close cut, his shoulders as square as his face, and his green eyes looked as if they held secrets no one would ever find out.

"Pleased to meet you, Tyson," Jasmine said.

"And this is Sam, Dexter, and Buddy." Ace pointed as he introduced the other three.

"We're glad to have you on the ranch." Sam stepped forward. "It's missed a woman since Ace's grandma died back when he was just a kid."

His voice was deep and very Texan.

Dexter and Buddy nodded in agreement.

"I hope you like the Double Deuce as much as we do," Tyson said.

"I'm sure I will. I've always loved ranches," Jasmine said.

"Ever lived on one?" Sam asked.

"No, but my best friend, Pearl, who married Wil Marshall, grew up on one and I loved visiting her," Jasmine answered.

"Well, we'd best get on back to the bunkhouse. We just wanted to congratulate you two and welcome Jasmine to the Double Deuce," Sam said.

"We're just stopping by to drop off Jasmine's truck and then we're on our way to the folks' place. They've never met her," Ace said.

Sam chuckled down deep in his chest. "She looks like she can hold her own. Let me open that door for you, son."

Sam swung the screen door open, and Ace scooped Jasmine up in his arms and carried her inside. He kicked the door shut with his bootheel and set her down in a huge living room. "Welcome home, Mrs. Riley."

She looked up to say something about him calling her by that ridiculous name, only to find his dreamy blue eyes already locked on her lips. She rolled up on her tiptoes. Their mouths met in a hungry clash, devouring and tasting, nibbling and teasing until they were both panting.

"Whew!" he said when they broke apart.

"That cannot happen again, Ace," she mumbled.

"Felt pretty good to me." He grinned.

"That's why." She took a step back. "Which way to my room?"

Ace whistled down the hallway. Four doors opened off to each side with a fifth right at the end. He slung open the first one on the right. "My room."

Then he pointed at the other. "Your choice. Each side has two bedrooms, but Gramps only put in one bathroom. It's a big one at the end of the hallway. Two sinks, shower and tub separate. I expect you'll be up before I am so that won't be a problem."

"I'll think about the rooms while we visit your

folks and make a choice when we get back. Should I change?"

"What you have on is fine. We're laid-back ranch folks, Jazzy. We ain't fancy-pants people."

"Is that what you think I am?" she asked.

"Hell, yeah! You are way out of this old cowboy's league, but I've got you for a year, so my younger brothers can all drool. Even if it is for only a little while, it'll be right nice," he said with one of his mischievous grins.

"Ace Riley, I am not out of your league, and that's probably a line you feed your women. But it won't work on me. I'm not a fancy-pants person. Are you ready to go, or do we need to wait a while longer so the guys think we're in here doin' something other than talking?"

Ace threw back his head and roared. "You got them pegged just right, Jazzy. I'm goin' to enjoy my year of marriage."

"Don't get comfortable, darlin'. It's only for a year and then we'll get one of those amicable divorces where you keep what you had when we married and I keep my assets," she said.

"But what if I want part of the Chicken Fried and all of your ass...ets?" He wiggled an eyebrow.

"Be careful. We didn't sign a prenup. I can take part of the Double Deuce."

That wiped the grin from Ace's face. "Don't tease me about that."

"Don't tease me about my café."

He took a step toward her, pushed her dark hair back from her neck with his fingers, and outlined her lips with his thumb. His touch was a combination of fire and ice: heat so hot that it would melt steel and chills racing down her backbone at the same time. His kiss was tender and left her wanting more.

"Why did you do that?" she whispered.

"We can't go to the folks' house fighting. Momma is going to be a hard sell as it is, and she could spot a fight a mile away. So we'll go with that kiss on our minds." He put his hand on the small of her back and escorted her up the hall.

She felt white-hot heat and saw pretty sparkling fireworks all the way to the door.

Chapter 6

JASMINE COULD HEAR THE NOISE OF LAUGHTER and conversation before she and Ace reached the house. The porch was wide and wrapped around three sides, but in size, it reminded her of Ace's house. Ace opened the door, took her hand, and led her inside. People were everywhere in the great room comprised of the living room, kitchen, and dining room. But the very second that she stepped inside, a bone-chilling aura surrounded her and Ace. She tried to tell herself that it was her imagination and that she'd expected the worst and they were just waiting for Ace to introduce her.

Ace looked around the room. "Are we having a family reunion, Momma?"

Dolly Riley shook her finger at Ace. "Don't you joke with me right now. You should have brought Jasmine to meet us before you married her."

Jasmine clamped her jaw shut before she said something that would cause a war right there in the midst of his family.

The smile on Ace's face faded. "Okay. Everyone, this is Jasmine, my wife. If you've eaten at the Chicken Fried in the past year and a half, you've eaten her cookin'. And, Jazzy, this is my mother, Dolly, and my father, Adam."

Jasmine extended her hand. "I'm very pleased to meet you."

She was surprised that her words came out lukewarm and not icy cold.

A tall woman, Dolly looked down on Jasmine. Her hair was jet-black, her eyes brown, and her skin lightly toasted. Her handshake was quick, and Jasmine half expected her to wipe her hand when it was done. Adam's handshake was downright rough, and Jasmine gave him one just as bone-crunching. His eyes were the same shade of gray-blue as Ace's, but his hair was as black as Dolly's. When he let go of Jasmine's hand, the corners of his mouth twitched in a grin.

"Okay, get ready for the rest of the zoo." Ace introduced her to his three older brothers and their families first.

Everyone tipped their heads toward Jasmine, and she smiled at each one. If they thought they were going to win the war, then they'd best make a fast run through the kitchen and pick up a brown-bag lunch because it was going to take more than a cold stare. She'd given her word and she'd stand by it. They could like her or not. Frankly, my dear, as Rhett Butler said in *Gone with the Wind,* she didn't give a damn. It would all be over in a year and they could have their precious womanizing son back.

"Before I go on, any one of you three got anything to say?" Ace looked over at his three older brothers: Garrett, Justin, and Tony.

Tony spoke up. "Just that this was pretty quick. Last week you told me you were dating a different woman every week and had your red book nearly full. Momma says you didn't even get a prenup."

Ace grinned. "Hey, I'm in love. I don't need a prenup. Don't it show?"

"Not so much," Tony said.

Jasmine wrapped both arms around Ace's neck and pulled his face down for a long, lingering kiss right there in the middle of the living room floor. She might not be his wife of the heart, but she was on paper, and they weren't getting away with implying that she would ever take her best friend for a financial ride. Besides, she'd had enough explaining for one day and she was tired of it.

Ace's toenails curled; his curly hair came close to straightening; and his heart missed two full beats during the kiss. He was blushing scarlet when he pulled away.

Jasmine looked right at Tony. "How about now?"

"I'd say she's in love even if Ace ain't," another brother said from the shadows.

"That would be Blake, the baby in the family," Ace said, but he couldn't wipe the grin off his face. He'd been right about Jasmine being strong. Not even the whole Riley clan had intimidated her.

Jasmine nodded briefly at the handsome cowboy in the corner. "Pleased to meet you, Blake."

"And I'm Dalton, and this is Creed. We're the tag-alongs. Momma had the three older boys, waited four years, and still wanted a daughter. So she had Ace and he sure wasn't a girl. So she waited six more years and tried three more times. Rileys make boys for the most part. And we're all dark-haired and brown-eyed except for Ace. He's the oddball."

Jasmine glued herself to Ace's side and hoped that's what a real new bride would do. "I'd say I got the handsome one. How in the world did someone with your curly blond hair come out of this family?"

Dolly finally smiled. "It was his Gramps Riley that gave him that hair. Granny was half-Mexican just like me. Black hair runs rampant in the Riley family, but Ace is a throwback to Gramps's side. He got his eyes from his daddy, though."

"So you always been a cook in a café?" Creed asked.

"No, not before I bought the Chicken Fried Café, but I've always loved to cook," Jasmine answered.

Ace led her to an empty recliner, sat down, and pulled her into his lap. Her breath caught in her chest, but she covered it with a small cough. That last kiss was impulsive, and the weakness in her knees was comeuppance for the stunt. But no one was going to treat Ace like that.

"What'd you do before that?" Dalton asked.

"I worked in Sherman at a corporation," she said.

"You goin' to keep workin' at the café or are you goin' to be a ranchin' wife?" Blake asked.

"That's something Ace and I haven't decided yet. Right now, I plan to operate the café."

Ace made a motion to stand up, so she stood with him as he said, "Okay, that's enough questions for one night. We're goin' on home now. We just wanted to stop in so Jasmine could meet y'all."

"I understand there's a reception at your folks' place in Sherman?" Dolly asked.

Jasmine nodded. "Momma says it's not a real marriage unless it's performed in Texas, so it will be a full-fledged wedding, not a reception. Second Sunday in July. I'll let you know the details when Momma tells me."

"I agree. Those Las Vegas things ain't real marriages. You tell your momma to call me if she needs anything," Dolly said.

"I'll do that." Jasmine nodded.

Dalton, Blake, and Creed all picked up their straw hats and followed the newlyweds toward the door. Dread and doom crept up Jasmine's fingertips to her shoulders and then to her scalp, which tingled like it always did when something horrible was about to happen.

Ace stopped dead still halfway across the floor. "Where are y'all headed off to?"

Blake shrugged. "Not a single one of us got those

jobs we thought we had at that horse ranch in Waco. Owner sold it off and the new man brought in his own crew, even for the summer. Creed is working for Rye and Austin over in Terral so he'll only be at your place this week, but you don't have to hire your usual summer help. We moved into the spare bedrooms. Didn't know you were comin' home with a bride until after we'd already moved in. Didn't even know where you'd gone until we saw it on the television last night. We won't interfere none. We'd stay out in the bunkhouse, but we'd have to sleep on the floor. And besides, Sam snores like hell," Blake said.

Jasmine waited until they were in the pickup before she exploded. "How in the hell do we fix this? They'll expect us to…" She couldn't finish the sentence.

"It's really not so big a problem. I've got a king-sized bed and we slept together last night. I'll put pillows between us if you are afraid you'll attack me and try to force your body on me in my sleep." He chuckled.

She sucked in a lungful of air and let it out slowly. "Don't laugh. It's not funny."

"No, it's not. I'm sorry, Jazzy. It was supposed to be a simple thing and it's turned into a big mess, but we'll get through it, I promise. I think we ate our horny toads tonight. Nothing else can happen now, and thank you again from the bottom of my beat-up old cowboy boots," he said.

She crossed her arms over her chest. "You are still grinning and it's not funny. And you promised me in Vegas you would never, ever say that nothing else could happen."

"I've always been the lucky Riley son," he said. "Garrett, Justin, and Tony worked their butts off for their land, and they are all still making payments to the bank. I inherited mine—house, land, and cattle—all free and clear. I guess it's time for me to pay some dues, and sneaking around from one bedroom to the other is a small price to pay. I only hire extra help during the summer months. Creed will be gone in a week or two, and Dalton and Blake will be packed up and gone the first of September. Then it'll just be me and you in the house at night, and you can have all three of those rooms for the rest of the year, I promise."

Dalton pulled in on one side of Jasmine's truck and Ace parked on the other side. She didn't wait for him to be the gentleman and open the door for her but scuttled out of the truck and headed toward the house.

Ace was barely out of the truck when his ringtone signaled that his father was calling.

He stopped in his tracks and answered it.

"Son," Adam's deep voice said.

"What do you need, Dad?"

"I got a call from Cole that disturbs me. I didn't share it with your momma or brothers. Figure that it would just stir up trouble that you don't need. Is it true?"

Ace's scalp tingled. "What?"

"That you married that girl to keep Cole from getting the ranch? Gramps never told me that he put that in the will. I thought the ranch was yours with no strings attached."

"I didn't ask her to do it, Dad. She offered and I accepted. Can we keep this between us?"

"Got to stay with it a year, do you?" Adam asked.

"Yes, sir, I do."

"You'll do it right, won't you? No cheating on her with other women. It's a big undertakin' that she did. She must be a hell of a good friend," Adam said.

"She is."

"Well, then we'll see what the year brings before we go worryin' your momma about the whole thing. And I told Cole if he goes spreadin' around a bunch of rumors that they'll just make him look stupid after that trouble with Megan all those years ago, so he'll keep his mouth shut."

"Thanks, Dad."

"One more thing, Ace. You going to go through with this wedding here in Texas?"

"Guess I am. Don't see any way out of it."

"I guess you are right. Like I said, a year can make a big difference in the way folks see things. I liked Jasmine. She's got spunk. It'll take that kind to keep you on your toes. Good night, Son."

"Good night, Dad."

Jasmine stopped inside the front door. Ace's house was nothing like the Riley ranch house. Theirs was much newer and had wide-open spaces. Ace's front door opened into a wide hallway that ran the width of the house from the front door to the back door. Two doors opened off to the right: one into the living room, one into the enormous country-style kitchen/dining room combination. On the left a long hallway split off leading to the bedroom wing. Straight across from the kitchen door, one opened into an office/den-type room. Hardwood floors shined like new money, and not a speck of dust rested on the foyer table.

Ace walked inside the house and answered the question on her face before she asked it. "Gramps said that he built it like this because he wanted to catch the evening breezes. It was built before air-conditioning so that was important. That's why the windows are so tall. When the weather is nice, we can get breezes all through the house."

"You ain't never been here before?" Blake asked.

"Of course, but I've never had the grand tour," Jasmine said. She wasn't lying. She had been in the house long enough for Ace to drop her bags and to look at four bedroom doors.

Blake pointed. "The living room is right through that door with the kitchen behind it. Big dining room is on this side of the hall, and there at the back is Ace's office. Down the hall are four bedrooms because Granny and Gramps planned for this big family but they only got Daddy out of the deal, and then Gramps got Ace most of the time after Granny died. At the end of the hall is the bathroom. Back when he built the house, multiple bathrooms were unheard of," Blake explained.

Blake was over six feet tall, maybe an inch or two taller than Ace. He had hazel eyes and black hair, a round face that could in no ways be described as a baby face, and a deep dimple in his left cheek when he grinned.

"I hear you get up before the crack of dawn, so we'll let you have first shot at the bathroom," Dalton said.

Standing at least three inches taller than Ace, Dalton had lighter hair than Blake but it was still a rich dark brown, light brown eyes the color of a Yoo-hoo chocolate drink, and a square face with no dimples in the cheeks or in the chin. His chest was broad, his biceps huge, and his waist narrow.

He reached up and touched the faint semicircular scar running from his eye to his jaw. "Blake did it."

"Oh, don't start that crap! She's not going to feel sorry for you. Besides, if you hadn't dared me to jump off the picnic table to prove I could fly with that towel around my neck, then I wouldn't have dared you to jump off the shed roof," Blake said.

Ace led Jasmine into the living room. "Come

and see this part of the house so you know where things are in the morning. And it wasn't Blake's fault. Dalton fell on one of those old metal coffee cans. He didn't have to take the dare."

Dalton followed them. "But if I hadn't, you would have told everyone I was a big momma's baby."

"Children, children!" Creed said in a deep voice. "Are you going to argue all night? Jasmine will think she's married into a family of fighting Irish or maybe Apache Indians."

Dalton made a faint snorting noise behind her, and Blake stopped on a dime and folded his arms across his chest.

"Just because you are the oldest one of us three don't give you the right to act like the big daddy figure," Blake said.

Ace chuckled. "Turn on the television and hush your bellyachin' with one another."

"I'm going out to the bunkhouse to see if the guys have a poker game." Blake headed out of the house with Dalton right behind him.

"Worked that just fine. Now I can watch whatever I want." Creed chuckled. "Want a sandwich, Jasmine? I'm a great bologna sandwich maker."

"With tomatoes and lettuce?" she asked.

"And mustard and dill pickles." Creed nodded.

"Sounds wonderful."

Ace's phone rang again and he fetched it from his hip pocket. "Hello?"

"So you and the instant bride are home. Will the license be at the lawyer's in the morning, or do I have to come to the ranch?" Cole asked. "By the way, I talked to your father."

"I'm taking it to the lawyer in the morning soon as he opens up shop, along with pictures. You can see it there, and I've got nothing to hide so talk to whoever you want to talk to," Ace said.

"I still don't think this is a real marriage, but like you say, all you have to do is produce a marriage license that is valid. The will didn't say that you have to prove you are in love."

Jasmine touched Ace on the arm. He looked as if he could chew up railroad spikes and spew out tenpenny nails.

"Cole," he mouthed.

Jasmine reached for the phone, and he put it in her hands. "What is your problem?"

"I'm not a fool. I can tell if a couple is in love or if they are faking it."

"Darlin', come on up here. We'll prove that we are in love right after Garrett whips your sorry ass." Jasmine walked down the hall as she talked so Creed couldn't overhear what she was saying.

"You are a bitch!" Cole growled.

"Yes, I am, and I'd love to help Garrett. Shall I expect you tomorrow morning?" Jasmine asked.

"Go to hell," Cole said and hung up on her.

She leaned against the wall. "Did he really come to the ranch to visit when he was a kid?"

"Oh, yes," Ace said. "Every summer his folks dropped him here for a week. He wouldn't do anything that got his hands dirty. Hell, he might have to get two manicures in a week if he did. Mostly he sat on the porch and read his books. My older brothers remember him well. Ask them about him sometime."

"What does he do?" Jasmine asked.

"He's a technical engineer in Dallas."

"How old is he?" Jasmine need to know more.

"Just over forty. About Garrett's age."

"Plain potato chips or barbecued?" Creed yelled from the kitchen.

"Plain," Jasmine yelled back.

"Barbecued," Ace hollered.

Creed had the sandwiches arranged on paper plates and sitting on the coffee table when they returned.

"It's been a long day and we got very little sleep last night. You guys mind if I take mine to the bedroom?" Jasmine asked.

"Not at all. You want to take yours too, that's fine. I've got a movie rented that I'm going to watch before I go to bed," Creed said. "What time do you get up, Jasmine?"

"Five. Open the doors of the café at six for breakfast."

Creed nodded. "You are welcome to have breakfast at the bunkhouse, but Dexter don't serve it up until seven."

"At seven the café has already been open an hour and we're in full breakfast mode, but thank you."

Ace picked up plates and followed her into his bedroom. He set them on the chest of drawers and went back out to get their bags. When he got back, she was sitting in the middle of the bed eating a fat sandwich.

"Delicious," she said.

"Creed is a good cook if you like bologna sandwiches, but that's the extent of his abilities."

She ate every bite of her food and grabbed her bag, fished out boxers, a tank top, and her toothbrush, and headed out toward the bathroom. She was surprised when she returned to find Ace stripped down to boxers and holding the top sheet up for her to crawl into the bed. When she was lying beside him, he covered them both and pulled her close to his side.

"Well, we just lived through the first set of family," she said.

"One down. One to go. Thank you again, Jazzy. Good night." He kissed her on the top of her head and rolled over to his side of the bed.

It was a long time before she went to sleep.

Chapter 7

Only two days had passed.

Two days before, on Saturday morning, Jasmine had unlocked the doors to the Chicken Fried Café just south of Ringgold, and it was a normal day.

On Saturday afternoon she had flown from Dallas to Las Vegas, and it was a normal flight.

On Saturday evening, June 2, she had married Ace Riley, and what happened in Vegas was sure supposed to stay in Vegas. It should have been a normal night in Vegas.

Now it was the second Monday in June and everything looked normal again.

"But looks are deceiving and there's no such thing as secrets," Jasmine said.

She mixed up two chocolate cakes and three pecan pies to offer for dessert that day. While those baked, she made biscuits for the breakfast rush and started a slow cooker full of sausage gravy.

Bridget, Jasmine's only employee, rushed into the café like a whirlwind, jogging from across the dining room floor and coming to a skidding stop in the kitchen to wrap Jasmine up in a fierce hug.

"Pearl called Lucy, and Lucy called me, and it's so

exciting and romantic. I'm so happy for you. I cried when Lucy told me. I knew he was always around, but I had no idea y'all were even dating, and you are going to keep the café, aren't you? I love it here and I'd hate to lose the best job in the whole county," she gushed.

Bridget looked far different than she did the first time Jasmine had seen her. She'd shed the extra pounds she carried six months before, and she had a bright smile to go with her newfound confidence. She wasn't that same little mousy woman who'd spent two years with an abusive husband. Now she walked with self-assurance and credited Jasmine and Lucy with every bit of her newfound happiness.

"So you think Ace is a good man? You don't think he'll turn out to be..." Jasmine put Bridget to the test.

"Ace Riley has the kindest eyes of any man I ever met. Now, Ace likes to flirt and carry on with the womenfolks, but he's not an evil man. Believe me, I can spot them and you got nothing to worry about. Besides, if he was to ever hurt you, either you'd kill him or I would. But you don't have anything to worry about. He's a good man and you're going to be married the rest of your life. Now tell me all about it and promise me again that you won't sell the café."

"I'm keeping the café and you have a job,"

Jasmine reassured her. "The marriage was a spur-of-the-moment decision and we'd really planned to keep it a secret for a few months, but I guess when it airs on public television the secret is out."

"Well, I'm tickled for y'all. You sure enough sprung it as a surprise. I bet your momma and daddy was shocked," Bridget said.

Jasmine nodded. "That doesn't begin to cover it. Momma says I have to get married again in the state of Texas."

"But them Las Vegas weddin's is legal, ain't they?" Bridget frowned.

"Oh, yes! In everyone's eyes but Momma's." Jasmine sighed.

"Well, I don't see nothing wrong with that. Ain't you the only child?"

Jasmine nodded again.

"Then do it for your momma. Me and the sum-bitch I was married to, we run off to Dallas and got married. Daddy never did like him, and Momma, well, she said he was a worthless bastard. They was right on the money, but it took me a month to figure it out and another two years to get out of it. Ace is a good man. He won't mind havin' another weddin' for your momma."

"It's not Ace. I don't want to do it," Jasmine said.

"Then tell her no."

Jasmine smiled. "It isn't that easy."

"Ain't it the truth! But remember, if Momma

ain't happy, ain't nobody goin' to be happy. There's the first of our coffee drinkers comin' in to gossip. I swear menfolks is twice as bad as the women. Hang around their table and you'll find out more than you ever can around a bunch of women." She tied an apron around her waist, picked up an order pad, and headed out to the dining room.

People yelled from the checkout counter or popped their heads through the kitchen door to congratulate Jasmine all morning. By ten o'clock, her plastered-on smile was hurting her face and there were still four hours before closing time.

The morning lull came at ten thirty. Bridget poured a cup of coffee and propped a hip against the table in the kitchen. She kept a trained ear tuned in to the bell on the door and an eye in that direction while she kept up a running monologue about her softball team that was playing that weekend.

"I been meanin' to ask you to come with me and play because there's this feller that plays for the Henrietta team that I just know you'd like but he's done missed out because Ace slipped in the back door and sweet-talked you into marryin' him. There's the bell. Too late for breakfast, so I guess he's here for either coffee or lunch."

Bridget set her cup down and breezed out into the dining room, a big smile on her face and a swing in her walk.

"Good mornin'. Sit down anywhere you want to.

Menu is on the table. Want some coffee?" She followed him to a back table.

"I came to see Jasmine, so tell her I am here," the man said bluntly.

"Well, she's busy, but I'll be glad to take your order."

"I'll only give her my order." His nose flared out in a snarl when he looked at Bridget.

Her blood ran cold but she wasn't going to let him or any man intimidate her again. "Do you have an appointment?"

He eyed Bridget up and down and snorted as if he was looking at a pile of trash. "No, but she'll talk to me. Just tell her Cole is here."

"And she'll know who that is?" Bridget asked.

"Oh yes, she will definitely know who I am. This is a pitiful little place. She came up in the world over the weekend, didn't she? I'm sure she'll be more than interested in what I've got to say."

Bridget went to the kitchen and sat down at the table. "You got a man out there that's mean and hateful. Says his name is Cole. I asked him if he had an appointment just because he was so ugly to me. Says he won't give his order to me and he has to talk to you."

"Well, crap! What do you mean... appointment?"

"He looked at me like dirt and talked down to me, so I asked him if he had an appointment when he said he'd only give you his order. I'm sorry if you know him," Bridget explained.

Jasmine wiped her hands. Her wide mouth turned into a narrow slit as she set it firmly and her hands balled up in fists.

"You could've shot him on the spot, and I'd have helped you tote his sorry carcass out the door. Hell, I'll bring the shovels if you want to do it now. Don't apologize, and he will give his order to you or he can starve to death." Jasmine stomped out of the kitchen.

Bridget wiped her forehead with a paper napkin. "Whew!"

Jasmine spotted Cole the minute she looked across the room. Other than a table of old cowboys who sat by the front window every morning and had coffee until eleven when they placed their order for lunch, he was the only person in the dining room. But that wasn't why she would have known him. He had the same dark hair and body build of the dark-haired Riley brothers. The difference was in the face. His was round and didn't have the character or rugged good looks that the other Rileys shared.

"I'm Jasmine," she said.

He started at the toes of her Nikes, traveled up her bare legs to her knees where her khaki shorts started, stalled out at breast level for a second, and then took in her face and hair. His eyes said he wasn't impressed.

"I'll have steak and eggs..."

"Is that the only reason you called me out here?" Jasmine asked.

Cole's eyes met hers in a frigid gaze. "Of course it is. I thought you'd be delighted to see me. After all, we are related now."

Jasmine glared at him. "Does Garrett or Ace know you are in town?"

His grin was one-sided but not friendly. "Darlin', there are two sides to every story."

"Well, *darlin'*"—she drug out the last word into six syllables—"Ace and I are married. You don't get the farm. Everything is being filed this very morning at the Montague County Courthouse. It's over, Cole. Go back to Dallas and lick your wounds."

A thick layer of ice covered his already dead-cold eyes. "I have to accept it. I don't have to like it. Living with Ace won't be easy. He's always liked the ladies, and a quickie Las Vegas marriage license won't change that. You can't tame him. When you get tired of his cheating, call me. We'll pull the rug out from under him and share the profit. Now I want the steak-and-egg breakfast and a short stack of pancakes before I head over to Montague. Did you think I'd take your word for it, or the lawyer's either? Men can be bought. I'll see the papers for myself."

"Bridget, will you please take this man's order?" Jasmine yelled.

"I could hang around for days and make your first week of wedded bliss miserable," Cole said.

Jasmine leaned close to his ear and whispered, "You don't intimidate me one bit. Stay and you'll learn all about misery. I'll invite Garrett and Megan for supper tonight. Then tomorrow night we'll have the rest of the clan to clean up what they leave behind."

Bridget was at her elbow when Jasmine stood up.

"Steak and eggs and a short stack of pancakes," he said through clenched teeth.

Jasmine didn't even look back. She went straight to the kitchen and slapped a steak on the grill. Bridget brought the order and hung it on the revolving wheel.

"That was intense," she said.

Jasmine noticed that he wanted his steak rare so she flipped it over. "He is pure evil."

"He's beyond evil. My ex was evil. That man out there has sold his soul to the devil," Bridget whispered.

Jasmine nodded.

"Here lately I've learned that if I had to do it, I could take my ex down with one hand tied behind my back. I wouldn't take on that man out there with a tire iron in one hand and a claw hammer in the other. What's his problem with you?"

"I married Ace," Jasmine said.

"I'll get the shovels. But we need something more for his kind. You got a stake hidin' in the pantry? We'll need to drive it through his heart. I reckon I could do it with the shovel if you haven't got a sledgehammer."

Jasmine giggled and part of the tension floated away.

Ace wiped at his sweaty forehead with his shirt-sleeve. The air-conditioning was out in the tractor he was using that day, and the temperature was near a hundred degrees. It was going to be one blistering hot summer in more ways than one.

Rye said that his whole life changed in a second when he first saw Austin on the riverbank sifting her grandmother's ashes between her fingers into the water. Ace's changed when that Vegas preacher told him to kiss the bride. Nothing had been the same since that moment. He thought back on all the women he'd enjoyed: flirting, dating, the chase, the sex. All that was over.

No more flirting.

He liked Jasmine too much to give her a cheating husband even if it was a fake husband.

No more dating.

Jasmine wouldn't cheat on him so he'd be good.

No more sex.

Ah, that one was painful, but the ranch was worth it.

A wedding, a big one, with a reception and he was the groom.

Saying the vows in Las Vegas wasn't like saying them in front of a real Texas preacher, parents, friends, and even God. That made it pretty real.

He'd slept with Jasmine two nights with no sex.

He had not planned on sleeping with his bride in his bed in his house without sex. That was the bed and the room he'd saved for his real bride, should the time ever come around that a woman got past the tat on his bicep and made her way to his heart.

His mind had run around in circles all day as part of the crew cut hay; part of them raked what was already down; and the last third baled other fields. Hay and his situation were the same; like wiping his rear end on a wagon wheel, there was no end to it. He'd been too busy to take a break and go to the café that afternoon, and he wondered how Jasmine fared. When he saw her park her truck in the front yard in the middle of the afternoon, he wanted to stop for the day, but there was plenty of daylight left and he'd wasted a couple of hours that morning going to the lawyer's office.

The marriage license hadn't been filed in the state of Nevada until the courthouse opened there, so it was after ten when the fax came in to the lawyer's office. The lawyer checked it and declared it legal, and Ace signed another round of papers. He and the lawyer walked over to the courthouse and closed out his grandfather's will. Ace paid the man with a check and made it home at noon. He'd been on a tractor ever since.

It was pretty cut and dried. It was over. The ranch was now legally his unless he didn't stay married for a year, and then Cole would have to file the necessary papers to contest the will. Too bad his life couldn't be so easy, because in that area nothing made sense anymore.

Jasmine parked beside Ace's truck and hauled in another suitcase of her things. She was still stomping mad when she unpacked it, hanging her things beside his in the closet, putting her underpants, bras, and nightshirts in a drawer right below his. She kicked off her Nikes, went to the shower, and soaped up twice. Still she could feel the insolence in the way Cole looked at her, so she poured another puddle of shower gel into the washcloth and started all over again. She stood under the cool water and forced herself to think of something else.

Bridget was right. Ace's eyes were warm and kind. He'd never look at her like Cole.

"Don't think about him," she said sternly.

Ace was a playboy for sure. He liked women, but he'd never...

"Don't go there," she yelled at the top of her lungs.

Okay, little girl, looks to me like you need a good dose of housework. Get that dustrag and get busy.

Since you can't clean his looks off your body or put his memory in the trash can, then clean something else and take your mind off him. Granny Dale's voice whispered so close that Jasmine threw back the shower curtain to see if she was right outside.

She turned off the water, dried herself, and dressed in cutoff jean shorts and a ragged T-shirt and headed for the kitchen. The oven was a holy mess with the ashes of too many boiled-over TV dinners still crusted on the bottom. The refrigerator was almost as bad with sticky grape juice turning to gcl on one shelf and something brown that looked suspiciously like spilled sweet-tea stains running down the side.

She found cleaners under the kitchen sink, sprayed the oven and shut the door for the prescribed thirty minutes, and went to work on the refrigerator. Everything, shelves and drawers included, came out and went into a sink of warm soapy water. She brought the trash can from the utility room and tossed everything that was out of date or growing layers of fuzz into it.

There was a galvanized milk bucket in the utility room, so she filled it with cleaner and water and went to work on the refrigerator, mumbling that homes should have to pass the same inspection codes that restaurants did.

"Can't eat a hamburger in a café that has a speck of mildew on the door of the fridge, but you can grow enough bacteria for biological warfare in a home's fridge. Don't make sense to me. But then I guess it's like they say about a license. Have to have a driver's license to drive a car; have to have a fishin' license to drop your line in the water; but anybody who can breed can have a baby. Cole is living proof that that law needs to be changed."

Don't go there, Granny Dale said firmly.

Okay, okay. Now doesn't that look better, and next on to the oven. Gramps Riley was right. A ranch needs a woman.

When Ace and the guys dragged their tired butts through the door at seven, she was sitting on the sofa with her bare feet propped up on the coffee table.

Ace kissed her on the forehead.

"What is that smell?" Creed asked.

"It's the smell of clean, and the next time one of you boil something out in the oven or spill something in the fridge, you'd better clean it up," Jasmine said.

"You didn't throw out that container of dirt, did you?" Blake asked.

"If it wasn't edible, it went in the trash," she said.

"Well, crap! That was my rose hips I was working on germinating," he said.

"Go look in the trash bin. I tossed container and all," she told him. "And if you want to grow something in dirt, do it in the bunkhouse."

"Dexter would kill me," Blake said.

"I rest my case," Jasmine told him.

Creed laughed.

"It's not funny. I gathered those rose hips last fall, and I'm just waiting on them to sprout," Blake said on his way out the back door to retrieve his precious seeds.

"So he's a horticulturist?" she asked Ace.

"Which kind of horti are you talkin' about?" Dalton chuckled.

Jasmine felt the blush begin to sting her neck but she willed it away. Hell, she'd stood up to Cole. She could force a blush into oblivion.

"I get the shower," Dalton said.

Creed nodded. "You can have it. I'd forgotten how much the first day of hay haulin' can work on my muscles. I'm getting into a tub of warm water and soaking my aches away. What time is supper, Ace?"

"Dexter says it'll be on the table in half an hour."

They both took off down the hall toward the bathroom.

"What put you in such a cleaning mood? I told you that you didn't have to do anything around the house since you work all day at the café," Ace asked.

"Cole."

"Cole?" Ace asked.

Jasmine told him about the day and how badly she'd wanted to poison his steak.

Ace sat down on the sofa and threw an arm around her. Sweat, remnants of the morning shaving lotion, and soap blended together into a heady combination. The dirty bad-boy image didn't usually appeal to her, but Ace sure did. She felt safe and warm and something else akin to steamy hot.

"That sumbitch. He had no right to come to your place of business," Ace growled.

"I took care of it. He's gone. He said he was going to the lawyers or the courthouse to see the license because he didn't trust y'all. I thought about bleaching down the chair where he sat and throwing the plate he used in the garbage," Jasmine told him.

Ace fetched his cell phone from the carrier on his belt loop and punched a few buttons. "Understand you've been harassing my wife."

A second of silence then he said, "I really don't care."

Another few seconds of silence.

"That remains to be seen. I know Jasmine and she is..." He caught himself before he said, "As good as her word."

"She's what?" Cole's raised voice came through the phone loud and clear.

"She loves me." Ace chuckled. "Why else would a woman marry a straggly old cowboy like me two times?"

He snapped the phone shut and looked at Jasmine. "He told us to go to hell."

"No, thank you. I'm not spending eternity with him anywhere around me."

Ace kissed her on the cheek. "He won't be back. Wouldn't have surfaced this time if Gramps hadn't put that in his will. And Dexter says supper is on the table at seven thirty so we'd better get a move on it. I'm going to take a quick shower. I smell like sweat and dirt," Ace said.

"Supper?" Jasmine asked.

"Summer schedule is breakfast in the bunkhouse, sandwiches out in the field at noon that we take with us from this house, and supper back in the bunkhouse. Dexter stops a couple of hours before we do and gets it ready," Ace explained. "It'll be nice to have a woman at the table."

Chapter 8

RICH COOKING SMELLS WAFTED OUT FROM THE bunkhouse and across the yard between it and the main house. The three younger Riley brothers walked ahead of Ace and Jasmine, the scent of their shaving lotion mixing with the aroma of baked bread and something with cinnamon coming from the bunkhouse kitchen.

Ace had been quiet since the phone call with Cole. Jasmine had given him his space like she'd learned to do back at the first of their friendship. In those days, he would pull up a chair in the kitchen and she'd slap a burger on the grill. In a while he'd start to talk and they'd hash out whatever was on his mind, but he had to have time to mull it over.

The wind whipped her hair into her face, and she tucked it back behind her ears several times before they reached the porch. The guys had already gone inside and she could hear male voices talking and laughing. Just a hint of the cool air that had escaped when they opened the door still lingered on the porch, but the hot summer night was replacing it rapidly.

She stopped just shy of the porch and pulled her

phone out of her pocket when it rang. She hoped she could make it short, but the caller ID said it was her mother, and she always talked forever.

"Hello, Momma," she said.

"Where are you? I hear cows and men's voices," Kelly said.

"Ace and I are about to walk into the bunkhouse. Dexter makes supper every night, and it's ready." She hoped her mother would get off the phone.

"Dexter?" Kelly asked.

Jasmine's stomach growled. "Ace has four full-time hired hands. Sam has been here for forty years, Dexter and Buddy for about twenty years, and Tyson just got hired last year. Ace's brothers also work for him in the summer. His younger three brothers are working here this summer. Well, at least two of them are here for the whole summer. Dalton and Blake will be here until fall. Creed is only here for a week or so. I'm hungry, Momma, and they're waiting for me."

"They won't start without you. Younger three? How many are there?"

"Six. Three here and with Ace that makes four, plus four full-time guys that live in the bunkhouse. I'm living in a testosterone-filled world of cowboys, spurs, boots, and bullcrap," Jasmine said.

"That's no way for a new bride to talk in front of her husband and all his hands. God Almighty, Jasmine." Exasperation came through the phone.

Jasmine could see her mother's expression without shutting her eyes. The only time that she got God Almighty-ed was when she'd done something like watering down John Richland's prime whiskey, or when she and Eddie Jay Chandler broke up the year before. Those two times got her a God Almighty in bright, flashing neon colors. It floated in the air for a full five minutes after her mother raised her voice and put it out there. Evidently mentioning testosterone and bullcrap was a sin as big as breaking up with a cheating son of a bitch or watering down high-dollar whiskey. Her mother should have given her a book when she stepped over into puberty entitled *God Almighty Sins*.

If a book like that existed, it would be as secret as Ace's rules-of-the-town book in Vegas! Both were secret books and could never be found in common bookstores.

"Well, aren't you going to say a word?" Kelly asked.

"I was thinking about a couple of books," Jasmine said.

"Jesus, Mary, and Joseph! I swear, you are more like your father every day of your life."

Kelly King only hollered for help from Jesus and his parents when "God Almighty" had failed. They were held in reserve for really tough times. And it took a long time to work her mother through those times.

Jasmine sat down on the step.

Ace sat down beside her.

"Well!" Kelly said.

"Sorry, Momma. Have you seen Marcella yet?" Jasmine changed the subject. Get her mother onto the wedding plans and everything would be fine.

"Of course I have. I called her last night and she's been here since morning. We've been sitting at the kitchen table making plans all day. You should be here," Kelly said.

No, I definitely should not be there. We would yank each other's hair out if I were there because my idea of a real wedding is what Liz and Raylen did. Propose, go stand before the judge the same morning, and be married by noon. What Ace and I did in Las Vegas was too big to suit me.

"Are you going to say a word?" Kelly asked.

"Momma, I'm sure you and Marcella will do a wonderful job. Tell me what you decided today," Jasmine said.

"This morning we decided on invitations. I need a guest list from your fiancé, and that's what he's going to be to me until you marry him in a real church in Texas... I need his list by the end of the week. I have the King and the Dale lists already done. We have two invitations picked out. I'll send them to you over the internet and you can make the final decision. One is ecru with apricot ribbons and pearls; the other is white with embossed doves on the front."

"Which one do you like?" Jasmine asked.

"The white one. It's more formal."

"Then that's the one I want. You aren't planning on apricot dresses, are you?"

"What's wrong with apricot? It's a summer wedding after all," Kelly said.

"I was thinking about red with multicolored bouquets," Jasmine said.

"Dear God!"

That wasn't quite as bad as the God Almighty, but it was only a notch down the ladder. Jasmine smiled up at Ace.

He pointed at her hip where the John Deere tat was located.

She smiled at him. "I guess that means green is out of the question. Then how about a very formal wedding with metal colors? Pewter, gold, silver, bronze, and calla lily bouquets."

Silence.

Her stomach growled again.

"If you don't make up your mind, I'm going to starve to death with food not fifty feet from me. If that happens, you can bury me in the wedding dress and all the bridesmaids can wear their apricot dresses and stand behind the casket for a picture to go above the mantel. Do you want Ace to weep into a hanky or sit on the end of the casket?"

"God Almighty! Jesus, Mary, and Joseph! That is a horrible thing to say to your mother. I was thinking that I like the idea of the metal colors. I'm picturing it in my mind, but Marcella and I'll have to go back to the drawing board for the invitations. Something in a very formal off-white with gold lettering. Oh, yes, I can see it all now. Go eat your supper, and don't you ever say that about a casket to me again! Marcella is still here and we've got the books out on the table. I expect that list by Friday. We have to put a rush order on the invitations as it is in order to get them out two full weeks before the wedding."

"I trust you and Marcella to figure it all out. How many bridesmaids do I need?"

"Pearl will be the maid of honor, so we'll need at least five more since your groom has six brothers. If he has some very close friends, don't be stingy. I don't care if you have a dozen of each. It will make a lovely picture to go above the mantel. Not a word. Not a single word, Jasmine Marie, and I mean it. Let me know dress and shoe sizes by Friday too."

"I promise I will. Goodbye, Momma."

Ace chuckled. "That was slick."

"What?" Jasmine giggled.

"You know very well. That casket thing was ingenious."

"You know me much too well, my friend. Now that I gave Momma something elegant to work with, she'll be off and running and I won't hear from her for days. But..."

"That 'but' is about the dress, right?"

She nodded. "Pearl is too big to traipse around looking for a dress. Liz and Raylen are at a horse thing in Dallas this weekend. Lucy can't leave the motel on Saturday afternoon. Please, Ace...will you go with me?"

"Sure. We'll all knock off early. Dalton and Blake will like that so they can have more time to get all spruced up to go tomcattin'." Ace owed her far more than an afternoon looking at wedding dresses. Hell, she'd just saved the ranch.

Blake poked his head out the door. "Dexter says he's puttin' it on the table and cold gravy ain't worth eatin'."

Jasmine slipped her phone into her hip pocket. "What was Cole saying on the phone?"

"That you wouldn't even stay around the full year and he'd made you a proposition. Half the money from the sale to leave me."

"Why should I give that son of a bitch anything? I can get half by leaving you anytime I want. We don't have a prenup, darlin'." She looped her arm through his. "Lead the way, Ace."

"I'm dreading meeting your momma." Ace groaned.

"Why?" she asked.

"If she can control you, she's Superman's daughter."

Jasmine was smiling when she stepped inside with him.

The bunkhouse was unlike anything she'd ever seen. The living room and kitchen were one big oblong room with two closed doors on each side. The big room had a long table at one end with benches on the sides and a heavy chair at each end. Cabinets made an L with an enormous refrigerator on the short end of the L and the stove and sink in the longer leg. A couple of comfortable sofas faced a fireplace that was stone cold in the middle of a Texas summer. Everything was in pristine condition, down to the rag rugs in front of the sofa and the fireplace.

"Welcome to supper, Miz Jasmine. We hope to see you out here every night," Dexter said.

Size-wise, he looked more like a bouncer than a cowboy. His huge head was shaved bald, and the back of his neck lay in enormous folds. Biceps as big as Ace's waist and a chest about an acre wide looked out of place in a snap-front western shirt. His jeans bunched up over the tops of buff-colored cowboy boots with sharp toes. Maybe a bouncer in a honky-tonk instead of a big-city club.

"Thank you. It sure smells good. I'm not used to sitting up to a table with food that I didn't cook," she said.

Dexter motioned for her to sit at the end of one of the benches. "This'll be your place. When the boss died, we gave Ace his place at the head of the table. Sam sits at the other end because he's been here more than forty years now. Me and Buddy and Tyson take the other side and the boys can line up beside you. Now Sam, it's your turn for grace."

In his deep Texas drawl, Sam thanked God for a new woman on the Double Deuce and for the food they were about to eat.

Jasmine was so busy thinking about her mother's God Almighty and whether He'd accept the farce wife sitting at the table with all the men of the Double Deuce that she didn't hear Sam say, "Amen."

Ace touched her arm and she raised her head to see the men all looking at her.

"Sorry," she mumbled.

They continued to look at her as if waiting for her to deliver a speech or maybe sing a song. Well, they were going to have a long wait for either. Jasmine King, now Riley, could not sing, and she wasn't too fond of speeches either.

"You start the food around," Ace whispered out the side of his mouth.

"I see. I'm used to being in the kitchen, not in the dining room. I'll know next time." She picked up the platter of meat loaf, put a chunk on her plate, and handed it to Ace. Conversations began as the food went from her fingers to Ace's, brushing in the transfer and sending more of those spicy shivers down her back every time.

"You evvvver worrrk on a rrranch?" Buddy stuttered.

He was as tall and lanky as Sam, but where Sam's thick hair was silver and curled up on his shirt collar, Buddy's was dark brown and clipped close to his head. His arms filled out his shirtsleeves, but the waist bunched up in pleats where he'd tucked it inside his jeans.

"No, but my best friend, Pearl, who married Wil Marshall last year, lived on a ranch. So, I spent lots of weekends on one," Jasmine answered.

"D-d-d-rive a trrractor any?" Buddy asked.

"Oh, yeah," Jasmine answered with a giggle.

Tyson looked up from across the table. He was the youngest of the hired hands. Thirty years old and had spent twelve years in the army—three tours of Iraq. His carrot-red hair was still worn in a military cut, and his shoulders were still squared off in military posture. His eyes reminded her of a two-way glass in a police station. He could see out but no one could see inside. She wondered what secrets were back there and if that haunted look would ever be released.

Ace chuckled. "She and Pearl sampled John Richland's fancy whiskey and refilled the bottle with water. When he found it, she and Pearl got to plow a whole week in open-cab tractors."

Tyson nodded, but he didn't smile. "Been on one since then?"

"Oh, yeah. Pearl lets me drive Momma Tractor sometimes just so I don't forget how," Jasmine said.

"What's a M-m-momma trrractor?" Buddy asked.

Jasmine looked across the table at Buddy and wondered if he'd stuttered all his life or if something had set it off at a particular stage somewhere along the way. "She and Wil bought three tractors one day and she calls them the Poppa Tractor, the Momma Tractor, and the Baby Tractor. She's the only one that gets to drive the last one. She's selfish that way."

Dessert was an apple cinnamon cake that did bring the hint of a smile to Tyson's face and lit Buddy's up like a neon sign.

"I thought I smelled cinnamon floating out across the yard," Jasmine said when Dexter set the Bundt cake in front of her and handed her the knife to cut it. "It looks scrumptious."

Tyson held his plate across the table. "I want a fat piece."

"You'll learrrrrn," Buddy stammered. "He llllikes cinammmmon."

"Do you?" Jasmine asked.

Buddy nodded and held out his plate. She cut a fat piece out for him and looked at Sam. "How big?"

"One of the slim pieces. I like it but I like meat loaf better, and I'm pretty well stuffed."

Dexter brought a full coffeepot and cups to the table, and Creed passed them around. When they reached Jasmine and she filled her cup, the pot was nearly empty.

"This is wonderful," she said when she finally tasted the cake. "I'd love to have your recipe for meatloaf and for this cake."

"Sure thing," Dexter said. "You need to use fresh apples," Dexter said. "They had some good Granny Smiths at the grocery store this week. Bought enough for a cake tonight and a couple of pies later in the week."

"Sounds great to me."

Dexter nodded.

Tyson, Creed, and Blake shared the last two inches of the cake, and Jasmine picked up the plate to carry to the cabinet. She didn't mind cleanup after a good meal like that. She'd wash and she'd make Ace do the drying and putting away.

Dexter took the plate from her and shook his head. "Oh, no! It's Blake and Tyson who does the cleanup tonight. Tomorrow it'll be me and Sam. Then Buddy and Dalton on Thursday. You and Ace get the chore on Friday night. Saturday and Sunday we don't have supper out here. I'll write off the recipes for you."

"Mind if I use them at the café?"

Dexter smiled. "I'd be right honored. You two run on now. Honeymoon ain't much as it is."

Jasmine was propped up on pillows watching the Cooking Channel when Ace waltzed into the room wearing nothing but a towel around his waist. She raised an eyebrow, but it did absolutely nothing for her racing pulse.

Dammit! She'd gone a year without sex, so why were those pheromone things flooding her body now? And why in the hell did they decide to multiply and attack with Ace? He was so sexy standing there with water droplets still clinging to his broad back and his curls kinked up to his scalp. She needed to fan her face at the naughty thoughts racing through her mind, but she couldn't figure out a way to do it without him realizing just how hot he made her.

"I forgot my sleepin' clothes. I'm not used to having a woman in the house and sure enough not in my bedroom," he said.

He opened a drawer and pulled out a pair of boxer shorts and a white gauze muscle shirt. He slipped the boxers up under the towel but she caught a glimpse of his butt cheeks when the towel dropped before he got the boxers up around his waist. He turned around as he put on the shirt and then stretched out on his side of the king-sized bed.

"What?" he asked.

"You're not used to a woman in your bedroom? Come on, Ace, I'm your best gal pal and you expect me to believe that?"

"Jasmine, I swear on my granny's grave, there's not ever been a woman in this bedroom. I saved it in case someone got past the barbed-wire tat and into my heart. This has been my sanctuary and it's never been open to women. Now what are you watching?"

She was stunned. So the playboy had a severely romantic side and he'd left one door closed to the women in his life. Knowing that she was the first one in there put a little extra kick in her heartbeat.

"Well?" he asked.

"Oh, sorry. I'm watching the Cooking Channel. Paula Deen is making gooey cake tonight. I'm going to make it for dessert on the day I make Dexter's meat loaf at the café."

Ace didn't care what she was watching; he just wanted to hear her voice. It was clear and sweet, like a soprano singer's. You'd think with a voice like that and a body like she had, plus that beautiful face, she'd be the next big thing in Nashville, but she could *not* sing. He'd caught her singing along with Miranda Lambert's "Gunpowder and Lead" one afternoon when she didn't know he was in the café. And that clear, sweet voice was all over the musical scale.

"What are you thinking about?" she asked when he just stood there staring at her.

"Food," he lied. There was no way in hell he'd tell her that she couldn't sing. "You said you were making meat loaf and cake. Whenever you make it, let me know. I love Dexter's meat loaf and I never met a cake I didn't like."

She looked over at him at the same time he looked at her. Their eyes locked and in one swift movement she was in his arms and his lips were on hers. Sweet at first, then teasing and finally deepening into something that erased every sane thought from Jasmine's head. It was more than the wedding kiss, more than the kiss in the living room of his parents' house the night before. It made all the kisses she'd ever had combined pale in comparison. She leaned into it and pressed her body against his, wanting more and more.

It set her ears to ringing and created liquid spasms down deep in her gut that threatened to explode like a volcano. The heat was unbearable, and yet she was drawn to it like a starving woman to a box of chocolates.

Stop! Right now! You are not a real bride. This is Ace and he's not a real husband and you're about to ruin your friendship.

She shut out the inner voice and ran her hands over his chest, teasing his nipples into peaks as the blistering-hot kisses kept fueling that liquid heat in her gut.

His hands moved under her shirt and up her back. They were rough as sandpaper and felt like firebrands as they massaged her skin, moving around to cup a naked breast already begging to be touched. "You feel like you are made out of silk."

"You feel like you are made out of leather." She tangled her hands into his damp hair and pulled his face back down to hers.

"So we're leather and lace." He covered her mouth with his.

She'd always figured if she kissed Ace it would feel like she'd just kissed her brother. It sure did not feel like he was kin to her. His tongue made love to her, and she closed every single bit of space between them. Her body was plastered to his, and the heat continued to ripple through her like ocean waves lapping up on the sand. She could think of nothing except release, and there was only one way to get that. She ran her fingertips across the tight muscles on his chest and was headed for pay dirt down below his belly button when that little voice named conscience set up a howl. She ignored it and kept right on inching downward.

Ace gasped when her cool hands encircled his more-than-ready erection. His lips found hers in another string of steamy kisses that kept shooting jolts of desire through his body. He couldn't think about a friendship going into a train wreck; he had to have Jazzy.

"God Almighty, that is..." he mumbled into her ear.

His warm breath was like throwing gasoline on

a raging bonfire. "I know," she whispered between kisses.

"Are you sure?" he asked.

"Are you?" She nibbled on his neck right below his earlobe.

"I'm dying," he admitted.

"Me too. I want you, Ace Riley."

He rolled over on top of her and peeled her nightshirt up over her head, taking only seconds away from the fiery kissing session to throw the shirt at the nearest chair. Boxer shorts and underpants were quick to join the shirt.

"One more time, Jazzy. Are you sure?"

She didn't trust her voice because she was panting so hard, so she nodded and felt a moment of pure joy when he began a series of long, slow teasing thrusts that brought her to the edge of a climax without letting her take the long tumble at least four times. Finally when she couldn't stand another moment of the heat, she growled his name and with one final thrust, they both found release.

"God!" he mumbled. He couldn't move a muscle. There was nothing left in him but loose connected bones and muscles with no power.

"I know," she said. He felt so right lying on top of her.

"What just happened?" he asked.

She was searching for an answer when someone pounded on the door and they both froze.

Blake yelled through the door. "Hey, sorry to bother you guys, but Ace left his phone on the kitchen table and Momma has called a dozen times. Thought he'd best call her back."

Ace groaned and rolled to the side and then off the bed, opened the door a slit, and stuck out his hand. "You could have called her back for me," he growled.

"I did after it rang for the tenth time, but she said she had to talk to you." Blake blushed. "Sorry, man."

"Next time throw the thing out in the yard," Ace said.

Jasmine slowed her breathing to something that faintly resembled normal. At least she wasn't panting in the background when Ace returned his mother's call. But she'd wanted more of the afterglow. More than just a few seconds for him to hold her. Much more than a few words. After that earth-shattering sex, she'd wanted the golden lights and the sweet nothings for at least half an hour before they fell asleep in each other's arms.

Ace leaned on the chest of drawers with his back to Jasmine and waited for his mother to pick up the phone. His boxers looked like someone had put the ridgepole for a pup tent inside them, and looking at Jasmine lying on the bed with her bee-stung lips sure didn't make it go away. He finally turned around and stared at the blank wall.

"Momma, what is so urgent?" he asked.

Jasmine listened to the one-sided conversation with one ear and tried to tune the other one in to the cooking show on television. Paula Deen was talking about frying chicken using her own special mixture for the coating.

Ace said, "Yes, all six of them. Yes, they can wear their western tuxes that they wear to the cattle-sale dance every year. And while I've got you on the phone, Jazzy's momma needs your invitation list by Friday with addresses. Jazzy will send you her mother's email address and you can send them directly to her. That'll save Jazzy playing middleman since she's so busy." He turned his head around and put his hand over the phone. "Give me your mother's phone number. We'll let them take care of it all between them."

"What was that?" Dolly asked.

"I'm getting the phone number for you. Her name is Kelly King and she's already planning things. Just call her and you two can hash things out between you about what you each need to do. Here it is." He held the phone out toward the bed.

Jasmine rattled it off.

"Got that?" Ace asked.

"I do and tell Jasmine thank you. Hope you two weren't asleep already," Dolly said.

"We were watching the Cooking Channel," Ace said. He added, "Good night, Momma," and ended the call.

Jasmine blushed. "We were not watching the Cooking Channel."

"Yeah, we were right before our bedroom got fired up hotter'n Miz Paula Deen's oven." Ace fell back on his pillow. "Now where were we?"

Our bedroom. He said our *bedroom,* Jasmine thought.

"Ace, I… We can't do this anymore. We've been friends because…" she stammered.

"We are married, Jazzy. We can do this and it's even legal."

"And when it's over next summer, a beautiful friendship that I value very much will be completely ruined. We've got to think this through," she said.

He plopped down on the bed and fell back on his pillow. "Thank God for a king-sized bed. This isn't going to be easy, Jazzy."

"I know," she whispered. "Good night, Ace."

She rolled over with her back to him and shut her eyes. Her breathing returned to normal, but the pheromones kept moaning and groaning for another hour.

Chapter 9

Ace slept on his side with one hand up under his pillow. His light-brown lashes rested on his cheekbones and he needed a haircut. The cowboy could charm the stripes off a skunk when he was awake; asleep, he made Jasmine wish she could snuggle up to his back and wake him with steamy hot kisses.

She sighed, crawled out of bed, and headed to the bathroom, making a mental note to bring her terry bathrobe from her apartment that evening. So many things she'd taken for granted, like running from bathroom to bedroom with nothing but a towel tucked around her, or sleeping in the nude.

After a quick shower, she dried her hair, pulled it up into a ponytail, and twisted it into a sloppy bun that she secured with a big clamp. The coast was clear when she peeked out the door so she hurried back down to the bedroom, opened her duffel bag, and found clean clothes for the day. When she was dressed, she picked up her purse and slipped out into the hallway where Blake bypassed her on his way to the bathroom. He mumbled something that sounded like *Have a nice day*. She smiled at him and kept going. When she got to her truck, she found the recipe for Dexter's meat loaf tucked under the windshield wiper.

There are three seasons in Texas. Winter and spring, which means warm; fall, which means hot; and summer, which means scorching hot. June falls in the summer months, and before Jasmine made it the café to open the door that morning, she'd broken a sweat. How on earth people ate heavy food like sausage gravy and biscuits and steak and eggs in that kind of heat was a mystery to Jasmine. She usually skipped breakfast except for two to eight cups of coffee, depending on how busy things were in the kitchen. That morning was barely a one-cup morning. Evidently no one wanted to heat up their own kitchens and everyone made an excuse to leave the house so they could have breakfast at the café.

Gemma ran in for breakfast at about nine that morning. She plopped down at the small kitchen table and ordered a stack of pancakes and a side order of bacon. There was finally a lull so Jasmine poured two cups of coffee and stretched six pieces of bacon on the grill. She picked up the pitcher of pancake batter and poured four out on the other end of the grill. When the pancakes had bubbles on the top, she flipped them over, turned the bacon, and reached for a plate. In less than five minutes she set the order in front of Gemma and took a short break.

"Missed you yesterday." Jasmine pulled out a chair and sat down.

"Had to clean house and do some grocery shopping. Dewar sucks at both." Gemma poured blended melted butter and hot syrup on the pancakes and let out a little moan when she put the first bite in her mouth.

Jasmine sipped her coffee. "Why do you buy food? You and Dewar eat in here most of the time."

"If I could get you to stay open twenty-four hours like one of those truck stops on the highway, we wouldn't have to buy anything but beer and pretzels," Gemma said.

"Where is Dewar this morning anyway?" Jasmine looked around to be sure he wasn't already in the café.

"My dear brother, bless his heart, is hauling hay. It's June in Texas. All ranchers are either cutting hay, hauling hay, plowing, or planting the next crop of alfalfa to make more hay. Your husband included. Whoever put out that urban myth about brides and weddings being perfect in June never did live in Texas. I'm getting married in the wintertime when the hay is in the barn or lined up in the fields."

"It's either hay or deer hunting," Jasmine said.

"Well, crap! I forgot about deer hunting. Maybe my sexy cowboy will fall right out of the sky from a planet that only makes steamin'-hot cowboys, and on his planet the cowboys do not go deer hunting and cattle and horses live on fairy dust," Gemma said.

"A planet that grows fairy dust, the men don't hunt deer, and you expect your cowboy to be straight?" Jasmine giggled. "Oh, Momma has narrowed the wedding invitations down to a short list and she's looking at dresses. And you really are a bridesmaid. I talked her out of apricot organza dresses so you can thank me for that," Jasmine said.

Gemma clapped her hands. "I'd wear baby pink to be a part of a big wedding party. Are all of Ace's brothers serving as groomsmen? Even Creed? I think he's plumb hunky but he's got a girlfriend so I can't ask him out. When is this big foo-rah happening? Nothing makes a man hornier than bridesmaids at a wedding. It's even better than Mardi Gras, I swear!"

Jasmine was glad someone was looking forward to the wedding.

"Second weekend in July in Sherman. Momma will reserve half a hotel for all the out-of-town guests, and since you are in the wedding party, you will have to be at the rehearsal and the dinner afterward. And yes, all of Ace's brothers are groomsmen and I think Rye is the best man. So I have to come up with seven bridesmaids. I've got six if you can convince Colleen to come home for the weekend. She wouldn't have to be here for the rehearsal, and they don't run the carnival then, do they?"

"Oh, she'll be here, trust me. They were playing out around Austin last week and coming east so it shouldn't be that big of a drive for her. Can I ask her when I talk to her later today or do you want to?" Gemma asked.

"Please do it for me," Jasmine said.

"Who are the bridesmaids? Me and Colleen, Austin, Pearl, and Liz?"

"And Bridget and Lucy. That makes seven. I'd forgotten Lucy. How could I do that? She keeps me in help."

"Lord, honey, it's a wonder you remember your name as much as you've got on your plate. I can't imagine being married already and getting used to a man in your bed and planning your wedding at the same time. That's enough to set a woman to drinking."

And a man in your bed that makes you hot as hell and you know better than to have sex with him again. Bring on the Jack Daniel's! Jasmine thought.

A rush of hot air brought in four cowboys with jingling spurs on their bootheels and sweat running down their necks.

Jasmine stood up. "Time to go back to work. That bunch looks like they could eat a whole hog. They sure don't look like their horses and cows live on fairy dust."

Gemma shot her a look, then giggled. "Even with all that sweat they do look yummy though, don't they?"

"I'm not answering that," Jasmine said.

Bridget put up four orders, picked up four large plastic tea glasses, filled them with ice and sweet tea, and carried them to the cowboys' table.

Jasmine pulled four steaks from the refrigerator. Slapping the rib eyes on the grill brought back an image of Cole, with his condescending attitude, in her dining room the day before. Her full mouth clamped down into a firm line.

"Who pissed you off this mornin'?" Ace asked.

She whipped around to find him sitting on the bottom step of the staircase leading up to her apartment. "Where did you come from?"

"Snuck in the back door. A husband has that right, don't he? A best friend does, so I kinda figured a husband should."

"What are you doin' in town?" she asked.

"Came after a good-mornin' kiss from my new bride. Might sweeten up her attitude. What happened to make you look like you could chew up a full-grown steer and spit out hamburger meat?" he teased.

"Cole ordered steak and eggs yesterday. The noise of the steaks hitting the grill reminded me. Why in the hell did your grandpa put that in his will anyway, and why is he makin' you stay married a whole year?"

Ace chuckled. "Want me to go to Dallas and whip on him for makin' you mad? If I leave now, I can wipe up the streets of Dallas with him and be home in time for supper. Would that make you feel better?"

Jasmine's face broke into a brilliant smile. "No but picturing you doing that is funny. And you didn't answer me about the will."

Ace shrugged and stood up. Spurs jingled and she looked down at his boots.

He poured a cup of coffee and sat down at the small kitchen table. "I promised Raylen that I'd help break a few horses today. Gemma usually helps, but she's got hair-fixin' goin' on all day. I'm on my way to Raylen's place. Now, to answer your question about the will, Grandpa never told me why or even that he had put that in his will, but things he said that year before he died kind of make sense now.

"He kept telling me that a ranch needed a woman; that she was the icing on the cake. Ranch could run without a woman, but it was a hell of a lot sweeter with one on the place. And he said that first year of marriage was a booger bear but that if a man could make it through the whole year, then he could make it through fifty and each one got sweeter. Guess he figured the Double Deuce needs a woman, and if I stay married to her a year, it'll last fifty."

She cracked eight eggs into a bowl and whipped them frothy before pouring them out onto the grill. "He was telling you without telling you, wasn't he?"

"Looks like it. Been a lot easier if he would have just spit it right on out and hadn't beat around the bush," Ace said.

"Steak and eggs and pancakes," Jasmine said as she set four plates on the shelf between the kitchen and the dining room and took down the next order.

Bridget waved through the window at Ace and set two plates on a tray. "Couldn't stay away from her, could you?"

Ace grinned. "You got it. Got to make sure all the other cowboys in Ringgold know that she's my wife."

"You fell into the husband role mighty fast," Jasmine whispered.

"And you are doing a fine job too, thank you very much, Mrs. Riley," Ace threw back.

"Two days down, three hundred and sixty-three to go," she said.

He turned up his cup and gulped down the last of the coffee. "Got to run, darlin'. Horses got to be broke. Hay's got to be raked. See you at suppertime. Now don't be beggin' me to stick around and kiss on you all day just because we are still newlyweds. A man has to make a livin' for his woman and there's things he has to do in the daytime other than sit around dreamin' up new ways to have sex in the evenin' when she gets home from work."

She looked up to tell him that he'd better get out the back door or else take a beating with an egg turner for that little speech—just in time to see his lips coming toward her. She didn't have time to turn or run, or even get ready for the electricity that zapped her when his tongue teased her mouth open. The kitchen got fifty degrees hotter, her belly clinched up in knots, and her knees went weak.

Then he strolled out the back door as if it hadn't affected him at all.

She melted into a chair. "And I've got three hundred sixty-three days more until the divorce. I'll never make it that long, not without seducing him or letting him seduce me. And then I'll fulfill every one of his dreams."

Ace's hands were trembling as he gripped the steering wheel. Blake Shelton had a song out a couple of years before titled "Delilah," and it fit that day perfectly. The song talked about a girl who had a best friend who was always right there to listen to her and listen when her love life went south. Only the best friend was in love with her and really wanted her to love him.

That's where Ace was that morning. He'd realized after he married Jasmine that she was his Delilah. She'd never let him down. She'd been right there in front of him, every day for a year and a half, while he moaned and groaned about the women in his life and how they were all so clingy and he just wanted a good time, not a permanent commitment.

Ace looked at the barbed-wire tat on his arm. He'd bragged about no woman ever getting across his barbed-wire fence and into his heart. How in the devil had Jasmine snuck under it without him even feeling a twinge?

He slapped the steering wheel. "It's going to be a long year."

At the close of the day, Bridget locked the doors and began her daily ritual of getting things refilled and cleaned up for the next day. Jasmine picked up the broom and started at the back side of the dining room, sweeping crumbs and sweetener wrappers from under the tables.

"Guess what? I've got a date for Saturday night. Divorce is final. Ex-husband has put out the word that he's going to marry that floozy he's been livin' with, and I've got a date. Who'd have thought that when I walked in this place six months ago?" she said.

"That's good. Just don't be fallin' for the same abusive type you got in trouble with before," Jasmine said.

"Not me. That man done broke me of bad-boy types. Daddy likes Frankie James, even, and

Momma thinks he hung the moon. He was this bashful kid in school who never said a word. Made good grades but didn't play sports or go out drinkin' and partyin' on Saturday night. We're going to dinner at a steak house and then to a movie," Bridget said.

"Where did you meet him?" Jasmine asked.

"At a softball game. I ain't played since I married because my ex was too jealous to let me play that first year and the second I was too fat. Me and Frankie are on the same coed team and we play on Friday nights. Frankie said that he liked me in high school but he was afraid to ask me out because he knew I'd say no. And he's right. In high school, I would have never gone out with him, but things is different now," Bridget said.

"Well, I hope you have a wonderful time. But save the second weekend in July for me, please. That's the weekend of the wedding."

Bridget's eyes went wide. "I got that marked on my calendar. I wouldn't miss that for nothing. Who all is standing up there with you, again?"

"Austin, Pearl, Liz, Gemma, Colleen, and Lucy. I think you should wear the silver dress. It would look good on you. What do you think?"

"What other colors is there?" Bridget asked.

Jasmine leaned on the broom. "Momma is picking out metal colors like gold, bronze, pewter, and silver. She'll insist that Pearl wear the gold."

"I don't care if I have to wear orange with purple

spots on it, I'm just so tickled that I get to be one of the bridesmaids. Can I bring Frankie if things work out between us?" Bridget asked.

"Sure you can, and to the rehearsal dinner too."

"Wow!" Bridget shook her head as if she couldn't believe it.

Both of them looked up when they heard a hard tapping on the door window and saw Gemma and Austin on the porch. Bridget was closest to the door, so she unlocked it.

"We was just talkin' about the weddin'. Y'all decided what color you are wearing?" Bridget asked.

"You were serious about that wedding? You are already married," Austin said.

"I know that. The state of Nevada knows that, but my momma, Kelly King, says it's not legal without the white dress, seven bridesmaids, and a reception that is so gaudy that no one will ever forget that I'm married," Jasmine said.

"You weren't kidding on Sunday, then? We all thought you were making a joke about your mother planning a wedding. Figured it might be a reception. I never heard of getting married before the wedding," Austin said.

"Second Sunday in July. I've got to shop for a dress this weekend, and Momma says if it's not fancy enough she'll have a backup one on hand."

"And I get to be a bridesmaid. Gemma is one, and there's seven of us altogether," Bridget beamed.

"And I'm a bridesmaid too. It'll be fun. A wedding when the bride and groom are already married." Austin shook her head. "I bet Ace just loves that idea."

"If he wants to get along with his new mother-in-law, he'd better pretend to love it even if he doesn't," Jasmine said.

"How'd you come up with seven?"

"Ace has six brothers and Momma says they are all going to stand up with him to show that they support our marriage. And he's going to ask Rye to be his best man since they've been best friends forever."

"What about Wil?" Austin asked.

"Eight." Jasmine rolled her eyes. "Ace has probably already talked to Wil and Pearl is the matron of honor. I need one more."

As if Kelly could read her daughter's mind, the phone rang.

"Hello, Momma," Jasmine said.

"You sound tired. You're doin' too much, runnin' a café and a ranch. You're goin' to have to quit that café, girl, or you'll never get pregnant," Kelly said.

"I'm not quitting my café," Jasmine said.

"Have it your way, but if you look tired and worn out at my wedding, I'm going to be really upset. I called to tell you that we are still looking at invitations. We just can't make up our minds. Oh, and how many dresses are we going to need to order?"

"Looks like we need one more than I told you. I forgot a groomsman. How about Marcella's daughter, Jenny? Think she'd like to be in the wedding? And Momma, you can pick out a couple of flower girls. How about Marcella's two granddaughters?"

"Oh, Jasmine, that is so sweet of you. Marcella will be so tickled. I've got to go to the kitchen and tell her all about it. Jenny is going to be dancin' on air. Goodbye, now." Kelly hung up.

"I'll need that Jenny's name for the bachelorette party," Gemma said.

Jasmine threw up both palms. "Oh, no! I'm already married. No party, please!"

"Oh, okay," Gemma grumbled. "But you won't talk me out of a baby shower when the time comes."

Jasmine did a fake shudder from her shoulders to knees. "I'm only married a few days. Don't be talking baby showers to me now."

"Pearl is having twins. Your momma is already behind," Austin reminded her.

Jasmine shuddered again, this time for real.

"Bachelorette party don't sound so bad now, does it?" Austin laughed.

"Hey, Rye knew the judge so y'all got married on Christmas Day. How'd you do that anyway?" Jasmine asked.

"Like I said, Rye knew the judge and he was at the courthouse on another matter that day, so he married us. My two little elderly friends in Ryan threw us a big reception. Ask Gemma about Molly and Greta."

Jasmine looked over at Gemma.

Gemma smiled. "They were all thrown out of the same mold as Pearl's Aunt Pearlita and Austin's Granny Lanier about eighty years ago. God made women even more sassy and bossy then than he does now. We couldn't begin to be as tough as those women."

Bridget changed the subject. "So what color dress are y'all going to wear?"

"Better be decidin' before next Sunday. We're meeting at Pearl's to choose colors and get sizes," Jasmine said.

Chapter 10

Jasmine was dragging by Wednesday night. Everything was set up for the first morning rush at the café. Bridget had gone home and Jasmine was heading home to the ranch. It hadn't rained since before the Las Vegas trip, and she broke a sweat just going from café to truck. She looked forward to a long, lazy bath in the big claw-foot tub while the guys were all out of the house. Put on some Josh Turner music and sink down into a foot of bubbles and think about absolutely nothing. She needed a couple of hours to refuel after running out every ounce of emotional energy the past week.

"Lord, has it only been a week? It seems like a month." She talked to herself on the way to the gravel parking lot.

The air conditioner in her little truck had barely cooled the cab down when she reached the ranch house. Normally, Ace's two old Catahoula cow dogs were either out with him or else they'd meet her at the truck. That day they were lazed out on the porch, tails thumping on the wooden floor, but they didn't offer to move out of the shade.

"Too hot to work this afternoon, ain't it?"

Jasmine stopped long enough to pet them. She'd couldn't tell them apart, but Ace said that Old Bill was fatter than Little Joe. She eyed the two dogs and they still looked like identical twins to her.

"A set of bathroom scales would have trouble telling the difference in you two," she said. "I bet he can't tell the difference either. He just says that he can."

She didn't stop in the living room but went straight to the bathroom, turned on the water in the big, deep tub, and added vanilla-scented bubble bath. She was glad that whenever Ace's grandfather remodeled the bathroom and put two sinks in the vanity and a shower in the corner, he'd left the tub. She stripped out of her jeans, Nikes, socks, and shirt and dropped them on the floor. She added panties and bra to the pile and sank into the water, letting the bubbles cover everything but her head.

"A tub deep enough that the water covers boobs and knees. Either Gramps or Granny knew the way to a woman's heart." She rolled a towel to go under her neck and let the sloped back of the tub cradle her. With her eyes closed, she could feel the warm water ease the tired tension from her muscles.

Her eyes popped wide open. She had forgotten about Sam, Dexter, Buddy, and Tyson. Ace would have to put them in the wedding, and that meant more bridesmaids. Unless they could serve as ushers.

She lay back. That would work. They'd need at least four ushers, and the guys could do that job. The only thing left was someone to sit at the registration desk...and that was on her shoulders.

"I hate this," she mumbled. "I'm asking Ellen and Nellie."

Your mother will pitch a fit, Granny Dale whispered softly. *Two eighty-year-old women in her wedding. It ain't happenin', child.*

The only way she could get away with it would be to pull out the Cousin Candace card. She could hear the conversation playing in her head like an old radio soap opera.

"But, Mother, I suppose Cousin Candace is..."

That's all she'd have to say.

Kelly King would go off on a tirade that would scorch the hair out of Lucifer's ears. "I will not have that hussy in your wedding. She's a disgrace to the King name with her tattoo parlor down there in Dallas. God Almighty! Jasmine, what are you thinking about? Don't you have another friend?"

"Well, there are two sisters, Ellen and Nellie, but..."

"Do either of them have tat sleeves or a nose ring?"

"No, they do not have tats or piercings."

"Then Ellen and Nellie it is."

Jasmine opened her eyes and giggled. "And that's the way it's done."

"What's done?" Ace was sitting on the vanity bench not three feet from her.

Her knee-jerk reaction was to come straight up out of the water. Her second was to gather what bubbles were left into strategic places. It wasn't until she reached the third that anger set in.

"What in the hell are you doing in here? What are you even doing in the house at this time of day?" she asked.

Ace shrugged. "Watching you sleep in the bathtub. You talk in your sleep. You said something about that being the way it's done. Got a phone call. Came home early to get cleaned up, and when I came to the bathroom I found you. You are so cute I couldn't make myself wake you up. Is the water still warm? Mind if I join you?"

"No! Water is cold and I'm getting out. So turn around and shut your eyes while I get a towel around me."

"Wives aren't supposed to be so skittish. I bet sex would be good in that tub with you all slippery wet," he teased.

She raised a hand out of the water and pointed at the wall.

He shut his eyes tightly, but that didn't stop him from picturing her leaving the tub with water sliding off her naked body, bubbles still hanging on her firm breasts and clinging to her butt. He heard her wet feet hit the floor and the towel snap open. He smelled the sweetness of vanilla. And the arousal started just like it had every single time Jasmine was anywhere near him. Ever since the wedding, that's the way it had been. Before the wedding, he saw her every day without a problem. Now he just had to think her name and he got an instant erection.

"You can open them now. I'm going to the bedroom and get dressed," she said.

The water gurgled as it swirled down the drain and the bathroom door closed, but it didn't take all of Jasmine with it. Her smell and the picture in Ace's mind stayed behind as he turned on the shower. He tossed his dirty clothing on top of hers and wondered if that was an omen. Underwear, shirts, jeans, even socks all tangled up together; did that mean that his and Jasmine's lives would be tangled up like that someday?

As he washed the dirt and grime from his hair and body, he was thinking about what it would be like to share his entire life with Jasmine. He certainly didn't expect to find her sitting fully clothed on a vanity seat when he threw the shower curtain back.

"Need some bubbles?" she asked.

His knee-jerk reaction was to grab the washcloth and cover his package. His second was to reach out and pull her into the shower with him. It took ten seconds to reach the third, which was laughter.

"A towel will do fine, ma'am."

She handed him a towel and fought back the blush. It had sounded like a wonderful plan to get back at him when she was dressing in denim shorts, sandals, and a sleeveless cotton shirt. But it had backfired when he threw open the shower curtain and there stood a real, breathing, flesh-and-blood Greek god before her.

Whoever was responsible for sculpting those statues sure hadn't had Ace for a model; that much Jasmine could vouch for. Before they went to chiseling out the lower extremities of those statues, they should have come on across the waters and found a blond-haired cowboy. That would have really made the ladies drool.

Ace whipped the towel around his waist and stepped out onto the worn throw rug. "Guess I forgot to tell you about that phone call, didn't I?"

"Your mother or mine?"

"Wil, actually. Pearl has been trying to call you for the past hour. No, make that an hour and a half now. Why didn't you answer your phone?" Ace asked.

Jasmine reached for her hip pocket, then checked the jeans on the floor. "Guess it fell out in the truck seat."

"Well, her water broke and she's at the hospital and she says she isn't calling her mother until you get there, because she can't deal with Tess without you," Ace said.

Jasmine popped up off the bench, her hands went to her hips, and she took a step forward until she was nose-to-nose with Ace. "And why didn't you tell me this before now? I could have already been halfway there. Hell, if I'd driven fast I could be there. *Dammit!* If Tess isn't there when Pearl has those boys, I'll get the blame. And if she's there and I'm not, Pearl will kill me because I promised that I'd keep Tess from driving her crazy while she's in labor."

Ace bent slightly and kissed her hard without touching any other part of her body. "You're really cute when you are mad."

"Ace Riley!"

"Okay, I didn't tell you on purpose because I needed to get cleaned up and because I want us to go together," he said.

Her lips were so hot she was amazed that her words didn't fry as they left her mouth. "Well, you'd better hurry up because if you aren't ready in five minutes, I'm leaving without you."

"Yes, ma'am." He grinned.

She stepped back, and her foot landed in the middle of the dirty clothing on the floor. She bent down to gather it up to take to the laundry room and touched his bare leg with her cheek. It immediately fired up as hot as her lips.

"I'm sure Pearl would understand, us being newlyweds and all, if you'd like to make a side trip to the bedroom," Ace said.

"That's a dream, cowboy," Jasmine said.

When she stood up with the clothes in her arms, he brushed a quick kiss across her cheek. "Thanks for taking care of mine with yours."

"Four minutes. You'd better hurry up."

"He's disappointed. I tell you that for sure. He might not even cooperate when you want him to," Ace said as he followed her down the hall toward the bedroom.

"Honeymoon must be over," she quipped and kept walking.

He dressed faster than he ever had, finger combed his curls back away from his forehead, and jammed his feet down in boots. He was lacing his belt through the loops on his jeans as he made his way across the yard to his truck where Jasmine was already sitting in the passenger's seat with the buckle fastened.

"Ten seconds to spare. I'm on my way," she said into the cell phone and snapped it shut.

"Am I forgiven?" he asked.

"Depends on whether we beat Tess to the hospital. She called fifteen minutes ago to check on Pearl, who happened to be right in the middle of a contraction, so Tess grabbed her bag that's been packed for a week and is on the way. You can bet that if she gets stopped, she'll talk the policeman into giving her an escort complete with sirens all the way to the hospital. If you get me there first so I can run interference for Pearl, I might forgive you," Jasmine said.

"I figured Rye and Austin would be ahead of us. They were on their way when the call came. Raylen and Liz were headed for the house to get cleaned up too." Ace started the truck engine and fiddled with his seat belt.

Jasmine tucked her head down and rolled her eyes up at him. "You, Ace Riley, better hope I'm the first one there."

"Or what?" he asked.

"Pearl keeps two shovels in her barn. I keep two in my pantry. You've probably noticed them before. They are right there beside the broom and mop. We are prepared at any time, night or day, to dig a six-foot hole. Need I explain further?"

He stomped the gas pedal all the way to the floor and hoped all the Texas Highway Patrol troopers were having doughnuts and coffee at the local Dairy Queen. He made it from Ringgold to Henrietta in record time, went through the first traffic signal on yellow, and the second one had barely turned green when he slipped through it. When he braked in front of the Henrietta hospital, he left skid marks on the pavement.

"Get out in a hurry. I passed Rye and Austin back there at the second red light. Hurry up and get in there first," he said.

Jasmine took time to touch his shoulder. "You are forgiven."

Chapter 11

Only one other truck was parked under the awning at the burger joint, but then all the midweek church traffic would have long since come and gone, and most teenagers had an early curfew, especially in the middle of the week.

Liz and Raylen waved through the window when they saw Jasmine and Ace nose into the other side of the parking spaces. Liz held up a hot fudge sundae and smiled.

"So will it be pickles and ice cream?" Ace asked.

"No, thank you. After that experience, I'll buy my babies. I knew it hurt like hell, but Pearl cried real tears," she said.

"But there was that big grin on her face when she was holding those boys," Ace said.

"I don't know how she did it, Ace. I really don't. I hurt for her there at the end when she pushed until her face was as red as her hair and she cried."

"Then no pickles on top of your ice cream?"

She shook her head. "One of those chocolate sundaes like Liz is eating will be fine. And a cup of black coffee."

"This late at night? You'll be awake all night, and

I'm too tired after all that waiting on Pearl to birth them two boys to even think about a romp in the sheets," Ace said.

"No more sex for me. I saw the end result of that fun right there in that delivery room," Jasmine told him with a soft shiver.

"Tess was more than a little bit jealous that Pearl wanted you in there to hold her hand," Ace told her.

"I know, but Pearl would have raised up out of those stirrups and strangled her mother. It was best that I stayed in there with her and Wil. I stayed up by her head and Wil got to actually watch the babies coming out. I did chance a peek or two at the mirror and that was enough for me. Tess forgot all about anything when he went out with a baby on each arm and she got to be the first one to hold the boys."

"Where were you when he brought the babies out?" Ace asked.

"Holding Pearl's hand and telling her that they were beautiful, that they had black hair and I couldn't tell if they were going to have blue eyes or green ones, and that she did a fantastic job. She was squeezing my hand and telling me that it hurt like hell, she wasn't doing it again, and that I could never endure it, to go buy my kids even if they had 'Made in China' stamped on their butts."

"Why couldn't you endure it?"

"She says I'm not as tough as her."

"Are you?"

"Oh, yeah. I'm every bit as tough but she just pushed two six-pound boys out of her body. I wasn't going to argue with her." Jasmine smiled.

"John and Jesse. I like the names, but they looked just alike. Think they'd better tattoo their names on their butts before they take them home so Wil don't get them mixed up?" He steered her toward the table where Liz and Raylen were sitting.

"You ever get Old Bill and Little Joe mixed up?" she asked.

"What's that got to do with anything? But no, I do not. Old Bill is six months older than Little Joe. They had the same parents but they aren't even littermates. They just look alike. I keep telling you Old Bill is fatter."

"Well, I don't reckon Wil's going to get his boys mixed up either. Maybe Jesse will be fatter." She laughed.

It had been a long evening, and by the time the twins were born, the waiting room was packed with friends and family. It was almost midnight when Ace and Jasmine left and they were both starving.

"What are you thinking about?" Ace asked.

"The look on Pearl's face when she held those babies."

"It was pretty awesome. I was standing in the doorway. We'd followed the nurse down there with them. Just looking at Wil and Pearl with those two babies made tears in my eyes," Ace said.

Jasmine looked at his face to see if he was joking. "You are serious."

"I am serious. Rye and Wil are my best friends. They have been since before we ever started school. Me and Wil and Rye were inseparable. Fatherhood looks good on both of them," he said.

"Ace, you're a romantic at heart," Jasmine said.

"Yes, he is," Liz said. "We're just getting finished so you two can have the table. We'd stay with you but we've got to get up early. How many of those squallin' bundles do you want?" Liz asked as she slid out of the booth.

"As many as I can buy," Jasmine teased.

"I want a house full. Momma swears she'll steal one of my kids from me and turn her into a carny," Liz said.

"I wouldn't put it past her one bit." Jasmine smiled.

They had barely gotten out the door when Ace kissed Jasmine on the cheek. "Darlin', I'm not just a romantic at heart. I'm a romantic all over my body," he said with a wicked gleam in his eyes.

"You are a rogue."

The waitress took their order and in minutes was back with their ice cream. "Make up your mind. Am I a rogue or a romantic?"

"Depends on whether you are being sweet

or trashy." She dipped into the hot fudge and ice cream and shoved it in her mouth. When she'd swallowed, she said, "We didn't have supper. I want a hamburger when I finish this."

"Your wish is this bridegroom's command. Just speak the words," Ace said.

"Bet you say that to all the women."

"Only the ones I marry in Las Vegas. The rest have to order their own burgers." Ace slurped up chocolate malt through the straw. He'd been too excited about the whole waiting-for-the-babies-to-be-born process to realize that he hadn't eaten, but a burger did sound good.

"How do you take yours? On the rocks or neat?" he asked.

"We still talkin' about burgers?"

"Yep, on the rocks is mustard and onions. Neat is mayo and no onions."

"On the rocks with a large order of onion rings," she said.

"Something to drink with that?"

"No, this coffee will do just fine," Jasmine answered.

He held up a hand and the waitress came right over. He put in an order for burgers and onion rings and added a Coke for himself. "Now, tell me again about how you are going to show up Pearl and have triplets the first time out of the chute."

Jasmine didn't know it was possible to choke on

ice cream, but she did. "Tell me how you want to be buried? Face up or butt up?"

"I'll have to think about that. Should you ever dig me back up, do I want you to kiss my butt or my sexy lips? Hard decision to make, ma'am," he answered with a wide grin.

"Believe me, if I ever put you in the ground, I will not be digging up your sorry old ass. I'll leave it there under the rosebush forever," Jasmine declared.

Ace had to swallow fast to keep from snorting chocolate malt out his nose. He'd never met a woman like Jazzy, who'd give him right back whatever he threw out. Lines that had most women swooning made her laugh. Come-ons that brought women to their knees caused her to tilt her chin down and give him a look that would fry a weaker man, leaving nothing but belt buckles and boots in the wake.

Maybe that's why he'd fallen in love with her.

Whoa, pard'ner! Pull up them reins. Just because I want to take her to bed every time I kiss her doesn't mean I'm in love with her. Crap! That just means I'm attracted to her. Hell, I'm attracted to women, period. I like the smell of them, the taste of them, and even the way they feel all soft and sweet. But love? That's for Rye and Wil. Raylen and Liz can have it too, but not this cowboy. I just want to make love to her. Long and slow and lots of times. That marriage thing sets my sex door to swinging; the one with the L on it is still fastened up tight.

"What are you thinking about? Your jaw is set and your face looks like it is set in stone. Wishin' I'd ordered the neat burger so you don't have to ride home with onion breath?" Jasmine asked.

Ace always had a comeback. Always! But his mind was completely blank. All he could see was that big red L on the door with four dead-bolt locks and a two-by-four length of oak nailed across it at an angle.

"Well?" Jasmine asked.

"Swallowed a hell of a big air bubble and couldn't say a word until it decided to go up or down." He forced a smile.

"It's a sympathy burp for the twins," she teased.

It's a lie, but it wasn't bad when you were staring at that picture in your head, that aggravating inner voice said. *What are you intending to do about all this?*

I'd like to seduce her tonight. Once I've made love to her, then I'll know for certain that it was door number one, the sex door that is thrown wide open, and not number two, the L door, or number three, the father door.

"Hell, I don't know," he said aloud.

"Don't know what? We were talking about burping babies," she said.

"Brain freeze. My crazy mind is thinking one thing, and my ears are hearing you and they are getting confused. I think it's an acute disease, one of those somethingmiotis things that I can't pronounce. It's not fatal. It'll pass when I get onions in my mouth," he said.

Jasmine brushed her teeth and went straight to bed. Blake and Dalton were still up when she and Ace got home so Ace stayed behind in the kitchen and told them all about the twins. When he made it to the bedroom, she was curled up on her side, her breathing steady and shallow and her back to his side of the bed.

That negative little niggling voice started the argument when he dropped his jeans on the rocking chair on top of hers. If he had sex with Jasmine, it would not change their friendship. It would prove that he could have sex with her without thinking about any kind of permanent relationship. And he wanted her oh so bad.

He peeled out of his shirt and tossed it on the chair and the battle got hotter. By the time he was down to his boxers, desire had taken over his better sense. He eased into bed and wrapped his naked body around Jasmine's. He nuzzled his face into her neck and was surprised as hell when she flipped over and snuggled right into his arms.

"Mmmm," she mumbled.

Jasmine was dreaming that Ace was cuddled up

with her and his hands were playing her body like a pianist on a finely tuned baby grand piano. She could hear the faint strands of "Last Date" by Floyd Cramer as Ace made big lazy circles on her back with one rough, old callused hand and cupped her breast with the other.

She'd never realized just how well her breast fit into his hand, but as she stood back in the dream and analyzed the situation, it seemed as if she'd grown breasts in her teens especially for him. She wiggled in closer to him and let her fingertips walk across his broad expanse of back.

"God, that feels good, Jazzy," he said.

Her eyes popped wide open at the sound of his voice.

"I was not dreaming, and you are naked," she said. Her breath was already ragged, and molten fire filled her lower body. It was turn back quickly or damn the torpedoes and full speed ahead.

"And so are you except that tank top and those cute little boxer shorts which I plan to take off with my teeth," he whispered hoarsely.

She damned the torpedoes.

He dived under the covers, grabbed the waistband of her boxers, and slowly removed them, his hands continuing to play all the way to her ankles, as his teeth pulled the elastic further and further. At the bottom, they hung up on her toes so he used his fingers to dislodge them.

Jasmine groaned when he started back up with wet kisses, tasting one inch at a time, stopping to graze several times along the way until she was groaning and arching her back for him.

"You are one sexy woman, Jazzy," he whispered when he finally ended the journey at her lips. He nibbled the lower one, teased her teeth apart with his tongue, and made love to her all over again with his mouth.

Jasmine had been kissed. She'd had sex. But she'd never had kisses so hot that they brought her to the brink of a climax.

When he moved on top of her, she was more than ready. She tangled her hands in his hair and held on for fear that when she did reach the apex of the climax she'd fall right off the earth into eternity. The rhythm intensified with each thrust and her moans became louder. She moved her hands to his butt cheeks and dug her fingernails into his flesh. She'd never had sex when it became the center core of everything and she could think of absolutely nothing else.

"You make me so hot!" The words came out one at a time with pauses between.

Ace had the reputation for having had sex with dozens of women, and he'd never done a lot to discourage the rumors. Truth was that he'd had only a handful of relationships and what he experienced with Jasmine was surreal. There were only two people on the face of the earth that evening.

Ace and Jasmine.

And Ace didn't care if it stayed that way forever.

"Ahhh, Jazzy!" he said in a deep Texas drawl and collapsed on top of her.

She could not breathe for a full minute and it had nothing to do with Ace's weight on her body. It took that long for her body, soul, and mind to reconnect after the blazing sex.

He finally rose up and covered her mouth in a string of passionate kisses that fanned the embers still hot in the ashes of the hottest sex she'd ever known.

"Ace, we can't. Another bout like that would kill me graveyard dead," she rasped.

"Me too, but I love your lips," he said.

"It isn't like kissing your sister then? I mean, since we are best friends?" she asked.

"I don't have a sister but hell, no! Why would you say that? Was it like making love with your brother? Crap! Jazzy, is that what you get out of our sex?"

"Hell, no! I don't have a brother, but I'm sure what we just did wasn't like that. It's just that we've been friends so long, and Liz said that when she kissed Blaze, it was like kissing her brother.," she explained in short gasps.

Ace kissed her softly on the forehead. "Well, darlin', we left friendship on the other side of the bedroom door."

"Then was it booty sex?" she asked.

"No! I can't believe you'd say that. And it wasn't because we came from the hospital where two of our best friends just had babies either. I can't tell you what it was, Jazzy. I can just tell you that it was awesome and it felt right. Hell, it felt better than right. Oh, crap!"

"What?" she asked.

"I got so involved and so hot that I didn't even think of protection. This time or the first time either. My mind doesn't work when I'm in the bedroom with you."

She blanched and then began to count days in her head. "It should be all right this time. I'm regular as clockwork and this is not ovulation time, but..." She left the sentence hanging.

"Yes, ma'am." He smiled. Was she about to say, "but next time"? He could sure enough live with that idea.

He drew her into his arms and kissed the top of her hair.

She wiggled down deeper into his embrace, listened to his heartbeat, and enjoyed her afterglow which was absolutely fantastic.

It was the strangest feeling. Afterglow. Friendship. Talking about how it felt to have sex with him. Birth control. All rolled up into one conversation that felt right. Was there something weird about that?

"Good. So I'm going out on a limb here and asking an old cliché question. How was it for you?"

"Wonderful. Steamy. Hotter'n hell. Felt right. Best ever." She yawned and fell asleep, still curled up against his side.

He still had a grin on his face when he finally went to sleep.

Chapter 12

Jasmine worried all day about the fallout from the best sex she'd ever had…twice now! She felt like Old Bill with a big ham bone, burying it in the yard and then digging it up to chew on it some more before digging another hole and hiding it again. Bridget would hang up two or three orders and she'd busy herself filling them, thinking only about whether to put mashed potatoes and gravy on the plate or french fries. Then there would be a lull in business and she'd pour a cup of coffee, sit down at the table, and worry over the sex issue again.

She picked up an order pad and scribbled.

Thursday: Ace told about the probability of losing his ranch to the villain, Cole. Slimy bastard. Ace is right about him. One week to find wife. I proposed.

But, did he play me? He knows me better than anyone other than Pearl, and he had to have known that I would do anything to help him.

Friday: Plans made. He asked a dozen times if I was sure I wanted to go through with it.

Reassurance so that later he could say I was given multiple chances to back out.

Saturday: To Vegas. Boom!

One kiss and I was hot for him. Again, he knows me. Was that the beginning of a subtle seduction?

Sunday: Home. He wins. I move out to the ranch. Brothers move in.

Hell of a lot of coincidences. I don't even believe in fate... Well, maybe except for Pearl and Wil and maybe Raylen and Liz. But not for me. Hell no! I believe I make my own decisions and live with the consequences. But wait, I decided to marry Ace, and now these are the consequences. I'm talking in circles again. It's time to bury the bone and get back to work.

Bridget peeked through the window separating the kitchen and dining room. "You makin' up next week's menus? The meat loaf today is really going good. You might want to make it again."

"I was thinking the same thing," Jasmine shoved the order pad into her apron pocket and picked the papers off the clips.

"Orders ready," she called out as she set the two plates on the window shelf.

Bridget grabbed them without commenting and Jasmine went back to her notes.

Last night: Awakened from dream before midnight and had sex. Why?

Why did he choose that time to make his move? Was it because he wanted the marriage consummated two times so that it was real? So that if his grandfather's memory ever haunted him, he could say that he'd found a wife in every sense of the word before the time was up?

Today: Proof?

I can't prove that. I've been hot for him all week so maybe I gave off vibes. He's a lady's man, a good-timin' cowboy who is sexy as hell. He could smell a vibe from a mile away.

"You look like you are fightin' a legion of devils," Bridget said from the order window. "Got a late customer who wants the chicken-fried dinner. Hot as it is, I swear I don't know how they eat such heavy food."

Jasmine nodded. A legion of devils was right.

Business ended at two. Bridget came into the kitchen and drew up a glass of sweet tea, sat down at the table, and folded a laundry basket full of napkins for the next day.

"You get those dragons slayed?" Bridget asked.

"Got 'em on the run," Jasmine answered.

"Good. Even when things are good in a marriage,

there comes a time when you wake up and think, 'Crap! What have I done?' Don't let it get to you. We all do it. Even when the husband ain't a bastard who hits on you and tells you how worthless you are. We had a counselor tell us that. Lucy got her to come speak to us one Sunday. Was you havin' one of those times?"

"I guess I was," Jasmine answered.

"Ace loves you. I can see it in his eyes when he looks at you. Don't worry none. It'll all be fine by tomorrow and you'll be all glad that you married him," Bridget told her.

Jasmine nodded. Bridget had gotten part of it right because she was thinking that very line: *Crap! What have I done?* Not over marrying Ace, but for having sex with him.

"Well, that job is done and ready for tomorrow. I'm going home now unless you want me to stay for something else," Bridget said.

Jasmine shook her head. "I'm going to whip up a couple of banana puddings for tomorrow and then I'm going home."

Home! She'd called the ranch home! Did Bridget have any words of wisdom about that word?

"See you in the morning, then." Bridget untied her apron and tossed it into the empty laundry basket. "Kind of like it is at home. Laundry and dishes never get completely caught up."

Jasmine's cell rang the minute Bridget was out

the door. "Redneck Woman" meant it was Pearl. She needed to hear gushing about how beautiful the twins were and how much they ate and how Tess was driving Pearl crazy. The notes tucked away in her pocket didn't seem so much like a big black cloud.

"Hello. I'm so glad you called. Tell me about motherhood," Jasmine answered.

"It's... I... God...help...me... Jasmine!" Each word came out in a heartrending sob that stopped Jasmine's heart and put her imagination into overdrive.

Something was wrong with the babies.

Wil had been killed.

Pearl had killed her mother.

Nothing but sobs came through the phone line. Jasmine fought to keep from yelling when she said, "Talk to me. What is it?"

"Come... quick." The weeping continued and the hiccups began.

Jasmine picked up her purse. "Hospital or home?"

"Home, but I need you. God, it's horrible."

"Did you kill your mother?" Jasmine asked on the way to her truck.

"No, she's wonderful and she's helping. I couldn't make it without her and..."

"Is it Wil?"

"No, he's there, but they can't save it."

"Stop it right now before I have a heart attack. Shut up your caterwaulin' and tell me what has happened!" Jasmine said sternly.

"You sound...like graduation...night. I'm not... drunk. And I didn't...have sex...with Roman," Pearl declared between sobs.

"I know you didn't and it's not graduation night, but you are acting like it is and you were drunk. Are you drunk now? Good Lord, Pearl, you aren't supposed to be drinking yet. Now, where is Wil and what is so horrible?" Jasmine talked as she started the truck and backed out of the lot.

"The Longhorn Inn is burning to the ground," Pearl whispered.

"Is Lucy all right?"

"Yes."

"Did she get the cat out?"

"Wil says Delilah is in the truck."

"Do you have insurance on the motel?"

Silence.

"Do you?"

"I'm sorry. I was nodding," Pearl said.

"Then shut up. It can be rebuilt or the mesquite can take over the land again. It's not worth getting so upset," Jasmine said.

"I knew you'd understand, but I can't stop crying." Pearl hiccupped. "Lucy will be devastated and she'll need a job and Wil proposed to me in the kitchen of my apartment and I met him in the lobby and my old doofus bowlegged cowboy on the sign just fell down and it's even gone."

"That crazy-lookin' cowboy is old enough to go off to the neon heaven in the sky. And if you'll hush, I'll put Lucy to work. Now shut up and go look at your two precious sons. I'll be there in ten minutes."

Jasmine turned north. When she reached Highway 82, she made a left-hand turn and hit the gas pedal. Traffic slowed to a crawl in front of the inn, on the east side of Henrietta. The inn was more than fifty years old, built of wood that had weathered to the color of ashes and must've gone up like dry tinder. There was nothing left but rubble, and the firemen were spraying the remains of the old neon sign of a bowlegged fifties-style cowboy pointing down at the Longhorn Inn sign.

Pearl had inherited the inn when her great-aunt died. She'd quit her job at the bank in Durant and told Jasmine that she was an entrepreneur. When Jasmine saw the place, her first reaction had been that Pearl had inherited the motel from *Psycho*.

Pearl had only been there a few months when a former employee dropped Lucy on her doorstep. Lucy was on the run from an abusive husband and in bad need of a healthy dose of confidence as well as a job. Pearl gave her both. When Pearl and Wil married the previous year, she'd turned managing the Longhorn Inn over to Lucy.

Lucy used the motel as an underground for

abused women. Bridget was one of her strays and still went faithfully to the Sunday afternoon meetings Lucy had organized. Now the motel was gone and Lucy would be far more worried about all the women she was instrumental in keeping out of another abusive relationship than the job she'd lost.

Jasmine made a right-hand turn on the west end of Henrietta, drove a couple of miles, and made another right onto Wil's property. By the time she parked the truck, Tess was on the porch and motioning her inside.

"Thank God you are here. She can't stop crying. It's more than that motel, but that's what she's blaming it on and I don't know what to do with her. She just keeps saying that Jasmine can fix it," Tess said.

"Where is she?" Jasmine asked.

Tess pointed. "Living room."

Jasmine went straight to the sofa and gathered Pearl into her arms. "I told you to shut up."

"You can't tell me what to do. I just had two babies last night, and I'm tougher than you are." Pearl scooted out of the embrace.

"You were tougher than me last night but today I get to be the strong one because having babies and your motel burning down all in twenty-four hours is too much to happen to you," Jasmine said.

Pearl swiped at the tears with the back of her hand. "It's all right now. You are here. And you'll fix it for Lucy. Wil just called and they just left. The firemen said that there wasn't no need in trying to get back in to save anything. They think a gas line broke and blew the whole thing up. Lucy heard a blast and thought it was a car wreck out on the highway. She ran outside to see about it and left the door open. That's how Delilah escaped. Lucy said when she turned around, the whole lobby was blazing. She's got the clothes on her back and Delilah. You can fix it for her, can't you?"

"Of course I can fix it. I can fix anything," Jasmine said. "Now hush. I'll take Lucy home with me and everything will be fine."

Pearl grabbed Jasmine by the shoulders. "You won't fire Bridget. Lucy would just die if you fired Bridget."

"I won't fire Bridget. I need to make a couple of phone calls before she gets here, though. So if you will stop this carryin' on, I'll fix it," Jasmine said.

Pearl inhaled deeply. "If you can fix it, I'll be all right."

God Almighty! Jasmine suddenly understood why her mother said that when things were tough. It was like pushing a button in the brain and letting a little bit of the pressure off before your head exploded.

Jasmine stood up and punched in Ace's speed-dial number on her way to the front porch.

"Hello, darlin'. Sorry I wasn't awake this morning when you left," he said.

"Oh, Ace, I have terrible news," she said breathlessly.

"What?" His heart stopped and then kicked back in with a thud. "Are you all right? Did you have an accident? What happened?"

"I'm fine. It's the Longhorn Inn. It burned to the ground and Lucy is hysterical and Wil is bringing her here and I want this settled before she gets here. And I want us to hire her to work for the ranch so Pearl will stop worrying about her. She can cook for the crew or clean the house."

"Okay," Ace said.

"Really? You mean it?"

"Yes, hire Lucy. She can start today and do whatever you want to hire her to do. You want me to call Dexter and tell him?" Ace said.

"I'll do it if you'll give me his number. Will he be upset?"

Ace rattled it off. "I imagine he'll be relieved, not upset."

"Thank you. I'll be home when this is settled and I'll be bringing Lucy with me."

Ace's heart did a double somersault. Jasmine had said she'd be *home*. Not that she was coming to the ranch but that she would be *home*.

Jasmine punched in the numbers for Dexter's phone, and he picked up on the second ring. "Hello?"

"Dexter, it's Jasmine. I need to know something

quickly. Do you cook because you really like it or do you cook because you have to?"

Dexter chuckled. "Miz Jasmine, I cook the meals because Buddy and Tyson would burn water tryin' to boil it and the devil couldn't eat Sam's cooking. It's been self-preservation ever since Ace's granny died. I'd rather be out in the fields or taking care of the animals. Why are you asking? You going to sell the café and take over the cooking for us?"

"I'm about to hire a cook because she needs a job. The Longhorn Inn burned in Henrietta and Lucy is without a job," Jasmine said.

"She that little lady who helps out women who get knocked around?" Dexter asked.

"Yes, she is. You boys got a problem with a woman in the bunkhouse to do the cooking?"

"No, ma'am. Not this cowboy. And if the others do, they can take it up with me. When can she go to work?"

"Tomorrow morning. And thank you, Dexter," Jasmine said.

"No, ma'am. I'm thankin' you," Dexter said.

Wil drove up in the yard and Lucy got out of the front seat slowly with the big yellow cat held closely to her chest. Delilah started to wiggle the minute that Digger, Wil's dog, left the porch with his tail wagging.

Jasmine rushed across the yard. "Put her in my truck. I'll turn on the air conditioner for her."

"Please don't take her away from me," Lucy said.

"She can stay in the house with Lucy," Wil offered.

"I need to talk to Lucy for a few minutes before we go inside. I think Pearl could use your shoulder right about now, though," Jasmine explained.

Wil nodded seriously.

"I can't be in your wedding now because everything I had burned up." Lucy's voice was hollow. "I'll have to move away because I don't have a job."

"To begin with, the wedding is three weeks away and you'll have plenty by then. And I want you to come work for the ranch so you have a job. Creed moved out of his bedroom yesterday. He'd planned to stay all week and maybe part of next week but Rye needs him over in Terral. The new stock came in faster than he planned, and anyway, that's another story. What I'm getting at is there's a spare bedroom at the ranch house." Jasmine swallowed hard. That was supposed to be her bedroom as soon as Creed moved out.

"It's just one room and not an apartment like you had, but we might work out something bigger later on. Remember I asked you one time if you'd leave Pearl and cook for me? Well, I promise I didn't set fire to the motel to get you, but I really do need your help. We've got a full crew running this summer. Four men out in the bunkhouse. Three in the house now that Creed has left. We need someone to cook breakfast. They take their lunch with them but then we need supper on the table at seven thirty in the summer and maybe six in the wintertime when it gets dark quicker. I was going to ask you next week if you had a stray in need of a job."

Jasmine was lying big-time about that, but Lucy wouldn't ever know.

"You can bring Delilah with you, and she can have run of the whole house. In between breakfast and supper, if you could do some cleaning and laundry in the ranch house, that would be good."

"Kind of like Wilma does for Liz and Raylen," Lucy asked.

"Except that it's seven old, cranky cowboys instead of just two people. It's a bigger job than what Wilma does, and for a while you'll only have one room and not a whole big house of your own like Wilma has. But if you like the job, we could maybe talk about putting a trailer out near the bunkhouse next spring for you so you could have more privacy." Jasmine made plans as she talked.

"I can have Sunday afternoons off for my meetings?" Lucy asked.

"After Saturday breakfast, the rest of the weekend is totally yours. The guys take care of themselves on Saturday night and Sunday. They usually only work until noon on Saturday if things are going well, but after breakfast is done, you don't have any responsibilities other than maybe shopping for food for the next week."

"Yes," Lucy said. "My truck blew up with the garage. You got something out there I can drive to my meetings?"

"You can use the ranch work truck to go wherever you want to go, or you can use mine when I'm not using it," Jasmine said.

Lucy brushed away a tear. "Thank you."

Jasmine reached across the seat and hugged her. "Don't thank me. You're going to have to work around seven old, grouchy men."

Lucy managed a weak smile. "I can do it. Pearl taught me that I can do anything. I reckon we'd best make a stop at the Dollar Store on the way, though. I'll need to buy a few things. I didn't even get out with a toothbrush or a pair of clean underbritches. And poor little Delilah will need her fancy canned food."

Later that night, Ace wrapped his arms around Jasmine and pulled her close. "You really do fix things, don't you? You ever thought of being a mediator?"

She wiggled until she was comfortable lying next to him, sharing the same pillow, their noses and lips just inches apart. "No, thank you. I think

Lucy is going to be an asset to the ranch. Getting used to so many men will be a chore for her, but it's what she needs."

"Didn't Wil tell me she was dating a fellow?"

"Luke got transferred to Kansas. They went out to dinner and parted with a hug. She says he was good for her because he taught her all men weren't like that bastard who beat her. But that she didn't love him."

"Dexter showed Lucy all around the kitchen and handed over the ranch credit card so she can do the grocery shopping. You think she'll do all right starting out Monday morning? That only gives her tomorrow to work with Dexter and the weekend to get settled in." Ace yawned.

Jasmine reached up and pushed a blond curl off his forehead. "You like my chicken-fried steak at the café?"

"Hell, yeah."

"Well, it's her secret recipe."

"About last night," he said, abruptly changing the subject.

"I was going to bring that up next," she said.

"And?" he asked.

"Did you seduce me because you wanted the marriage to be consummated before the final minute was up?" she asked.

Ace shook his head emphatically. "No, Jazzy. You are my best friend. I never thought I'd have a best friend that was a girl, but I've told you things and whined on your shoulder about things that even Rye and Wil don't know. You know my heart and my soul better than anyone. So believe me when I say that last night had nothing to do with our marriage. It had to do with the fact that you are so hot that I can't keep my hands off you. It's like friend and lover rolled up into one. I can't wrap my mind around it so I can't explain it."

She understood exactly what he was saying. "But how did this happen, Ace? We went into this knowing it was for a year. That's all I want. I'm happy running my café and with my life. What happens at the end of a year when we have to end it?"

"We'll shake hands like Lucy and Luke, sign the papers, and go have dinner to celebrate," he said.

If that's all she wanted, then that's what Ace would give her. He never intended it to be anything more than a paper marriage anyway. But the turmoil deep inside him said that he wanted a lot more than empty vows and a few nights of blazing sex.

Jasmine bit the inside of her lip. She would not cry. It was her day to be the tough one and she would keep the tears at bay, but it had sure enough had been one hell of a day!

First the doubts and worries all day about having sex with Ace. Then seeing her best friend have a meltdown. Pearl was pure piss and vinegar with a little kryptonite tossed in. She was stronger than Superman. To see her upset was like watching *Armageddon.*

Lucy coming to work at the Double Deuce and getting her and Delilah settled into the spare bedroom had been a good thing. But now hearing Ace say that they'd shake hands and walk after a year was almost more than she could take.

A year and a half ago when Jasmine quit her job at Texas Instruments in Sherman and bought the café, she'd had a kick-ass attitude that entered the room before she did. But lying there on Ace's arm that night, she feared that she'd lost some of her kick-ass.

"It's been a hell of a week," she said.

Ace didn't answer.

She looked up at him. He was asleep with a half grin on his face, and the action behind his eyes said that he was dreaming. She wondered if he was dreaming about her, or if some other woman danced through his dreams as she waited for the year to be over.

Chapter 13

"You ready for this? You look like you'd rather be tossin' hay bales into the barn," Ace said before he pushed the door open into the bridal shop in Wichita Falls.

"If I had a choice, I'd tell you to hand me the hay hooks and gloves," Jasmine said.

"Tell your mother no," Ace said.

"I can fight with her on anything else, but not this wedding. She's preached about it since I was born. And we've only got two hours to find the dress because these shops will close at five."

Ace removed his Stetson and opened the door. A rush of cool air came out to greet them, and a cute little salesgirl smiled at Jasmine and gave Ace two quick scans before rushing to their side.

"When is the wedding?" the lady asked Jasmine, but her eyes had stalled out on Ace's silver belt buckle.

"Three weeks," Jasmine said.

"Oh, my! Well, you look like a perfect size six so that shouldn't be a problem."

Just how she got Jasmine's size right by studying Ace's belt buckle was a mystery bordering on the supernatural.

"Would you have a theme in mind? Big bell gown, mermaid, Grecian goddess?" She finally looked at Jasmine.

"Just need a dress," Jasmine said.

The salesgirl pointed at a velvet chair in front of a round platform with mirrors on three sides. "You can sit there while we get her all ready," she told Ace.

Ace sat down, right boot cocked up on his left knee, hat on his lap.

Wedding dress number one: Jasmine's mother, Kelly, would love it but sweat flowed down between her boobs like the Red River in flood season, and her hair was sticking to her neck like she'd gotten hold of superglue instead of mousse that morning. If she was sweating inside an air-conditioned store, she'd melt in a church with three hundred people watching her tempt the hand of God a second time. She had to have something she could at least breathe in.

However, if she said this one would do just fine, then the day would be over and she could go home. She turned around to tell the woman she'd buy the hot bell gown with a train all the way to Ace, only to see her flirting blatantly with Ace. Actually, leaning forward to whisper in his ear. Jealousy and heat mixed together into a raging blaze that would make a wild prairie fire look like a match flame.

"Not this one. I'd be dead of sweat dehydration just walking down the aisle. What else do you have?" Jasmine asked.

Ace liked all that satin, lace, and puffy stuff and imagined how much fun it would be to undo every single one of those little covered buttons down the back. The saleslady was definitely flirting with him when she asked if he liked white silk. He brushed her off with a shake of the head, but Jasmine wanted to slap her.

Wedding dress number two: Jasmine held her arms up while the saleslady, Kyla, with the wandering eyes, pulled it down over her body and hooked elastic thread over dozens of small buttons up the back. Jasmine shook her head in the dressing room, and the dress with all its satin roses on the skirt and scattered on the train went back to the rack.

"Third time is a charm," she whispered when the woman brought in the third choice, a watered-silk strapless, fitted to a long waist with a train that could be fastened up to make a bustle.

She walked out from the fitting room and Ace shook his head. "It's not you, Jazzy. You look miserable in it. When the dress makes you look like you did in the Las Vegas one, then you've found it."

She didn't even step up on the revolving platform. She and the woman went right back to the dressing room to remove it.

"Is that your brother?" Kyla asked.

"No, ma'am."

"Your best friend?"

"Yes, ma'am."

"Is he gay or something?" Kyla asked.

"Hell, no!"

"Then why in the world is he shopping with you for a wedding dress? We never have men come help a lady pick out her dress. Usually it's the bridesmaids or maid of honor."

"He's my husband." Jasmine was amazed at how that slipped off her tongue so easily.

Husband!

She was married. It didn't sound strange at all, and that was downright frightening.

"He's what?" Kyla gasped.

Jasmine held up her left hand with the wedding band. "He's my husband. We got married in Las Vegas a week ago, but my mother insists on a Texas wedding."

"Well, that's a first for me. Never sold a dress to a lady who was already married with her husband watching from the sidelines," Kyla said.

"Thank you for all your help," Jasmine said.

"No problem. Come on back if you change your mind," Kyla said.

"Next store?" Ace asked when they were back outside with hot sunshine bearing down on them.

"Right around the corner. We could walk to it," Jasmine said.

"Lead the way, darlin'. Sorry you didn't find one in there. I don't know why you couldn't use that one you wore in Vegas. I liked it and you liked it.

Tell your momma she can have the wedding but you already got a dress," he said.

"It's complicated, like I said. It's got to be perfect and she thinks that dress is tacky. Okay, here we go for the second round." She pointed to the next bridal shop.

"I'd rather have a second round of something a hell of a lot more fun," he teased.

"Is that a line?" She giggled.

"Dammit, Jazzy, you are ruining my ego. That works every time," he said.

She laughed again and reached to push the door, only to have it swing open and wedding music begin. "Wow, talk about promotion," she mumbled.

Debra was middle-aged with her dark hair pulled back to the nape of her neck in a tight bun. She wore no jewelry, too much makeup, and glasses perched on the end of her nose. She didn't even notice Ace's belt buckle.

Dress number one: An ivory silk with long fitted sleeves, a square neckline, and no train. Kelly would hate it but of the four she'd tried on, Jasmine liked it best.

She looked at Ace who shook his head. "Your eyes aren't all dreamy."

Number two: Tight-fitting bodice covered with pearls and rhinestones, strapless, flowing skirt with a twelve-inch ruffle around the bottom that matched the bodice, and gold bells on the underskirt that tinkled when she walked. She swished several times in front of the mirror.

"This is a hoot, but I wouldn't be able to stop giggling. I sound like wind chimes." She giggled.

Ace laughed with her. "This isn't working, Jazzy. We can try again next week if they close before you find one. How about coffee and cheesecake from that Starbucks we passed on the way here?"

"I'm ready," she said.

She couldn't get out of the dress and into her khaki shorts, sandals, and red T-shirt fast enough. Debra was still getting the dress back on the hanger when Jasmine thanked her for her time and escaped out the door to a faster and more upbeat version of "Here Comes the Bride."

"Redneck Woman" started playing in her purse and Ace chuckled.

"What's so funny?"

"From fancy to trashy all in two minutes," he said.

"Don't let Pearl hear you say that. It's her ringtone," she said as she fished the phone from her purse and answered it.

"Did you get it yet?" Pearl asked.

"Tried on several and didn't fall in love with any of them," Jasmine answered.

"I'm so sorry I can't be there. You helped me pick out mine."

"Yeah, some friend you are! I helped you and

then you go and have babies before me and I have to listen to Momma whine about both your wedding and your babies," Jasmine said.

"Oh, hush! I was being nice. Is Lucy with you?"

"No, Ace is."

Pearl gasped. "You know he's not supposed to see the dress."

"I don't think that matters since he's already seen one dress," Jasmine argued.

"This is so bizarre. Not even a soap opera would write it into their script," Pearl said.

"You got it, sister!"

"I'm remembering how much fun we had the day we shopped for my dress. We picked it out in half an hour and spent the rest of the day in the western wear stores, remember?" Pearl's tone was wistful.

"Yes, because you wanted those fancy boots to go with your dress. What shop was that? I might need some to go with my dress if I ever find it," Jasmine said.

"Have you opened Kelly's email? She sent all of us bridesmaids the dresses she picked out. She did a wonderful job. You've got to see them. Open your mail and call me back. Could be that you don't have to shop anymore today," Pearl said.

"Honey, I'd wear a burlap bag and carry ragweed if I didn't have to try on another dress. I'll call you tonight with an update."

A few minutes later, Jasmine stopped in her tracks and gasped and said, "Holy crap!"

"What?" Ace asked.

"Sorry. Momma sent the bridesmaid's dresses and they are pretty," she said.

She sat down on a bench in front of a shop with "Kiddie Land" written on the front window and opened the second email from Kelly. She had to scramble to catch the phone as it dropped at the same time her jaw did. Her mother's backup dress was elegant. It looked like something a Grecian goddess might wear. It had a high waistline, spaghetti straps, and a skirt that flowed from the waist in soft pleats into a very short train at the back. The description said it was made of satin and chiffon, and the straps were rhinestone crystals.

Kelly's note said: *No veil. Just a magnolia blossom on one side with your hair pulled back behind your ear. No high heels. Very skimpy flat sandals of white kid leather that lace up around your ankles.*

Ace sat down beside her and reached for the phone. "Let me see."

"No, it's bad luck for the groom to see the dress, even if he is the husband, and this is the one. No more shopping today," she said.

"Look at me, Jazzy," he said.

She looked up.

He smiled.

"Yep, that's the one. Your eyes look right. Call

your momma and tell her she's the queen of shopping today."

She pushed a speed-dial button and winked at Ace while she waited.

"Hello, Momma, I just found the perfect wedding dress."

The pause was so long that Ace cocked his head to one side and raised an eyebrow in question.

Jasmine held up a finger.

"But, Momma, it's perfect."

Another wait.

"Okay, okay, Momma. I found the dress on my phone. It's the backup dress. I love it. I was just teasing you. Yes, ma'am. Size six and you can use my dress from Pearl's wedding for the hem. It's still hanging in my bedroom closet. I know we don't have time for a fitting or two. But that one is hanging in the closet at your house, and it was the perfect length with flat-soled shoes. And I like the idea of the hair thing and the shoes. I was thinking white cowboy boots."

The phone went dead.

"What?" Ace asked.

"She hung up on me when I mentioned the boots," Jasmine said.

"I'm glad I never had sisters."

"Why?"

"My mother would be in jail for murder if my sister was like you."

"Is that a warning? Do your sisters-in-law walk on eggshells?"

"Just be glad when they were passing out baby girls in Texas that they gave you to Kelly King and not Dolly Riley."

It was hotter inside the truck than it was outside. Jasmine didn't care if she ever saw another sauna or spa in her life right then. Little black birds hopped out of danger, proving it was even too hot to fly. The cab hadn't even cooled down when Ace pulled into the Starbucks parking lot. Jasmine hopped out and pointed to an advertisement poster picturing a mocha smoothie and a sandwich in the window.

"I want that," she said.

Ace held the door for her. "I figured you'd want black coffee."

"Too hot for trying on wedding dresses or for drinking hot coffee, and I'm hungry."

And sitting in close quarters with you, fighting the urge to kiss you whenever you hold the door and I catch a whiff of your shaving lotion, which is sexy as hell. And the way your hand burns an imprint on my back. It's too hot for all of it, Ace Riley!

Other than one old fellow wearing faded overalls and a chambray shirt, they were the only customers in the place. When the order was filled, Ace carried the tray to a corner table. The old fellow raised his coffee cup and nodded at them.

"Afternoon," Ace said.

"Hot one, ain't it?"

"July and August ain't even here yet. It'll get hotter," Ace answered.

"And September. Lord, used to be it started to cool down in September, but these days it's just as hot as August. Back when I was a boy, we was butcherin' hogs come November first. Nowadays, kids is playin' football in their short-sleeved shirts on Thanksgiving Day," the old fellow said.

"Then winter hits us in February," Ace agreed.

Jasmine sipped at her icy smoothie.

"Good!" she muttered.

"I shoulda got me one of those things, but I sure do have a cravin' sometimes for their coffee. Reminds me of the time we was runnin' some cattle from here up through Randlett to the sale. It was back when I was a kid during Depression times and my grandpa brewed up coffee in a pot right over the stove. He'd put in a cup of grounds and fill up the pot. Then when it was boiled down to about half-full, he'd taste it. Sometimes it had to boil another half an hour, but most of the time he gauged it about right.

"I miss that good strong flavor, but this place has got it down pretty good. And I miss a real cup instead of these paper things. A man can't wrap his hands around a paper cup and get warm in the winter like he can with a real coffee cup. But it does taste mighty good. I asked the girl back there if they had a fire going out in back of the store. She looked at me like I was a crazy man. Decided I'd best not go on or she'd be callin' them boys up to haul me off." He winked at Ace.

"My grandpa liked his coffee strong enough to blister paint off the side of a house," Ace said. "He used to call it 'murdered water' if it didn't melt the silver off a spoon when he stirred it."

"Good man, your grandpa. They don't make them like that no more. Well, I'd best get on home. I told Momma I was goin' to town to buy feed and I'd be home in time for supper. I reckon she's just about got the biscuits ready." He grinned. "Us old cowboys is a dyin' breed. All this newfangled world is too fancy for us. Coffee with names like latte and capa-whatevers. It's more than our old brains can take." He threw his cup in the trash and waved as he left.

Ace watched out the window until he was gone. "He reminded me of my grandpa."

"Was your grandpa that size?"

"Oh, no, he was tall and lanky. Blond hair like mine with the same color eyes I've got. Granny was the short little part-Mexican lady. She was pretty round when she died, but I don't think Grandpa ever saw her as anything but the exotic girl he fell in love with." Ace sipped at his cup of dark roast coffee.

"Did he call her 'Momma'?" Jasmine asked.

"Oh, yeah."

"Don't you ever call me that."

"Why?"

"I'm not your momma. I have a name."

"Don't think we'll ever have that problem, Jazzy. Old folks didn't call their wives 'Momma' until the kids came along. It happens when they start sayin' things like, 'Go on in there and Momma will fix that scrape on your elbow,' or 'Momma is fryin' chicken for supper, so you better not have another cookie right now.' Since we ain't really married and since we ain't really goin' to have kids, then we don't have anything to worry about, do we?"

Please say there's a possibility that you'll change your mind about a divorce. Crap! Where did that come from? I don't want to be married, ever, he thought.

"Guess you are right," she said.

Evidently, that barbed wire around your arm is for real. You don't want a woman in your life no matter what.

He changed the subject. "So what now? You've decided on the dress and we've had something to eat. What would you like to do the rest of the day? Take in a movie and then have dinner?"

How about we check into a motel? Maybe order a pizza delivered when we're ravenous from too much sex, she thought.

"Let's go visiting."

Ace raised an eyebrow.

"I want to go check on Pearl and talk wedding with her. Then I'd like to go see Liz and show her the dresses Momma picked out. If Liz is still exercising horses, I might catch a ride. And then we'd better get on home to make sure Lucy isn't feeling too abandoned on her first day at the ranch."

Ace cocked his head to one side. "Okay, but now that I think of it, why isn't Lucy shopping with you instead of me?"

"Lucy spent the morning getting her recipes ready for the week and is doing grocery shopping this afternoon in Bowie. She's very organized. She stopped by the café on her way to the store and asked me to buy a hundred-pound bag of potatoes and a few other things from my produce man. That way she'll get them at a better price. Tomorrow she and Delilah will sleep in and in the afternoon she'll have her meeting in Henrietta and stop by to see Pearl on the way home," Jasmine explained.

"Wow!"

"I told you she'd be an asset to the ranch. You won't be sorry a day that you hired her. She'll have things runnin' smooth as..." She grinned.

"As silk?" Ace finished for her.

"As a baby's butt." Jasmine giggled.

"But what about working around all the menfolks? Is that going to stress her out?"

"I hope not. That's the only thing I worry about and why I don't want to leave her all alone tonight.

So visiting for half an hour at each place and then home?" she asked.

She'd said it again: *home!*

His heart swelled, and he fairly well strutted out the door with his arm thrown around her shoulders.

Make up your mind, cowboy. Do you want to be married or not? To Jasmine or not?

Chapter 14

Lucy's hands were on her hips, and her stance said that Blake and Dalton were in deep crap. The sports channel was broadcasting a golf game behind her, but she didn't care. Right then she was about to call down the wrath of God upon those two worthless cowboys if one of them didn't own up to his thievery.

Jasmine and Ace walked in on the scenario and stopped in their tracks just inside the living room door.

"What in the hell is going on in this place?" Jasmine asked.

Lucy shot daggers across the room at the two brothers. "One of them is a thief, and whoever stole it is going to make a trip into town before next Friday night."

Blake and Dalton looked like two little boys who'd gotten caught with their fingers in the cookie jar.

Ace could barely contain his laughter. "What did they steal?"

Lucy pointed at the coffee table where two empty cans of Vienna sausage sat along with beer cans and half a bag of pretzels. "Right there is the evidence. I wouldn't make an accusation without proof."

"But we didn't know they were yours. Everything in the house has always been community property," Dalton said.

"Yeah! And get away from the front of the television, Lucy," Blake said.

Lucy glared at him. "Stealing from Delilah and bossing me too. Boy, that ain't going to happen."

"Don't call me 'boy,'" Blake said.

"Don't boss me. Who stole her treat?"

Neither one said a word.

"Then you will both go to Bowie to the Walmart store this week sometime. I expect to see two cans of that very brand on the shelf come Friday. She gets one can a night and I bought enough to last until next Sunday. Two are missing. Don't be buyin' Delilah no cheap generic crap. She likes her viennie weenies in that brand."

"Ace," Dalton pleaded.

Ace threw up both hands. "Don't look at me. I didn't steal the sausages that Lucy buys for her cat."

"Shhh," Lucy said. "Don't say that so loud. I've convinced her that those are canned mice."

"Yuk!" Dalton's nose snarled.

Blake threw a hand over his mouth. "Crap! Lucy."

"No, not crap! She wouldn't eat that. They are prime-quality canned mice with the guts and hair removed." Lucy's big blue eyes twinkled. "And every night before she goes to bed she gets a can so come next Friday night there had better be"—she looked down the hall to be sure Delilah was still in the bedroom—"Vienna sausages in the pantry, or I swear I'll dose a batch of brownies and you'll think crap."

"Okay, okay! I'll make sure I replace them, and believe me, after hearing you call them mice, I'll never eat the things again." Dalton sighed. "Is there anything else we aren't supposed to touch?"

Lucy shook her finger at them. "Don't be eating her special food in the bag. It might smell like party mix but it's hers and it's marked C-A-T on the outside. And the stuff in the cans with a cute yellow cat on the front belongs to her. Other than those three things, the rest of the pantry is open."

Delilah chose that moment to sashay into the living room, her big yellow tail held high and her long hair brushed to a sheen. She sniffed the air and went straight to the coffee table. She sniffed the cans and looked up at Lucy.

She picked up the cat and held her close. "I know, baby. Those two mean old boys ate your special treats, but we have more in the pantry and there will be replacement cans for the end of the week or else they are going to trap, skin, and gut some real mice for you."

Dalton shivered.

"Not too fond of going rat huntin', are you?" Ace asked.

Jasmine was giggling so hard that her ribs ached. She followed Lucy into the kitchen and watched her put Delilah on the cabinet before she opened a can of Vienna sausage. Delilah got a whiff of the can and jumped from the counter to the floor and weaved in and out between Lucy's legs.

Jasmine leaned on the counter. "I was afraid all these menfolks would intimidate you. Guess I was wrong."

"Ain't no man alive going to ever intimidate me again. And those two won't be stealing from Delilah again, I'll guaran-damn-tee it." Lucy laughed.

"Well, if I'd been the sorry culprit that had just fought with you, I'd never eat another little weenie again."

Lucy was a small woman—petite, delicate-boned. But when she got really tickled, her laughter sounded like it was coming out of a three-hundred-pound truck driver.

"What?" Jasmine asked.

"You just said you'd never eat a little weenie again? I was wondering about Ace and just how big..." Another spasm of laughter had her pounding on the counter with her fists.

Jasmine gasped. "God Almighty!"

Dammit! I'm sounding more and more like my mother. Does this happen to all women? Do they turn into their mothers when they get married?

It started as a giggle in Jasmine's throat and soon

she had her arm around Lucy and they were both carrying on like they'd just finished off a whole fifth of good Jack Daniel's whiskey.

Ace poked his head in the kitchen door with Dalton and Blake right behind them. Lucy looked up and got tickled all over again. "Wonder if all Riley men have little..."

"Little what?" Blake asked.

"Brains," Jasmine said quickly.

Lucy wiped her eyes with a dish towel and picked up Delilah, who had licked her plate clean.

"Good girl. You ate all your little..." She looked over at Jasmine.

That brought on another burst of laughter from Jasmine and Lucy both.

"What is so funny?" Dalton asked.

"Lucy just told you."

Lucy rolled her eyes. "Their brains are definitely little. Maybe it's a sign."

"Inside joke or something?" Ace asked.

"Well, it's sure not funny to me," Dalton said.

"It wouldn't be. Anyone who'd eat my cat's mice wouldn't have a sense of humor," Lucy said.

"Quit calling them that! They are just little weenie things," Blake said.

"Takes one to know one." Lucy's eyes glittered.

"Know what? What in the hell are you talking about?" Dalton asked.

Jasmine looped her arm in Ace's. "Shall we leave

the children to their bickering and take a walk out around the place?"

"You're going to leave us in here with that devil-woman?" Dalton asked.

"Be careful what you call me. I might trap some rats and fix you a fine dish of spaghetti."

Lucy was still twisting them up in knots with her bantering when Jasmine and Ace left the house by the back door.

The temperature hadn't cooled down with the setting of the sun. There was a faint breeze that tickled the tree leaves, making them do a slow country waltz, but it was not enough to create a big stir that would shake them like they were line dancing.

They'd left the house behind them and were on their way to the hay barn when Ace finally broke the comfortable silence. "So what was so funny back there about canned sausage? Is Lucy losing her mind over the fire after all? Kind of like that posttraumatic stress thing that soldiers get? Tyson has it, but it made him just hole up inside himself. Dexter is his uncle and he thought that hard work would help him work through frustrations. Quietness would help him work through it in his mind. Sometimes I wonder if it's working at all and with Lucy it's only been two days. Maybe the shock is just now setting in for her."

Jasmine stopped at the edge of a small creek and sat down, pulled off her shoes, rolled up her jeans, and put her feet in the water. "Lucy is just fine. She's a strong woman, and believe me, PTSD won't ever get a hold on Lucy."

Ace jerked off his boots, pulled up the legs of his jeans, and joined Jasmine. The clear running water was cool on his toes, but when he moved his foot over to flirt with hers, his foot was suddenly hot.

Jasmine swished her foot in the cool water, but it didn't work. When she brought it back to the comfortable resting place and touched his, the heat was still there. If she could harness the electricity sparked by their feet touching, she could save them an energy bill at the ranch.

"Why do you say that Lucy won't ever feel the aftereffects of that fire? It took everything," Ace said.

"She told me on the way to the ranch that she had less and she had more. She had more pride, more confidence, and a cat that she didn't bring with her before. But she had fewer bruises and aches, pains, and fears. Fire had destroyed what she'd accumulated for the past year and a half in the way of material things; it had done nothing to destroy all the things she'd accumulated in spiritual things. So she wasn't too worried about it because material things could be replaced. As long as she had Delilah, a job where she could still have her meetings on Sunday, and a place to live, then she was still a blessed woman."

"You are right. She's made out of steel," Ace said.

Jasmine eased back on the grassy bank and

hoped that there were no chiggers. She sure didn't want to wake up with little itchy, red bite marks all over her body the next morning.

"Want to go skinny-dippin'?" Ace changed the subject abruptly.

Jasmine shot a glance toward him to see his eyes glittering and a big grin on his face. She forgot all about chiggers when a vision materialized of a naked Ace lying beside her in the sandy-bottom creek with the cool, clear water flowing over them. "Water's not deep enough for skinny-dippin', but we might go skinny-stretchin' if you think the children won't follow us to tattle on each other."

Ace chuckled. "Skinny-stretchin'? Ain't never heard of that."

"Shuck 'em all off and lay down in the water, let it bubble over us like a Jacuzzi with cold water instead of hot," she said.

He peeled his T-shirt over his head and tossed it back farther on the bank with their boots and shoes. "We were doing fine with two boys, but you had to bring that mouthy girl into the picture. She's the one that is causing all the trouble."

Jasmine unbuttoned her sleeveless cotton shirt and threw it over her shoulder. "Well, your two boys need to leave her toys alone."

Ace leaned across the space and tipped her chin up. The kiss was gentle and then deepened into hard, and when his tongue reached into her mouth to flirt with hers, it became so intense that liquid spasms vibrated in Jasmine's lower belly.

That's it! It's the kiss. No wonder so many women flock around him. It's the way he kisses. Like fire and ice mixed together. Sweet and demanding at the same time. Twisting up my mind, heart, and soul into a braided rope. We'd never kissed before the wedding! It's his addictive kisses that make me feel like a real bride.

He jerked the snap loose at the top of her jeans, unzipped them, and tugged them down over her well-rounded butt. "Ah, lacy panties."

"That do something for you?" she asked.

"Yes, ma'am."

Whew! He even whispers with a sexy drawl.

"Everything about you gets my attention." His jeans came off in a blur.

She reached behind her back and unfastened her bra. "Is that a line?"

"No. I only say that to the women I go skinny-stretchin' with. Let me do the honors with those cute little panties."

Kneeling in the grass, he ran his tongue around her belly button and down to the edge of the panties before hooking his forefingers in the sides and slowly taking them to the ground, tasting every inch of her legs along the way.

Her knees trembled and she needed the cold water over her body by the time he scooped her up and carried her to the middle of the sandy-bottom creek. She gasped when he sat down with her in his lap. He was fully aroused and the cold water didn't do a thing to take the heat out of either of them.

The creek water made a blanket for Ace's body from the waist down and covered the parts of Jasmine that weren't resting in the crook of his arm. Snuggled up to him with water flowing around them was almost as sensual as Ace's kisses. The water cooled her body; his thumb heated it as he made lazy circles on her back under the water.

"Waterbed," she said.

Ace even chuckled in a Texas drawl so sexy that it would make a woman's hormones go from zero to the speed of light in less than a split second.

"Yep, I guess it is, but I like this one better than any of the others I've tried," he said.

"Oh?" She looked up at him, his strange gray-blue eyes looking even eerier by the light of a full moon hanging on the top of the willow trees lining the creek bank. She'd never noticed before how mesmerizing they were.

"Never did like a real waterbed. Too much movement. But this sandy bottom and water just deep enough..." His words trailed off as his hand roamed down her back to cup a butt cheek and squeeze gently.

She squirmed free of his hands, threw a leg over his body, and sat down on his belly. She could feel his erection against her hip. She leaned forward, breasts brushing against his chest, and kissed him hard.

One of his hands snaked up around her neck and he tangled his fingers in her dark hair, holding her head in place to keep her lips on his. The other hand wrapped around her waist and held her so close that a cup full of water couldn't get between them. He moaned when her breasts pressed tighter into his broad chest.

She broke the string of steamy kisses and slid backwards on his wet body, rose up slightly, and with a wiggle slid him into her. One hand on his tight abs and the other behind her on his tense thigh, she began an easy rhythm.

He smiled. "Oh, yes, I do like this waterbed better."

"So do I," she gasped between words.

"You are beautiful in the moonlight," he whispered.

His words were as hot in her ears as his body was to her touch.

"Who needs...a fancy...hotel...with..."

"A Jacuzzi." He chuckled as he grabbed her around the waist and flipped her over and began a rhythm of his own, faster, harder, and more furious than what she was delivering. The cool water rushing around him with each thrust was as heady as the kisses she demanded, her fingers tangled in his wet hair.

"Ace!"

"Now?" he asked.

"Please," she whined.

He brought her right up to the very tip of the climax and then fell over the top with her.

He buried his face into the hollow of her neck and nibbled, whispering sweet words into her ear. The cool water, the warmth of his breath, and listening to him tell her just how beautiful and sexy she was sent chill bumps down her naked body.

He started to roll to one side, but she wrapped both arms and legs around him and held on tightly.

"Don't go. I like the way you feel on my body," she whispered.

"But darlin', we're sinking into the sand, so it is either roll over and hold you or suck water up my nose," he said hoarsely.

She held on as he moved to his side, keeping her in his embrace. The water flowed around them again as they settled comfortably into the sandy creek bottom.

"That was pure, unadulterated ecstasy," she whispered.

"Jazzy, you are better than drugs and even more addictive. And I don't say that to all the girls," he said.

"Can we sleep here all night, or do we have to go back to the house?" she mumbled as her eyes fluttered.

"Come morning, the children will come looking for us if we aren't at the house," he said.

"Rotten kids." She giggled.

Chapter 15

"GOOD MORNIN', BEAUTIFUL," ACE SAID WHEN Jasmine opened her eyes on Sunday morning.

She caught a whiff of coffee and bacon and looked around. A tray with two pieces of toast, bacon, scrambled eggs, and coffee was sitting beside her on the bed. She sat up carefully so she wouldn't spill anything, picked up the coffee, and sipped.

"Mmmm, thank you," she said.

Ace was already dressed in jeans, boots, and a football jersey with the number 13 on the front. He had a day's worth of scruff on his face, and his hair hadn't even seen a comb. And she thought he was sexier than ever.

"I can't believe you brought me breakfast." She picked up a piece of bacon and nibbled on it.

"It's midmorning. Lucy said you have to get up because y'all are going to Pearl's place for wedding crap. My brothers are all over at Momma's so I'm goin' over there to play Sunday football," he said.

"I never sleep this late," she said.

"Guess last night's skinny-stretchin' wore you plumb out."

She smiled. "I suppose it did. What would it take to wear you plumb out?"

"Ain't never been there yet. But if you want to give it a try, we could both stay home all afternoon," he said.

"Lucy would be beatin' in the door."

"It's that girl child causin' the trouble," he teased.

"If I remember, the boy child beat on the door when your momma called a few nights ago," she reminded him.

Ace kissed her on the forehead and grabbed a piece of bacon from her plate. "So what time will you be home?"

"Soon as I can get it all talked through. I'm sick of it, Ace."

"I know, darlin', but it'll all be settled and finished soon and then we can get on back to normal livin'," he said.

Yeah, right. Normal flew right out the window at Cupid's Wedding Chapel.

"Hey, Ace." Dalton knocked on the door.

"See, rotten boys!" Jasmine grinned.

"Got a fence down and two cows on the highway. We got to go get them in and fix the fence."

Jasmine waved him away. "Can't have two cows gettin' hit on the road. I know how to eat by myself. But, Ace," she said as he was rushing out of the room, "thank you for breakfast."

"You are very welcome, beautiful lady."

She giggled.

"What?"

"You and your lines. They are so corny that they are cute."

"It's not a line, Jazzy."

"Yeah, right. Go get the cows. I'll see you later."

Jasmine turned on the truck radio as she and Lucy started toward Henrietta. Lady A was playing "Can't Take My Eyes Off You." Hillary Scott, female lead singer for the group, sang about the bridges she'd burned that left her with walls and scars. Jasmine kept time to the slow beat by tapping her thumb on the steering wheel. Hillary sang that she was falling fast and that she wasn't scared all because he had climbed her walls.

"Sounds kind of like you and Ace, don't it?" Lucy said. "Y'all can't take your eyes off each other. He walks into a room and you just automatically look at him, long and hot-like. And he does the same thing."

"You've got romance on the brain." Jasmine laughed. But her thoughts went back to the creek the night before and how she hadn't been afraid as she'd cuddled up in his arms. Ace Riley had climbed her wall of defense. The one she'd worked so hard to construct after the fiasco with Eddie Jay.

She'd put on an I-don't-give-a-damn attitude and pulled it off with everyone. Knowing that he and Jadeen had been together the whole time he was with Jasmine, that they had a baby together, and still Eddie Jay let Jasmine believe that they had a future. She'd put herself on the wagon and hadn't fallen off until Ace kissed her.

Now she was defenseless, in a fake marriage, planning a fake wedding, and like Hillary said in the song, she couldn't take her eyes off Ace Riley. And he had a barbed-wire tat around his left arm to remind her daily and nightly that no matter how good the sex was, he was never letting a woman past the fence and into his heart. Lust, yes definitely. Love, hell no!

On his way back to the house, Ace turned on the radio. Lady Antebellum was playing a tune they'd had out a couple of years before called "Can't Take My Eyes Off You." He waved at Jasmine and Lucy when he passed them turning out onto the highway while he turned back toward the ranch.

The lead singer was female and she reminded him of Jazzy with her dark hair and full lips. The chorus said that she just wanted him to lay beside her, to hold her and never let go, and that the feeling was something she'd never known. And then it finished with saying that she couldn't take her eyes off him.

"Turn it around to be a guy singer and it's my song," Ace said.

Ace's blood had run cold when she'd said that she was falling fast and the truth was she wasn't scared at all because he'd climbed her walls.

"I didn't see it coming," Ace muttered. "And now that it's here, I don't know what to do. Two weeks ago you were my best friend, Jazzy. Looking back, you'd already climbed the walls. I wish I could go back and start all over. Take you out on real dates. Have the boyfriend and then the sex experience. Not the marriage one first. But it can't be undone and it's ruined forever."

"This is the craziest thing I've ever heard of," Lucy said when they were on the outskirts of Henrietta. "A wedding after a marriage."

"Me too. I wish it wasn't even happenin', and I'm already tired of the whole thing. Changing the subject, do you think you are going to get along all right working around so many men at the ranch?"

Lucy answered with a grin. "If they leave my cat's food alone, and I think they will now."

"I thought maybe you were flirting with Dalton," Jasmine teased.

"Those two remind me of a couple of my brothers. Girl don't flirt with her brothers, not even in Kentucky," Lucy said.

Her deep southern accent had softened around the edges since she'd been in Texas, but not much. Kentucky came out *Cane-tucky* in four or five syllables even yet.

"And the guys out in the bunkhouse?" Jasmine asked.

"Sam is a sweetheart. He reminds me of my uncle Cyrus. Not a lot of words and only opens his mouth when he's got something to say. Dexter scared me at first. Lord, that man looks like he could tear a barn down in thirty minutes with his bare hands, but he's got a heart of gold. And Buddy is a teddy bear. His stuttering just makes him that much sweeter."

"What about Tyson?" Jasmine asked.

Lucy squirmed in her seat enough that Jasmine shot a look her way.

"Tyson has demons. His soul is haunted. He reminds me of the abused women I work with. He's going to take some work," Lucy finally said.

"Like you did?" Jasmine asked. "I never did hear that whole story."

"It's short. I married at sixteen. That's not so unusual in the backwoods of Kentucky. I was pregnant and Cleet's momma said that was the only reason he married me and she said it wasn't his baby anyway. But it was because I'd never had sex with nobody else. He had a temper, a bad one, and anything could set him off. If I had chocolate cake for supper and he wanted peach cobbler, he'd jerk that belt off and whoop me with it. I lost the baby and was glad because she wouldn't never have to grow up and make a big mistake like I did with Cleet.

"I saved my money, hoardin' it back by pennies and dimes until I had enough to get out of Kentucky. I faked my death and used my money to buy bus tickets as far as it would go, and then I started walkin' west from over in Gainesville. This sweet lady named Rosa gave me a ride and deposited me right in front of the Longhorn Inn. Pearl gave me a job and a place to live."

"Cleet never did come around?" Jasmine asked.

"Nope. After Pearl married Wil, she got in touch with a lawyer who got me a divorce. When it was final, I called my momma. She was glad I wasn't dead but told me to stay out of Kentucky. If I ever came back, Cleet would probably kill me."

"Why? Because he didn't get any insurance money if you weren't dead?" Jasmine asked.

"We was too poor to have insurance. Cleet worked with his daddy in the coal mines up there. I expect he was good at his job or they'd have fired him for as much work as he missed. He'd kind of tally up what he had to make for a week and that's how much work he'd do. Rest of the time he hunted and fished with his other worthless buddies," Lucy explained.

"Then why would he kill you if you went back?"

"Because he lost his cook, his house cleaner, and his wife to beat on when he was mad. And because he'd take that as an insult. Cleet would shoot a dog for barking too much. Think what he'd do to me if I ever went back. Momma didn't have to warn me, though. I made a vow I'd never set foot back there when the Greyhound bus I was ridin' on went over the Kentucky state line. If I die on the Double Deuce, you bury me in Henrietta, Texas. This is my heaven, right here."

The front yard at the Riley ranch looked like a used car lot for pickups. Ace parked at the end of the long row, got out, and shook the legs of his jeans down over his boots. Adam was sitting at the far end in an old straight-backed chair. The chair's back leaned against the house, and the front two legs were jacked up in the air. Adam's legs were propped on the porch rail and crossed at the ankle. He held a sweating bottle of beer in one hand and fanned his face with his straw hat with the other.

Ace propped a hip on the porch rail. "Hot day."

"Yep. Don't see any mention of any snow comin' our way. You and that woman of yours has stirred up a hornet's nest. What in the hell was you thinkin', runnin' off to Las Vegas? You knew your momma would pitch a hissy, and her fit ain't nothing compared to Jasmine's momma's. Lord, them two women spend every waking minute on the phone. I'm so sick of hearing about weddings I could run away to Las Vegas myself and not come home until it's over. Your momma wanted a girl baby so we kept on trying to get her one but I got to admit, I was always glad to see another boy. Know why? So we didn't have to worry with weddings. And look what you've done."

"Sorry about that, Dad. We didn't intend to cause a stir," Ace said.

"Your older brothers had weddings, but all we had to do was show up and smile for a couple of pictures. Your momma stewed around about a dress and how to fix her hair, but it wasn't nothin' like this hoorah. Eight men to stand up there with you. God, boy, are they expecting that maybe that many can keep you in the church if you decide to run? They sure don't know a Riley, if that's their thoughts. And besides, if you did run, what the hell good would it do? You're already married," Adam said.

"Does seem like overkill, doesn't it?" Ace said.

"Yep, but then it's makin' them two women happy as a preacher at a baptism." Adam grinned.

Ace pointed to the beer. "Got any more of them

out here, or do I have to wade through the groomsmen to get one?"

"Get to wading, Son. I only brought two with me and I done finished the first one." Adam waved him toward the door.

Jasmine stopped at the first traffic light in Henrietta. They'd driven right past the ashes of the Longhorn and neither of them had even looked that way. She made a right-hand turn at the far edge of town, and then a couple of miles farther up the road she made another right onto Wil and Pearl's ranch.

"There's old Digger. I like that dog, but Delilah hates him so bad, I reckon she could claw his eyes right out of his head. Pearl says it's because Wil had him with him that night when they first met, and the crazy dog bayed at Delilah like she was a coon. Guess she figures any sorry-ass dog that don't know a queen from a coon don't deserve his sight," Lucy said.

Jasmine laughed. "Looks like we're the last ones here so let's go plan my Texas wedding. I'm glad my parents stayed together and Daddy didn't move off to Tennessee or Louisiana, or I might have to get married three times."

Pearl met them at the door before Lucy had time to knock. Her kinky red hair was pulled up in a ponytail, and she wore a flowing lime-green sundress with a smocked top and spaghetti straps. "Y'all come on in. We're in the living room. We've got iced tea and beer."

"Beer for me." Jasmine tugged the bottom of her jean shorts down and adjusted the straps of her bright-orange tank top. "I didn't know we were dressing up."

"I'm not dressed up. It's the only thing that will fit me that isn't maternity, and I'm so tired of those clothes that I gave them to Momma when she left to take to her church rummage sale next week," Pearl explained.

"You shouldn't have done that," Lucy said.

"Why?"

"You did what?" Liz yelled from the living room.

"She gave all her maternity clothes to the church rummage sale," Lucy answered.

"Every single one? You didn't even keep the one you wore to the hospital the night the twins were born?" Bridget asked.

Pearl shook her head.

Bridget shook her head seriously.

"Why?" Pearl asked again.

"Give all your maternity clothes away, and you'll be pregnant again real soon," Bridget explained.

"What?" Pearl blanched.

"Old wives' tale, but I've seen it work too many times to chance it. I'll keep one thing in the closet forever if I ever have kids," Lucy said.

Jasmine pulled a folder from her purse and laid it on the table. "Don't let them worry you. It's superstition."

Pearl picked up her phone and called Tess. "Momma, you still got my maternity clothes at your house?"

A pause.

"Keep it. Don't let anyone talk you out of it."

Another short pause.

"You knew and you didn't tell me! I may fire you from being a grandmother," Pearl said. "You better hang on to that one last shirt or you are in big trouble."

Jasmine patted her on the arm. "You're safe now."

Pearl wiped her forehead. "It'd just be my luck to have twins again. And besides, it's your turn."

"Not mine. Liz got married before me!" Jasmine said.

"I'm almost ready so save that one shirt for me," Liz said. "I promise I'll give it back when I'm done with it."

"Okay, here we go," Jasmine said. "Dresses."

She spread out copies of the dresses that she'd printed off that morning in Ace's office. Four colors: gold, pewter, silver, and bronze. All in Grecian style like her wedding dress but without rhinestone straps or a train.

"You are changing the subject pretty fast. Come to think of it, this was a speedy wedding. You got something you haven't told me?" Pearl asked Jasmine.

"I'm not pregnant," she said.

And other than that, yes there is something I didn't tell you, but I can't. I'm not sure what the statute of limitations is on lying to your best friend, but that has to play out before I tell you.

Pearl laughed. "Well, that answers that question. Now show me the dresses. Do I get to really wear gold?"

"Yes, you do. There's two each of the bronze and silver, and three of the pewter. Pick your color and write your size on the sheet so Momma can get them ordered," Jasmine said.

"I want bronze," Lucy said.

"Me too," Gemma said.

Liz pointed to the silver. "That's mine."

"I'll go with Liz," Bridget said.

"Guess that leaves pewter for me and Colleen," Austin said.

"I'd wear turtle-crap green if I had to. That's why I didn't pick first because it don't matter to me, so if anyone wants to change it's fine by me," Bridget beamed.

Jasmine tossed another printed sheet out on the table. "Flowers. One calla lily with the colors of all the dresses in satin streamers? Or a nosegay of white roses with the same steamers?"

"What are you carryin'?" Bridget asked.

Jasmine laid a picture on the table. "Momma says it's magnolia blossoms in a bed of soft fern with long white streamers. The florist says the bouquet will have to be kept in the refrigerator until the minute the wedding starts so the magnolias won't turn brown."

"Then it should be the calla lily," Pearl said.

"Everyone in agreement?" Jasmine asked.

"What would you carry?" Lucy teased Bridget.

"Honey, I'd carry a bouquet of stinkweed to get to be in the wedding," Bridget said.

"Jewelry?" Pearl asked.

"Momma says that no one is to bring jewelry. My present to each of you will be your jewelry that day and you will get it at the brunch, which will be held in the church kitchen at ten o'clock that morning. We will eat. Gemma will do our hair. Then we'll go back to the kitchen for a finger-foods lunch. After that we'll get dressed and the photographer will do a million pictures of us."

"That sounds like so much fun," Bridget said.

"I'm glad you think so. Pearl, how are you going to manage with the twins?" Liz asked.

"Momma is coming with me, bless her heart. She and Daddy said they'd help with the boys," Pearl said.

"Shoes." Jasmine spread out four different pictures on the table. "Momma says that they don't all have to match but for each one of you to choose a style you like and put your name and size on the paper. They are all satin which will be dyed to match your dress color."

Three minutes later Jasmine gathered up all the papers. "Did I forget anything?"

"Wil and I won't need a room. We'll be staying at Daddy's ranch, but what about all these other folks?" Pearl asked.

"Momma has arranged rooms at the Hampton. Thanks for reminding me. She needs your name and number of people staying in your room and whether you want a room with a king-sized bed or one with two doubles."

"Here's a piece of paper for that." Pearl ripped a piece out of a notebook beside the phone. It went from woman to woman and Bridget handed it back to Jasmine. "Is that it, then?"

"I believe we've covered it. I've got printed directions to the church for each of you. Be there at four thirty on Saturday for the rehearsal. Then Momma and Daddy will lead the convoy to the restaurant where we'll have dinner. She and Marcella are still working on that. Anybody here vegetarian?" Jasmine asked.

Gemma laughed. "Honey, if you live in Texas and don't like steak, you are in big trouble."

"If that's it, I'll take the keys to the truck, Jasmine, and go on to my other meeting," Lucy said.

Jasmine handed them to her.

"And if that's it, I get to hold one or both of those babies." Liz pointed toward the two blue bassinets in the corner of the living room.

"Not if I get there first," Gemma said. "If you had been nicer when you read my fortune last winter, I could already be married and have one of those on the way."

Liz laughed. She'd been raised in a carnival and had read fortunes for a living before she inherited her uncle's property and traded in her wings for roots. Nowadays, Colleen, Gemma's older sister, told fortunes in the carnival. She'd fallen in love with Blaze, the engineer for the carnival, last winter and given up her roots for a set of brand-new wings.

"Patience, my dear sister-in-law." Liz patted her on the shoulder. "When your cowboy comes along, he's going to sweep you off your feet."

Liz had wondered when she read the cards for Gemma's future if the cowboy might be Ace, since she'd visualized him with blond hair, but it was evident that Ace and Jasmine belonged together, and in reality, Gemma's cowboy could be tall, dark, and handsome instead of a blond.

"I hope he appears wearing nothing but a Santa hat and a big smile and he is ready to be a daddy because I want a house full of these things," Gemma said as she picked Jesse up out of his bassinet.

"Be careful what you wish for. What would you

do with a naked cowboy in the middle of winter?" Liz laughed.

"I could think of a million things and none of them involve clothes," Gemma said.

Pearl reached across the space left on the sofa when Gemma stood up and she touched Jasmine's hand. "You okay? Is Kelly drivin' you insane?"

"When this whole wedding thing is out of the way, I will be," Jasmine said.

"Got to remember we are only children and our mothers have looked forward to planning our weddings for years and years."

"Be thankful Wil didn't have six brothers and two best friends." Jasmine sighed.

"And that we weren't married before the wedding." Pearl smiled.

"Think Momma will ever get over the Vegas wedding?" Jasmine asked.

"Oh, yeah. In a year no one will even remember that you got married in Las Vegas. There will be the big picture of you and Ace hanging above the fireplace in the living room, and that's the wedding everyone will remember."

"How'd Austin get away with it?"

"I think down deep her mother still hopes she'll come to her senses and move back to Tulsa. No picture above the mantel. Nothing ever happened." Pearl laughed.

"Amazing theory. Does it work when people get

divorced? Take down the picture and it never happened?" Jasmine asked.

"Yep, that's the first step. Take down the picture. Call the lawyer. And poof! It never happened. But we don't have to worry about that. Wil and Ace would be dead cowboys if there was ever a divorce. Our mothers wouldn't even hire a hit man. They'd just borrow our two shovels and take care of the problem themselves. The bodies wouldn't ever be found. Speaking of Wil and Ace, I wonder what our husbands are doing right now."

"Playin' football while we slave over wedding plans!"

Ace was still propped up on the porch railing when more than a dozen men and boys shoved their way outside into the bright, hot, sunny day. Six brothers, two friends, and all of his nephews ranging in age from ten to sixteen.

"Granny says for you to get your hind end in the house so she can talk to you. Make it fast. We're going to play football out in the pasture," his nephew, Garvin, said.

"She didn't say 'hind end,'" Luke yelled.

Dalton threw a fake punch at Ace's bicep. "She said your slow ass."

Luke threw a football toward Dalton, and Ace

reached out over the railing and caught it. "I'm on Garvin's side. We'll be right out and whoop y'all, Blake."

"Bring it on, big boy!" Blake hollered.

Boots and socks began to fly into a pile at the end of the porch. Ace tossed his over the side in with the rest and padded barefoot into the house. He found his mother and three sisters-in-law, Megan, Mary Sue, and Holly, at the kitchen table with a notebook and multiple pictures strewn around.

"There you are. You're late. I swear to God, you'll be late for your own funeral. You are just like Grandpa Riley. He ambled around like he had all day to get somewhere and about drove poor old Granny to swearing," Dolly fussed.

Ace chuckled. "It didn't take much to drive Granny to swearing. She could blister the paint on a brand-new pickup truck when she was mad at Gramps. Now what do I need to do before I go out there and whoop Blake and his team in football?"

"Kelly has picked out a bridal bouquet for the wedding. But that's your job and you should pay for it. Are you okay with what she picked out?"

Ace nodded. "Whatever she wants, she gets. Send the bill over to the Double Deuce for anything I'm supposed to pay for."

"As the groom's parents, we are supposed to pay for the rehearsal dinner. We don't know anything about Sherman, so I've asked her to pick out a restaurant and make arrangements. Do you have any input on that?" Dolly asked.

Ace shook his head. "You two make up your minds. Us guys would like a steak house or else a good barbecue place. Please don't ask us to eat Cornish hens like we had at Garrett's dinner. No offense, Megan, but I'd rather have steak. And Momma, you and Dad don't have to foot the bill. I'll take care of it."

Dolly's black eyes said as much as her words. "No you won't. We've done our part for the older three, and we will for the rest of you."

"Megan, Mary Sue, and Holly are serving at the reception and Raylen and Dewar are ushers," Dolly said. "Have we missed anyone who should have a part in the ceremony?"

Ace opened the refrigerator and took out a bottle of beer. "Nope, I think that covers it. I asked the guys out at the bunkhouse if they wanted to be in the wedding, and for a minute I thought they were all going to quit right there on the spot. Barely got them talked into attending it. Can I please go out and play now, Mommy?" He whined like a two-year-old.

"Oh, shut up that nonsense. I don't have time for jokes today. One more thing: we are responsible for the groom's table," Dolly said.

Holly flipped her red hair back behind her ears. "That's the table with your cake and punch. Do you want a flat cake with your names on it? Or how about a two-tiered round German chocolate?"

"Hell, I don't know. I liked what y'all did at Tony's wedding when him and Holly got married. Remember that stand-up thing with tiers on it and slices of different kinds of cheesecake?"

Holly smiled. "That was my idea. We do that up in Waurika at weddings pretty often."

"I'll put that idea to Kelly. I expect she'll like it fine since she's going for elegant," Dolly said.

"Now can I go out and play?" Ace asked.

"Yes, get out of here and don't you come whinin' like a little girl if the big boys take you down." Dolly giggled.

The grass was hot on his feet as he ran out the back door and to the pasture where teams were already chosen. But at least the grass wasn't brown and crunchy yet. That would come in August if they didn't get the right rains. "You ready to work up a sweat? We're goin' to make you work for every touchdown you get." He joined his team: Garvin, Kyle, Rye, Raylen, Dewar, Dalton, and Justin.

Adam stood in the middle pasture with a cowbell in his hand. "Y'all are goin' to play fair. No elbows in the eyes. No knees in the balls. Fair tackles. Keep it clean, or I'll set you on the sideline and your team will be a man short. You hear this cowbell, you can bet there's goin' to be a penalty. So huddle up, boys, and let's play some good old Sunday afternoon Riley football."

Chapter 16

MONDAY WENT FAIRLY SMOOTHLY, BUT JASMINE was antsy all day. Something wasn't right, and yet she couldn't pinpoint a single thing that was wrong. Bridget wasn't fighting with Frankie. Pearl hadn't called in hysterics because something was burning down. Liz and Raylen stopped by for lunch and everything was fine there.

After work, she went straight to the ranch rather than making the desserts for the next day, and she grew more agitated with every mile. By the time she parked her truck, she was sure the whole world would come crashing down on her shoulders.

Old Bill and Little Joe were asleep on the porch and didn't even wake up to wag their tails at her. She made sure they were both breathing and went on into the house. She poked her head into the living room to find Dalton and Blake watching television. Chips and a container of salsa were on the coffee table, but there were no empty cans of Vienna sausage in sight. Lucy must've made believers out of them.

"Where's Lucy?" she said.

"Gone to the store over in Terral for cinnamon.

She forgot to get it over the weekend in Bowie. Guess she's makin' cinnamon rolls for supper," Dalton said.

"What are you two doing in the house?" she asked.

"Ace has got to do book work this afternoon. He's back in the office. We finished a couple of hours early so we quit for the day," Blake said.

The door to Ace's office stood ajar so she peeked inside. "Got time for a walk?"

"I'm two weeks behind on computer entries. See you later," he said without taking his eyes from the screen.

"Then I'm going back to the café. It might be late when I get back. I probably won't be back in time for supper. I'll just grab a plate of leftovers there."

He raised a hand and kept working.

She'd lived in the apartment above the Chicken Fried for a year and a half. She'd come in and out of the empty café dozens of times, but that night the silence was eerie. She turned on the kitchen light and took down the recipe for Black Forest cake, lined up the ingredients, and greased six round pans. Working with her hands left her thoughts free to go wherever they wanted, and they kept drifting back to Ace brushing her off. She knew him well enough to know when he was brooding about something. And he always, always found time for her.

She mixed, whipped, beat, and poured the batter

into the pans. She set a timer, checked her watch to be double sure, and climbed the stairs to her apartment. Everything was the same as it was before she married Ace, but the place seemed empty, as if it had given up on her ever coming back. Picking up the remote, she turned on the television, thinking maybe noise would help.

It didn't.

Ace had been in her life for eighteen months. There had been days when she hadn't seen him and didn't even think about it. Then he'd pop back in with a story about some woman who'd thought she could tear down his barbed wire; he'd point at his tat and Jasmine would tell him that no woman would even want his scraggly old cowboy heart. And she'd make him a hamburger and they'd laugh.

"He was too serious to even look at me, so something is way the hell wrong and it has to do with me," she said.

And then the light bulb went off and the anger set in.

They'd had sex and he was afraid that she would consider that a declaration of love or expect a permanent relationship. Her eyes narrowed and she stomped back down the stairs into the kitchen. Fifteen minutes left until the cakes were done. She'd planned to make the icing and frost them that night, but they were going to wait until morning. She paced the floor and checked the clock every thirty seconds. Finally, the timer dinged and she jerked the cakes from the oven.

Ace was sitting on the porch with his feet propped on the railing when she drove into the yard, braking hard and slinging gravel halfway to Bowie. She stomped up on the porch and left no doubt that she was madder'n the devil in a snowstorm. He knew he was in trouble when she stopped right in front of him, propped her hands on her hips, and drew her green eyes into nothing more than slits. Well, she could bring it on because he had a few things to say to her too!

"We need to talk," she said.

"Yep, we do."

"We might need to take a walk because I might get loud," she said.

"How about we ride down to Bowie and get some ice cream? You look like you could use a coolin' off."

"It'll take more than ice cream to cool me off. I've been thinkin' and it's not pretty," she said.

"Well, so have I, and it ain't pretty neither." He stood up slowly and brushed past her on the way to his truck. Without even a gesture of cowboy manners, he got inside and waited on her to open her own door.

He'd turned onto the highway heading south

toward Bowie when she exploded. "You jackass! We had sex and now you are ready to throw me in the trash like you've done with all the others."

His jawbones worked knots into his face. "You think that about me? You think I'd do that to you?"

Her voice raised two octaves. "Not that you would, Ace Riley. You did! What was I? A big conquest. Rinky-dink me into proposing to you..."

He pulled into an abandoned car lot on the west side of the road, stomped the brakes hard enough that he left skid marks and the smell of hot rubber, turned off the engine, and turned to face her.

"My conscience is clear. I did not rinky-do you into jack crap. We had amazing sex, but I'm not ready to put you in a trash can! God Almighty!" Ace growled.

"You sound like my mother!" Jasmine said through clenched teeth.

He raised his voice to match hers. "And that's the problem."

"What? That you sound like my mother?"

"Hell, no! That you are the strongest woman I know, but you won't let go of your mommy issues. You don't want to have this big farce of a wedding. I can see it in your face and hear it in your tone. You say she always gets her way. Well, darlin', that's because you let her. If you don't want to have a wedding, then tell her no. As long as you let her control you, then you won't ever..."

"Ever what?" she whispered.

"Ever really be your own person." He reached across the seat and cupped her face in his two rough hands. "If you want this big thing, then that's fine. I'll do it for you because you've done so much for me and I care about you, Jazzy. But if you don't, then have the balls to say no, and I'll back you up with my momma too. You decide. It's been playin' on my mind all afternoon. Everyone is acting like we aren't even married and we are, and neither one of us even wanted things to go this far, much less mushroom into all this full-fledged wedding crap."

"A-damn-men!" she muttered.

He kissed her softly, then harder, and then with so much heat that she almost whined.

"We could compromise. A barbecue at the ranch on the day your momma wanted to have a wedding. Dexter could smoke ribs and Tyson can grill steaks. You and Lucy can come up with the rest. Or we'll call a caterer to do the whole shebang," he said.

"No caterers. That's too much fanfare. Kelly King could make even that into a million decisions. Lucy and I can make desserts and the rest of it."

"So?" He shifted back to his side of the truck.

She leaned forward and pulled her phone from her hip pocket and hit the speed-dial for her mother.

"Speak fast. Marcella and I are finishing the last touches on the invitations and getting all the information down for the dresses," Kelly said breathlessly.

"Hold the presses," she said.

"No! No changes this late in the game."

"Big changes. No wedding."

Ace reached across and closed his hand around hers.

"That is bullcrap, Jasmine Marie! You are already married so you can't back out of an engagement like you did with Eddie Jay."

Jasmine took a deep breath. "And that's why I'm not doing it again. We are married. It does not have the Texas stamp on the paper, but it's legal and this is ridiculous, Momma. There is not going to be a wedding and I'm dead serious. If you order that dress, you'd better get it in your size because you will be the one who's wearing it."

"But..." Kelly stammered.

"We are having a party. A big Texas-style barbecue out on our ranch, the Double Deuce. You can use the list to send out invitations for that. Same day as you planned the wedding. From noon until the food and beer is all gone or until everyone goes home. Put a note at the bottom of the invitation that says, 'No gifts. The presence of your company is the best gift you can give Jasmine and Ace.' Or something like that."

"You can't do this to me," Kelly said.

"I have done it. I mean it, Momma. No wedding. No church crap. No presents. Everyone can come to the ranch and have a big time. Ace will send you the ranch logo, which is his brand, if you want to put it on the invitations. I don't care what they look like. They can be regular old post office postcards run out on Daddy's computer printer for all I care."

"God Almighty!" Kelly King said.

"I mean it, Momma." Jasmine felt like a weight had been lifted from her shoulders.

"Jesus, Mary, and Joseph! You can't do this, Jasmine Marie!"

"We can and we did," Jasmine said.

"I hope you have five daughters who all disappoint the hell out of you," Kelly yelled.

Ace heard that and grinned.

"I hope if I do that they all elope to Las Vegas, and I was actually thinking seven daughters and then maybe one son."

Kelly hung up on her.

She looked at Ace and started to giggle.

"How'd that make you feel?" he asked.

"I sure feel sorry for Daddy tonight because she's going to be in a royal blue-blooded snit. And I actually feel sorry for her. It can't be easy to lose control like that."

"But how do *you* feel?"

She squeezed his hand. "Like King Kong on steroids!"

"Why?"

She looked into his eyes. "Because I don't have to worry with all that wedding crap. Now it's your turn. Call Dolly. I'll tell Pearl tomorrow, and she can put the word out to the rest of the bridesmaids. I'm glad I didn't ever say anything to Nellie and Ellen, but I do want them invited to the party."

Without a moment's hesitation, Ace dug his phone from his shirt pocket and hit the right button.

"Hello, Son," Dolly said.

"We're callin' off the wedding."

"Is Jasmine leaving you?"

Jasmine heard that and held up her wedding ring.

"No, ma'am. But it's got way out of hand and it's crazy. We are married and the license is valid and we don't want to do it. We've decided to do a big party at the ranch on that day so both families and all our friends can meet each other. From noon until the food is gone or the visitin' is finished."

Long silence.

Jasmine playfully smacked him on the arm.

"Did Jasmine talk to her mother?" Dolly finally asked.

"She did."

"And?"

"She wasn't happy but we've made up our minds and we're not changing them. We're not having a wedding but we are having a party and Jasmine says no presents either. Kelly is sending invitations from the list and it will be on there about the presents."

"Then we won't have to do the rehearsal dinner?"

Ace could hear what was coming next so he stopped her. "Dexter and Tyson are doing the barbecue and steaks. Lucy and Jasmine will do the desserts. It's not going to be a catered thing."

"Put me down for enough potato salad, coleslaw, and baked beans to feed an army. I'll get the other girls to help with it and send Dalton and Blake home that weekend. You'll need the house for her family," Dolly said.

"Thank you."

Jasmine raised an eyebrow.

"Done. She's bringing potato salad, coleslaw, and baked beans."

"You got off easier than I did."

"Remember that when you have five daughters and want to plan a wedding for them. Maybe you'd rather trade them in on five sons before you even get started." He chuckled.

"Las Vegas has this beautiful little wedding chapel I will book and all it takes is a phone call to book a flight there," she teased.

"Ready for ice cream?"

She nodded.

All was right in the world. Jasmine was sorry that she'd disappointed her mother, but Kelly could get over the disappointment. Ace wasn't mad at her because of the sex and he was whistling. Jasmine was hungry for the first time in days.

When they rolled up to the Dairy Queen window, she ordered a double dip of homemade vanilla on a waffle cone.

Ace ordered a double dip of chocolate on a waffle cone.

The lady handed the ice creams out the drive-through window, and Ace drove through Bowie to a motel on the east side that reminded Jasmine of the Longhorn back before it burned down. The Wildcat Motel did not have a doofus old neon cowboy on the sign, but like the Longhorn, it was set up in a U-shape popular back in the fifties.

"What are you doing?" she asked when he stopped in front of the lobby instead of turning around in the parking lot like she expected him to do.

"I've missed you. I liked coming into the café after hours and having you all to myself for an hour while I ate a burger. But lately everything has been about that wedding and there's always dozens of people around. Let's get a room for a couple of hours and leave our phones in the car. I don't care if we just watch reruns of something on television or if we talk the hours away." He grinned.

She looked down at the last dip of ice cream and a wicked plan magically materialized. She tossed her phone on the dash and said, "Yes, and please hurry. Leave the air-conditioning on."

She hadn't finished her ice cream when he came out of the office holding an old-time key with a big chunk of plastic on the chain with it. A burst of hot air escorted him into the truck, and he tossed the room key over in her lap.

"Number 112, all the way to the end of this side." He backed out slowly, drove to the end, and parked in front of the right door.

She slurped up another bit of ice cream, jumped out of the truck, and hurried toward the door so her ice cream wouldn't melt. She unlocked the door while he was still swaggering from the truck to the room.

It was semi-cool inside, so she headed across the room to the air-conditioning unit under the window and turned the knob to high-cool. Immediately, the thing began to rattle out enough noise to raise the dead, but it cooled down the room fast and that's what Jasmine wanted.

Ace grabbed the remote control, kicked off his boots, and plopped back on the bed using both pillows as a backrest. He flipped through channels until he found CMT and tossed the remote over on the nightstand.

"Come lay down beside me," he said.

She handed him her ice cream cone. "Hold this for me and don't take a single bite."

Trace Adkins's video of "Honky Tonk Badonkadonk" started playing on the television and she shot Ace a wicked grin.

"What?" he asked.

"Shhh, just don't eat my ice cream." She began a slow, sexy striptease, kicking her sandals into a corner and unfastening her jeans to the beat of the music.

When the jeans were lying over beside the bathroom door, she crawled up onto the bed and caught a bit of ice cream running down the side of the cone with the tip of her tongue. Then she went back to the floor and wiggled and squirmed out of her shirt and then her bikini underwear before crawling back up his legs to wrap her tongue around the ice cream again. When he reached for her, she shook her head.

"Can't touch and can't eat my ice cream. Your job is to hold it for me."

She finished the strip by tossing her bra over the lampshade and turning around to give him a real honky-tonk badonkadonk in full dancing motion.

Next video was Blake Shelton's "Hillbilly Bone." Jasmine couldn't have had better luck if she'd called the station and requested the two songs be played back-to-back at that very time.

She locked eyes with his and did a slow crawl up his long legs and undid his belt buckle. "Let's see if your hillbilly bone liked that dance," she said and licked off more of the melting ice cream.

"Oh, yes, the bone and I both liked that dance very much," he said.

She undid his zipper and pulled his pants down to his ankles, taking socks and all off as she went. They landed in the corner with her sandals.

"I believe you did like it." She took her ice cream from his hands. "Looks like he could use a cooling down."

Ace's eyes widened. Hell's bells! He never knew what to expect from Jazzy. One minute he thought he knew her well; the next he found out just how little he did know.

She dumped the ice cream in her hand like it was lotion and tossed the cone into the trash. Her eyes were sparkling when she looked into his.

"You aren't going to—?" Ace gasped.

"Oh, yes, I am. A baked Alaskan right here in this room. Only reverse. Hot on the inside, cold on the outside." She covered his erection with the ice cream and then slowly and deliberately licked every bit of it off.

By the time she was finished, he was moaning and trying to flip her over.

"Oh no, you don't," she said.

"Then it's my turn." He grabbed her hands and one by one licked her fingers clean, wrapping his tongue around each one and savoring every bit of ice cream.

By the time he finished her thumb, she was

panting. She wiggled to settle him inside her and began a fast ride.

"You going for eight seconds?" he gasped.

"I'm going for something to stop this aching desire," she admitted.

He grabbed that honky-tonk badonkadonk in his hands and flipped her over. "Then let's get it done."

It lasted more than eight seconds but nowhere near eight minutes.

He collapsed with a groan.

She managed to snuggle in close to him when he rolled to one side, but that took every ounce of her energy.

She shut her eyes and Ace traced them with his finger, then her lips and her jawbone.

"I'm too tired for another round," she said.

"Me too. But don't go to sleep. I want you to hear this, Jasmine."

She forced her eyes open.

"I could never throw you in the trash, darlin'. I like having a wife, but I can live without one. Girlfriends are nice, but I can live without one. I can even live without the best sex I've ever known. But I cannot live without you. So kick that crap out of your head."

"It's gone," she whispered.

"Promise?"

"I promise," she said.

"We're okay now?"

"We're okay."

"Was that sex like King Kong on steroids?" he asked.

"That was King Kong on a cup of coffee. I'm saving the steroids for something really big. Don't let me sleep past five. I've got three cakes to put icing on," she said.

Ace chuckled and held her close. In that moment he knew he wanted to live with Jasmine the rest of his life. Now all he had to do was convince her. At least he had a whole year to get the job done.

Chapter 17

JASMINE HUMMED WHILE SHE SHOOK A LITTLE lemon pepper in green beans. She sang along with the old country song "Good-Hearted Woman."

"Good-timin' man," she said aloud.

She'd been thinking about Ace being such a ladies' man and then she was humming. The song talked about a good-hearted woman lovin' a good-timin' man. Jasmine wasn't a good-hearted woman, but Ace was sure enough a good-timin' man.

The words to the fast-beat music said that through teardrops and laughter they pass through the world hand in hand. She and Ace had already done that. But then it said that when the party was over, she'd welcome him back home again. Not Jasmine! Cheating husbands only had one place to go if they lived with Jasmine, and that was out the door.

"I'm falling for that good-timin' cowboy," she whispered.

She poured out five pancakes on the grill and had just flipped them when she got a whiff of Ace's aftershave. He slipped his arms around her waist from behind.

"What did you say?" Ace whispered softly. "You were humming and then I heard something about a good-timin' cowboy."

"That's what you are," she said.

"Are you my good-hearted woman, and am I your good-timin' man? Waylon said that you ain't supposed to complain about the bad times or the bad things I've done," Ace teased.

"Darlin', my heart ain't that good," she said.

He kissed her on the back of the neck. "This good-timin' cowboy is on his way to Bowie to take the books to the accountant. See you at supper? Think Lucy might serve ice cream tonight?"

The mother of all blushes filled her cheeks with crimson. "If she does, let's take ours to the creek and see what happens when we combine skinny-stretchin' and ice cream sex."

"You are killin' me, Jazzy!" He twisted her around until they were face-to-face, and he kissed her hard. It did nothing to erase the blush from her face or put out the heat in her belly. "Sorry I ain't been a model husband this past week but..."

"Gotta make hay while the sun is shining, right?"

"You got it, darlin'. You would make a wonderful rancher's wife, as understanding as you are about the busy season when we work from breakfast until midnight and come draggin' in with barely enough energy to get a shower. Thank goodness for Lucy. At least I can keep Dexter in the fields and he doesn't have to go back in to fix meals. Next year I'm hiring one more person for summer help."

"Thank you. I've missed talking to you at night, Ace." She looked up into his weary eyes in time to see them slowly closing and his lips headed her way.

Bridget stuck her head in the kitchen. "Hey, can we start serving lunch early? Is that a PDA in the workplace, I'm seeing?"

"Yep, couldn't keep my hands off her. Ain't she the cutest thing ever this morning in these cute little cutoff jean shorts and that green shirt the same color as her sexy eyes? And the apron, man, that really turns me on," Ace teased.

Bridget giggled. "You are a lovesick puppy, Ace Riley."

Ace dropped another kiss on Jasmine's forehead and moved toward the back door. "See you at supper. I'll ask Lucy about that ice cream. Vanilla, right?"

Jasmine shook her fist at him. "Get on out of here before I make you wash dishes. And Ace, I'm an accountant. You might remember that."

"Lunch?" Bridget asked.

"Chicken and dressing won't be ready for thirty minutes. If they want that, then the answer is no," Jasmine answered.

"They are orderin' chicken-fried steaks, mashed potatoes, and green beans." Bridget said. "Is that much done?"

"It will be by the time the steaks are fried," Jasmine said.

"Then I'll hang the order and take those pancakes out to table three," Bridget told her.

"Will do," Jasmine said.

Bridget made the rounds with the coffeepot and then made a pass back through the kitchen. "Are those steaks about ready?"

"Puttin' them on the plate now," Jasmine said.

"Folks that ordered them said they'd like for you to bring them out," Bridget said.

"Who are they?" Jasmine asked.

"Don't know. A middle-aged couple. Maybe someone wantin' to congratulate you that don't get in too often and just heard about the weddin'," Bridget said.

Jasmine set the two plates on a tray, wiped her hands on her apron, and backed out into the dining room. She glanced up at the clock hanging above the order window. Eleven o'clock on the button. Breakfast rush was over and dinner rush would hit hard right before noon. Chicken and dressing was cooked and on warm in the oven, and the hot rolls were ready to cook a pan at a time so they'd be right out of the oven for the customers. There were only four tables with lingering customers that hated to leave the air-conditioned dining room.

"Over at table eight," Bridget said.

Jasmine headed toward the table in the far-right

corner without even looking at the customers sitting there. Her mind was on all the phone calls she'd already had that morning. Pearl had been elated that the wedding was off and had volunteered to call everyone, but Bridget, before Jasmine even asked.

Jasmine had already told Bridget when she walked in the café that morning. And she'd been sorely disappointed until she found out that she and Frankie were invited to the barbecue. "Well, that sounds like fun. Maybe we'll get us up a softball game out in the pasture."

Austin offered to bring a case of watermelon wine.

Gemma said she'd be the bartender for the barbecue.

Lucy agreed that she and Jasmine could make desserts but thought they should have a real wedding cake just to make Jasmine's mother feel a little better about the whole thing. One of the women in her meetings made wedding cakes on the side and she'd have her make it.

She set the tray on table seven, gathered her wandering thoughts, and really looked at the couple. "Oh! I… This is a surprise… What are you doing in Ringgold?" She stuttered and stammered.

"Hello, Jasmine Marie," her mother said.

"Hi, kiddo." Her dad, Walt, grinned.

Jasmine set the plate down in front of her father

and gave him a kiss on the cheek, then did the same for her mother. "I've been tryin' to get y'all to come over and see my business for a whole year. You should have called, Daddy. I'd have made peach cobblers instead of cake for today's dessert. And Momma, if you are here to try to talk me into changing my mind about the wedding thing, it's not going to work."

She pulled up a chair and motioned for Bridget to bring her a glass of sweet tea.

"Very good," Walt said after the first bite of his steak.

"Momma?" Jasmine asked.

Kelly King laid her fork down, sipped at her Diet Coke, and said, "Your cooking has always been fine, but you know what this means to me and I've given you a week now for your little rebellion and tomorrow is the absolute last day I can get the invitations ordered. We could put it off for one week, have it on the third Sunday in July."

"Ain't goin' to happen. Ace and I don't want a big farce of a wedding. We are plannin' a summer barbecue," she said.

Walt sipped his iced tea. "Can't talk you into the big wedding, then? Your mind is made up and we can't change it?"

"No way in hell," she said. She should have known her mother wouldn't give up so easily, that she'd gather all her forces and attack from a different angle when Jasmine least expected it.

"Okay," Walt said. "What's the secret on this steak?"

Kelly shot him her meanest look. "He's been watchin' the Cookin' Channel on television and he fired Carlotta. And I'm not finished with the wedding idea, so don't try to change the subject, Walt. Jasmine, you cannot just call me up and say it's off when I already had invitations ready to order and the dress picked out. What in the hell went wrong?"

Jasmine raised an eyebrow. "Who is Carlotta?"

Walt shrugged. "Her newest cook. Woman couldn't boil red beans without burning them. I can cook better than she could and save that much money."

Kelly shook her head. "He's gone crazy since he retired. Most men go out in the garage and build stupid little lawn things or birdhouses. This man has gotten into cooking."

Walt tasted the green beans and shut his eyes. "Bacon, a little onion, and is that lemon pepper?"

Jasmine smiled. "A dash and fresh green beans, not canned or frozen ones. I can get them year-round from my supplier."

"You two are exasperating me. Stop talking about food and let's plan the wedding again. So, you had your moment of rebellion. All brides get cold feet a few days before the big day. You've had yours. I want pretty pictures."

"I have pictures, Momma. I'll send you a disk

of them and you can pick out whichever one you want, have it blown up to life-size, and hang it on the mantel. You really like the steak, Daddy?"

"Very, very good. Tender. Good crisp outer layer; nice moist inside without being undercooked."

Kelly threw up her hands in defeat. "I'll pay off this café if you'll have the wedding."

"Can I see the kitchen later?" Walt asked.

"Sure. There's a table back there where you can sit and talk to me while I work."

"You can't shut me out," Kelly hissed.

"Momma, you are beating a dead horse. I'm not having another wedding. Ace and I are legally married and we are not doing it again. So why keep going over it? My answer is no. Remember what Granny Dale used to say."

"I never did like that," Kelly pouted.

"What?" Walt asked.

"She said that when she said no that it meant no and it was never changing to yes, so stop asking," Jasmine said.

Kelly exhaled loudly. "Okay, Walt, you win. Now we'll go to plan B."

"And that is?" Jasmine asked.

"I'd like to see your apartment," Kelly said.

Jasmine's neck crawled as if ants were marching from her backbone to the top of her head. Something wasn't right and she had a notion it had to do with plan B.

Kelly smiled.

That made the ants crawl faster. A stress headache hit Jasmine right between the eyes. She'd take aspirin later, but for the time being she pinched the bridge of her nose. It wasn't as if she never went home and never saw them after she moved to Ringgold. She spent Sunday afternoon with them at least once a month, just like she had when she lived right there in Sherman, barely five miles from them.

"We are driving over to Pearl's to see the babies and coming back to the ranch to see it. I'm going to take a look at the apartment while you and your dad play in the kitchen. Why anyone would want to get all hot and sweaty over a cookstove is beyond me. I was so glad when your dad finally made enough money to hire a cook that I could have kissed his feet," Kelly said.

"I'll call Lucy and tell her to set two extra plates for supper. She was making roast tonight and her loaded mashed potatoes," Jasmine said.

"That would be great!" Walt said. "Does she give out recipes?"

Kelly sighed heavily.

Six big, burly ranchers with the sleeves cut out of their shirts, jeans tucked down into the tops of work boots, and hay in their hair saved her from any more conversation or trying to figure out what her parents were really doing in Ringgold, Texas.

"Got to go to work. I'll send Bridget out with dessert and refills for your drinks," she said.

"One waitress is all you have?" Kelly asked.

"It's all I need," Jasmine answered.

"If you'd spruce it up and advertise, maybe get a website like that place you told me about in Thurber, you'd need more and maybe even a real chef," Kelly said.

And if pigs flew, we'd all be covered in crap, Jasmine thought. But she kept her mouth shut and hurried off to the kitchen.

Bridget looked up from the counter, where she was folding flatware inside napkins. "They ready for dessert?"

"Anytime you want to take it to them—and the bill is on the house, Bridget. They are my parents," Jasmine said flatly.

"Holy crap! Did you know they were coming?" Bridget asked.

Jasmine shook her head. "No! And I wasn't paying attention and didn't even know they were there until I got to the table. And they are coming to the kitchen when they get finished. I'll introduce you then. I don't think Momma is nearly finished bitchin' yet."

Jasmine was in the middle of six chicken-fried steaks when Walt and Kelly came through the swinging doors. Walt went straight to the coffee machine and poured two cups while Kelly settled into a chair.

"It's hot in here," she said.

"It's a kitchen, Momma," Jasmine said.

"Don't get sassy with me. You could put an extra air conditioner in the window or maybe update the one for the whole place. It wasn't as cool out in the dining room as it could be. Those poor working men need to at least eat in a comfortable environment," Kelly said.

Jasmine busied herself with the steaks. "This is a little country café, Momma. Not the Ritz."

"Can I help?" Walt asked.

Jasmine looked around to see him with an apron tied around his waist. Not once in her thirty years had she seen her father wearing an apron. Very seldom had she seen him in anything other than a suit. In the summertime he did take the jacket off for supper, but never the tie. To see him in khaki pants and a three-button knit shirt was strange enough, but wearing an apron?

And Kelly? Was she really wearing jeans out in public? Jasmine squinted, but the jeans didn't turn into pleated dress slacks and the knit shirt didn't become silk.

Surely calling off a wedding wouldn't cause them to go crazy, would it?

"I suppose those are the stairs that go up to your apartment? Well, while your dad plays chef, I'm going up to look at it." Kelly picked up her cup and was gone before Jasmine could speak.

"What can I do?" Walt asked.

"Remember what your plate looked like?"

"Oh, yes!"

"I'll put the steaks on the plates. You add potatoes, green beans, and a slice of tomato."

"I can do that," he said. "Your cake was wonderful. I suppose you have a cookbook full of the recipes you use here?"

"Okay, Dad, what's going on? You and Momma are scaring the crap out of me," she said.

Walt laughed. "Your mother and I've been doing some talking. Lots of it since you called her and canceled all her plans. She was pretty pissed and said that if she came over here, you wouldn't be able to tell her no to her face, that you'd break down and let her go ahead with the wedding. I was proud of you," he whispered.

She did a quick bow. "Thank you."

"I knew there would come a time when you just flat-out said, 'No more.' I was hoping it would be before she decided what to name your children, and I never did like all this wedding stuff going on again after you was already married."

There wasn't anything spectacular about Walt King. He was average height at five feet ten inches, not too fat but not lanky, brown receding hair, and a square face. All but his eyes. They were the same shade of green as Jasmine's, the color of spring grass with just a touch of mossy green around the rims.

When he laughed, they sparkled, and ever since Jasmine had sat down at their table, Walt's eyes had been twinkling.

"So?" Jasmine asked.

"I'm retired. Kelly has her friends and her church so she wouldn't want to leave Sherman permanently, but she's ready for a lark. I'm tired of being retired with nothing to do. After a year I'm bored to tears. But I've found a passion I didn't know I had and that's cooking. Guess you got that gene from me and it's been lyin' dormant for years. So there's going to come a time when you don't want to run a café and be a rancher's wife both.

"When the babies come, it'll be too much. So your momma and I want to buy your café. We'll live upstairs like you did and we'll go home to Sherman on Saturday afternoon so your momma can go to church on Sunday and see her friends. After a year or so, I expect she'll have a whole new group of friends over here and we'll sell the property over there and build something right here," he said.

It was more words than Jasmine had heard her father speak at one time in her entire life. And she wasn't totally sure she hadn't just imagined everything he'd said. Did he really say he wanted to buy the Chicken Fried?

"Order up," she called to Bridget who was refilling tea glasses.

"So?" Walt asked.

"I'm not selling the café," she said.

"Your mother has her heart set on it now. That is plan B. She says we'll keep it country. She liked that little sign you talked about last Christmas. The one that said something about countrified and satisfied. She's already planning all kinds of ways to improve it. She'll be the hostess. Seat people and take money. We'll have two waitresses and I'll cook," Walt said.

"I'm not selling," Jasmine said.

"Of course you are," Kelly said from the bottom of the stairs. "Maybe not today, but you will sell it, Jasmine Marie. And when you do, your father and I want it. That way we'll be close enough to enjoy our grandchildren. Which I need to talk to you about. Tess is already ahead of me. She got twins and I don't have anything. But I've got one over on her. By the time you have the first baby, we'll be living here and I can spend all the time I want with them, where Tess has to drive more than a hundred miles. Walt, I like the apartment. It reminds me of the one we had when we were first married. I've already got ideas about how to give it some major cosmetic help. And we won't need a cook since we'll be taking all our meals right here. I'm liking this more and more."

"I can run a café and a ranch at the same time. Besides, I just hired Lucy and she's helping me at the ranch," Jasmine argued.

Kelly patted her on the arm. "Walt, take that apron off, and let's go see Pearl's twins so I can hold babies. Next year I'm getting mine and Tess won't be all superior. And Jasmine, we aren't in a hurry. Just whenever you decide to sell, we are ready to buy it. I'm going home, and Marcella and I are going to get out the home-decorating books. I'm so excited about it all. We aren't getting any younger and I want to enjoy my grandkids while I'm young enough to play with them, not watch them play from my wheelchair."

Bridget caught a moment between orders and went straight to the kitchen to introduce herself.

"Hello, I understand you are Jasmine's parents. Well, I'm Bridget. I been workin' here about six months and it's the best thing that ever happened to me. Your daughter should be a counselor. She's taught me a lot and it all don't have to do with business. Nice to meet you. More customers. Got to get back to it."

"We need to get to it too." Walt pulled off his apron, hugged Jasmine, and whispered, "Don't sell it to anyone else."

"We'll see you later." Kelly bussed Jasmine on the cheek.

Bridget poked her head in the kitchen when they'd left and found Jasmine slumped in a kitchen chair with her head on the table.

"Bad?" Bridget asked.

"You don't know the half of it."

Chapter 18

ACE CUSSED THE TRACTOR.

Blake kicked it.

Tyson picked up a wrench and used all his muscles.

But the rusty nut would not budge.

"Lard," Lucy said from the back door.

"What in the hell are you doing out here?" Tyson asked.

"Don't talk to *me* in that tone. I brought a gallon of cold sweet tea and some throwaway cups so y'all could have a drink, so don't take that attitude with me." She set the tea down on the tailgate of the ranch work truck and shoved her finger close to his nose.

Tyson smiled for the first time since Lucy had been there. "Then pour us some tea and leave us alone."

The smile or the slight twinkle in his eyes did not escape Lucy. "That's a little bit better. Still needs some work but it's progress, Tyson. Lard is what you need. Put some lard on it, and I don't mean none of that vegetable oil. Then sit back and drink your tea and when you get done drinkin', it will let go."

Ace picked up the jug and poured. "You got any lard? We'd try anything right about now."

"I got bacon grease left from breakfast. I never throw out good bacon drippin's. Accordin' to my momma, that would be sinnin'. And I done already tested God's mettle enough in my life so I ain't goin' to be takin' chances," she said.

"Well, bring it on out here," Ace said.

Lucy went back into the bunkhouse and returned with a coffee cup of bacon grease. She dipped her fingers into it and rubbed it all over the nut.

"Anything else you got that needs a greasin' before I wash my hands?"

Ace shook his head.

Tyson hurried toward the back porch. "I'll get the door for you, Miz Lucy."

"Thank you. I appreciate that. Y'all enjoy your tea and cool down a little before you go back to fixin' that tractor. The heat makes everything worse," she said. She'd get Tyson trained and take that haunted look from his eyes if it was the last thing she did. But no man was ever going to talk to her like that again. She watched them from the window above the sink and giggled when Ace applied the wrench to the nut and it twisted right off.

Jasmine tried to call Lucy several times from noon until two thirty when she locked the doors behind Bridget. She tried as many times to call Ace, but every time all she got was their voice telling her to leave a message. She didn't want to talk to a machine; she needed desperately to talk to either or both of them.

She pulled out of the café parking lot at two thirty-five, drove home, and made a quick dash through the house before jogging out to the bunkhouse. She found Lucy singing a Loretta Lynn song. The smell of roast in one of the ovens and something that smelled like cinnamon in the other filled the whole bunkhouse, and Lucy was setting the table.

"Hey, I didn't hear you. You are really early today," Lucy said.

"Been trying to call you for an hour," Jasmine said.

"I didn't even bring the phone with me out here. We need to put a second line out here. Hang one on the wall over there by the fridge. What do you think?"

"I think I needed to talk to you." Jasmine's tone was short.

"You sound cranky. It's this blasted heat. It ain't supposed to get this hot until August. Them men out there were tryin' to cuss a nut off of the tractor. Heat gets to us all. Want a glass of tea?"

Jasmine melted into the corner of the sofa at the other end of the room. "Yes, I've had a tough day. Yes, I'm cranky as hell. And yes, please, to the glass of tea."

Lucy filled two glasses with tea and carried them to the coffee table. She sat down on the other end of the sofa and said, "Talk to me."

Words exploded like a bomb out of Jasmine's mouth. "Momma and Daddy want to buy the café, but I can't sell it and I can't tell them why, and Momma says she wants to live close to me because she wants to see her grandchildren whenever she can, and Daddy is into this cooking crap and thinks he wants to be a chef, for heaven's sake. He never cooked before he retired, so why can't he do what Momma says and go build a birdhouse?"

She stopped to suck in some air and went on just as fast and furious. "And they are coming for supper and I tried to call you to tell you to put on two more plates because I knew there would be plenty of food because you always overcook, but I couldn't get through to you and I'm falling for Ace and he's a good-timin' man like Waylon sings about and I'm not a good-hearted woman because if he ever cheated on me with a woman I wouldn't welcome him back home again"—she gasped again but it barely slowed her down—"and he will cheat because he's Ace and he likes women and I knew it when I married him, and who am I to think he'll settle down and not flirt around other women, and I've got to talk to someone or I'm going to blow up like a stick of dynamite and I can't tell anyone because I promised Ace I wouldn't and now Momma wants babies and it's all going to be over in… Nothing… I can't tell anyone."

"You done?" Lucy asked.

"I don't know."

"I hear the worst stories in the world, Jasmine. I counsel abused women. You can talk to me," Lucy said softly.

"I've got a tattoo on my butt," Jasmine blurted out.

"And your momma saw it and that's got you this twisted up? Lord, I thought the world was coming to an end," Lucy said.

Jasmine pushed her hair back with both her hands and held her aching head. "Momma didn't see it, but it's a tat of the John Deere logo. I'm supposed to be strong enough to take on anything, but I told her no on the wedding and now she wants to buy my café and I couldn't even sell if I wanted to because I'll have to have it back in a year because…"

"Go on," Lucy said.

"It's got to be confidential. I promised Ace, but if I don't talk to someone, I'm going to fall to pieces right here, and Momma will be here in an hour so she and Daddy can see the whole place and Ace don't even know it."

"You promised him that your parents would never come on the ranch?" Lucy asked.

Jasmine's hands fell to her lap. "Confidential, Lucy?"

"I'm bound by my own inner code just like them doctors or lawyers is bound by the vow they take to be in their jobs. I tell my girls that they can tell me anything and you can too. Wild horses couldn't drag it out of me," Lucy said.

"I proposed to Ace," Jasmine started.

"I don't think that's a hangin' sin in today's world. But your momma don't have to know, and I'm sure Ace isn't about to tell them."

"No, that's not it. I told him I would marry him because there was a codicil on his grandpa's will," Jasmine explained.

"A what?" Lucy frowned.

"A part in small print that said Ace had to be married in two years or this son-of-a-bitch cousin, Cole Nelson, would get the ranch. Anyway, Ace didn't read the will when his grandpa died so he didn't know about it until the lawyer died and this fancy-pants lawyer found it and contacted Cole to see if he was still living. Cole is still livin' and he said he was selling the ranch to the highest bidder and if Ace wanted it, then he had to buy it back. Ace had one week to get married and I didn't have any intentions of getting involved with anyone for a helluva lot longer than a year so I said I'd marry him. It was supposed to be a secret, but then it got put on television," Jasmine said.

A huge weight lifted from her shoulders.

"Oh!" Lucy clamped a hand over her mouth.

Jasmine nodded. "And he has to stay married a year or it's not any good."

"Oh!" The second one came out muffled from behind her hand.

"Yeah!" Jasmine nodded.

The hand came down. "And your parents want to buy the café and they want grandchildren and you're in love with Ace?"

Jasmine nodded.

"Dear Lord." Lucy gasped. "Now that is a first-rate pickle that bacon grease won't fix for sure. What are we going to do?"

"Hell if I know. But Momma and Daddy will be here any minute, and Ace don't even know they are coming because he didn't pick up his phone either."

"Hello!" Kelly yelled from the front door of the bunkhouse. "Anyone in here?"

"Smile pretty and we'll talk about this later," Lucy said.

"We can fix it, can't we?"

"Jasmine, you can fix anything. Look at what you did for me. You are Wonder Woman. Hello! Come right on in here! We're in here," Lucy yelled and stood up.

"Thank you," Jasmine said.

"Don't mention it. We are strong women. Between us we could take on King Kong."

Jasmine smiled at Lucy's choice of words. But right then she sure didn't feel like King Kong on steroids; more like a mouse hiding in a corner.

Kelly marched across the floor and extended her hand. "I'm Kelly King and this is my husband, Walt. We knocked on the door at the house but no one answered, and then we saw Jasmine's truck parked out front so we walked on back here. You must be Lucy."

Kelly's dark-brown hair was cut in a feathered back style, and her makeup was perfect. Her eyes were brown and her smile sweet. Lucy could see where Jasmine got her height, her hair, and her pretty lips, but her green eyes came from her father.

Lucy shook her hand and said, "Yes, I'm Lucy. I work here for Jasmine as chief cook and bottle washer. Delilah, my cat, and I have a room in the ranch house but I spend a lot of my time in here cooking for the crew. Would y'all like a glass of tea or a cup of coffee?"

Walt King stuck out his hand to Lucy. "It's a pleasure to meet you, Lucy. Jasmine has talked so much about you and her other friends that we feel like we already know all of you. And thank you for the offer, but we just had something cold."

Kelly nodded. "We had coffee and drinks with our lunch, then Pearl insisted that we have tea at her place, and on the way back over we had to stop for gas, so I had a Diet Coke. I'm addicted to them. I'll admit it."

Jasmine stood up and hugged both her mother and her father. "Welcome to the Double Deuce.

Remember when I was a kid and wanted to live on a ranch like Pearl? Well, I got my wish."

Lucy winked at her and that gave her courage to go on.

"As you've already figured out, this is the bunkhouse where our permanent crew lives. They each have a bedroom and bathroom behind those doors. This is the great room where everyone eats together at breakfast and supper. They take sandwiches to the field with them at lunchtime. All those wonderful smells floating around are from Lucy's cooking. Daddy, you'll have to talk recipes with her. You almost beat me here. I just got in from the café."

Lucy pointed at the door. "Ace and some of the guys are out there working on a tractor so you can go meet them now and, Mr. King, I share all my recipes. Maybe we can talk cooking later on after you have a tour of the place."

Before Walt could answer, Ace slung the back door open and carried the empty tea jug inside. He had black grease smears on his forehead and sweat rings on his dirty T-shirt that had the sleeves cut out. His barbed-wire tat right out there in plain sight, and his jeans looked like they'd been pulled through a mudhole backwards.

"Hi, darlin', you are home early. You didn't tell me you were bringing home company today," he said.

Jasmine crossed the room, tiptoed, and kissed

him on a clean spot on his cheek and said, "Ace, meet my parents, Kelly and Walt King."

He set the jug on the cabinet, wiped his hand on his hip pocket, and extended it toward Walt. "Glad to meet you, sir. Just got finished fixin' a tractor so I'm not cleaned up. Still got a few hours of work left. Want to tag along with me?"

"Be glad to, son. Used to like to go over to John Richland's place for an afternoon and work with him," Walt said.

Ace turned to her mother, took Kelly's hand in his, and brought it to his lips. He brushed a kiss across her fingertips and said, "You don't look old enough to be Jazzy's momma. You'd pass more for her sister. Me and Walt are going to leave you womenfolks alone. Jazzy, darlin', give your momma the tour up at the house and show her all around. I'll be in to clean up in a couple of hours."

He and Walt were talking tractors and cows when they shut the door behind them.

"Oh, my!" Kelly gasped. "He is a charmer, isn't he? Even in his work clothes, I can see where you would be attracted to him, Jasmine. And all that pretty curly hair. I've always wanted a granddaughter with Shirley Temple curls and blue eyes. I can already see her in a frilly little pink Easter dress with a big bow in her hair. And Christmas, oh how pretty she'll be."

Lucy butted right into the conversation. "If y'all

will excuse me, I need to check on my roast and get some hot rolls started for supper. Jasmine, I reckon you want to show your momma the house, don't you? I'm thinkin' we'll have supper at five tonight. These folks won't want to be drivin' too much in the dark. Unless y'all was plannin' on spending the night? I could sleep on the sofa if you wanted to stay over."

"Oh my, no! We didn't come prepared to stay. We're just visitin', but it would be nice to have supper at five. I'd like to stop at the Gainesville Mall on the way back to Sherman. Maybe I'll just glance at the little girl dresses." Kelly gave Lucy a broad wink and locked arms with her daughter. "Lucy, you call me Kelly. When anyone says 'Mrs. King,' I think they are talkin' about Walt's momma. Jasmine, let's go see your new house. I bet I can come up with all kinds of ideas to spruce it up."

Jasmine mouthed "Thank you" at Lucy and led her mother off toward the house.

Later that night, after her parents had gone home and the rest of the house was quiet, Ace drew Jasmine into his arms and kissed her on the forehead. She smelled of coconut-scented shampoo and sweet-smelling soap.

"That went fairly well, even if I didn't intend to

meet your folks looking like I just went swimming in a fresh hog wallow," he said.

Jasmine threw an arm across his broad chest and sighed. "They want to buy my café, Ace. If she can't have a wedding, then she'll just buy my café and make me have babies. I can't sell my café, and I can't tell them why. And I tried to call you but it went straight to voice mail."

"Tell her no. Simple as that. Besides, I don't think she can make you have babies. I might be able to do that, but not your momma." He chuckled.

Jasmine slapped him playfully. "It's not funny."

Ace propped up on an elbow. "Yes, it is. If anyone deserves to be in a pout, it's me. I felt like crap, them seeing me the first time all nasty and smelling like bacon. I would have liked to make a better first impression than that. So don't get on your high horse with me, Jazzy."

"Men, especially ranchers, can be all dirty and... Why did you smell like bacon?"

"Because I couldn't budge a nut off a bolt on the tractor and Lucy said that bacon grease would take care of it so she smeared it up good with grease and then I twisted the nut off and got it all over my hands. Then I wiped my hands on my jeans."

"Ranchers can do things like that and it's okay, and my dad liked you so it doesn't matter," Jasmine said.

Ace moved to her side of the bed and pulled her back into his arms. "And your mother?"

Jasmine frowned. "Let's see. The house was nice, but it did need redecorating. A few of those big gold mirrors and some silk flower arrangements on pedestals would be helpful; and of course it really had to have another bathroom or two and maybe a kitchen makeover. Old Bill and Little Joe surely did not ever come into the house, and Delilah was not given the run of the house, was she? Animals should not be allowed in the house with babies, and her granddaughter did not need to have nasty cat hair or dog dander on her sweet little body."

"And what did you say?" Ace asked.

"That it was my home; that I loved Delilah and the dogs; and when wintertime came, Old Bill and Little Joe could curl up in front of the fireplace at night if they wanted or sleep at the foot of the bed with us. That I absolutely hate gold mirrors and I'd take the kitchen makeover under consideration later. And that when and if I had a daughter, she was going to be surrounded by animals and she was going to be at home on the ranch."

Ace heard *my home* loud and clear and smiled. "You done good, Jazzy."

"I don't feel like I did good. I'm tied up in knots," she said.

"Roll over on your tummy," Ace said.

"Why?"

"I'm going to work those knots out for you and then you are going to get a good night's sleep. You didn't sleep much at all last night. We were too busy playing and then all this went down today. Roll over while I go in the bathroom and get that vanilla-smellin' lotion of yours," he said.

When he returned, she was on her stomach with her shirt off and her boxers resting under her butt cheeks. She heard him chuckle and looked up.

"What?"

"Nice pose there." He poured cold lotion in a long stream from neck to butt and rubbed it in before he kneaded the knots out of her neck and shoulders. He moved down by inches, using more lotion along the way. Her body was silk beneath his callused hands without lotion. With the sweet-smelling lotion, she was warm butter dripping though his fingers. Touching her aroused him, made him want to taste all the places he massaged, and more.

"I feel like a wet noodle. Thank you, Ace." Jasmine yawned.

Ace kissed her softly. "Good night, darlin'."

"You sure?" she asked.

"You need sleep worse than sex. Go to sleep now and we'll talk again tomorrow."

"You are wonderful," she mumbled.

Even with the massage, she didn't sleep well. She had nightmares about big gold mirrors with her mother's distorted face watching every single move she made. Instead of the alarm clock flashing in her face to wake her the next morning, it was her cell phone. She threw her legs over the edge of the bed and blindly fumbled on the nightstand.

"Please don't be Bridget telling me she's too sick to work," she mumbled.

"Hello."

"Thank God. I was afraid you'd run off the road and was layin' off in a bar ditch half-dead. You are never ever late and I was going to get in the car and come find you if you didn't answer the phone, and where are you? Are you broke down in that spot where there's no phone reception? Just tell me… why are you answering your phone if there's no reception?"

"I overslept! I'm just fine. I'm getting around right now."

"Thank God! Want me to start the biscuits and get the sausage frying?"

"Yes, please! I'll be there in fifteen, I promise." She grabbed her jeans, threw her cell phone at her purse, and missed, knocking the bag off the chair beside the bed and scattering its contents everywhere. She hoped that she'd scooped everything back into her purse as she hurried outside.

Chapter 19

It was a Murphy's Law Friday. If it could go wrong, it did! A can of cherry pie filling slipped out of Jasmine's hands and splattered all over the floor. The chicken-fried steaks she'd already put into the skillet burned while she was cleaning that up, and she had to start the orders all over. Her mother called six times before lunch to see what she thought of lace curtains for the apartment window; to tell her that she needed the menus a week ahead of time to put on the new website she was designing; that she'd seen a lovely pose for her granddaughter at age three in a field of Texas bluebonnets; that her father had ordered a new set of cookbooks especially for country cooking; and two other times to ask if she'd changed her mind yet about the café. Jasmine told her each of the six times that the café was not for sale.

If it couldn't go wrong, it did anyway! Her produce order was short and she had adjust her menu or she'd never have enough potatoes to last until the next week. Every time she had a spare second, Bridget wanted to worry and pout about Frankie not calling her. Ace didn't come by all day long and she missed him.

By closing time, Jasmine was ready to give the apartment, the café, *and* Bridget to her mother, run away to the beach, and pick up seashells for a living. She locked up behind Bridget, plopped down in the nearest chair, folded her arms on the table, and laid her head on them. Used to be that she thought her life was boring. How could it have gotten so complicated in such a short time?

She sat there five minutes before she went to the kitchen and whipped up desserts for the next day. She expected something to go wrong the rest of the day and was surprised when it didn't. Thinking that she must have finally broken the bad-luck streak, she removed her apron, picked up her purse, and started home. She took two steps on the porch, stumbled, and caught herself on the railing, but her purse went flying, stringing the contents from one end of the porch to the other.

"Dammit!" she swore. "Twice in one day is not fair!"

She bent over and crammed things back inside: lipstick, a flash drive with the café business backed up on it, wallet, two-year date planner so she wouldn't forget birthdays, keys, little red book…

"Whoa! What is this?" She picked up a worn leather red book. She'd never seen the thing before. It was barely bigger than the palm of her hand. She turned it over to see gold initials on the outside right corner: A. R.

She sat down on the porch steps. "Ace Riley."

She wiped sweat from her forehead with the bottom of her T-shirt and turned the book over a dozen times. She knew exactly what she was holding, but opening it would be unforgivable. It was his little black book of women's names, addresses, and phone numbers.

Just how detailed was it, anyway? And how many names were in it? Did a woman get her name in the playboy's book of sin the first time they went out, or did she have to put out first?

Jealousy abounded and she couldn't help it.

Where did he get it? Surely he didn't buy this thing. Some woman gave it to him. Was her name in the book? *Crap! I sound like a wife.* Maybe it was empty. Some two-bit hussy gave it to him, but he never wrote a single name in it. If she just fanned through the pages she could see if it was empty or if there were really names in it.

Holding it in her left hand and using her right thumb, she fanned.

Enough little black stars flew past her eyes to light up a galaxy or two.

Stars! He had graded each woman. How did it work? One star for sex; one for humor; one for looks? If she only looked at the first page, she'd at least know that much. She didn't have to look at their names or how many stars they got.

She shut her eyes tightly and opened the cover.

Lightning didn't shoot from the sky and zap her. Thunder didn't roll in warning. Snow didn't start to fall right there in Ringgold, Texas, in the middle of June. She looked down at the first page.

From Mallory, who gives Ace the five-star maximum for sex. All the rest is window dressing.

She snapped the cover shut.

"What would I rate him?" she whispered.

If five stars is the maximum, you'd give him a good solid ten.

She crammed the book down into her purse, picked up two pennies, a dime, and a quarter, and looked around to make sure she hadn't left anything lying on the porch. Tires crunched the gravel in the parking lot, so she looked up, hoping that it wasn't Ace. She didn't want to face him until she'd decided how to deal with the book.

How did it get into her purse to begin with? Did he put it there to torment her? Or to leave a not-so-subtle reminder that he had no intentions of a long-term relationship with anyone? Did he want her to look inside it?

"Hey." Liz crawled out of her truck. "I'm on my way to Ryan for a load of feed. I saw your truck and thought I'd stop and tell you that the O'Donnells can bring the music to your party. Granny is all excited about it."

"Thank you and tell Granny thank you," Jasmine said.

"You sick? Or is it just this unbearable heat? We need a good rain for sure to cool things off a bit. Hate to even think about August when it's this hot in June." Liz fished around in her purse and found a rubber band, whipped her hair up into a ponytail, and secured it, and then she sat down on the top porch step in the shade.

"No, I'm not sick, but it is hot. Want to go inside?" she asked.

"No, you done shut up for the day. Why aren't you already headed home?" Liz asked.

Jasmine told her about the little red book. "It's not the book itself. I'm just wondering why it's in my purse and if Ace put it there to tease me. If so, it's not a funny joke. And if he put it there…" She stopped before she blurted out that he was making a statement about her not being a real wife.

Liz fanned her face with her hand. "When Raylen and I went out on our first real date, we were eating at the Olive Garden over in Wichita Falls and the waitress said she hadn't seen Ace in a while. Raylen and I were laughing about how he should have to put a tattoo on all the women he'd dated so other women could spot them. I'm not surprised that Ace has a book with his women in it or that they've got stars. What I am surprised about is that he hasn't destroyed it. You are my friend and I wouldn't say a thing to hurt you, but darlin', you knew Ace better than anyone in the world. You knew what you were getting when you married him, so why does that book bother you so much? Burn the thing or give it to him and tell him you'll burn him at the stake if he don't set it on fire."

"Did Raylen have one?"

"Yes, he did. I never saw it, but one day I caught him burning something in a metal can out in the barn. Spooked my horse, Star, and he was pitching a fit in his stall. When I asked Raylen what he was doing, setting a fire in the barn, he laughed and told me he was burning his past because he sure didn't ever want me to find it. You really aren't going to look in it?" Liz asked.

Jasmine shook her head. "I flipped through it and saw all those stars and then I read the first page. Here, you read it." She pulled it from her purse and handed it to Liz.

"Oh, my!" Liz said when she read what Mallory wrote. "Is he that good?"

"Is Raylen?"

"Point taken." Liz handed the book back.

Jasmine dropped it into her purse. "Now I remember! I spilled my purse twice today. This morning and a few minutes ago. It was dark this morning and some of the stuff went under the bed. I scooped it all up with my forearm. I must've gotten that book in with my stuff then. But why was it under the bed?"

Liz shrugged. "Maybe he dropped it or kept it stuck between the mattress and the box springs like a little boy with his stolen girlie magazines and it fell out when y'all were bouncing the mattress."

Jasmine would have shot him right there if he'd been standing in front of her and she had a gun. He'd had all those women right there under them when he was making passionate love to her. He could have at least put them on the top shelf in his closet in a shoebox of rodeo memorabilia. *Dammit!*

She almost opened it to the K's to see if Jasmine King was in there, but she couldn't. Just thinking about it put a burning blush on her face. If she only had two stars by her name after the ice cream sex, she'd be so mad she'd go up in flames and prove that spontaneous combustion was indeed a possibility.

"I'm glad I didn't ever find Raylen's book. I've never heard of a Mallory so you'll never have to meet her. She's probably someone he met on the rodeo rounds, maybe a groupie. I read somewhere that they are always buying their cowboys presents," Liz said.

"You are probably right."

Liz stood up. "I've got to go or I won't make it to the feed store before it closes. Just wanted to stop and offer our music for the party. Call if you need to talk."

"I will and thanks again for everything," Jasmine said.

"Sure thing." Liz hurried across the lot to her truck.

Jasmine followed her and hopped inside her own truck, turned the key, and adjusted the air-conditioning to the highest notch. Heat came off the highway in waves, distorting images like special effects in a movie, and it took a full minute for the air conditioner to blow anything but hot air.

She had her hand on the gearshift to put it in reverse when her phone rang. The ringtone was "Redneck Woman," which meant Pearl was calling.

"I'm glad you called. I just found out today that I've married you. Does Wil see a good therapist and is he taking new clients?" Jasmine asked.

"Whoa, girl! What are you talking about?" Pearl gasped.

"I found Ace's little black book, only it's a little red book, and I didn't read it but I flipped it and there's more stars than the galaxy in it, and some woman gave it to him named Mallory and she gave him five stars for sex," Jasmine said without taking a breath.

"And that means you married me?" Pearl asked.

"No, I married the male species of you. You were the party girl of north Texas. It looks like Ace is the good-timin' cowboy of the whole state," she said.

Pearl giggled.

"What's so funny?" Jasmine asked.

"Two things. One is that you didn't go into this

blind, girl. Ace was the good-timin' cowboy of the whole state like you said, but you knew that. Hell, you knew his secrets and the women's names. You could have blackmailed him but you married him, so don't come bitchin' to me about findin' his past. And two, I was thinkin' of my little purple book."

"And what happened to it?"

"I gave it to Lucy the day before the wedding and told her to make sure it was burned to nothing but ash. I sure didn't want Wil to find it. Which brings me to the reason I called, now that we've established that you did not marry me. I've got two things in that category too. Number one: How is Lucy doing out there on the ranch?"

"Great. She fit in from day one like she'd been there her whole life. I think she's even going to bring Tyson back to the living with her cooking and patience. I'm wondering how the Double Deuce ever survived without her. Now back to the book. What should I do with it, in your opinion?"

"Give it to Lucy and then tell Ace what you did," Pearl said.

"Or?"

"No 'or's in this case. Just do it. I'm surprised you haven't called me to carry on about his women callin' every hour all day like they used to do."

Jasmine got angry all over again. His women probably were calling. She tuned back in to hear Pearl saying, "But then when your marriage is broadcast over national television, I guess most of them know he's branded and leave him alone. Still there would have been a few who wouldn't care if he was married or not. Only advice I've got is to give it to Lucy."

"Okay, y'all are still coming to the party, aren't you?"

"Of course," Pearl said. "I still can't believe you stood up to Kelly like that. If it wasn't for the fact that you are selling her the café, she'd probably be commissioning someone to build a gallows to hang you from. Which brings me to item number two."

It was Jasmine's turn to gasp. "I'm not selling her my café. She wants to buy it, but the Chicken Fried is not for sale."

"She's going to gripe and complain until you get pregnant with her grandbaby. You might as well go on and sell the café to keep her mind off you for a while," Pearl told her.

"No, thank you! And what's item two?"

"Your dad asked me how much you still owed on the café. He said that he was using the wedding money to pay off the café for you and that they were going to give you fair market price for it too, since it would be an investment. He's got it all figured out and I got the check for the café today so you now own it, lock, stock, and barrel."

"Holy crap!" Jasmine said.

"No, just a check. Been a pleasure doin' business

with you. And here's a beep. It's Momma and if I don't answer, she'll be in the car driving over here. Goodbye and good luck holding on to that café."

The line went dead.

The year before, Pearl had loaned her the money to buy the café and Jasmine had made regular monthly payments. Now it was paid for with her wedding money. More and more complications! She flipped her phone shut and tossed it in her purse. She put the truck in gear and headed home. She didn't notice that there was an extra pickup truck parked in the line in front of the house until she was already on the porch. Then she turned around and counted with her forefinger. Four. That meant they had company. She slung open the door and stepped to find a tall blonde with her arms around Ace in what looked like a pretty serious hug. The hussy was dressed in a white strapless sundress and had a killer tan, big blue eyes, and long, long legs.

The scenario stopped the earth from turning as if someone had pushed a pause button on life. The sun stood still. Everything and everyone froze in place. The fly that had been buzzing around Jasmine's head stopped. The hug went on and on.

And then the woman stepped back and smiled at her. "You must be Jasmine. Acey said you'd be home pretty soon. Tomorrow, then?" She looked back at Ace.

At least he had the good grace to step back two steps and blush. "Honey, this is Mallory. She's a photographer from over in Wichita Falls. She'll be here tomorrow to take pictures of me for next year's cowboy calendar. I'm Mr. July," he said.

Mallory laid a possessive hand on his arm. "We've been doing this for ten years now. Acey makes a wonderful Mr. July."

"Tomorrow?" Jasmine was stunned to hear even one word come out sounding normal and that she hadn't slapped that grin off Mallory's face. Would this day never end?

"We got plans?" Ace asked.

"No," she said. But if she'd had some forewarning, they would have definitely had plans.

"Good. Then I'll see you about three. I'll bring the flag for the backdrop for Ace. You wear the same as last year. We'll take them in the old barn this year rather than out in the field for something different. Blake, we might do yours by that old rusty tractor out behind the barn, and Dalton, I'm thinkin' of yours in the hayloft," Mallory said.

She breezed past Jasmine leaving a cloud of expensive perfume in her wake. When she was gone, Jasmine looked at Ace who threw up his hands defensively.

"I forgot that she was coming by. It was written on the calendar in my computer but I haven't looked at it in weeks. We've done this for years. Blake is Mr.

June and Dalton is Mr. August. I'll be wearing jeans, but the top button will probably be undone, and no shirt, but I'll have my boots on. You got a problem with it?" Ace folded his hands across his chest.

"Of course not. Why would I? I'm doing a hot rod calendar. I'll be wearing little red velvet hip-slung short shorts and no top, but the photographer is shooting it from behind and my hair covers most of my back. Last year, it only showed the shadow of my boobs. The hot rod I get to lean back on this year is candy-apple red so I'll have to shop for some lipstick that color. Want to go with me this Saturday, or should I ask Lucy to shop with me while you get ready for your photo shoot?" The outlandish lie got bigger with every sentence.

"You will not! You are a married woman. I don't want men looking at you half-naked." He raised his voice.

"Deal with it, darlin'." She deliberately and slowly brushed her body across his on her way to the living room.

He glared at her.

She ignored him.

The living room smelled like a Stetson cologne factory had exploded right smack in the middle of it. Blake and Dalton lazed on the sofa with their feet propped on the coffee table. They wore clean jeans, ironed shirts, and polished boots.

Jasmine turned and realized that Ace was dressed

up, too. "What's going on here? Are we having a party no one told me about?"

"Nope. Just Mallory coming by," Blake said.

Jasmine's hands clenched into fists. "And you forgot?"

"Remembered this morning when I looked at the calendar," Ace said coldly. "Why are you so jealous? We've all been doing this for years."

"Ten? Right?" Jasmine asked.

"Right. How long were you modeling for the hot-rod calendars?" he shot back at him.

"Since I was sixteen," she lied again.

"What's going on in here?" Lucy came in the back door. "I can feel the tension all the way in the yard. Was that one of your girlfriends that just left, Blake? I swear if another of your bimbos lets Delilah out the front door like the last one did, I'm going to put a curse on you."

"Jasmine is all hot under the collar because Ace is going to model for a cowboy calendar. He's been posin' for years, but this is just me and Dalton's second time to get to do it," Blake said. "That was the photographer, Mallory, who takes the pictures. She catches all three of us at one time."

"Yep, the hottest cowboys in Texas in the hot summertime," Dalton said.

Jasmine shot him a stinging go-to-hell look.

Dalton held up both palms in a defensive gesture. "What? That's what she said, not me."

"Acey?" Jasmine stepped up into his face.

"Boy, you are in a heap of big-time trouble," Lucy said. "You and Jasmine better go on to the bedroom and get this settled once and for all."

Jasmine dug in her purse and tossed the red book across the room to Lucy.

"That's mine!" Dalton tried to catch it in midair.

Blake tackled him for it. "No, he's married, and I get it."

Lucy picked it out of the air above their heads like a football pass into the end zone. "This what I think it is?"

Ace stared at the book and wondered how it got from under the lamp on his nightstand into Jasmine's hands.

Jasmine answered Lucy, but she looked straight into Ace's eyes. "I found it hiding under the bed this morning. I understand you know how to cremate those things. Wash out one of Delilah's fancy-cat-food cans and put the ashes in it. Seems like a fitting urn, doesn't it?"

Lucy nodded seriously. "Does this belong to you, or Ace?"

It was the first time that it occurred to Ace that Jasmine might have a book filled with stars and names like his. Just thinking about another man rubbing her back after a stressful day's work at the café made his chest clinch up in knots.

"It's mine," Ace growled with his gaze locked

with Jasmine's. "I promise I'll burn it and spread the ashes over the hog lot. My chasing women days are over."

"Ah, man, give it to me. Don't waste all that good research," Dalton said.

"A man has to do his own research. Now your turn, Jazzy. Where is your book?" he asked.

"Already gone," she said. It wasn't really a lie. It had never existed, so it was gone.

"You really going to pose for that hot-rod calendar?" he asked.

Blake looked up from the sofa. "Wow! Do you model for hot-rod calendars, Jazzy? I'll buy a dozen for my friends."

"You really going to pose for the cowboy calendar?" she asked.

Ace nodded. "This year. I won't next year."

"Then I won't next year either," she said.

"Now, there! We've got a truce." Lucy smiled. "But I still feel some tension so you two get on back in your room and don't come out until the fight is really finished."

"After you." Ace motioned toward the door.

"Thank you, Acey," she said.

"Enough!" he said.

She pointed her finger at his nose. "Not yet, darlin'. When I hear you tell your sweet Mallory that this is your last time to model, then it will be enough… Acey."

He picked her up like a sack of flour and tossed her over his shoulder. "Married people don't fight in front of the children. We'll finish this in the bedroom. We'll be in the bunkhouse in plenty of time for supper, Lucy, and she'll have a smile on her face."

"You are full of bullcrap!" Jasmine had trouble breathing and her words came out in short spurts.

"So are you, Mrs. Riley," he whispered as he carried her down the hall and into the bedroom. He kicked the door shut with his bootheel and tossed her on the bed.

She bounced twice before he landed on top of her, his lips connecting to hers in a clash of passion that sent sparks dancing around the room and heat flowing over every inch of Jasmine's body.

"I'm still mad at you," she said.

He propped up on his elbows. "And I'm still mad at you for telling Lucy to burn my book."

"You put stars in front of their names, Acey baby!"

"You actually read it!" He gasped.

"No, but I flipped through it."

A wide grin split his face. "You got more stars than any of them, darlin'."

She blinked so fast he was a blur. "I was in that atrocity?"

He lowered his lips to brush across hers. "Now you will never know unless you go out to the hog lot and sift through the ashes or else tell Lucy you want it back."

She wrapped her arms around his neck and

nipped his lower lip. "Don't tease me, cowboy. Kiss me right," she whispered.

"My pleasure." He devoured her lips, tasting, teasing, tempting until he was so aroused that he couldn't bear it another minute.

He didn't know when it happened, but she had his belt buckle undone and her hand around an already hard erection. He wondered how something so small and as cool as her hand could have so much heat and power over him.

She wasn't aware of when he'd unfastened her bra, but suddenly his mouth left her lips and was kissing its way toward her breast. His tongue was velvet heat when it found its destination, and she arched against him.

"Still mad?" he asked.

"I'll be even madder if you don't finish what you've started," she panted.

"This is going to be a helluva year." He chuckled.

"I'll make it hell tonight if you don't get those jeans and boots off," she threatened.

He wiggled out of his jeans at the same time she did hers. Ace didn't like underwear and he was more than ready. He looked like a Greek god bathing in the sunlight that filtered through the sheer curtains in the bedroom.

She was in love with him and didn't care about tomorrow. She just wanted him to ease that deep ache inside her body as only he could do.

His kisses were hot and demanding, sweet and sensual, and in minutes they were both panting. Then he slid into her without stopping the kisses, building her up into a panting frenzy. She dug her nails into his firm butt and held on as she bucked against him.

"Bull riding, are we?" he teased. "Well, you are the most beautiful bull rider I've ever seen, Jazzy."

"Call it what you want, cowboy. I just need you right now," she whispered hoarsely.

"Fight over?" he whispered as he nibbled on her ear.

"Hell no!"

He ran his tongue around the outer edge of her ear. "Then we'll just skip supper until it is."

She whimpered and he increased the rhythm.

They reached the climax within seconds of each other, and she called out his name at the same time he said, "My God, Jazzy."

"Stars?" she asked when she could breathe.

"A whole galaxy."

"Fight is over, darlin'. Hold me tight. We've got thirty minutes before we have to go to supper."

"I don't have enough ink to make that many stars on the page with your name," he groaned.

"I love this part," she whispered.

"The end?" he asked.

She kissed him, soft and sweet on the lips. "No, the after part when we cuddle. I love it."

"Confession time," he whispered. "Mallory

wasn't the same Mallory who gave it to me. That lady is married and has three kids now. The Mallory who takes pictures isn't in the book. I've never even been out with her but Dalton has." He chuckled.

Jasmine slapped him on the butt. "That was mean."

"Yep, it was, but you made me mad when you said that about posing for a hot-rod calendar. I don't want other men looking at you," he said.

"Well, I don't want other women looking at you," she told him.

"Then this is our last year to model for calendars?"

"It's your last year," she said.

His blue eyes turned dark.

"Don't get your underbritches in a wad, darlin'. I never did pose so it isn't my last year or my first. I was jealous so I lied," she admitted.

"To begin with, *darlin'...*"—he drew out the endearment in a sexy Texas drawl—"I don't wear underbritches and you know it. And to end with, you don't play fair." His eyes went all dreamy again.

"No, I don't play fair, and don't forget it," she said. "And thinking about what's under your jeans makes me very hot, and it's not a vision of underbritches either. We still have twenty minutes and the children don't sound like they are fighting. Cuddle or a second helping?"

"I think a second helping is in order. This ranch ain't called the Double Deuce for nothing, darlin'."

Chapter 20

Jasmine took the steps up to her apartment two at a time. She took the quickest shower of her life and dressed faster than she'd ever done in the past. She had taken time to iron her shorts and halter top and put on makeup. Mallory was not going to steal the show that afternoon, not if Jasmine had her way. She was on her way out to her truck when her phone rang.

"Hello," she answered without looking at the caller ID.

"Hey, it's Lucy. You want to go grocery shopping with me down in Bowie this afternoon so you won't be on hand when the photography thing is going on at the ranch?"

"Thanks, but no thanks. I wouldn't miss this for anything. I want to be standing right there when Ace does his half-naked shots," Jasmine said.

"You're jealous?" Lucy asked.

"Oh, yeah, and I'll even admit it to you. What are the guys doing? Has she arrived yet?" Jasmine asked.

"She's not here, but this place is like a beauty parlor for the menfolks." Lucy laughed.

Jasmine got to the ranch ten minutes before

Mallory was due, but she'd broken every speed law in Texas to do it. She hadn't even known her truck could go that fast or could corner so well until that day. When she entered the house, she got a nose full of shaving lotion and hair product. She should have escaped to the grocery store with Lucy, but a team of wild mules couldn't have forced her away from the ranch that day.

It was pretty evident that all three grown men had primped and spent hours in the bathroom that morning, but they were sitting in front of the television acting as if they weren't even thinking about doing photos that afternoon.

Dalton looked up. "Lucy said she was picking you up to go with her. She was going to one of those meetings. What is it? AA?"

"No, SM," Jasmine answered.

Blake frowned. "SM!"

"Stands for Stupid Men," Jasmine said.

"Oh," Blake said flatly.

"It's a support group for abused women. Lucy has kept many of them alive, I'm sure. But today, if you'd been listening to her rather than primping for Mallory, you would have heard her. She's gone grocery shopping," Jasmine said.

"So you decided not to go?" Ace asked.

She bent down and kissed him on the forehead. "Honey, I wouldn't miss this afternoon for half the dirt in Texas."

"Blake, have you got your hair fixed just perfect?" she asked.

He nodded.

"Then you'd better be careful pulling that T-shirt up over your head. Acey, darlin', why didn't you tell him to wear a button-down shirt like you?"

Blake jumped up and headed down the hallway.

Dalton squirmed around for a while like a little boy who wanted to go outside and play but had to eat his brussels sprouts first.

"How do I look?" he finally asked.

"You look plumb sexy." Jasmine headed toward the kitchen.

Ace followed her.

She wore cutoff denim shorts so short that her legs looked like they went all the way to heaven. Wedge-heeled sandals added three more inches to her height. Her dark hair floated around her face like a halo, but Ace had living proof an angel did not live in that body. More like the devil's sister. An orange halter top tied around her neck, leaving half of her back bare.

He wanted to touch her skin, smell her hair that was all shiny with a fresh shampooing, but most of all he wanted to kiss her so bad that it hurt. When she reached up into the cabinet to take down a glass for iced tea, her skimpy little shirt rode up and her belly button showed.

All the air left his lungs.

"What time is five-star Mallory getting here?" Jasmine asked.

Ace leaned back and propped his elbows on the cabinet. "Three, but I wouldn't know anything about stars. You'd have to ask Dalton about that."

His jeans were faded but they stacked up over his boots just right. His blond curls were all shiny and clean but without the mousse that Blake and Dalton had put into their hair. Ace's curls would blow in the summer breeze and women would drool over Mr. July. She could visualize them reaching out to touch the picture and run a finger over his hair.

"Well?" Ace asked.

"What?" she asked.

"Why did you call her a five-star?" he repeated.

"Three men don't gussy up like y'all are for less than a five-star."

She started to remove the tea pitcher from the refrigerator and noticed a six-pack of beer. It looked a helluva lot better than tea, so she pulled out a bottle and twisted the top off. She took a long draw and handed it to Ace.

"Good and cold. I don't want a whole one. Want to share?"

He turned it up. Anything to cool down the heat sending him into semi-arousal. It wouldn't do to have a bulging zipper in the pictures.

"Thanks." He handed it back to her and turned to look out the kitchen window.

She walked up behind him, ran her hands up under his shirt, and kissed him between the shoulder blades. Even through the cotton shirt she could feel his muscles tensing and his quick intake of breath. Her hands skimmed over his chest, her fingers tracing the outline of his pecs.

"Turn around!" she said.

He turned and she unbuttoned his shirt.

"Dammit! What have you done?" she squealed.

"What?" he asked.

She went to work on the buttons of his shirt, threw the sides back like they were trash, and stared, unbelieving even after she blinked a dozen times. "You shaved your chest!"

"Of course I did. Did you not understand this is for a calendar, Jazzy? Women don't like hairy men. They like big muscles and tight abs. Mallory brings a bottle of special oil that we rub on our chests and then she sprays us with a mister to make it look like we're sweating," he said.

"I like the hair on your chest. Running my fingers through it makes me hot. You'll be all bristly for weeks," she whispered.

"Hey, Mallory just pulled up," Dalton yelled.

Ace quickly buttoned his shirt and shrugged. "You going to stay here and pout or go with me?"

She narrowed her eyes. "Let's go. And FYI, I do not pout."

Mallory stood just inside the door with Dalton

to one side and Blake leaning on the wall in a seductive pose. Tomcat number one had already dated her. Tomcat number two was posing for her.

Ace nodded toward her, grabbed Jasmine's hand, and brushed past all of them on his way out the door. "We're going to walk up to the barn. We'll meet you there."

"Hello, Jasmine." Mallory nodded.

"Hey." Jasmine stopped and Ace's hand slipped out of hers.

"So I guess y'all are ready to get this done?" Mallory asked, but her eyes were locked with Jasmine's.

"Guess so." Blake had changed his shirt and made sure his dark hair was perfect.

"Jazzy and I'll meet y'all down at the barn. You all right with doing mine first, Mallory? Jazzy and I have a date this afternoon so I'd like to get done early so we can go." Ace laced his fingers back into Jasmine's and his thumb gently massaged the top of her hand.

"No problem," Mallory said.

He led Jasmine out the front door, around the house, and toward the barn. Mallory, Blake, and Dalton all got into her truck and followed the path from the house to the barn.

"I wasn't aware that we had a date," she said.

"I planned it for a surprise," Ace said.

"When? Right then?" Jasmine snapped.

It was going to take a long time for her to get over that shaved chest. Not that it wasn't sexy all smooth and muscled up. She didn't even have a problem touching it, but knowing that he'd shaved it for another woman stuck in her craw and wouldn't go down.

"FYI," he said with sarcasm. "I planned it a couple of days ago. I know you are upset about this, Jazzy, but as long as you and I are together, I promise I will not do this again."

As long as we are together. Just exactly how long were they going to be together after all? A year? Forever?

"Should I change for this big mystery date?"

"No, ma'am. I want you to watch this photo shoot, not go back to the house. Besides, you are dressed perfectly, except for the shoes and they don't matter."

"Why do you want me to watch the photo shoot?"

He squeezed her hand. "So that later Dalton or Blake can't tease me and make us fight again."

The temperature had reached a hundred degrees at noon and it hovered there, right happy with itself. A breeze stirred the trees and fluffed up Ace's hair just like she imagined. Sweat poured down her neck, took the path of least resistance between her breasts, and rolled on down to her belly button where it pooled up. When that place overflowed, it traveled on to the waistband of her shorts.

"Where are we going?" she asked.

He stopped and looked down into her green eyes. "On the date or long term?"

"Date. I don't discuss long term with men who haven't even got hair on their chest yet," she answered.

He lowered his lips to hers and kissed her so passionately that she gasped. When he broke away, he ran his palms down her arms from shoulders to fingertips.

"It will grow back. I promise." His Texas drawl was husky with desire.

She smiled. "Is our date in the bedroom?"

"No, ma'am, it's a real date."

"Dinner and a movie? I'll have to change," she said.

"No movie but dinner, yes, and I don't want you to change. You are sexy and beautiful just like you are."

When they got there, Mallory and Dalton already had a flag attached to the door of the barn and several bales of hay pulled up in front of it. She was setting her camera on a tripod and attaching a remote trigger. She looked up and motioned them toward the hay.

"Ace, sit here, undo your shirt, but don't take it off. Here's the oil. Rub it on your chest and I'll spray you with the mist. Throw that shirt back a little farther. I want to tease the women into buying more calendars. I'm glad you wore a red shirt. It goes with the setting so well. Okay, here comes the spray and it's cold," Mallory said.

Jasmine watched his nipples perk right up when the water hit his chest. Ace gave her a lopsided grin and Mallory squeezed the trigger. "Keep looking at Jasmine. Yes, like that. The twinkle in your eyes is priceless when you are looking at her. I like this time of day. It puts your face in half shadow and the wind is picking up the curls on your collar."

She squeezed as she talked, and in five minutes, she shaded her eyes with her hand and looked at the images on the back of her digital camera. "Got plenty of really good ones to choose from. Dalton, let's take you on down toward the creek. I saw an old dead tree down there that would make a great prop."

"That's it?" Jasmine asked.

Mallory nodded. "Unless you want some pictures with Ace. I could take some for y'all and you could come by next week to pick out a package. I'm reasonable on prices and you do look like a modern-day Daisy Mae in that getup. It would be perfect out here in this setting."

Jasmine shook her head. "No, thank you."

"Okay, maybe another time. I think you'd be very photogenic, Jasmine. Hey, Dalton, help me take down this flag and we'll move this operation on down to the creek. There's a container of wipes in the passenger seat, Acey, darlin'. That oil will ruin your shirt if you don't get it off," Mallory said.

Dalton hurried to help. The sidelong glances he gave Mallory did not escape Jasmine.

"See you next year?" Mallory asked as Jasmine and Ace started toward the truck.

"This is my last year. Give my Mr. July spot to some other rancher. Creed might be interested," Ace said.

"Take good care of him, Jasmine. He's a keeper," Mallory said.

"I think he might be." Jasmine nodded. "Maybe we could hire you to come around next week on Sunday afternoon and take some pictures of our reception. Momma wants a picture to go above the mantel, and she hates my wedding picture."

Mallory raised an eyebrow. "I loved that dress and the hat and veil. Saw it on the news that night. It was different and I'd love to take pictures of you out by the barn if we could sneak away for a few minutes. I have tons of pictures of brides in big dresses in a church setting, but that would be something different for my portfolio."

"Sounds like fun. Can you be here then on Sunday?" Jasmine asked.

"I've got a christening that morning, but I could be here at one thirty."

"Good. Bring a date and have a good time after you take a few pictures."

"Thank you. I'll do it," Mallory said.

Ace wiped the oil from his chest, buttoned his shirt, and grabbed Jasmine's hand again. "I did not see that coming."

"You aren't the only one with surprises, Ace."

He pulled her close to his side. "No 'Acey,' darlin'?"

"You kept your end of the bargain. I'll keep mine."

Chapter 21

"WE'RE GOIN' FISHIN'?"

She knew a fishing boat when she saw one, and that wasn't a cabin cruiser hitched up to the back end of his truck.

He opened the passenger-side door for her and kissed her on the forehead.

"Kind of," he answered. "Things are about to get crazy on the ranch. These next two weeks are going to be hectic and then we've got the party week. We are going to get away for a day of quiet and peace before it all kicks off."

"Party week?"

"Oh, yeah, the Sunday before our party, we have a church picnic, then July Fourth is at Momma's, and if you're a Riley and you ain't in the hospital or funeral home, your presence is required; the next Sunday is our party, but today is for us to be alone."

She could think of a dozen things she'd rather be doing than fishing on her day of quiet and peace. If she'd been given some notice, she would have at least brought along that thick romance book by Amelia Grey that she'd been reading in snippets when she had time.

"Where?" she asked.

"Red River. Maybe we'll catch a big catfish for our supper."

"If we don't?"

"Then I guess we'll have sex on empty stomachs." He grinned.

"Who says I'm ready to have sex with a man that shaved his chest?"

He chuckled. "You like it. You're just mad because I did it for a calendar and not just for you."

Jasmine couldn't keep the grin off her face. "For the calendar?"

"Hell, yeah! I wouldn't shave my chest for anyone, not even you. Itches like hell when it's coming back in, but the volunteer fire department gets a percentage of all the sales on that calendar." He pulled out on Highway 81 and turned north.

"Okay, confession! I like it, but I like it better with hair," she said.

"Oh, yeah?" He drove about six miles and pulled off on a dirt road leading down to the river.

"I like your chest. I like your abs. I like everything about you, Ace," she said.

"Why, thank you, ma'am," he drawled. The bridge was on their right and the muddy waters of the Red right ahead when he backed the truck as close to the water as he could and shut off the engine.

She crawled out, kicked off her shoes and tossed

them into the boat, and waded out into the cool water. It was shallow, barely reaching her knees. Ace climbed into the boat, reached out and picked her up like she was as light as a feather, and set her in the boat.

He'd taken off his boots and rolled his jeans up before he unhooked the boat and raised the trailer to let it slide into the water. He slung a leg over the edge of the boat, opened the bench seat in front of them, and pulled out a bottle of sunblock lotion with a rubber band stretched around it.

"What is that?"

"Band is to get your hair off your neck. Sunblock is to keep you from burning. You put up your hair and I'll lather you up good with the lotion before I start the motor and we get on down the river. There's a deep hole about three miles from here where the catfish might be biting."

She finger combed her hair up into a ponytail and secured it with the rubber band. "You think of everything."

"When I'm taking a beautiful woman out on a date, I do my best. When it's my wife, I do even better."

His touch was light when he applied lotion to her back and arms. He handed her the bottle and said, "You'd better do your legs. I get that close to your underpants, I'll have to fight the desire to take them off."

"You are a rogue." She giggled.

"No, I'm just an old cowboy who's married a beautiful woman with the sexiest legs in Texas. No, wait—in Texas and Oklahoma, because we are officially in Oklahoma when we are floating in the river." He pulled a cord and the engine roared to life. He kept it at a slow, steady speed for twenty minutes before he killed it and let the waves float the boat back toward the bridge at a lazy pace.

"Now what?" she asked.

"Now we fish." He raised the bench lid, took out a container of worms, picked out one, and threaded it on a hook. "You want me to bait your hook?"

"I'm a big girl. I've been fishing a couple of times in my life, so I know how to lace a worm on a hook." She picked up the second rod, unwound the line from around the rod, and took a fat earthworm from the black dirt in the container. She laced the worm onto the hook, held the button down on the reel, and snapped the rod forward, letting the lead weight carry the red and white bobble out into the water.

"Not bad," he said.

She wasn't a bit squeamish about handling the worm. She'd even had her own special way of baiting the hook that impressed him.

He flipped his hook out into the water on the opposite side of the boat. "Who took you fishin'?"

"Pearl's dad likes to fish. He took us out a few

times. He made us bait our own hooks and told us if we caught a fish we had to learn to clean it. We were bored to death and after the first time we took a book to read," she said. "Is it ever going to rain?"

Ace put his rod in a holder attached to the boat and opened the bench seat again. He brought out a worn straw hat and settled it on his head and a bright pink cap for Jasmine. She flipped the ponytail out the hole in the back and crammed it down until the sweatband was across her forehead.

"Thanks," she said. "What all do you have in that bench?"

"Everything we need," Ace answered.

Jasmine nodded and watched the red and white bobble dancing on the water. In the quietness, her thoughts went to Ace, and she questioned things like why hadn't she gone out with Ace when he asked her the first time they met?

Because I thought he was teasing.

Why hadn't she made a first move?

Because I didn't know how his kisses and touch would affect me.

An hour later the bobble blurred and her chin hit her chest. Ace let out a whoop that scared her awake. She jerked her head up so fast that she almost fell out of the chair.

"Jazzy, you've got a bite."

The rod was easing out of her hands as the fish swam away taking the rod and reel with it. She grabbed the rod and held on so tight her knuckles turned white. "What do I do, Ace? I never caught a fish."

"Thought you'd been fishin'."

"Been fishin'. Never caught a thing because I didn't want to learn to clean it. Help me."

He put his arms around her and reeled the fish in, then let it have a few inches of line before he reeled some more. "It's a big boy. Don't know if it's something for supper or a big old gar, but you've got to reel it almost in and if it's still fightin', you got to give it some line to play it out, and then reel it all the way in."

He let her have control of the reel but he kept his arms around her. She reeled the fish up nearly to the boat and looked at its big head swishing back and forth. "Look, Ace, it's not a gar!"

"I can see that. Looks like a big old blue cat to me. Easy now. Don't lose him. That's enough for supper and another meal at home."

"You do it!" she squealed.

"It's your fish. You either catch it or lose it," he said.

"Get that net back there. I'll bring it up close and you catch it in the net," she said.

"You sure you don't want to flip him up in the boat like a real fisherman?"

"No, I want to eat, not play," she said.

Ace grabbed the net, reached down, and scooped

up a five-pound catfish. "Yep, you are definitely bringing home the bacon tonight, Jazzy. And since you are supplying the food, I'll do the cooking."

"Does that mean the date is over and we're going home? I'm not ready to go home, Ace. It's not dark. Can't we fish some more?" she asked.

"Darlin', it means the date is barely starting."

She drew her bare feet up in the chair to keep the fish from flopping on her. "Then we are going to fish some more?"

"Nope, now we go to shore and tie up the boat and I cook," he said.

"Out here?"

"Best fish in the world is what is cooked on the banks of the river," he answered.

He jerked the rope and started the engine again, steered the boat up the river a mile or so and then back to the shore where he hopped out and tied it to an old tree stump. She stepped out over the side into ankle-deep water and looked back at the fish.

"How do we get that thing to shore without losing him?"

"In the net. You carry this blanket and get comfortable up under that willow tree and leave the rest to me. Take a nap and when you wake up, supper will be ready."

"Are you teasing?" she asked.

"No, ma'am. I won't eat all your fish. I'll wake you when it's done. You were played out just before you got that fish. You worked hard all morning. Let me pamper you the rest of today," Ace said.

"That is so sweet," she said.

"That's me. Good-timin', sweet cowboy," he said.

"Yes, you are." She carried the blanket to the shade where she flipped it out and sat down. He made one trip from boat to shore to bring the cooler and a strange-looking black pot; another trip to bring the second blanket and a jug of oil; and a third to tote in the big fish.

Jasmine sat on the blanket and watched. She was tired but she couldn't sleep. Watching him working so hard to pamper her really was so sweet. He started a small fire with twigs that he'd gathered near the site, set up a rigging that the black pot hung from, and poured it full of oil. While that heated he cleaned the fish, rolled the fillets in a cornmeal mixture he brought out of the cooler, and laid them on a paper plate.

She pointed at the cooler. "You got a beer in there?"

He pulled out an icy-cold one and carried it to her. "You were supposed to be sleeping. How can Prince Charming awake Sleeping Beauty if she's wide awake?"

"Honey, this is not a fairy tale," she said.

Ace sat down beside her. "Peaceful, ain't it?"

She nodded and handed him the beer. "Have some. It's peaceful, but it's still hot as the devil's pitchfork. Cold beer tastes really good."

"Not as good as that fish is going to taste," he said.

She slung a leg over him and sat in his lap, drew his face down to hers, and kissed him hard. "Ace, this is a wonderful date."

He chuckled, picked her up, and set her down beside him. It was either that or forget the fish and make love to her. And he'd planned much more before that happened. "Ten minutes and you'll have the best fish you've ever eaten. Oil should be hot enough to float it in that length of time."

"Float it?"

"When it floats, it's done. I'll scoop it up and bring it to you. You never cooked fish?"

She shook her head. "I like it but I don't cook it. Tried a couple of times but it came out soggy."

He dropped the breaded fish into the hot oil and it bubbled. While it cooked, he went out to the boat and brought a big paper bag back to the blanket. From that he produced paper plates, a roll of paper towels, a loaf of bread, and a container of tartar sauce and one of coleslaw.

"Forks?" He pulled plastic ones from the sack.

"You're pretty good at this," she said.

By then the first batch of fish was done. He scooped it up from the hot oil onto a paper-towel-lined plate and carried it to her. He picked up a piece of fish and held it up to her mouth. "Taste."

"Mmmm," she mumbled as she chewed.

It was hot and then it was *hot*. Something in the cornmeal had added spicy hot to the fire hot, giving the fish a wonderful flavor. She wrapped the next piece up in a slice of bread and added tartar sauce, making a fish sandwich.

"Not bad for this time of year. Sometimes it gets muddy-tasting when the river gets low, but the early rains this spring helped keep the river flowing."

"What makes it hot?" she asked.

"Fire." He laughed.

"You know what I'm talking about."

"Good fisherman doesn't share his secrets. Not even with his beautiful wife. Got to have something to keep her coming back for more. If she knows how to cook hot fish, then she wouldn't need him anymore."

"You didn't share with any of those five-star women?" she asked.

"Darlin', I've never cooked fish for another woman. This is usually one of those BFF things that men do while you women do one of your girls'-night-out things. And let me tell you something about that book. It don't matter how many names are in the book. The only one that matters is the name that makes a man burn it."

Jasmine looked into his eyes. She knew him well, and he was not teasing. He was dead serious. "Even if the man didn't want to burn it but was forced into it because his brothers were sitting in the living room and they'd find out the marriage wasn't what it appeared to be on the surface?" she asked.

Ace ran his forefinger down her jawline.

Every nerve ending in her body was suddenly hotter than the fish.

"Darlin', if I'd wanted that book, I wouldn't have let Lucy burn it. I'd have slipped around behind your back and talked her into giving it back to me. Yours was the name that made me ready to get rid of the book. Keep eating. Date night is not over until curfew. Isn't that about midnight when there's kids in the house?"

She giggled. "Sounds about right."

"The sun is beautiful when it sets over the water this time of year. Ever made love on the banks of the river under a willow tree?"

"No, but I betcha I'm about to find out what it's like," she said.

"All in due time, sweetheart. Now we eat, then we skinny-dip, and then we make love and wallow around in that afterglow stuff before we go home."

"You really are a romantic, Ace Riley."

"Of course I am. Good-timin' cowboys are always romantic."

"Egotistical, too!"

"Now, don't be startin' a fight, darlin'. Eat your fish and then we'll take us a nice nap until the moon comes up."

"What's the moon got to do with anything?" she asked.

"It's a surprise."

They ate and he packed the rest of the fish fillets into the chest with the ice.

They napped with her snuggled up against his side, even though they were both sweating hot, and he awoke her with sweet kisses and a nod toward the west where the sun was setting over the river in a whole array of browns, oranges, and deep yellows.

"There is the moon," she said.

"Yes, so it's time to go skinny-dipping in the moonlight. I've been lookin' forward to seeing you all wet in the moonlight again ever since we made love in the creek," he said.

"Are you serious? Is it deep enough to swim?"

"Right here it is, and since I'm pampering you, I get to take those cute little shorts off and untie that thing behind your neck."

She giggled and sat up. "Have at it. I like this pampering business."

They skinny-dipped and he wiggled through the water like a fish, nibbling at her toes and making her squeal when he ran his hands up her inner thighs. Like two innocent children romping in the water, they played and Jasmine loved every minute of it.

And then he carried her back to the blanket. They were wet and naked; cool on the outside, hot as hell on the inside. She sat on her knees with him in front of her with a foot of space between them. He leaned forward and licked a drop of water from her lower lip. She leaned forward and put so much passion into the kiss that he was instantly aroused and ready.

"Slow," he mumbled.

"Slow it is, but closer. I want to feel you."

He opened his arms and she moved into them.

His hands splayed out against her back.

Her fingers tangled into his wet hair and pulled his mouth back down to hers for more wet, wild kisses. Just how slow was slow, anyway, she wondered.

"You are so very lovely in the moonlight," he said.

She didn't even think about that being a line. His tone and his body language said that he was talking to her, not reciting pickup lines.

"You are a wet Greek god," she muttered as she ran her hands over his slick chest.

"Never been called that before," he said. "But I like it."

He covered her mouth with his and tasted the remnants of fish and river water. "I want you so bad, Jasmine."

She wrapped her legs around him and didn't even see the possum stealing bread from the other side of the blanket.

It wasn't sex.

They made sweet, passionate love.

And the climax brought an afterglow that

wrapped itself around them like a golden aura and they slept again in a world where no words were necessary.

When she awoke, he was propped on an elbow staring down at her, his eyes softer and dreamier than they'd ever been before. "You truly are beautiful, Jazzy," he said hoarsely.

"So are you, Ace."

"Beautiful?"

"Handsome, sexy, beautiful, and one very, very hot cowboy."

"Even with a shaved chest?"

"It's only hair. It'll grow back." She ran a hand over his sleek chest and kissed each nipple. "This was the most wonderful date I've ever been on."

"Me too, Jazzy."

Chapter 22

On Tuesday Wil called Jasmine to ask a favor. It was hay season in his world too, but he was caught up until the end of the week and Pearl needed a girls' night out. She was stir-crazy and bone-tired after three weeks of twins.

"And she's weepy. Help me, please," Wil said.

"How about I bring Gemma and Lucy and we watch the boys and let the two of you have dinner and a movie?" Jasmine offered.

"Sounds wonderful, but I want her to have a night away from it all. I've talked to Rye and Raylen and they're willin' to come help me out," Wil answered.

"Okay, I'll call in the troops. What night are you thinking?"

"Tomorrow," Wil said quickly.

"Then tomorrow it is."

"I owe you one, Jasmine. She'll be so excited."

So on Wednesday night, Rye, Wil, and Raylen were left behind at Wil's ranch house with two baby boys, one baby girl, a list of instructions, and the remote control.

Wil kissed Pearl at the door and told her not to worry about anything and to have a good time.

"I can't go, Wil. What if they need me? What if Jesse wants to be rocked at bedtime and you can't get him to sleep? What if one of them gets sick and you have to take him to the hospital? I can't go," Pearl fretted.

Jasmine looped her arm through Pearl's. "Three strong men can take turns rocking Jesse, and if one of the boys gets sick, we're barely thirty minutes away and you can even keep your cell phone on all night, which is against the rules on girls' night out. You are coming with us so stop your worrying."

Wil mouthed a thank-you to Jasmine as she talked Pearl out onto the porch.

Rye kissed Austin and whispered that he was a pro at the father business and he'd take care of everything.

"I've got faith in all of you, but remember the first time I left Rachel?"

"Oh, yeah!" Rye grinned.

Raylen kissed Liz and told her that he'd miss her horribly.

"Will I ever be like that?" she asked.

"Oh, yes, you will," Rye answered for him.

Three women crawled into the front of the club-cab truck and three into the back seat.

Pearl dabbed at a tear.

"Stop it!" Jasmine said. "You'll mess up your makeup, and you need this night out with us."

"We all need it," Liz said. "We need to go bitch

about our husbands and boyfriends not having a spare minute for us since hay season started, right, girls?"

"Amen, sister! And don't fret, Pearl. Wil can always holler at Rye. He's an old hand now at the baby business," Austin said.

"I ain't never been on a girls' night out before. What do we do?" Lucy asked.

"Tonight we are going to a Chinese restaurant over in Wichita Falls because Pearl can't drink, and besides, all of us are married except you and Gemma. So it would not be a good idea to go clubbing," Austin said.

"Dammit!" Pearl said loudly. "I didn't read the marriage license close enough. Did it say, 'I promise to never go clubbing again'?"

"That's the spirit." Jasmine laughed.

Liz leaned forward and tapped Jasmine on the shoulder. "You're the one who got married last. Have the vows changed? Do they say, 'I promise to burn my little black book when I get home and never go clubbing with the girls again'?"

Lucy laughed. "No, they say 'I will give my book to Lucy to burn.' Gemma, you need anything cremated after you get married, you just bring it to me. I've got an old galvanized milk bucket that I use to cremate the remains of the past."

"And do you say a curse on anyone who comes back to tempt the newly wedded husband when you scatter the ashes?" Gemma asked.

"Hell, no!" Liz said. "That's my job. I'm the gypsy carny woman. I can tell your fortunes or put a curse on the cremated remains of a black book. Your choice for five bucks."

Pearl giggled.

Jasmine could have stopped the truck and hugged all the girls for that one giggle.

"I've got a five in my purse. I'll dig it out when we get to the restaurant. I want the curse," Jasmine said.

"Okay, are we only talking about black books?" Gemma asked. "Can you put a curse on things other than black books, Liz?"

"Hey, I might be interested in that five-dollar deal if I ever find a black book in Rye's stuff," Austin said. "But I think we've missed something, Lucy. Did you burn someone's address book or what?"

Lucy smiled. "Last year Pearl brought me her address book and told me to burn it and make sure the ashes were scattered far and near and there wasn't a bit of anything left with a name on it for Wil to find. I got to tell you, girls, it was a thick book. That girl was flat-out a party girl. Wil must be a strong man to tame her down."

"Believe me, he is." Pearl nodded. "I'm just going to make one call to see if everything is all right before we get too far out of town."

Everyone was quiet and the call only lasted a few seconds. "Wil says I can only call once an hour from now on."

"Good man," Jasmine said.

Lucy went on. "Couple of days ago Jasmine had bad luck all day. Started off with her alarm clock not waking her up and didn't get no better. Mr. Murphy, that feller who controls bad luck, poured out an extra supply on her head. Way I figure it is that two people don't get to sit down on a blanket in a pretty little field of yellow daisies with blue birds hoppin' around singin' songs in the trees above them and just flat-out fall in love. If they did, it would be boring as hell. So the good Lord employs Mr. Murphy to come around and throw a little heat at two people who are in love. It toughens them up so that when the big storms come later, like raisin' teenage boys or even boys in their twenties like Blake and Dalton, that those people in love can weather the storm. So Jasmine and Ace got a little bit of heat blown on their cute little world when Jasmine found his little black sin book with all the women's names in it that he's known, kissed, or screwed around with." She went on to tell the rest of the story in her southern accent, tossing in Kentucky wisdom along the way.

Pearl laughed first, and then suddenly giggles echoed off the windows and the ceiling sounding like a playground full of third-grade girls telling secrets.

Lucy wiped her eyes and continued. "And so here I am with this little pile of ashes and two blobs of gold. Would you believe those initials were real gold, not just painted on with gold glitter from the hobby store? Well, they were! They had little thumbtack-lookin' things on the back that pinned them right into that red leather. And they melted into a couple of bubbles of gold. I hated to pour that out in the hog lot. All those women's names and stars burned up into ashes was one thing for the hogs to root around in, but those two little gold shiny things in the wallow... Why, they'd be tellin' all their other hog friends that they had a gold-studded wallow at their place."

Gemma got the hiccups. "Lucy, only you would think of such a thing. You should be a writer."

Lucy held up her hands. "Not me. I can't put two words together on a piece of paper without wearin' out an eraser. Hated English in school. But Momma could make a story out of anything, so I guess I got that from her. Anyway, here I was thinkin' about the hogs gettin' all uppity because they've got gold in their wallow and I just couldn't do it. So when it all cooled down, I fished out the two little nuggets and brought them with me on our girls' night out. Pearl, would you roll down the window just a little bit so I can throw them out?"

Lucy leaned across Pearl when the window was half-open and flung the tiny bit of gold out.

Immediately, red, white, and blue lights flashed behind them and a siren began to blow.

Lucy groaned. "I killed myself and got away with it, and now I have to go to jail because I threw out pure gold? This ain't fair. And besides, it's my first time to get to go on girls' night out, and besides all that, I don't get to be in a wedding. Life sucks, girls!"

"Don't mess with Texas." Gemma pointed straight ahead to a roadside trash can with those words emblazoned on the front.

Jasmine eased over to the shoulder and rolled down her window. The trooper was standing at the side of the truck before the window reached the bottom.

"License and registration, please," he said.

Jasmine fished her license from her purse and Pearl found the registration in the glove box.

"You ladies realize there is a fine for littering?"

"Officer, that was me doin' the litterin'," Lucy said. "You see, I had to burn up Ace Riley's black book this week, and when it was all burned, there was some of the gold from the initials on the front..."

"Wait a minute. Gemma, is that you back there?" he asked.

"It's me, Sammy, and she's tellin' the truth. All she pitched was a tiny little gold nugget so the hogs in Ace's pen wouldn't feel superior to the other hogs in Montague County because they had a gold-studded wallow." Gemma hiccupped.

"Y'all been drinkin'?" Officer Sammy asked.

"Sober as a sinner on Judgment Day," Lucy said.

"You serious, Gemma? This woman really burned Ace's book? Who married Ace Riley? Did you, Gemma?"

"Hell no, Sammy! I did not marry Ace. He's like a brother." Gemma hiccupped again.

Lucy's blue eyes popped wide open. "No, sir! Not me. That would be Jasmine, this woman right here."

"How about that? Aren't you the one who owns the Chicken Fried?" Sammy asked.

"Yes, sir, I am."

Sammy shook his head in disbelief. "And you burned that famous red book?"

Lucy raised her hand slightly. "I did that, sir."

"I know men that would have sold their souls to Lucifer for that book. Hell, I would have mortgaged my truck and tomcat just to get to a copy of it." He chuckled. "Y'all get on your way and don't be litterin' no more. Not even gold from a black book."

"Thank you, sir," Jasmine said.

"And Gemma, if you are lyin' to me about drinkin', at least promise me you won't drive."

"Sammy, darlin', I ain't lyin' but I promise I won't drive tonight." Gemma crossed her heart.

"Okay, you ladies be careful and no more littering." He went back to his patrol car and followed them for a mile before he took the next off-ramp into Wichita Falls.

"I was scared out of my underpants," Lucy said.

"I thought for sure he'd haul me to jail, and what would Tyson do for breakfast tomorrow morning?"

"You are sweet on him, aren't you?" Jasmine asked.

"I could be, but it's too soon to be tellin' just yet. I got to figure out if I'm tryin' to save him from himself or save him for myself before I decide if I'm going to put him in my black sin book. Come to think of it, he'd be the first name in the book. How did you say that star business went, Jasmine?" Lucy said and then cracked up with giggles. "You talk now, Gemma. How did you know that policeman?"

"Well, it's sure not as funny as the hog lot story. I dated him a couple of times. Remember when he followed you to the Halloween party last fall, Liz?"

"Oh, he's that officer. I remember him now."

"Yes, he's the one, but he wasn't *the* one. Liz done promised me a cowboy, not a policeman, by Christmastime, and I'm holding out to see just how strong her voodoo is."

Liz patted her on the leg. "Honey, you just wait. He's being groomed for you right now and he'll be here for Christmas. It was written in the cards."

"Wearin' nothing but a Santa hat and boots, right?" Gemma asked.

"I conjured up the cowboy. You got to ask Santa for the rest of it, and that'll depend on whether you are a good girl or a very good girl," Liz said.

"What if I'm very good at being very bad?" Gemma asked.

"Then I'd say you'll get your cowboy with nothing but a Santa hat and cowboy boots," Liz said.

"Hey, I just realized Bridget ain't here with us," Lucy said.

"She and Frankie are making up after a fight they had earlier this week. She whined for days but yesterday she was all spicy," Jasmine said.

"Takes a while to get some kids raised up, don't it, Pearl?" Lucy asked.

"Girl, if you are talkin' about yourself, I'd say you were pretty easy to raise. You pretty well had things figured out when I got you," Pearl said.

"I'd figured out some of it, but you helped me a lot."

It was well after midnight when Lucy and Jasmine made it home. They both had early mornings so they tiptoed down the hallway. Lucy went to her room and Jasmine eased into the bedroom with intentions of peeling out of her clothing in the dark and being asleep when her head hit the pillow.

"Oh, honey, you are so ready!" a high-pitched voice said.

"Mmmm," Ace mumbled.

The only light in the room was what filtered through the curtains from the full moon, but it didn't take a hundred-watt bulb to see that there was a woman in the bed with Ace or that she was naked as a newborn baby and had her body glued to his back. And where her hand was headed put a jealous streak the size of a football field right down Jasmine's back.

"Dammit!" Jasmine whispered.

Evidently one woman in Texas didn't know that Ace had burned his book and wasn't even smart enough to know that it was hay season and he was too tired for sex. Jasmine flipped on the light, and the woman sat straight up in the bed.

Ace sat straight up and rubbed his eyes. "Jazzy, that felt good. Why are you turning on the lights?"

Then the red-haired woman squealed and jumped out of bed, taking the sheet with her to cover her nakedness. "You are not Blake. What in the hell are you doing in his bed?" Her voice went from a mouse squeak to a full-fledged, all-out screaming fit.

She turned on Jasmine, pointing her finger, and nearly losing the sheet. "And who the hell are you coming into Blake's bedroom this time of night?"

Jasmine bit the inside of her lip to keep from bursting into laughter. "This happens to be my bedroom, lady."

"Blake is married? He didn't tell me he had a wife." The woman gasped and pointed at Ace. "And who are you? If that's his wife, then why are you in her bedroom? Does Blake know you are messing around with his wife?"

Ace had thought Jazzy was making a move on him. She'd kissed him between his shoulder blades and run her hand down his chest to tease him into a full erection, and she whispered that they were going to have hot sex all night. He really thought it was Jazzy and hoped that he had enough energy for at least one round of sex. He'd been so tired the whole past week that he'd barely kissed her. And then the lights came on. Now some redhead was screaming that he was messing around with Blake's wife?

Blake heard the commotion and came running across the hallway. Lucy opened her door and Delilah meandered down the hall and into the bedroom where she jumped on Ace's bed. He grabbed a pillow and covered his nakedness as both Blake and Lucy pushed into the room.

"What is going on in here? I heard screaming and it sounded like… It *was* two women. Ace Riley, you better start explainin'," Lucy said.

The redhead sneezed three times. "Cats! I'm allergic to them. Get that thing out of here."

Blake stared at the woman. "What are you doing in this room? And why are you even here? I told you I couldn't see you until Saturday night."

"You said your room was the one closest to the foyer on the right when we were having phone sex last night, and I thought I'd just surprise you tonight." She sneezed again.

Blake chuckled.

"Don't laugh at me. I went to the bathroom first and then made sure I opened the door to the room closest to the foyer. You did this on purpose, didn't you, Blake? Well, it's not a funny joke, and the joke is on you because I'm out of here." The redhead gathered up clothing off the floor as she talked and stormed down the hall with the sheet dragging behind her.

"I'd say that it's pretty plain what's happened. That woman don't know left from right. We need to get out of Ace and Jasmine's bedroom." Lucy led the way out with Blake right behind her. Just before she closed the door, she turned back to Jasmine and said, "This ain't Ace's fault."

"Hey," Blake yelled at the flow of blue cotton sheeting sweeping the floor ahead of him. "I'm sorry I didn't make it plainer which room was mine, darlin'."

"Don't ever call me again."

Lucy waited until the woman was gone before she turned toward Blake. "Next time you pick up a woman, be sure she's smart enough to know left from right. I'll buy you a little stamp with each word on it next time I get to the hobby store. You can ink the top of her hands and maybe this won't happen again."

"She did know left from right," he said coldly. "I just didn't tell her that it was on her left after she came out of the bathroom and her right before she went to the bathroom."

"Same difference. That could have been a train wreck in there. They're still on fragile ground and they didn't need this right after the red-book thing. Now where'd Delilah go?"

At the mention of her name, Delilah came out of Blake's room, her big fluffy yellow tail high in the air as she walked down the hallway like a queen to her room. Lucy giggled at the sight. It had been a night for sure. She had a lot to tell her momma the next time they talked on the phone. And this would make such a funny story that she could picture her momma wiping at her eyes with her apron tail.

"Good night, Lucy," Blake said.

"Night, Blake," she said and followed Delilah into her bedroom.

Jasmine sat down on the edge of the bed and removed her sandals. "Okay, stud, what have you got to say for yourself? Don't you even know your wife's touch? Someday when you really get married, that could get you in big trouble."

"Really get married? I'm married now. You're even a jealous wife. You said so when you met Mallory." He moved the pillow back to its rightful place, leaving himself without anything to cover his nakedness.

She scanned him from eyebrows to toenails.

"I was asleep and she snuggled up to my back and started to mess with me. I thought it was you," he said. Her green eyes stalling out midway down his body, and a whiff of her perfume was already arousing him again.

"Guess we need a top sheet since your bimbo went home with ours for a souvenir." She padded out into the hall and brought back a folded white sheet. She flipped it out over the bed and it floated down to cover him. She tucked the ends into the bottom of the mattress and then returned to undressing. Jewelry went on the chest of drawers. Khaki shorts and bright-yellow tank top were folded and laid neatly on a chair so she could wear them again the next day.

She was down to panties and bra when Ace started humming the traditional striptease song. She whipped around to find him grinning and the sheet making a tent right below his waist. She put a hand under the edge of her panties and teased him by pulling them down an inch and then back up, gyrating the whole time to the music he supplied. The girls had all talked about making Liz teach them to belly dance. Now she wished she did know how to do real belly dancing or had even watched those pole dancers better on television.

Ace reached out to her. The music stopped when she walked to the edge of the bed and he wrapped both arms around her waist and pulled her across him. Wrapped up in his arms, she forgot all about the redhead and looked up to see his lips on his way to hers.

A quick involuntary flick of the tongue wet her lips in anticipation. Ace's met hers in a clash of pent-up heat. He nibbled her lips, then moved to her eyelids and to the tip of her nose, and she got hotter by the second.

She let her hands roam over his broad back, every inch increasing the heat flowing from her fingertips to fuel the liquid heat in the pit of her stomach. She laced her hands around his neck and brought his lips to hers for a series of lingering wet kisses that sucked all the air from both of them.

"Jazzy, you are so hot and you make me hot as the devil just touching my skin," he rasped when they finally broke away to catch their breath.

He slid her panties down to her feet, peeled them off, and tossed them off the edge of the bed. Then he worked his way back up, tasting, teasing, and loving the way she wiggled and moaned. When he reached her mouth, he lowered his lips to hers and slid inside her at the same time.

"Oh! Oh! Now that feels good," she said.

"Am I forgiven?"

"Nothing to forgive you for this time. That

wasn't your fault, but you will be putting a lock on that door tomorrow morning."

"Yes, ma'am." He grinned.

He teased her until she was ready to scream, then he slowed down and let her cool off, then brought her up to the brink of a climax with intentions of playing the same game twice, but Jasmine had different ideas. She moved in unison with him, hips wiggling and kisses continuing to fuel the fire until he wasn't in control anymore. He exploded and all the air left his lungs again, leaving him gasping for air.

"Yes, yes, yes," she mumbled and buried her face in his neck.

When the alarm went off at five o'clock, she was still wrapped up in his arms so tightly that it took some fancy moving to get untangled. She grabbed a robe and stumbled to the bathroom for a wake-up shower. She'd barely lathered up the shampoo when she saw a shadow behind the shower curtain. She peeked around the edge to fuss at whoever was out there to find Ace with a big grin on his face and the bedsheet wrapped around him toga-style.

"Greek god!" She smiled.

"Good mornin', Mrs. Riley," Ace said as he dropped the sheet and stepped into the shower with her. "We fell asleep without our sweet-nothing time. I missed it."

He picked up a washcloth, poured her fancy vanilla shower gel in the middle, and washed her back.

"Sweet-nothing time?" she asked. The sensation of his hands on her back was almost as good as sex with him.

"You call it afterglow. I call it sweet-nothing time. It's after sex when we talk and cuddle. We were both so tired we fell asleep, and when I woke up, I thought it was still right after sex and it wasn't. So I felt cheated. Lean back and I'll rinse the soap from your hair."

"Mmmm," she moaned when his hands massaged her scalp.

"Like that, do you?"

"Oh, yeah! I'd give you five stars just for that."

"And for the sex?" he asked.

"On a scale of one to five?"

He kissed her neck. A wet kiss on wet skin, so sensual that she forgot what he'd asked.

"Yes."

"Yes, what?" she asked.

"On a scale of one to five." He chuckled.

"Eleven," she said without hesitating.

"Thank you, ma'am. I try to please. Now, sweetheart, it's time to dry your hair and get you ready for the café." He stepped out of the shower, held a towel out for her to step into, and wrapped it around her body, stopping to kiss each breast before he concealed them. He picked up her hair dryer from the vanity. "Sit down right there and I will do it for you this morning."

Warm air and his hands combined to make her scalp tingle. She was glad she was sitting on the vanity seat with a towel around her because every part of her body had goose bumps the size of mountains. And it sure wasn't because the air-conditioning was working so well.

He finished drying her hair, leaned over her shoulder, and kissed her on the cheek. "And now, madam, is there anything else I can do for you before you go to work? It is now five thirty so I suppose a morning romp in the bed or right here on this floor is out of the question?"

She wanted to say *yes* so badly that it hurt, but she had a café to run. And Bridget would be there in twenty minutes, right on time. She shook her head, stood up, dropped the towel, and pressed her body to his. "No, but I'll be thinkin' about it all day."

"Well, I won't," he said.

She cocked her head to one side and looked at him. "What?"

"Thinking about you makes riding a tractor or a four-wheeler or a horse almighty uncomfortable," he explained with one of his world-class grins. "What's it do for you?" He strung steamy hot kisses from her neck to her eyes, stopping along the way to taste her lips.

"Makes me hotter'n a Texas firecracker," she admitted.

"We got this physical stuff down pretty good, don't we?"

"Yes, and now I've only got fifteen minutes to get dressed and go to work." She pushed back and started toward the door.

"Hey, Jazzy," he said.

She turned around.

"I liked that sweet-nothing time almost as good as your afterglow," he said.

"Oh, yeah." She smiled.

Chapter 23

The last time Jasmine had been in church was in Sherman on Mother's Day. Several hundred voices sang and there was a big screen hung high above the preacher's head to project him bigger than life for those who couldn't see him from the back seats. A balcony behind him held the choir in brilliant blue robes, and the special music they presented was beautiful. The preacher stood behind a modern clear podium with a center aisle in front of him. It was where her mother had planned for her to get married with groomsmen and bridesmaids filling up the whole front of the church.

Not even two months ago, she had not planned on getting married until she was forty. That day she had not fallen smack-dab in love with her own husband. And that day she was not living a miserable lie.

It was the first time she'd been in the little white church in Ringgold. A row of pews on the left, one on the right with a center pew between them, and four short pews behind the preacher's antique oak pulpit where the choir members sat. They didn't wear robes and two of the men wore striped overalls. Grandpa O'Donnell grinned and waved at her when Ace led her to the front two pews on the right-hand side where the Rileys sat every Sunday morning. She sat down next to Dolly, who patted her on the shoulder and graced her with a big smile.

Dolly didn't know that she was taking her life in her own hands that bright, hot sunny July morning. There was every chance that lightning could zip through the window without even breaking it and fry everyone on the whole pew, leaving nothing but ashes. God did not take well to blowing the bottom out of any of his commandments, but the one about "Thou shalt not lie" was as big as a longhorn bull sitting on the front pew that morning.

Ace picked up her hand, laced his fingers through hers, and held it on his thigh. How in the hell was she supposed to corral wandering thoughts about wild, passionate sex under a willow tree or licking ice cream off…

Oh, crap! I'm in big trouble! But just touching his hand and his thigh sends my hormones into orbit. Okay, okay, think about anything, even selling the café to Momma. I'm not going to do it but think about that rather than making love to Ace in one of those choir pews. I could sit on his lap and unbutton his shirt real slow-like, kiss his naked little nipples until they perk right up, and he could… Crap! I'm in church and that man upstairs might run out of patience. I do remember my Bible stories about when someone made him mad and he torched the whole city.

Ace squeezed her hand.

The preacher cleared his throat. "'Tis a bright beautiful morning to bring in July. We'd like to welcome Ace's new bride, the former Jasmine King, into our congregation. Many of you will know her as the owner of the Chicken Fried and have eaten her fabulous weekday specials as well as her world-famous chicken-fried steak. She's caused me to commit the sin of gluttony many times in the past year and a half, and the bathroom scales tell God on me."

That brought on the laughter and he waited for it to die down.

"So everyone make her welcome when services are over. We've got a new baby in the back pew. Our love and welcome to Jasper Jefferson, the new son of Grady and Misty Cordova. He joins five older sisters and one older brother. Our young people are the future of our community, and we'll have a fine one if they are raised in church. Now the choir is going to sing to us and then I'll deliver this morning's message."

He sat down on a little short pew back behind the podium. Built for only two people, it was probably designed in the beginning for a couple of deacons to sit on. But the congregation was small enough in Ringgold that the deacons sat with their families in the congregation.

Grandpa O'Donnell was the first one on his feet, and then he extended a hand to help Granny. Their voices could be heard loud and clear as the choir sang "Farther Along."

The words fascinated Jasmine. In the church she had attended all her life over in Sherman, the music tended to go more toward praise and worship songs and alternative Christian music. The lyrics to the old gospel hymn said that farther along they'd know all about it. Grandpa winked at her when he sang that they'd understand it all by and by.

Tears came to her eyes when the song talked about death coming and taking their loved ones and leaving their homes so lonely and drear. Granny O'Donnell's voice was loud and clear when she sang, "Cheer up, my brother, and live in the sunshine."

Jasmine glanced over at Ace to see his Adam's apple working as he swallowed hard two or three times. She'd wondered if he was thinking of his own grandpa. Did they have his funeral right here in this little church? Did those same people, lifelong friends of Grandpa Riley, sing that song during the service?

The preacher took his place behind the podium and opened a well-worn Bible. "John fourteen, verses two through four. Jesus said that he was going to prepare a place for us and that he would come again. Farther along, my friends, we will know exactly what that place looks like and the glory of it all..."

Jasmine tried to listen, but when Ace tensed, she noticed that he was having trouble. She inched over closer to him and laid her head on his shoulder. He tilted his head to touch her hair and the tension eased.

Ace had gone to church sporadically since his grandfather died, usually when the family planned some big thing like Christmas or Easter that started off with church on Sunday morning and followed with dinner out at the ranch.

It was the first time he'd ever taken a woman to church. When Grandpa O'Donnell winked at her, he could almost see his own gramps up there in the choir singing perfect alto. And then Gramps started talking to him as surely as if he'd been sitting on the arm of the pew on Ace's left side.

You done good, boy, gettin' that Jasmine to marry you. I knowed you'd find a good woman and settle down if I made you do it. Man can only run around chasin' skirt tails so long and then he needs to make a home for the next generation. I like her. She's got spunk and she'll do to ride the river with.

"Ride the river" meant that she'd do to keep for a lifetime. Ace flinched, glad that Gramps only came to visit in church and occasionally when he was out riding a four-wheeler and checking on the cattle. And he was really, really glad that Gramps did not come around to talk to him when they were under the willow trees beside the river or in a motel room with a cone of melting ice cream.

Gramps, I've fallen in love with her and I don't know what to do.

He could hear his grandfather's deep chuckle. *I expected that you would. Figured it might take the whole year, but I'm glad it's happenin' right now. What are you goin' to do about it?*

Ace pondered that question for a long time. He didn't have to answer right away. Gramps had been a patient man in life. When he sat beside Ace in church or in the tractor, or behind him on a four-wheeler, and dispensed advice, he didn't mind waiting for Ace to work the question through his mind.

"We don't get the big picture all at once," the preacher was saying when Ace looked up. "Picture it like this. We're standing on the back side of one of those pretty needlepoint things you womenfolks make. It looks pretty tacky back here with all the ends of the threads showing and crossing over each other. We don't get to see the other side of the picture until life is finished and we look back at the whole thing. Then it becomes clear to us like our choir members were singing this morning. Farther along we'll understand why."

Amen, Gramps's voice whispered in Ace's ear. *You know what to do about it. Think about all the tomorrows for the rest of your life and who you want to share them with. It's not one of them floozies in that book that Lucy burned up, or you would have brought her to church with you when I was still living. The woman you stay with is the one you ain't ashamed to take to meet God. Got things to do now of my own, so I'm leavin' before the collection plate is passed around.*

Ace caught himself before he blurted out, "Don't go." He tried to listen to the rest of the sermon but his thoughts went to Jasmine. What was it Gramps told him to look for in a woman just before he died? Ace drew his eyes down and then smiled.

A woman who knows how to fry okra and make a decent chicken-fried steak in the kitchen. One who could sit a horse, run a four-wheeler, or drive a tractor all day and not whine about it. One he wouldn't be ashamed to sit down beside his momma in church. And one that could heat up his bedroom.

Jasmine could do all that and more. She'd been his friend and then his wife and lover, and he'd fallen in love with her. She'd said when she offered to marry him that she did not intend to get involved with any man again for a long, long time.

"Today," the preacher said in a loud voice to wake up anyone sleeping on the back row, "we are having our annual church dinner and anniversary out on the church lawn. The food will be in the fellowship hall and served buffet style. Everyone can help their plates and sit down in the hall as long as we have room, or they can take it out on the lawn and sit on pallets. There are quilts in the nursery for anyone who forgot to bring their own today. We'll have visiting and music from the O'Donnells until everyone is ready to go home or it gets dark, whichever comes first. Brother Cordova, would you lead us in the final prayer?"

"Are we staying for the dinner? I should have brought something," Jasmine whispered to Ace while Brother Cordova thanked God for the day and his beautiful new son.

"Momma brings enough to feed an army. And we'll stay if you want. If not..."

"I want to," Jasmine said.

Chapter 24

Dolly Riley not only brought enough food for an army; she brought enough quilts too. One for each of her boys and one for her and Poppa Riley. The yard would have been full with just Rileys, but everyone scooted their patchwork homes together and made room for the rest of the church family.

Sitting on that quilt with Ace, surrounded by his biological family and their friends, sent Jasmine on a worse guilt trip than thinking about having sex with him on the choir pews. She couldn't explain the feeling, but it was as if she was the sole member of the whole patchwork community who did not belong. And yet, her little six-by-eight-foot world was the second-most visited place on the lawn that day, coming in second to the crowded Cordova quilt with eight children and two adults. New babies and marriages—the future of a community.

She was eating chicken casserole that had crunched potato chips on top and thinking about asking for the recipe when a cute little dark-haired woman sat down next to Ace.

"I can't believe you got married. I didn't even

know it until today. I kept waiting for you to call me to go dancing with you," she said.

"Felicity Cordova, meet my wife, Jasmine," Ace said.

"Glad to meet you. Someday we'll have to talk. I just knew I had this cowboy roped in and ready to propose to me, and then I hear he's married today and from the pulpit of the church. I'm sure enough out of the loop, I tell you."

"Nice to make your acquaintance," Jasmine said. "I figured everyone in the whole area saw our wedding on television."

"Guess I was out with another cowboy tryin' to make this one jealous that night and no one told me. I'm Grady's sister, the one with the new baby. I bet y'all got married about three weeks ago? That was the night I was over at his place watchin' kids when Misty had that false labor. We were watchin' a Disney movie and I didn't see the news." She sighed.

"Move over, girl. I haven't kissed the groom." A petite blonde plopped down between Felicity and Ace and flat-out laid a kiss, tongue and all, on Ace.

He blushed a brilliant red.

Jasmine knotted her hands into fists.

The blonde ended the kiss with an extra little smack on Ace's cheek and looked at Jasmine. "You got a good one, honey. I was anglin' for him, but guess I didn't have the right bait. By the way, I'm

Justina Algood. I live up between Terral and Ryan, but my grandparents come to church here and I always come for the reunion dinner. Be seein' you around, Ace. If you decide you don't want him, kick him north. I'd still take him even though you got to walk down the aisle with him first." Justina went on to the next blanket to talk to Granny and Grandpa O'Donnell.

Felicity left at the same time and went straight to the Cordova quilt where she took the baby from her sister-in-law and carried him from blanket to blanket so everyone could see him.

Raylen and Liz brought their plates to Jasmine and Ace's quilt and settled down to eat. Jasmine hoped that their presence would act like bug spray and keep all of Ace's former women from lighting.

It didn't work.

"Hey, Ace, I saw your wedding on the television. Bad, bad boy! Getting married to someone else when I almost had you convinced we would be good together. Hello, Jasmine, I'm Kylee from down near Bowie. Grew up around here with all these wild cowboys. We'll have to compare notes on this one sometime." Kylee giggled. She didn't stick around long, heading next to the Cordova place.

"Tat stamps," Liz whispered.

"What?" Ace asked.

"Inside joke between BFFs," Liz said.

"Don't even ask," Raylen said between bites. "It would take a rocket scientist to understand what goes on between those two."

Jasmine shook her head slowly. "Is there a woman in all of Montague County that you haven't dated? I mean, here we are in a town of one hundred at a church picnic, and in the first fifteen minutes there's already been three who thought they would marry you, including one that kissed you right in front of me."

"Raylen, help me out here?" Ace said.

"Sorry, buddy. I can't think of any." Raylen laughed.

"I didn't date Liz or Gemma or Colleen. There's three right there," Ace said.

"Raylen already had Liz scoped out when you met her. Gemma and Colleen are like your sisters. Your words when we first met, not mine. Those three don't count."

"Pearl. She came to the ranch with Colleen way back before she ever knew Wil, and I didn't date her," he said.

"Well, praise God and pass the biscuits," Jasmine quipped one of her grandmother's favorite sayings. She drew her feet up under her and tucked the tail of her white eyelet sundress under her thighs to keep the south wind from whipping it up.

Liz tapped her on the arm. "I haven't heard that expression in years. My grandpa, the one who lives out in west Texas, says it."

"It was one of my granny's favorite adages. It made me think about her. She lives south of Sherman in Whitewright, a little bitty town where my momma grew up."

"I thought about my grandpa this morning in church," Ace admitted. Anything to get the conversation away from all the women he'd dated. "I swear Gramps was sitting on the arm of the pew right beside me. He was wearing his Sunday overalls just like Grandpa O'Donnell and whispering in my ear the whole time the preacher was talking."

Liz tucked the tail of one of her many multicolored tiered skirts around her thighs and nodded. "Sometimes my momma and aunt do that to me. Raylen thinks I'm crazy when I argue with them. All he hears is one side of the conversation."

"And it sounds kind of crazy when I don't know what they're saying to her on the other end. What did Gramps Riley say to you?" Raylen asked.

Ace stuttered and stammered before he could figure out an answer. "Basically the same things he's said forever. 'A ranch needs a woman.'"

"It does," Liz agreed.

"Yes, ma'am." Jasmine nodded toward Liz.

Liz finished off the last two bites of her dessert and touched Raylen on the thigh. "Granny is motioning to us. She's got our fiddles on the chairs and ready. We must be up first. What are we doing first?"

He stood up and extended his hand to help her. "'Farther Along' like they sang this morning or 'Amazing Grace'?"

"Whatever you want, Raylen. I'll follow your lead."

"If you do, it'll be the first time. Why couldn't we get one of those sweet little women who'd jump to do our bidding?" Raylen asked Ace.

"Sorry, but you don't get second chances. You got *me*. Be satisfied or be dead." Liz smiled sweetly.

"Tougher than nails." Raylen grinned as he led her toward the fiddles.

Ace turned to Jasmine. "How about you? Should I be *satisfied or be dead*?"

Vibes danced.

Everything sparkled.

Jasmine sweated.

"Well?" Ace pressed.

She wiped the moisture from her forehead with a paper napkin with fireworks printed on it. Mercy, how did she ever get in such a pickle and where were his old girlfriends when she needed them?

"All depends," she stalled.

"On?"

"On where we are in one year. I promised not to hold you past that."

"And if I release you from that promise?"

What was he saying? She wished whatever it

was he'd just spit it out and quit dancing around the patchwork.

"Let's just put it this way. I agree with Liz. My husband isn't going to be getting second chances. So don't be makin' any promises you don't plan on keepin'," she said.

"And that means?" Ace asked.

"Don't get caught up in the moment and regret it later," she said bluntly.

Ace leaned on his hand, barely an inch from Jasmine's. His little finger edged over and locked with hers, and that crazy feeling in the pit of his stomach said that the only thing he would regret was losing her. He simply had to make her feel the same way, and all his old tricks of the trade wouldn't work.

More than a ranch was riding on the line. His heart and soul were both lying out there in the ante pile.

Just his little finger touching hers had Jasmine ready to drag him back into the church to the choir pews and do wicked things to his body. But somehow while two fiddles whined away to "Amazing Grace," she was downright afraid to tempt the wrath of the Almighty.

She looked up to see Dolly coming toward her, holding a little blue bundle. When she reached Jasmine, she plunked the baby boy down in her arms.

"It's your turn. You've been waiting patiently for everyone else since you feel new here, but I brought him to you. Enjoy him while you can because there's lots of others who can't wait to get their dose of baby-holding today."

"Hey, Dolly, the kids are getting up a softball game over on the back side of the church. Would you unlock the room where the balls and bats are kept in the fellowship hall?" Adam yelled across the lawn at her.

Dolly headed in that direction with a motion toward Maddie O'Donnell to go with her. "You've got keys, right? I left mine at home."

"In my purse. Thought the kids might want to play ball. I'll get them out of the truck and meet you in the hall," Maddie said.

Jasmine undid the cotton blanket and looked at the plump little boy in her lap. His hair was jet-black, his eyes so deep that they were almost black and blinking at her as if deciding whether to cry or not. His mother had dressed him in a one-piece knit outfit that left both arms and legs bare and Jasmine counted toes and fingers.

Tick! Tock! Dammit! That is the first time I've ever heard the biological clock. I didn't even hear it when I held Jesse and John, so what makes the difference now? His name is Jasper... All J names, so that can't be the catalyst.

"Pretty cute. Reminds me of Creed, Dalton, and

Tyler when they were born. They looked a lot like that," Ace said.

"You ever want any of these?" Jasmine asked.

Jasper wrapped his tiny fingers around her forefinger, and the clock rattled so loudly in her ear that she could scarcely hear anything else.

"Oh, yeah! Bunch of them. I liked growing up in a big family. My older brothers have stopped at two or three each. I'd like five or six."

Jasmine swallowed hard. Raising five or six kids and running a café, plus helping with the ranch? She'd have to be Wonder Woman.

Hey, hormonal woman. He didn't say he wanted five or six with you, so don't be planning the future right now.

She sighed. *But I want a big family too. I always wanted a sibling, and Pearl filled that spot in my life really well. But I want my kids to have blood-kin brothers and sisters to grow up with. To eat breakfast with in the mornings, to fight over who gets the last pancake.*

Ace reached over and stuck his finger in Jasper's other hand. The baby latched onto it. "Look at that! He's got a hold on my finger like it was the rope around a bull. Betcha he's going to be a rider like his daddy."

"Oh?"

"Oh, yeah. Grady makes a little money on the side riding in the local rodeos."

"My sons are not doing something that dangerous," Jasmine said.

"Well, they aren't going to take ballet lessons," Ace told her.

"If they want to, they can. And if they want to paint pretty pictures or write books they can do that too," she argued. "Ain't that right, Jasper? You might have strong hands and legs so you can dance or hold a paintbrush."

Nothing but pure old fear that he wanted his children with someone who knew all about bull riding made her argue with Ace. If they argued, she'd get mad and then the feeling that she wanted babies with Ace would vanish, leaving her with a café and determination that she did not want a commitment with anyone.

"My turn." Holly, Ace's sister-in-law, squatted before them and held out her hands.

Reluctantly, Jasmine handed over Jasper and Holly stood up, crooning at him as she carried him toward the other two sisters-in-law, who were sharing a quilt under a different shade tree.

"So what do you think, Mrs. Riley, five or six boys?" Ace tested the waters.

"What do you think, Mr. Riley, five or six daughters?"

Ace shuddered. "Rileys throw boys."

"Tony got a girl unless he and Holly decided to name that last boy Melanie and dress her up like a girl."

"Melanie is a girl, believe me." Ace laughed. "But that's the only one."

"You're the odd child. Blond hair, pretty blue eyes. Maybe that means you won't be like the other Riley men and you'll have five daughters. Just think, Ace. Five girls to worry about when they're sixteen and driving to Bowie on Saturday night and meeting cowboys just like you were at eighteen or nineteen. There are at least two motels down there, and those boys will wear their jeans just right and their boots will be polished and they'll have a little red book with their initials on it to write stars in..."

Ace put his fingers on her lips. "Just thinkin' about that puts a vise grip around my heart."

Jasmine giggled. "Exactly."

Lucy's voice rang out from the parking lot. "Jasmine."

Jasmine turned and saw her coming toward them. "Hey, Lucy, come on over here and have a seat. Have you eaten?"

Lucy shook her head. "Just got back from the meeting in Wichita Falls. Didn't have time for lunch before I left. Had a few cookies and some coffee there, though."

"There's lots of food left. You can eat here, and besides, I want you to try this new chicken casserole that has potato chips crunched up on top of it if there's any left. Ace, I'm taking Lucy inside for some food. Do not be kissin' on the women," Jasmine teased.

Lucy shot him a look. "What was that all about? I thought I cremated those women and took care of their remains."

"One sat right down there and kissed him smack on the lips. Got him to thinkin' about havin' five or six little girls to primp for church on Sunday morning," Jasmine tattled.

"Where is the hussy?" Lucy looked around.

"She kissed and ran," Jasmine said.

"And I was not thinkin' about daughters. I was thinkin' about sons."

Lucy shook a finger at him. "Something wrong with us girls?"

Ace chuckled. "I'm not even goin' there. Y'all go on and find that casserole. I haven't seen Creed all week or my older three brothers since the day after we got married other than to nod at them in church this morning. I'll catch up with y'all later."

The fellowship hall was empty, but there was still plenty of food on the tables so Jasmine handed Lucy a plate and waited for her to load it up. She started to lead the way back outside when Lucy set her plate on one of the tables and sat down.

"I want to talk, just me and you, not out there with so many people," she said.

Jasmine sat down across from her. "Okay, shoot. Just please don't tell me you are leaving the ranch."

"Oh, no! I love the ranch even more than I liked the motel. Never thought I'd say that but I do. I like the solitude and the job and all of it. I've come a long way this past year and a half, Jasmine."

"That's an understatement." Jasmine smiled.

"I'm in love with Tyson," Lucy blurted out.

Jasmine was struck absolutely speechless.

"But you've only known him a couple of weeks," Jasmine stammered.

"I didn't say I was going to do anything about it tomorrow. I'm a patient woman. He loves me too, but he doesn't know it yet."

Jasmine finally found her voice, but it came out in a whisper. "How do you know?"

Lucy shrugged. "Same way you know that you love Ace. It's just there. A spark in the air when he walks in the room. I never had it with Cleet or with that Luke fellow I dated. Never would have believed it existed, not even when Pearl fell in love with Wil. But it's there and I want to know if that's going to be a problem on the ranch."

"Hell, no!" Jasmine said.

"Good. This is some really good chicken casserole. I can taste a touch of mayonnaise and potato chips. We got to get this recipe. The guys will love it with hot rolls and corn on the cob."

"Lucy, how do you plan to tell Tyson how you feel?" Jasmine asked.

"Same way you'll tell Ace. When the time is right and it comes up, I'll just lay it out there on the line for him. We've talked about things, Jasmine. Not love things, but things that he wouldn't want me to repeat. Things that happened over in the war that made him go inside himself. There's a light in his eyes these past few days. It's not a big light like one of the floodlights out back of the bunkhouse. It's a little flicker like a candlelight. But even a tiny light dispels some of the darkness, don't you think?"

"Yes, it does, Lucy. But what if you miss the time and the moment is gone forever?" Jasmine asked.

"Not me. I know Tyson. I can see into his soul when I look in his eyes, like you can Ace's, and when he says something that gives me an opening I will take it. When his hand brushes against mine at the supper table I catch plumb on fire. And when his leg touches mine under the table, it's about all I can do to keep from kissin' him. Wait a minute! You aren't askin' me about not speakin' up. You are talkin' to yourself. How many times have you let the opportunity get a mile down the road and didn't chase it down?" Lucy asked.

Jasmine cocked her head to one side and frowned.

"I'll put it another way. How many times have you already been in that moment and didn't speak up?" Lucy asked.

"Too many," Jasmine admitted.

Lucy dropped a piece of salad with red dressing on her white knit shirt. "Well, crap!" She looked up at the ceiling. "Pardon me, Lord. I been livin' around menfolks for nearly a month and I say too many bad words. Got any ginger ale back there?"

Jasmine pushed the big bottles of soda pop around until she found one of 7-Up and brought it to Lucy. She poured some in a cup, dipped a napkin in it, and had the stain out in no time.

Lucy went on. "Well, don't let the next one slip by you because you never know when the door will get shut and locked, and you don't get no more. So I been thinkin' that when the time comes, maybe me and Tyson could get a trailer and put it on the ranch and keep working at our jobs there?"

Jasmine's eyes popped open so wide that they hurt. "You haven't even kissed him and you are ready to move in with him?"

"The heart will have what the heart wants, but I'm preachin' to the choir, ain't I? Great dinner. I'm goin' on home now and see what's happenin' on the ranch. Thinkin' about makin' an apple cinnamon cake for tomorrow's lunch."

"Well, cooking all afternoon will put you out in the bunkhouse for sure, and since Tyson will be there, I'd say you're chasing toward opportunity, not after it when it's a mile down the road." Jasmine smiled.

"You got it. And if you'd keep Dalton and Blake out here for a while, that would be good too. I swear, raisin' them grown men is tougher than raisin' little boys, and I got the living room all straightened up in case the opportunity to take Tyson out there comes up." Lucy giggled.

"Yes, ma'am," Jasmine said. She sat in the fellowship hall for a long time weighing what Lucy had said. The woman had come to Texas the year before, abused, bruised, and not trusting a single soul. She'd certainly learned to speak her mind. Maybe that's what happened when an abused woman found her confidence. But what about a woman who'd never been abused? How did she stand right up to the man she loved and say the words?

"Jazzy?" Ace said so close behind her that his warm breath made chill bumps on her arms. Yep, Lucy was right; the chemistry was there between them.

She looked up and he bent down and kissed her upside down, his tongue teasing her upper lip.

"I was worried about you. When I came in, you looked sad," he said.

"Lucy is in love with Tyson," she whispered.

Ace sat down in the chair beside her and threw an arm around her shoulders. "And?"

"She was afraid it would be a problem on the ranch."

"Don't think so," Ace said.

"That's what I told her."

"Does he know?"

Jasmine shook her head. "She says she's patient and she'll wait until he figures it out."

"Smart woman."

"I'm in love with you," Jasmine blurted out.

Ace's heart stopped and he could not speak.

"You don't have to say anything. It doesn't have to change anything. If I was in love with anyone else, I'd tell you because you are my friend, but I'm not in love with anyone else. I've loved you as a friend for a long, long time, but this is more and it's deeper and..."

He picked her up from the chair and set her firmly in his lap and locked eyes with hers. "Shhhh." He laid a finger on her full lips and traced them gently with his forefinger.

The tingles that raced all over her body were almost more than she could bear.

Time stood perfectly still.

Ace didn't even blink as he opened up his soul through his sexy blue eyes and let her inside his heart. He cupped her chin with his hand and gently nibbled on her lip before kissing her with more passion and heat than she'd ever known. It was enough to bring tears to her eyes, and she was sure he was about to say that he loved her as a friend, even as a lover, but not the way that she did him.

When he broke the kiss, he pulled her close to his chest, her cheek resting on his racing heart, and whispered right into her ear, "I love you, Jazzy. I've loved you for a long time as the only real gal pal I ever had. But I fell in love with you when the preacher told me I could kiss my wife. I was afraid to tell you because you said you didn't want to get involved with anyone in a committed relationship."

"Guess I was wrong." She looked up into those mesmerizing eyes again. "I love you like I've never loved anyone in my life."

"Looks like Grandpa was right," Ace said.

"About what?"

"Everything."

His lips found hers and the world disappeared again. They were floating somewhere high above the earth on clouds, and nothing that went on below them mattered anymore.

Chapter 25

Ace's job was to keep the hot dogs turning so they wouldn't burn, to grill them to a perfect plump brown color, and then put them on the platter. Garrett was the hamburger cook, and Justin took care of the steaks. Tony, the gourmet, was in charge of the enormous shrimp and fish fillets. Four grills sending out delicious scents prepared everyone's stomachs for the upcoming feast.

Jasmine was in the house with the other four Mrs. Rileys. Megan, Garrett's wife; Mary Sue, Justin's wife; Holly, Tony's wife; and Dolly. They were hustling about putting the finishing touches on a Crock-Pot of gumbo, potato salad, baked beans, and all the side dishes that went with the meat the men were grilling.

"I love this holiday," Dolly said. "And just so you know, Jasmine, since this is your first Independence Day in our family, I always do Thanksgiving and this holiday. Easter is hit-or-miss. The Sunday before Christmas is here so that the married kids can have their own holiday at home. I don't think it's fair for kids to open presents and then have to leave them to go to their grandma's house. Usually

Adam and I make the rounds on Christmas, seeing everyone for an hour or so and having dinner wherever we land at that time of day."

"So Thanksgiving and July Fourth it is," Jasmine said. Thanksgiving she would still be married. She didn't know about next July. Sunday after the church picnic when she and Ace declared their love for the first time, she'd figured they'd have a night of sweet but passionate love.

Not so.

He'd gone straight to his office and she'd been asleep when he came to bed. When her alarm went off the next morning, she found a note on his pillow that said he was up early to go to a cattle sale in Chico. He'd see her at supper. Strange thing was that he had not mentioned a sale. She mulled it over until he came into the café that afternoon, all smiles and kisses, telling her about buying five new heifers with calves to add to the ranch stock.

Monday night she'd gotten home just as Lucy called supper. She and Ace had sat on the porch until long after dark talking about changes he'd like to make to the ranch. A new fence around the back forty where he'd like to keep the longhorns away from the Angus, but first he needed to bulldoze the mesquite so their horns wouldn't get caught in the brush. When they went inside, Monday night wrestling was on television and Dalton and Blake threw a fit for him to watch it with them. He'd kissed her and whispered "Love you, darlin'" and plopped down in the recliner to yell for his favorite wrestler. She showered and went to bed with a book, fell asleep with the light still on, and dreamed of him telling her that he'd been caught up in the moment and shouldn't have told her that he'd fallen in love with her.

Tuesday he showed up at the café in the middle of the morning with a bouquet of wildflowers in a mason jar. "I was walking a fence line and thought you might like them," he'd said with a big sexy grin.

That night he and all the guys worked until past dark on the new fence and Lucy held supper until nine o'clock. They moaned and groaned as they ate, but after a shower, Dalton and Blake talked him into watching a rerun of *NCIS* on television. She snuggled in next to him and when that episode ended, they started talking about the longhorns they wanted to raise and how they'd start some rodeo stock like Rye handled. Blake got out a pencil and paper, and they were drawing up all kinds of plans when she went to sleep.

She'd been aware of him carrying her to the bedroom and remembered that she had glanced at the clock to see that it was midnight. She had awakened that morning at eight o'clock and sat straight up in bed.

He put a cup of coffee in her hands and she noticed he was fully dressed. "We're supposed to be over at Momma's and Daddy's place at ten. Lucy made a late breakfast. You ready?"

"July Fourth," she remembered.

"Momma's special holiday. That and Thanksgiving is when she calls all her chickens home for the day." He sat down on the edge of the bed and cupped her chin in his hand, landed a kiss on her lips that set her whole body to humming, and then took off like he'd been shot with an excuse that he had to get a case of beer into the cooler.

And now she was standing in the kitchen, stealing glances of her handsome husband out there playing cook with his brothers and listening to the women gossip. And wondering what the hell was going on in her life.

She wished Lucy had come with her, but she and all the hired help said they'd rather stay at the Deuce and have their own holiday. Sam was going to cook steaks; Lucy had made side dishes and a special strawberry dessert; and Jasmine would bet dollars to fresh cow patties that Tyson liked strawberries.

Maybe this was what happened when two people really fell in love. Maybe they reverted back to the best friend status and sex was just something for Saturday night. If so, then she wished to hell Saturday night wasn't so far away. Hell, she might redo the whole calendar in his office and put Saturday on every single day. As of right now there would be no more Mondays, Tuesdays,

Wednesdays, Thursdays, or Fridays. Only Saturdays and Sunday, for him to rest up and get ready for another week of nothing but Saturday nights.

Dolly touched Jasmine on the arm and she jumped.

"You were a million miles away," Dolly said.

"Betcha she was thinkin' about that baby boy she was holding Sunday," Holly teased.

"Betcha she was thinkin' about how much fun it would be to make one of those baby boys," Megan said.

"Girls! Those are my sons you are talking about." Dolly laughed.

"Momma Riley, those are your sons, but they are our husbands and they're all sexy cowboys," Mary Sue said.

"So have you and Ace discussed children? I know you've only been married a few weeks but you looked so good holding that baby," Dolly asked.

"Briefly on Sunday. He said he wants five or six boys, which would just tickle my father to death. Momma doesn't care if grandbabies come in pink or blue, but I think Daddy would like boys. I told Ace that he could wind up with five girls."

And he hasn't had sex with me since. Son of a bitch! Is that what's going on?

"Not in the Riley family, darlin'. They throw boys. If I thought I'd have a daughter, I'd try one more time, even if I am forty," Megan said. "But after three boys, I admit defeat. I'd just get another Blake like you, Momma, and believe me, I'm not as strong a woman as you are."

"I'm a quitter too. I'd like a girl but I'm afraid I'd just get more boys," Mary Sue said.

Holly pointed toward the ceiling. "Melanie came with a price. I promised I'd be happy with a daughter no matter what. I didn't know I was agreeing to red hair that's a nightmare to fix for school every morning and a prissy little thing that doesn't know if she wants to wear cowboy boots or satin slippers."

Ace swaggered through the back door and over to Jasmine where he hugged her up close to his side. "Dogs are ready. Garrett is taking the steaks up right now, and Justin and Tony said to tell you their part of dinner will be ready by the time you get the food out to the table. Want me to call in the kids to help carry?"

"I'll do it." Dolly went to the back door and rang the old dinner bell hanging from the porch and yelled, "All seven grandsons and Melanie, y'all come help tote things out to the picnic tables."

It looked like a stampede with Melanie in the lead, but Landon, with his long legs, quickly overtook his younger cousin, swooped her up in his arms, and carried her the rest of the way. When they hit the back door, they split into groups and headed toward the kitchen sink and the bathrooms to wash up and were back in front of Dolly in record time.

Two trips for each of them and the tables were ready. Ace led Jasmine outside, his arm still thrown around her shoulders, and motioned for her to sit by him on one side of the picnic table. Creed sat on Ace's other side, and Blake pushed in beside Jasmine, crowding them so that Jasmine and Ace were plastered together.

Heat rises. That's a given fact. But when it doesn't have room to rise, it has to settle for burning up whatever is right there in its pathway. So the heat between them spread to places that it shouldn't be with a whole family gathered around them and grace being said.

Jasmine vowed right then that she was going to seduce him as soon as they got home that night. Ace was the only one who could put out the fire about to consume her. She reached under the table and ran a hand up his thigh. As tense as his leg was, there was no doubt his mind sure wasn't on the scrumptious food in front of them or the grace either.

Oh, yes! Tonight was ending the sexual drought. Jasmine was going to get satisfaction if it caused a snowstorm the next morning right there in Texas on July 5th.

Chapter 26

THE BATTLE BEGAN WHEN SHE SQUEEZED HIS thigh.

He retaliated by leaning over and whispering, "Higher, darlin'."

She blushed.

Chalk one up for Ace.

After dinner Adam declared he and Garrett were the team captains that year for the baseball game out in the pasture behind the backyard fence. Teams would be chosen by dropping everyone's name into a hat and the two captains would take turns drawing.

"So anyone who wants to play, write your name on one of these papers," he said.

Megan spoke up to tell them that today she was a cheerleader so she would yell for Poppa Adam's team. Mary Sue said she was sitting out this year because she'd hurt her ankle that week, and Megan said she had just gotten over a summer cold so she'd cheer from the sidelines for Garrett's team. Dolly told Landon to go bring four folding lawn chairs out to the pasture.

"I'll put your name in the hat while you are gone," she said.

Landon nodded and jogged toward the garage.

Ace looked over at Jasmine. "You playing, Jazzy?"

"What kind of ball are we talkin' about?" she whispered as she brushed his curls back from his forehead.

He blushed ever so slightly, but it was a blush.

Chalk one up for Jasmine.

"Baseball, darlin'," he said hoarsely.

"Of course I'm playin'. My team is going to whip yours," she announced loudly.

Names went into Garrett's straw hat.

"What if we're on the same team?" Ace asked.

"Then I'll get more home runs than you do," she said.

Blake slapped Ace on the back. "Sounds like she's throwing down the gauntlet, Brother."

"Sounds like she's making threats to me," Dalton said.

"What are we bettin'?" Ace looked right at her.

"If I win, I get to tell you later." She kept the rising fire from her face so she didn't have to give up her hard-earned point.

"And if I win?" Ace kissed her right there in front of his mother, father, and all his family. Tongue and all.

"Whatever you want." She wrapped her arms around his neck and pressed her body against his. All was fair in love, war, and seduction. Right?

Blake wiped at his forehead and whistled through

his teeth. "I hope I'm on your team, Brother. With that kind of bet, you're going to be playin' your best game today."

When all the names were drawn, Jasmine was on Adam's side and Ace was on his brother's team. She grabbed his hand as they started out to the pasture and tucked her thumb inside next to his palm where she made lazy circles.

"You are cheatin'," he said.

"What?" She acted all innocent.

"You know that drives me crazy. Anytime you touch me, I get hot as hell. You are already cheatin'. Just remember I can play the same way," he said.

"But I'm goin' to win no matter what happens," she said.

"We'll see about that."

Blake tossed a coin in the air, caught it, and slapped it on the back of his hand. "Tails. Daddy, your team is up first. Momma, you ready to ump?"

Dolly set her chair down on a slight rise and nodded. "Let the game begin. I call 'em the way I see 'em, and anybody has a beef with that they might as well know right now that it don't do you a bit of good to argue with the momma."

Ace played second base. Landon was on first and Garrett on third.

Jasmine was up to bat and she knocked it out into right field on the first swing. She dropped the bat and cleared first while Dalton was still trying to scoop up the ball, so she took off for second. She didn't slow down but rounded second and Ace reached out and squeezed her butt cheek as she went past him. She turned back to see the ball coming right for his glove. It was either go back or take a chance on a long slide. She came to a halt and barely made it back to second when Ace reached out and grabbed the ball right out of the air.

"Safe!" Dolly called.

"You cheated," Jasmine gasped with her hands on her knees.

"All's fair, darlin'." Ace laughed.

Landon's sixteen-year-old brother, Mark, came up to bat. He swung twice and missed with his younger brother, Luke, who was pitching for the other team, tormenting him every time. When Luke sent his best speedball flying the next time, Mark's bat made a solid connection. He let go of the bat and took off for first and didn't even slow down.

Jasmine ran for third with him right behind her and then on into home. Mark stopped on third and Megan jumped up and down, squealing that her team made a point. Adam blew a kiss at his granddaughter.

When Garrett's team went up to bat, Adam served as pitcher and Jasmine went to second base. Ace was first up to bat. He swung wide twice and the third time his bat connected, but the ball went straight up instead of out in the field. He figured Mark would catch it on first base so he jogged in that direction without a thought of making it. But the ball hit a mesquite tree limb on its way down and bounced out into left field. Ace picked up speed while Luke went running for the rolling ball.

He was grinning when he neared second base, thinking that there wasn't a thing Jasmine could do to him to slow him down, but he was wrong. The minute his toe touched the base, she flashed him. Jerked up that cute little halter top and gave him a quick peek at a set of beautiful breasts. He got tangled up in his own feet and barely got control when the ball flew over his head. Jasmine reached up and grabbed it and threw it to third base. Ace made it back to second seconds before the third baseman put it back in her glove.

"Safe!" Dolly called out.

"Momma, she cheated," Ace yelled.

"Safe!" Dolly said again.

"I'll take you down for this, girl," Ace said.

"I'll look forward to it," she told him.

When the game ended, Ace had made six points, and Jasmine had five. Ace had gotten three players out; Jasmine had gotten four out. Dolly called it a tie and announced that neither had won the bet so they were right back at square one.

The older Rileys grabbed a beer and melted into lawn chairs or stretched out on quilts under the shade trees in the backyard. Jasmine downed half a bottle of cold Coors and collapsed on a quilt. Ace did the same, propping up on one elbow so he could look at her. Her skin was slick with sweat and her eyes were shut, lashes fanning out on her cheekbones. Thinking about kissing her eyes open and making love to her all sweaty began to arouse him, so he forced his thoughts in another direction.

"You play softball in high school?"

"Yep."

"You play a pretty mean game even without the flashing. Lord, you about gave me a heart attack when I looked up and saw those boobs," he said softly.

"Good! When you grabbed my butt, my brain went stone-cold dead and I almost jumped your bones right there. Want to sneak off to the barn and let me do it now?"

He stuttered and looked around to see if anyone was paying attention to their conversation. "You are a tease. Know what happens to a tease?"

"They get their bones jumped?" She opened her eyes and locked gazes with him.

"No, they go to bed frustrated," he said.

The younger members of the Riley clan had popped open soft drinks or else had iced sweet tea, and as soon as it was gone, boredom set in. They brought out dominoes and Monopoly and set up the games on two of the picnic tables.

"Which one? Bet I could whip you at either," Ace challenged.

"I'm sleepy. I'm going to lie right here on this quilt and take a nap. You go on and whip someone else." Jasmine yawned.

He tucked a strand of hair back behind her ear and then traced the outline of her ear with the tip of his finger. It took all the willpower she could muster to keep from dragging him off to that hayloft.

"You are a tease," she countered.

"Yep, and I'll go to bed frustrated, right?"

"Not my idea at all, darlin'."

"I'm going to go play dominoes with Daddy and Megan."

"Have fun." She yawned again and shut her eyes.

With every nerve wound so tight that she couldn't think of anything but sex, she didn't think she'd fall asleep, but she did, and the sun was setting when Ace awoke her with a kiss.

"Time to wake up, Sleeping Beauty," he whispered.

She opened her eyes to see all seven Riley grandsons looking down at her and giggled. "I'm not Sleeping Beauty. I'm Snow White because I see the seven dwarfs."

"Yep." Landon smiled. "I'm Doc since I'm the oldest, and Mark is Grumpy."

"Well, Luke is Sneezy since he's allergic to everything, and Kyle has to be Happy. That boy is laughing all the time," Mark said.

"What about me?" Bart got into the game.

"You are Sleepy," Landon said.

"Why?"

"Because of your droopy eyes."

"Momma says the girls are going to like them someday," Bart said.

Jasmine sat up. "She's right. They'll tell you that you have bedroom eyes."

"Yuk," Bart said and took off in the opposite direction.

"Guess that leaves me to be Bashful," Hunter said.

"That's a big lie." Garvin laughed. His voice was at that crackle stage that came out in a high squeak part of the time and in a low growl the other. "And that only leaves Dopey for me, and I'm not dopey."

"I don't remember the dwarfs fighting in the fairy tale. What is happening now?" Jasmine asked.

"Supper and then fireworks out by the pond. Poppa already has everything set up, even the chairs," Hunter said. "He and Uncle Garrett take the boat out in the middle of the pond and set them off for us."

Jasmine raised her arms and stretched like a long, muscular wildcat. Just those movements about broke the vow Ace had made to himself after they'd made love the last time. Making it until Saturday night was going to kill him graveyard dead for sure.

Dolly brought out cold cuts and leftovers for

supper and served them buffet style in the dining room. Everyone was free to take their plates wherever they wanted. Jasmine carried hers outside to the pallet and Ace followed.

"Is Prince Charming aware that after he wakes the princess, they live happy ever after?" She dipped a hot dog in mustard and bit off the end.

"He is," Ace said. "Momma got boys, but we had to listen to her read a few girl books when we were little."

"So?" Jasmine swallowed and waited.

"You believe in happy ever after?"

She nodded. "I didn't but I'm willing to admit I believe in the possibility. I don't think it's all wine and roses. I think there are speed bumps along the way." She remembered telling Liz that she had to get over the speed bumps to get to her destination, which was Raylen.

"Speed bumps? Well, Jazzy, I'm working on a speed bump right now. Think you can bear with me until Saturday night?"

"What's that got to do with anything?"

"It's a test I set up for myself. I drive very fast and I have to slow down or else I'm going to crash and burn. I love you. I'm in love with you, but I'm not going to make love to you until I get over this bump."

"Why?" she asked.

"It's like this, Jazzy. I've loved you as my best

friend for a long time. Now I'm in love with you but I've just got to prove to myself that it's the real thing and not a sex infatuation. It's just until Saturday night, darlin'. Three more days. Will you wait until Saturday night?"

"It won't be easy," she muttered.

"No, it won't. It will be pure old hell," he said.

"I'll wait." She nodded.

He kissed her on top of her head. "Thank you."

Chapter 27

Thursday, after work at the café, Jasmine drove a hay truck, had a supper of sandwiches that Lucy brought to the field, and kept driving until midnight. Rain was forecast for the next day and the small bales of hay would be ruined if they got wet, so it was either get them into the barn or lose them. By the time they got the last of the bales in the barn, dark clouds were rolling in from the southwest with lightning and thunder off in the distance.

The first raindrops fell, hitting the dry dirt and throwing up dust from the force as Jasmine and Ace were driving from the barn to the house. The rain was coming down hard and steady when Ace parked as close to the front-yard fence as he could.

They ran hand in hand through the rain from truck to porch.

Ace shook his head like a dog, and water flew from his hair. "Looks like the drought is over."

"That one is," Jasmine said.

"What does that mean?"

"It's not Saturday night yet. Until then there's a drought in my body. I'm going for first shower and then you guys can fight over the bathroom." She took off before Ace could say a word.

She made it quick and found Ace standing at the bathroom door when she came out with a towel around her head and her terry-cloth robe cinched up at the waist. "Good night," she said.

"Good night, darlin'," Ace said.

She tried to go to sleep, but it was impossible. She sat up when Ace came into the bedroom and wished he was naked, but he wore boxers and a gauze undershirt that hugged his muscles, tempting her to reach out and touch his tight abs and broad chest. She laced her fingers together in her lap.

"Cuddle with me," he said as he slipped beneath the covers.

"That all?" she asked.

"For tonight. I miss holding you at night, Jazzy."

She snuggled up in his arms and sighed. Five hours until she had to crawl out of a bed that felt so good and so right and go back to the café. And she'd gladly spend all five of them in hot sex rather than sleep. She'd never felt like that with another man, not ever! All she could think about was Ace—his smile, his hair, his kisses, his hands on her body.

"Thank you," Ace said wearily.

"For cuddling? My pleasure." She laid a hand on his chest and settled into the crook of his arm even tighter.

"For that, for your patience in this other drought,

and for helping us with the hay. We wouldn't have got it in without you driving an extra truck," he said.

The rain hit the windows and the wind roared.

"Got 'em in just in time. I enjoyed helping, Ace. Reckon we're in for a tornado?" she asked.

"Sounds like a hard rainstorm, not a tornado," he said.

"They do sound different, don't they?"

"Jazzy, you know I love you."

She didn't answer. He waited, but all that answered him were soft snores that reminded him of a kitten purring. He shut his eyes and sighed.

Dalton and Blake moved back to the Riley ranch on Friday while Jasmine ran the café. Lucy cleaned their rooms thoroughly, and when Jasmine got home that evening, her mother, father, and Grandma Dale were already there.

Grandma and Lucy were in the kitchen with cookbooks lined up from one end of the table to the other. Kelly had driven to Bowie to pick up tablecloths and paper goods for the next day, and Walt had gone with Ace to Wichita Falls to buy everything they needed to work cattle on Monday after the party.

"Grandma! I didn't know you were coming." Jasmine crossed the kitchen floor in a few easy strides and gave her a big hug.

"I couldn't stay away, and I had to meet the man that finally got you to the altar. I like him. He's a fine young man besides being pretty. He'll make pretty babies," Grandma said. "Don't you roll your eyes at me, girl. I don't care if you are thirty. I can still take you down."

Jasmine smiled. Her grandmother wasn't quite five feet tall, had a mop of kinky gray hair that Kizzy made popular back when *Roots* came out, and wouldn't weigh a hundred pounds soaking wet with rocks in her pockets.

"I don't doubt it, and Ace *is* pretty. And Grandma," she leaned down and whispered, "he's sexy too."

"Hell yes, he's sexy. That boy would make your great-aunt Rosalee's underbritches wet, and honey, she's a preacher."

Jasmine giggled and pulled out a chair. "What have you two found to cook for tomorrow?"

"We've about decided. Grandma's been tellin' me stories." Lucy winked.

"And I like Lucy. Don't ever get rid of her," Grandma said.

"I don't intend to," Jasmine said.

"Well, I'm tellin' you if you do, then there's going to be trouble in our quarters." Grandma's eyes were barely slits.

"You pickin' a fight with me?" Jasmine asked.

"Nope. Just gettin' things said before your momma

gets home and can't no one get a word in edgewise. She's off to get tablecloths and centerpieces and all kinds of tomfoolery. She always did like to fancy things up. That comes from my sister. She liked things like that," Grandma said.

"I ain't sayin' a word. She can do whatever she wants since she didn't get her wedding," Jasmine said.

"That was the biggest bit of horsecrap I ever heard. You was already married and it was done with. I'm glad you stood up to her and said that you wasn't goin' through with it. Now, me and Lucy has decided on makin' two of these things here with the bananas and whipped cream and strawberries and cream cheese layered up with pound cake on the bottom. That way we can do them early tomorrow and they'll keep in the 'frigerator until Sunday. Then Saturday we're makin' chocolate sheet cakes, a couple of cobblers, and some cookies. How's that sound?"

Lucy smiled and held up her list. "Grandma has it all organized and we can use the oven in the house and the two out in the bunkhouse. I'm making soup on top of the stove tomorrow. Two kinds: vegetable and tortilla."

"Don't guess y'all need me, then. I'm going to take a bath," Jasmine said.

"That's what you need to do. You'll be relaxed when your momma comes in here all in a tear tryin' to boss everyone around. Don't let her rile you, Jasmine. It's just her way. She loves you and wants the best for you," Grandma said.

Jasmine kissed her on the top of her silver curls. "I know. I'll be back in a little while. Y'all are doin' great, and believe me, I wouldn't let Lucy go for nothing."

She'd barely sunk down in the tub when Ace poked his head in the door.

"Hey," he said.

"Come on in and talk to me."

He eased inside and shut the door behind him. "Want some company in that tub?"

"Sure, but the sex drought would be over if I see you naked," she said. "Want to talk to me about it?"

"No, ma'am. I'm saving it for tomorrow night. I'll pick you up at work."

"But we have guests," she said.

"No, we have family. They're going to be so busy getting things done that they won't even know we've run away for an hour. Three o'clock and, Jazzy, wear that pretty sundress you wore to church last Sunday for me."

"Okay, want to tell me why?"

"No, that's just what I want you to wear. Now lean up and I'll wash your back and your hair for you. Walt told me today that he still wants your café. He says it's all he thinks about and that your momma is already talkin' about selling their house in Sherman and building something in Ringgold, not too far from the café, maybe even out back of it if they could buy a couple of acres. She's even looking into making a garden so there would be fresh vegetables for the café."

"Dammit! I've got water in my ears. I didn't hear what I thought I did, did I? I can't even begin to imagine my mother in a garden," Jasmine said.

"Grandma Dale says that she'd probably be good at it, that whatever she sets her head to, she can do." Ace poured water through Jasmine's hair and lathered it up with shampoo. "I love your hair. It's like holding strands of silk in my hands."

The door to the bathroom was shut and locked, but even the air changed when Kelly got back to the ranch. She came in talking about her fantastic finds and asking Lucy and Grandma to help her make silk arrangements after supper that night.

"Don't tense up," Ace said. "Lean forward and let me rinse your hair and put in that conditioner stuff. Then I'll wash and massage your back. Just remember someday you'll be a momma."

"You are good for me as well as good to me, Ace Riley."

"Right back atcha, darlin'."

Saturday went by in a blur. Kelly called in the middle of the morning to ask about the flower arrangements she was making for the tables and to talk about the wedding cake table. Did Jasmine want a punch bowl on one end and the cake on the other with a big arrangement in the middle? Or did she want the cake in the middle flanked by the punch bowl and the arrangement? Kelly had to have an answer right away so she'd know how big to make the arrangement.

"Momma, I trust your judgment. You make it. I'll love it," Jasmine said.

"Thank you, Jasmine Marie. I appreciate that. Your dad is in the kitchen with Lucy and Grandma. I swear he looks strange wearing an apron, but I've fallen in love with him all over again in the last few weeks. Please think about selling us the café. We need something to keep this retired-type love alive and I think the café would do it," Kelly said.

"I won't sell it to anyone else," Jasmine promised.

Finally, at two o'clock Jasmine locked the doors. Bridget raced through her afternoon chores and was out by two fifteen, leaving Jasmine forty-five minutes to shower and get dressed.

She was more nervous than she'd been at the Vegas hotel when she dressed for the wedding. Ace had something big up his sleeve. She could feel it and couldn't, for the life of her, figure it out. She took a quick shower to wash away the sweat and cooking odors, used a dryer on her hair, and ran an iron over the dress she'd worn on Sunday. Shoes, boots, or sandals? The choice was there in front of her. She tried on a high-heeled shoe and a sandal and stood in front of the mirror. She kicked off the high heel and replaced it with the white cowboy boot she'd worn when she married Ace.

She checked her reflection in the mirror and decided on the boot.

She was walking down the stairs when she looked down and saw Ace staring up at her.

"Well?" she asked.

"You look beautiful. Love the boots. Are you ready?"

He wore a pair of creased jeans stacked up over his best Sunday boots and the same shirt he'd worn Sunday. When he hugged her, she got a whiff of Stetson, and a dot of blood on his jawline testified that he'd just shaved.

"You look pretty sexy yourself, cowboy. I have no idea if I'm ready because I don't know what we are doing, but I'm putting my hand in yours, Ace, and trusting you," she said.

"That means a lot to me today, Jazzy." He laced his fingers in hers and led her out to the truck where he tucked her safely into the passenger's seat and whistled all the way around to the driver's side. He turned north instead of south when he backed out onto the highway, then swung west on Highway 82, went a few blocks, and turned back north.

"Where are we going?" she asked.

"Just another minute." He pulled into the empty church parking lot and got out of the truck.

"We're going to the church?" she asked when he opened her door.

He looped her arm in his. "Yes, ma'am."

The front door was open but the church was eerily quiet.

"Ace?" she asked.

"To the front," he said.

When they reached the pulpit, he dropped down on one knee and looked up at Jasmine. "Jasmine King Riley, I love you and I'm in love with you. I've wanted you all week, but I had to be sure that I needed you as well. Want and need are two different critters. They're as far apart as black and white. Want is instant gratification. Need goes deeper. It's something that comes from the soul, not the body. And I need you in my life and in my heart to be whole. So I'm askin' you to marry me, Jasmine, right here in this church, right now."

Tears welled up behind her eyelashes. "Yes, Ace, I will marry you."

He picked up a faded velvet box from the front pew and snapped it open. "I've already given you a wedding ring, but on this day of our real marriage, I want to give you the pearls that Granny wore the day she married Gramps."

Tears streamed down her face. "Oh, Ace, they are beautiful."

Ace stood up, wiped away the tears with a clean white handkerchief he pulled from his pocket, and gently kissed her eyelids. He removed the pearls, fastened them around her neck, and said, "With these pearls from the box, I promise to give you my love, my respect, and devotion for the rest of our lives. I promise to be faithful and to love you with my whole heart, not only in this life but for all eternity."

She swallowed hard and touched the string of aged pearls around her neck. "Ace Riley, I accept the pearls and promise to give you my love, respect, and devotion for the rest of our lives. And I promise to cherish these pearls as much as our love, to be faithful and love you forever."

"And now I can kiss my bride," he said.

She slipped her arms around his neck and he sealed their marriage with a kiss full of love and passion.

"Honeymoon will have to wait until fall when things slow down," he said as they walked together down the aisle.

"Honeymoon, darlin', begins tonight in our bedroom at the ranch and will go through our whole lives. And Ace, tomorrow at the reception, I'm selling the café to my cousin. I'm ready to be a full-time rancher's wife," she said.

He stopped and hugged her to his chest. "I'm the luckiest man on earth."

"Tell me that after we have five daughters." She laughed.

He graced her with his sexiest grin. "Fine by me. Five daughters and five sons. Maybe we'll start tonight?"

She giggled and he scooped her up like a bride and carried her to the truck.

"I love you, Mrs. Riley." He kissed her long and hard before settling her into her seat.

"I love you, Ace. Now let's go home and lock the bedroom door."

Epilogue

One year later

Jasmine ran her hand over her bulging stomach. In just two more months she and Ace would be parents of a son. She hoped that he looked just like his father and was just the first of several children. Even though her swollen feet and sheer exhaustion told her she was crazy for even thinking about going through this again, she wanted a big family.

She had to admit, though, that she was glad she had sold the café to her second cousin, Jasmine Thurman. Growing up with the same name and being the same age sure made it difficult for them at family gatherings. Their hair being the same color and them being the same height, carried the confusion right over into their college years. Of course, since Jasmine was a fairly popular name the year that the cousins were born, there were two other young women who shared the same name in their dorm. That's when her cousin decided to be called by her middle name, Suzanne; another Jasmine used her initials, J.J.; and the fourth one followed by doing the same and being called J.R. Once they had graduated, Jazzy's cousin went back to being Jasmine. After all, J.T. and J.R. were off in other states, and the two cousins only saw each other a few times a year when the family got together for gatherings.

"We sure fixed that when Ace started calling me Jazzy, didn't we?" she whispered. "Now everyone has followed right behind him, and I'm Jazzy all over this area."

"Who are you talking to?" Her cousin came through the back door with a grocery bag in her hands.

"Me and this baby that's making me look like an elephant. I swear he's going to weigh ten pounds," Jazzy answered. "I was thinking back to when we were kids and..."

Jasmine butted in before she could finish. "What were our parents thinking when they gave us the same name?"

"Jasmine was our three times great-grandmother," Jazzy answered. "It's a wonder we didn't have more of us with the same name in the family."

Jasmine set the groceries down on the table, pulled out a chair and sat down. "Maybe I should revert back to Suzanne."

"Nope, I've already told everyone in the area, and we even put an ad in the Nocona newspaper about the café having a new owner, Jasmine Thurman."

Jazzy eased down into a chair beside her and propped her feet on one of the empty chairs. "I'm glad that this is my last day."

"I'm glad that when I open up tomorrow, I'll have waitresses coming in," Jasmine said. "Shall I pour us a glass of sweet tea to celebrate you closing the doors and handing over the keys to me?"

"Yes, please," Jazzy answered. She was going to miss the café and all the local folks who came in for good home cooking. "Do you think you'll change the name of the place after a few months?"

Jasmine pushed back her chair and filled two glasses with sweet tea. "Lord, no! I'm going to keep it the Chicken Fried Café forever. That's too good a name to ever change. Kind of like our names—they fit us. Suzanne worked for college, but it never did suit me." She handed a sweet tea to Jazzy and sat back down.

Jazzy reached across her belly and the table to clink her glass with her cousin's. "To a great first year for you."

"To enjoying motherhood to you," Jasmine said.

"Pretty good toasts," Jazzy said as she handed over the keys to Jasmine.

"Pretty sweet deal you gave me on this place," her cousin said. "I've got a business and a place to live, and your friends have been amazing. And to top it all off, I get to see Pearl sometimes. We were such good friends in college, and I love it that she keeps sending waitresses over here to help the women who need jobs."

"Pearl is a firecracker, but she's a sweet person," Jazzy smiled and set her half-empty glass of tea down, "and now look at all three of us. She's happy as a lark on her ranch, and I'm going to live on a ranch. On that note, I'm going to walk out the back door, and I'm not going to cry a single tear. I feel like I'm taking the first step on the path to a brand-new life."

"Me, too," Jasmine said, "and I'm very excited about it. See you tomorrow?"

"Maybe not tomorrow, but before too many days get past us," Jazzy promised. "Think you'll ever wind up on a ranch, that maybe moving to this area is an omen?"

"Oh, hell, no!" Jasmine said with a giggle. "You and Pearl got the good men. It would take a miracle to have three in a row."

"Miracles still happen," Jazzy said as she stood up and headed for the back door.

"Not to me, they don't," Jasmine said. "Lock the door behind you and enjoy your new life."

Jazzy left with a lump in her throat. The café had so many good memories, but she would make more precious ones on the ranch with Ace—and eventually they would have a yard full of kids. She wanted a daughter—or two or three—and her son needed siblings to argue with, take up for, and love him.

When she reached the farmhouse, Ace met her at the vehicle and opened the door for her. He leaned in and kissed her—long, lingering, hot, and passionate. "Welcome home for good, Mrs. Riley."

"I'm glad to be here," she said. "I thought it would be tougher than it was."

"You didn't cry?" He held out a hand and helped her out of her SUV.

"I got a lump in my throat, but I didn't shed a single tear. The past has been good, but the future with you and our family here on the ranch is going to be great," she said.

"Yes, it is," he agreed as he slung an arm around her shoulders and led her up to the porch where two rocking chairs waited for them. When she offered to help Ace out by marrying him, she had no idea that they would fall in love. Now she didn't even have to close her eyes to imagine them sitting in the same chairs fifty years down the road—with family gathered around them and grandchildren playing in the front yard.

About the Author

Carolyn Brown is a *New York Times*, *USA Today*, *Wall Street Journal*, *Publishers Weekly*, and #1 Amazon and #1 *Washington Post* bestselling author. She is the author of more than one hundred novels and several novellas. She's a recipient of the Bookseller's Best Award and the prestigious Montlake Diamond Award and also a three-time recipient of the National Readers Choice Award. Brown has been published for more than twenty years, and her books have been translated into twenty foreign languages.

She's been married for more than fifty years to Mr. B, and they have three smart, wonderful, amazing children; fifteen grandchildren; and too many great-grands to keep track of. When she's not writing, she likes to plot new stories in her backyard with her tomcat, Boots Randolph Terminator Outlaw, who protects the yard from all kinds of wicked varmints like crickets, locusts, and spiders. Carolyn can be found on Instagram @carolynbrownbooks, on Twitter @thecarolynbrown, on Facebook at facebook.com/carolynbrownbooks, and at her website carolynbrownbooks.com.

Also by Carolyn Brown

What Happens in Texas
A Heap of Texas Trouble
A Slow Dance Holiday (novella)
Christmas at Home
Summertime on the Ranch (novella)
Secrets in the Sand
Holidays on the Ranch
Red River Deep
The Honeymoon Inn
Love Struck Café (novella)
Bride for a Day
Just in Time for Christmas
A Chance Inheritance
The Third Wish (novella)

LUCKY COWBOYS
Lucky in Love
One Lucky Cowboy
Getting Lucky
Talk Cowboy to Me

HONKY TONK
I Love This Bar
Hell, Yeah
My Give a Damn's Busted
Honky Tonk Christmas

SPIKES & SPURS

Love Drunk Cowboy

Red's Hot Cowboy

Darn Good Cowboy Christmas

One Hot Cowboy Wedding

Mistletoe Cowboy

Just a Cowboy and His Baby

Cowboy Seeks Bride

COWBOYS & BRIDES

Billion Dollar Cowboy

The Cowboy's Christmas Baby

The Cowboy's Mail Order Bride

How to Marry a Cowboy

BURNT BOOT, TEXAS

Cowboy Boots for Christmas

The Trouble with Texas Cowboys

One Texas Cowboy Too Many

A Cowboy Christmas Miracle